PRAISE FO

Tom Lukas has crafte̶ ̶ ̶ ̶ ̶ ̶ ̶a̶n̶d̶s̶ far
and away above the pack: not just intelligent but intellectually
challenging yet at the same time consistently entertaining.
Imbued with a sophisticated comprehension of the darkest
workings of the human psyche reminiscent of Thomas
Harris' "Hannibal Lector" novels, Special Operations seethes
with the kind of tension that compels the reader to stay up
way past bedtime to find out how it will end. And what an
ending! This is a novel that will haunt you long after you've
turned the final page.

~ Pamela Marcantel, *An Army of Angels:*
a Novel of Joan of Arc, and V-Squad

Tom Lukas is a very talented visual writer. The settings of
many of his scenes—particularly the climactic confrontation
between his protagonist and antagonist were detailed and
vivid. I could see, smell and hear those scenes, and instantly
imagined them up on the big screen.

~ Laura Davis, author of the bestselling books,
The Courage to Heal and *Allies in Healing*

PRAISE FOR SPECIAL OPERATIONS

TOM LUKAS

SPECIAL OPERATIONS

Spycar Books
Seattle, WA

Story Illustrations by Tom Lukas

Cover Design by Tom Lukas, [collage on background image: Lucifer - torturing souls as well as being tortured himself in hell, from the 15the century Illuminated manuscriptTrès Riches Heures du Duc de Berry]

Published by SPYCAR BOOKS
and YANCASTEL INC.
3801 Brooklyn Ave NE Stevens Court L111
Seattle, WA 98105
spycarbooks.com / spy@spycarbooks.com

Library of Congress Cataloging-in-Publication Data:

Lukas, Tom

Special Operations, Paperback 1st ed.

ISBN 978-0-9911696-1-0

1. Fiction. 2. Thrillers. 3. Psychological.

First edition paperback: November 2013

1 2 3 4 5 6 7 8 9 10

Printed in the United States of America

The writing in this book is primal, rough, to reach the darkest recesses of the human heart. As well, this novel is infused with a brilliant light, not of the author's making, but shimmering nonetheless, to eradicate shadow and show hope and freedom anyone can share.

NOTES

Most gracious thanks to the government of Colombia, a place of natural beauty and welcoming, generous people. My editors Larry Soucy, Laura Davis, and John Paine all brought a different kind of magic to my finding my story, and to each of them, my warmest wishes.

Saludos! and deep thanks go as well to Malesurvivor.org, and to men and women survivors near and far whose courage lights the way. I wish also to thank my professors at the University of Virginia, for their patience and support and life-long lessons. May God bless The Sisters of the Holy Names, and the Campus Ministry at Seattle University, for their help with things of the Spirit. Also the University of Washington School of Medicine, and Seattle's Swedish Family Medicine, Cherry Hill -- for helping with all the other parts. Further gratitude goes to the Seattle Woodland Park Zoo, for help with research on animal behavior. To the Ludwig Vogelstein Foundation, I thank you for your generous grant in 2007 that helped make this book possible.

For helping me understand the dynamics of winter fog that lurks in Cape Cod cranberry bogs, I wish to thank Bill Simpson of the Taunton, Massachusetts wing of the National Oceanographic and Atmospheric Administration (NOAA).

My deepest gratitude goes to Detective Carl Westerman, for his expertise in law enforcement, and for being a lifelong friend who made the difference.

And all the many, many others who helped, a selfless band of scoundrels who shall go by the name, The Apaches.

Speaking of the best, the Literary and Textual Forensics techniques employed by the character Professor Canon Nailor of this novel were adapted from the authoritative book on the subject, Author Unknown, Tales of a Literary Detective, by Don Foster. The forensic techniques he developed have saved many lives. I hope I got them right.

TABLE OF CONTENTS

For Yannette

I will rid the LORD'S city of people who do evil.

Psalm 101:8

CHAPTER 1

Goddard, Massachusetts: a place of secrets.

In the final days of Simon Allengri's punitive surgery, The Illuminator's lair in her deceased brother's house has the transitory look of an encampment. Neat. Orderly. Yet ready to abandon once this stage of her Mission is complete.

A regiment of styluses line up like surgical instruments that wink morning light from a rosewood carry-case, at the ready on a worktable before the window. Beside the waiting styluses stands a selection of quills, and the mortar and pestle she uses to grind gall for making inks, these pigments a colorful array of crystal wells with silver caps that gleam. Sticks of charcoal lay scattered on a drawing tablet.

With the dawn stillness, Cassandra, The Illuminator, sits at this table before her laptop to monitor the patient who lies in the makeshift clinic at the far end of her house.

What she sees, satisfactory: Allengri's hand and leg restraints are holding, the head bandages fine. Some crimson blotches from tiny incisions wick through the gauze covering soft implants to augment the tip of his nose.

She clicks from the web cam to news and spies the headline,

MISSING TEACHER MAY HAVE FLED

Today an unnamed number of Pinecrest Academy students filed allegations of teacher Simon Allengri's history of sexual misconduct, spurring the Goddard Police Department to investigate whether Allengri has fled. According to G.P.D. Chief Phil Robertson, a missing person report was filed on the teacher two weeks ago, when Allengri did not show for classes at end of the Thanksgiving break. Simon Allengri has taught at Pinecrest Academy for the past eighteen years. The range of victim allegations are said to fall within this timeframe.

Administrators at Pinecrest Academy declined comment. A brief statement issued by The Headmaster's office in light of this week's student allegations reports that the school will be working in full cooperation with police, and that an in-depth internal inquiry on Simon Allengri is already under way.

Cassandra scrolls to check the forecast. She's hoping for good weather on the day of her patient's post-operative Debut. But here, another headline screams:

PINECREST BOYS SPEAK OUT:
MISSING TEACHER A PREP SCHOOL PREDATOR

No need to read the rest. She sips juice, wondering when the press will catch on, and carry stories about all the others.

She chases this from her mind. Much to do for this program of catch and release. With the cutting done, her current Subject will need a tuxedo; black loafers with thin soles; dark socks. The hand mirror she plans to leave with him – can't forget that. For his teeth, she already has etching solution and bonding resin. And the special blue light to cure it. The grinder as well.

Primed to complete this Subject, she clicks to close the weather report, devoting her attention to the clinic cam.

A chartreuse blaze flits across the screen . . .

Cassandra clucks her tongue, and smirks in recognition, but otherwise ignores the hummingbird's antics. She's focused on the patient's breathing, slow and shallow. He stirs.

Iridescent green blur darts after the first . . .

She thinks: *little show boat.* Just yesterday she had released the hummers into the clinic, her three little assistants – hoping the birds might boost her patient's morale, ease his spirits in recovery.

Feeling drawn to check Allengri in person, Cassandra zooms out the web cam and pulls on a white lab coat. But she pauses, taken by what she sees on the computer screen, marveling at her birds' zipping aerobatics.

Winged fireworks above and about her patient's stillness.

Inspired, she can't help herself. Reaching for a sketchpad on the worktable she dashes a few quick, light strokes with a charcoal stick to refine the crook of Allengri's nose, his chin. Then she adds a few sharp lines to lengthen the incisors.

Soothed by the tactile rasp of charcoal on textured drawing stock, stroke by stroke The Illuminator reveals the man's true self to The Light.

Day to day, she pivots according to task: from Cassandra, war-veteran surgical nurse – to The Illuminator, healer of the world. Preparing for each Subject, she feels The Light climb within: deep in her trunk and rising into her limbs. Bubbling throughout. Once she imagined it as a diver, in the dark and deep, a cone of gold shimmering through murk, then ascending, shined bubbles rising. At these times she's Guided, the glimmer drawn to the sliver part of her. The silver turns to sunlight, and it's begun: the Light seeping into her hands, ready to share it – to reach for the knife.

She starts down the hall. The ventilator makes a rhythmic pull, puff, and hissing reset. Beneath these sounds – once inside the clinic – she hears a buzzing. The birds' wings.

The Illuminator has rules. Always approach a Subject from behind. Neither Simon Allengri, nor any of her other surgical Subjects would ever hear her voice, or see her face, once The Work had begun.

For a moment the vision of this occupied hospital bed – the sounds of the ventilator – bring her back to the vision of her younger brother during his two final days in Intensive Care. Hardly enough time to say goodbye to him – though with less than half of his thinker remaining, he hadn't been much for conversation. Then again, he never had a chance to become his best.

The Illuminator bites down hard on her lip to hold off the memory and tastes blood. Refocusing on Allengri's I.V., she turns the plastic wheel, adjusting to day drip, the drip to keep him hovering.

A tiny flutter. The hummingbird Bolivar zips by her ear.

The monitor, strategically mounted on a wall bracket behind the bed, provided a full view of Allengri's new face, while preserving her own anonymity. While she regards her work, a second hummingbird, Antonio Nariño, lights for a moment on her shoulder, and then darts off.

Funny bunny.

With the black volcanic glass edge of an Obsidian scalpel, she has taught herself to write in flesh what words cannot fully convey. Even the fine Illuminated manuscripts she creates and leaves as calling card with each Subject cannot speak with the same clarity as a scalpel on skin.

Together, today, her message and Subject combine: word and flesh, the dispatch full-bodied, the graphic novel drawing breath, the text message pumping blood.

Touching a button on the *Versa-bed* touch pad, she lowers Allengri's head to clear his nasal passages. In a moment, the Subject's respiration returns to normal.

She easily acknowledges her unfair advantage over Simon Allengri. But she rationalizes his disembodied and depersonalized condition by what she considers unquestionable pretexts: Brother's suffering at the hand of this man. And the Religious laws by which she sculpts her Subjects' bodies.

The Illuminator acts by the law of Contrapasso, a concept Dante Alighieri illustrated in <u>The Divine Comedy</u>. By this law each punishment of Hell is tailored to the particular villainy at hand. Vengeance, Cassandra has read in the ancient texts, is a sensitive scale of moral balance, Perfected over time. She knows that Religions, mythologies, and nations still employ the precept to this day. Based upon words attributed to an Almighty who might bless wars' tortuous revenge. Yet allow predators and traffickers to roam the Earth, to feed on the weak.

Ever-resourceful, facing a world so imperfect, The Illuminator has adopted such tailoring as her medium of creativity. Any true art form is no end unto itself, but should inspire awe, interest, and knowledge.

A thorough caregiver, Cassandra, as The Illuminator,

never cuts corners. Gentle, preventing physical pain, she worthily abides every medical duty in the role of Seeing them Out.

Laying before her, open-eyed in his state of drug-induced dissociation, Simon Allengri had fully witnessed every slice and stitch. But he would not emotionally connect with these events until she chose to bring him back. She was saving that.

The Illuminator smiles, placing her charcoal rendering of her patient's new face, his *Contrapasso*, on the bed table where he'll be unable to avoid it.

Then she stands behind the head of his bed. Using a joystick to zoom in, she watches the teacher's eyes on the monitor.

It's unusual to catch a pure sociopath emoting. But each time she shows a Subject a sketch of his new face, there's that Sacred Moment.

There! On the monitor. She bears Witness. Mostly transparent, attempting escape.

His soul!

At first lightly visible, a flash like enflamed swamp gas blooms behind Allengri's irises.

Then it's hard against the cornea. The Soul trying to rip its way out.

But the Subject's still-live flesh still imprisons it.

At least it's *in* there. Hope.

Defeated, it sinks out of sight. She watches it recede. The shimmer of moral dust, the way toxic chemicals in smog can make a sunset seductive.

She knows that to show a Subject how his face will look is the only means of determining a clear fit, to confirm that he comprehends this Tailoring according to ancient Spiritual Law.

Cortez, the Scoppery Emerald hummingbird now hovers above the Subject, rushing and retreating from the charcoal sketch. Deciding whether to light, or to leave. He leaves, a fiery chartreuse flash, then perches at a sunlit feeder by the window to partake of its ruby-fluid. He had claimed this feeder as his own, and defends it like a miniature general.

Before leaving her patient to attend to other duties, The Illuminator hangs a second bag of clear I.V. fluid, so Simon Allengri can intravenously soak up enough food, water, and succinolcoline to sustain him another day. One more day of nursing before she will release him back into the wild. One more day before he'll fully confront the depths of his own Nature.

The Illuminator smiles at her three winged guardians as they flit and fly; their antics, her medicine. Then she heads down the hallway to exercise.

Cassandra practices Capoeira each morning, the non-violent martial art she learned during a volunteering stint in Brazil – brought from Angola by captive slaves. Running through her routine, she remembers one maestro who'd impressed upon her that even within danger's constant shadow, violence need not be a necessary evil.

But that was long ago – before Brother was lost.

At her vanity table she brushes on foundation and color. She looks younger than young, having left the years' aging back in the aesthetic salons of Cali, Sao Paolo, and Buenos Aires. There, a nurse with her wartime surgical experience could put up in a hotel for a few weeks and work a swap: scrub in as lead on money jobs in order to pay for her own transformation.

She stretches her lips before the mirror, poises her shoulders, and turns her cheek to the light. Pleased. She'd cut her hair, then her facial features – precisely to remake her boyish – to exactly resemble her brother. To become his keeper in body, mind, and Spirit. Her healing from the procedures completed only days before the phone call she knew to be inevitable – and then her hasty return from South America to say goodbye to his body.

During the last years of his life, the brother Cassandra had grown up with had slipped away. She had tried to keep up with his fade. But the more she grasped, the less of him she could grip.

Before the mirror now she considers her breasts. Their size pleasantly negotiable – small enough to flatten when The Work required, yet large enough to smuggle the three hummingbirds in the cozy space between. She loved to remember the five minutes clearing security – the warmth of the three tiny hearts beating above hers as she strode from the restroom at the gate to the waiting plane.

Then, inside the cramped airplane bathroom, she'd undone the silk bindings and set the birds free in her black mesh carry tote. Beneath its false bottom hid enough injectable drugs, needles, and plastic syringes to paralyze every person on the plane. Unnoticed by airport security x-ray, the narcotics had made her recall an old postcard that pictured a dirigible moored to a mast atop a skyscraper. She imagined the 747 hovering that way. But had serious plans for these vials.

After landing at Boston Logan, Cassandra had re-silked the birds and packed them back in her bosom. She had feared the Customs agent might notice her eyes, the irises so unlike Brother's in their burning hazel glow; groupings of green shards here, specs of red when the mood struck. Every other detail of her matched him. She'd made sure. And when she handed the official her brother's passport, she'd felt The Illuminator rise within her, had watched the agent's face as he studied the document, his eyes glancing up at her, the rise of his upper lip.

She had summoned The Light. Felt it spread through her, and slipped through. Proof, she decided, that she was Guided.

CHAPTER 2

Like every Thursday evening Chief Phil Robertson sat at home in his recliner, the wide-screen tuned to *Animal Kingdom*, keeping an eye on the twins.

Their mother, the chief's daughter Judith, was still at night school – working on a certificate in medical billing. Their grandmother, the chief's wife Francine, had aerobics Tuesday and Thursday nights.

The girls Kim and Kylie huddled over their homework at the dining table where the chief could be sure they kept it up. Or when they didn't, hitting the kitchen for snacks. Once, they used the telephone to call a friend about the assignment. After ten minutes' disappearance, Robertson had to lay down the law. Bribed them, more like it, with a promise of hot cocoa, and to tell another of the made-up police stories they loved to hear him tell. But not till their homework was done. And double checked.

Now Junior High age, the twins knew little of the details. How their mother's dream marriage went sour in its first year. Regardless of fault, the man who had been Chief Robertson's son-in-law owned the town's only new car dealership. His father was Braxton Jewell, owner of Jewell Eternities, the town's only mortuary – and who also served on the Board of Selectmen that governed the town of Goddard, Massachusetts. During his son's divorce, Jewell had tapped his access to the small town's better law firms, leaving Robertson's daughter with a handful of second stringers that the chief had met in the course of police work.

The setup left Judith Robertson, pregnant with twins, with a far from adequate settlement. The Chief and his wife hadn't hesitated a moment in bringing their daughter back home.

The girls Kim and Kylie had sprung from cagey stock. Through grammar school and growing into adolescence there was nothing they couldn't do, and do better than most of their peers: soccer; basketball; music; art; math; science; languages; and reading – often successfully engaged in more than one of these at a time.

The divorce had been twelve years ago, and by now never discussed.

What mattered was family.

Somehow through it all, Robertson had sidestepped conflict. Had held onto a solid job, now raising a second family at sixty-two and driving a squad car with the word "Chief" emblazoned in gold across the hood and along both front fenders.

Given the good family reputation, if Robertson's granddaughters could keep their grades up, they held excellent chances for a scholarship to Pinecrest Academy. And a future far brighter than Granddad's.

The twins looked to be deep in their studies when Robertson received the phone call from Pinecrest Academy's Headmaster. A teacher, named Simon Allengri. Harmed students, sounds like. Had disappeared. The Academy needed help.

The chief had to agree. The situation warranted delicacy. "Of course," Robertson told him. "Anything I can do."

"Look, Phil. If this Allengri bastard hurt our students, we're obligated to make it right. I want to know the full extent of it. Whether it stops with Allengri, or if there are more like him to root out," The Headmaster told him. He added, "Your First Detective Nick Giaccone's quite good."

"Nick's record is the best in the county."

"In the state," The Headmaster corrected. "I'm looking at a copy of his arrest and convictions rates."

"Then you must be aware Nick retires this week."

"That as well. Both his homes sold. Moving to Italy. A family homestead." The Headmaster had to be reading from notes.

The chief felt a tightening about his chest. His friend Nick Giaccone had put off retirement twice. On both accounts to save someone's hide.

The twins, by this point, are triumphantly marching about, waving their completed homework above their heads. They circle the dining table, chanting, "Co-coa! Co-coa! Co-coa!" Now the chief watches as they made their way toward his easy chair, their papers held out for him to check. Still calling for, "Co-coa! Co-coa! Co-coa!"

Robertson felt sad when he raised a hand to halt and hush the parade.

The Headmaster broke the silence, his voice almost friendly. "Is that Kylie and Kim Robertson I hear there in the background? Must be a handful, Phil. I hear good things about those two. . ." The Headmaster paused. Then his tone was back to business: "Phil. There are kids and families who've invested everything in a Pinecrest education. I'm asking you: **don't** make the mistake of giving this to Giaccone's replacement."

The chief kept his mouth shut and thought. After thirty-five years' service, such a dedicated cop as Nick deserved to get the Hell out of Goddard. And given current family obligations, Robertson would never see such a chance. Nick had earned the break.

But The Headmaster persisted. "I'm sure you can talk to your friend Nick. To get this out of the way might help clear him for takeoff. Selling two homes ... a lot can go wrong. . . but I know you and Nick go way back. We need Pinecrest to be strong for. . . . For the *future*. You have *family* to think of."

Chief Robertson understood everything he was being told. Because over the years he'd come to know The Headmaster, despite tonight's polite tones, to be a man with far-reaching political contacts who could have his pick: Federal law enforcement; elite "discreet" private security personnel; even a roster of Navy SEALs, at his discretion on certain matters. And when matters involved the safety of children and adolescents, The Headmaster's discretion was known to be certain, because he'd been around long enough to view these citizens as the nation's future, and thus basis of national security. "I see," was all Robertson could bring himself to say. Sighing, unable to rid the deep gray weight of it, the air in his lungs felt like a heavy liquid as he put down the phone.

Nick's exit from Goddard was at risk, thought the chief. All because of a teacher who, according to students' pained reports, couldn't have vanished soon enough.

CHAPTER 3

She wondered if she was rushing things, driving Brother's old pickup toward Detective Giaccone's house. She'd made up her boy disguise of an Ace bandage binder, red flannel shirt, and coveralls. Now burned to test it. And to size up Nick, up close.

The risk, she felt it tug.

Nick qualified as a Subject for treatment. But only in a *technical* sense, since he stood in a different moral hemisphere than the others. What she must excise from *him* would require handling of a different sort. *Nick's* would be a surgery involving words, histories, images – all related to the tragic loss of one Patrolman Jim Stevens, who the detective had brought into police work as a teenaged Police Cadet.

Jim's death had been explained away. In the style townspeople could live with. Simple. A fatal squad car wreck. No questions asked.

The Illuminator's work would be to reveal deeper causes.

Driving her brother's old truck into Nick's neighborhood would be a first step in delivering a special trail of breadcrumbs. Following, the detective and the entire town of Goddard were in for the lesson of a lifetime.

Many townspeople wouldn't get it. She could accept that.

Her target segment would be the ones with some personal connection to cases like Jim's –- or her own brother's. To *them*, the message would be clear as ice.

And she was betting all: that the detective would wind up head of the class.

Like a glacial fragment, by now Nick's loss of the young Rookie Jim Stevens had sunk between the lobes of the aging investigator's brain. She knew cops did that. Stuffed such things down.

Yet a death tragic as Jim's would chafe. No oyster grain – to be salved with time and coated benign.

No. The pearl, for policemen like Nick, was that the irritant becomes sustenance for the hunt.

To set her plan in motion – she'd soon unveil Simon Allengri, the surgical Subject who now lay in her clinic. Message number one.

And after that, with each further stage of The Work, the menace of Jim's death would work its way up through the folds of Nick's consciousness. She would see to it: the meaning of it would rise – the way a stone rises in a farmer's field – beneath daily rumblings of the plough – rattles of the harrow – soil-settling rain – and the heave of wicked frosts: inch by inch pushed up through root, fertilizer, and dirt – to one day bask on the surface in the sun. Scrubbed by the wind.

Walls built of stacked fieldstones like this gave New England its close-cordoned charm.

Other buried fragments would surely surface in Nick's mind as well. Yes. Perhaps the aging detective would face other Truths he'd avoided. In the end, she fully believed, he'd be thankful.

She'd done her homework. Had much in common with Nick. Both had served tours in Viet Nam.

She knew battlefield medicine inside and out. Surely he'd understand the way a field hospital operates. He'd certainly know the ways of the battle-shattered. How fearful the brave but shaken can be: fresh from bloodying front lines, fearing at first the administered cure would kill them.

Easing the rattling old pickup truck into the detective's street, Cassandra felt The Illuminator rise within, and then take over. Familiar now with the transformation, it began from the center of her breast, rising into the neck and shoulders, radiating to the tips of her fingers. She felt her arms tremble. Then everything tingled.

As a girl Cassandra had read of Christian Mystics in their cells. The Metaphysical poets who attained religious Ecstasy. Not the worldly sort, nor given to pleasures of the flesh. She'd worked it out. The flutter throughout her now came through service, of giving over her entire self to The Illuminator: physical, moral and Spiritual. An instrument of Righteousness tolerates no other agendas to compete, or distract. Pure as the snow she now drove on.

Parking out front of Nick's house, she checked her disguise in the mirror a last time. Then felt for the Taser in the pocket of her overalls, in case she's forced to defend all she so Justly causes.

The day she'd abducted Simon Allengri the campaign had begun. One day, the detective whose investigative obsession she was carefully seeding would come to understand. Then Nick Giaccone would join her. Also to work in The Light.

She stepped out of the truck in front of his house. A Holy Warrior on reconnaissance.

CHAPTER 4

Moving furniture out to his front porch, Nick stopped dead to glance out at his street, a narrow lane rare to see traffic.

Fresh tire tracks sliced the new snow crossways, ending in a skid where a road-salt-rotted Cheyenne pickup sat cockeyed, half in the street, nose against the split-rail fence beyond.

By that moment The Illuminator was already on her mark, on the vacant lot across from Nick's house. Ready to play her role of a young odd-job worker bolting a **For Sale** sign to the fence.

Relax, Nick told himself. He'd been told he'd need to learn it like a skill – to look at the world as something other than a crime scene, or else die of a heart attack within his first years in retirement. *Just a kid,* he decided to peg this. *Okay, that's the way, a kid trying to earn a couple bucks on a Saturday to save a shitbeat pickup from the smelter.*

Even so, Nick's paternal instincts took the reins. Decided the kid needed a hand – was too young – too small – to be grappling with the four-by-four post. Far too green to know enough to support it between shoulder and chin and then insert the through-bolt.

No. Let it be, he thought. That was another thing he'd been told. *Remember. Resist the duty urge; don't get involved so easily.* He walked back inside for more furniture.

Setting the kitchen table outside on the front porch he took another look.

The kid had dropped the nut in the snow. The post landed with a muffled thud, and then Nick heard "___k," her well-placed curse as he'd turned to go back for more furniture. He couldn't help himself.

"Hang on there. . . let me give you a hand," Nick shouted, setting an armload of chairs beside the rest, and then on down the front steps.

But already the youth had raised the post for another try.

Hurriedly crossing to lend a hand, Nick could sympathize, watching the kid reach frozen-fingered, fiddling a bolt that *again* slipped into the drift. The signpost coming down.

The wind bit Nick's face and burned through his sweatpants. Snow cascaded over the tops of his shearling moccasins, his steps silent beneath the howling wind and the grinding sound from a cordless drill she used now to enlarge the bolthole.

"Hey. . . hang on." The fine features and slight build made Nick wonder if this kid was even old enough to drive.

The Detective's ample face, she realized, his generous dark lashes and worrier's brow, was divided by another set of lines. And to look at Nick made her think of another face – from a Religious painting. The painting called *The Denial of St. Peter.*

To avoid appearing obvious she looked away, but was unable to strike it from her mind. The painting depicted

St. Peter's third disavowal of a condemned Christ on the morning of the Crucifixion.

A *sign,* she thought; it was Right to draw the aging lawman into The Work here in Goddard – part morality play, part study in accountability.

What took her own brother could have been avoided – had the protectors not looked the other way. That same pattern of pretending had resulted in Patrolman Jim Stevens's deadly car crash.

Facts and fragments about The Innocents – her brother, Jim, and others – had spun so many years in her mind.

Stepping through shallow drifts to lend a hand, Nick didn't notice the blocky shape of her Taser within the bulk of winter garments. But he did notice, she could tell, a length of rigged medical tubing on the old pickup's dashboard. Something, maybe the plastic's medical blue cast, had evoked a sharp discomfort. But the powder melting into his slippers and a biting gust swept this from his mind.

By now The Illuminator had enslaved Cassandra's host identity. But when she bent to lift the signpost, part of the disguise stretched, and then slipped loose inside her flannel shirt. A slight flush of panic, and for a split-second she was frightened Cassandra again.

Nick's gruff offer, "Let me hold that," landed on her ear as a plea and emboldened The Illuminator.

Yet again the young worker's hands fumbled. Again she felt her breast binding slip, and beneath that, Cassandra's heart hammering at having Nick so close. She dropped one of the bolts. "Damn."

"Now," Nick instructed, "Stand up and hold this."

"You'll get sick dressed like that," Cassandra replied,

making sure to use that boy-voice. On the old detective she could smell soap and sweat. And the snack he'd made of grilled cheddar with sliced artichoke and one or two anchovy fillets.

Nick patted his stomach. "Insulation." He knelt, sifted snow between his fingers, and came up with the fastener. "Keep it straight," he ordered, kneeling, and then with some effort bending his former wrestler's build to duck close to the snow and make sure the holes lined up right.

Pushing the bolt through he said, "Think I got it," slipped on the washer and started the nut. From the corner of his eye he saw the youth reach into the toolbox and come up with a ratchet wrench and Nick thought, *I've got to be crazy. The kid could bash in my skull and use the truck to empty my house.* But it didn't stop him from helping.

Now with both bolts in place, the nuts finger tight, Nick groaned standing up, "Use that wrench of yours to snub it up." He jerked a thumb toward home, "That's me over there. . . ." He added, "Temporarily. My buyers move in after New Years."

"She divorce you or something?" Cassandra asked it cruelly, fishing to see how deep lay his wince. Then she stooped to ratchet down the bolts.

"Cancer." Thinking of his wife Nora, Nick turned away and laid a hand on the rail fence. "What're they asking for this lot?"

"I'm not sure." The youth went about installing a cross-bar at the top of the post. "I think maybe, like, forty-five thousand?"

Way too high, Nick thought. Over the past couple year, prices had been falling. But this was only a kid putting up signs, he reminded himself. *Good kid,* he decided. Then he noted foot tracks beyond the fence, and asked, "You walk the lot?"

"Only the bounds." She reached to the crossbar and hung the **For Sale** sign on its bits of chain.

Strange. Nick was thinking. *Why's a kid who doesn't know values concerned with metes and bounds?* He hardened his eyes and stood a shade closer. "Why?"

Toying with the ratchet like a piece of unfinished business, the youth replied, "I had to clear away branches and stuff, my boss said, so people can walk the perimeter."

Nick softened his stance, but kept up the hard eye. He couldn't help notice flecks of red in the irises.

He supposed it was this stare that made the teen's face soften when he heard the confession, "And . . . I wanted to check it out for my father," the kid said, gathering his drill bits and replacing the cordless drill in its box. "If he can get better he wants to try building," he added, turning to place the equipment in the truck bed. "I don't know if we can afford this, though," he sighed and gestured resignedly toward the snowy parcel that appeared so perfect. "We're renting over in Spencer."

"My name's Nick. There're better lots. Got anything to write on?"

From the cab of the pickup the youth brought out a paper and pen and again Nick felt troubled by the rigged medical tubing on the dashboard. "Say, what's with the snorkel?" he asked, indicating the plastic, testing the kid.

The eyes went tense. "My father has a . . . a breathing problem."

Nick felt like an idiot. "Emphysema," he guessed aloud. "That's a tough one." He wrote 'Nick' then his mobile number and email address. "Tell your dad he can call me any time."

"Thanks," the youth replied sheepishly. But her heart hammered with thrill. The Illuminator's task almost finished, she climbed into the truck and turned the ignition key.

Only an electric click and stutter. With it, she heard the pump of blood in her ears. In the next split second, her every molecule scanned to assess risk. Felt edges of the hard, square shape of the Taser in her pocket pressed against her flesh. An all-out break down of the old truck might mean surprises.

"Sounds like the solenoid," Nick offered helpfully.

The Illuminator closed her eyes and in a moment stilled her heart, modulating breath. "Tired Bendix spring," she replied.

It was as if pronouncing the name of the auto part mystically repaired it. Because when she tried again, the motor caught. "Hey," Cassandra asked Nick while backing out, pushing the pitch of her voice to cheer, laying all bets on the sense that an old gruff like Nick would surely refuse, "Want help moving your furniture back inside?"

The Illuminator's instinct proved right.

"Not finished cleaning." Nick looked her over again. "I got all day. Retiring tomorrow."

Cassandra knew. And would study him daily. The surveillance cam, processor, and solar power collector she'd placed walking the lot's perimeter earlier that morning – would monitor Nick like an electric shepherd. As she put the truck in gear and let out the clutch, The Light bubbled inside her. With a broad smile she said, "Thanks, Detective Giaccone," and drove off.

"Don't forget to call on those lots," Nick called out above the clunker's rattling.

Waving, he noted the spin of tires bald as banana skins. *Too heavy on the gas.* He felt his back tense as he watched the truck skid, its rear end whipping loose before disappearing around the street corner.

"No sense."

Walking back toward his house his hackles still hadn't gone flat.

Thanks Detective Giaccone. He'd neither mentioned his last name, nor his life's work.

Let it go, he decided, reminding himself that in the past couple years, after thirty-five years' service as the town's sole detective, he no longer knew everyone in Goddard by name.

That fact had never settled right, amounting to one more reason for getting out.

Tomorrow, after the dedication of Goddard's new police headquarters, Nick's to-do list would be complete. And his retirement final. Today he must stay on task, ready his house for the buyer.

Back inside he hoisted Nora's wingback chair onto machine-gunner's shoulders to resume a thorough housecleaning.

CHAPTER 5

"Look at a case from *missing persons*?" Nick shot back to the chief. He cradled the phone on his shoulder, bending to retrieve veal cutlets from the fridge and thought of the news stories about the Pinecrest teacher gone missing, "It'd be a Hell of a lot easier once the guy's dead, wouldn't it?" Nick joked and moved to the sink to unwrap the meat. Rinsing, he speculated, "Say I review this Allengri thing and come across a lead. I'm done tomorrow after I dedicate the new headquarters – the construction of which canceled my retirement last time. You forget? *No* missing persons. *No* scumbag hunts!"

Nick lay out the three cutlets on a cutting board for tenderizing. He'd been hungry. But a taste like pennies now crept into his mouth. He knew it well: adrenaline.

The chief remained silent on the other end of the line.

The copper taste became intolerable.

Connections come to detectives in all forms. Bad tastes included. And one had better take note. Nick wondered: was it the mention of the name Simon Allengri? Or that rasp in Chief Robertson's voice?

He remembered the last time the chief's voice burned like this. Pre-dawn. New Years morning. Two years back. Same graveled rasp. Official-sounding words, "Officer down."

Things get linked. And the body remembers. By now the taste was so strong Nick wanted to spit.

He didn't have to think: Last time Allengri's name came up – the *only* time – Jim Stevens had uttered it. As a high school kid joining the Goddard Police Cadets program Jim had been a natural, and showed true interest in becoming a policeman. But to Nick it had also been obvious the kid was covering some major stress.

Those days nobody asked. Prying, they used to call it.

But given this week's news stories about Simon Allengri – Nick realized he should have done some of that.

Prying.

After all, he was a detective.

With silence still on the chief's end of the line Nick took up a knurled mallet and began pounding the three fillets.

It worked. The chief asked, "What's all the slamming?"

"Cooking a special lunch for myself," Nick answered, setting the mallet aside, then added sarcastically, "To honor my *re – ti - re - ment*."

"All that damned pounding," the chief chided. "Your cookbook named Cooking With Anger?

"Triumph of the Veal," Nick fired back. Then added, "I'd pay to see *that* movie."

"Cooking what?"

Nick heard sarcasm. "Scallopine. C'mon over. But leave the dossier there." He drizzled oil into a skillet and put a medium flame under it.

"Sounds tasty," answered the chief, from the sound of it reloading for another shot. "Veal. Fancy for a cop, isn't it?"

"I ate shit in the Marines." Nick growled, adding the mushrooms and sautéing. "And for six years after Nora died, not to mention thirty-five years on a cop's diet. I don't smoke any more. Don't drink. I cook. Eat. A lot, and often." He paused to taste the wooden spoon, considered the thought. "And oh, Chief – I'm not a *cop* anymore."

Robertson seemed to ignore the distinction as he sang, "*Nick Giaccone. Cooking.* I never would have thought. Plodding Detective Giaccone. You probably count every strand of spaghetti."

"Detectives cook with style once **retired**," Nick replied with emphasis. "It comes with eating our mistakes . . ." He dusted the three cutlets with spiced flour. They sizzled as they hit the pan.

The chief said, "We'll talk about Allengri tomorrow at the Dedication."

"Ask me wherever the Hell you want. Never going to happen." Nick had put off retiring the first time to help Robertson deal with the aftermath of Jim Stevens' death, and to make sure the Goddard Police Association got the Rookie's mother Mary settled. The second postponement had been last spring, when the chief asked Nick to act as a go-between in constructing the new police station.

He'd said yes to oversee the building of Headquarters, but only once the chief had explained that *this second delay* in retirement would end in the building's dedication to Patrolman Stevens.

Like nobody in Goddard, Nick could pop open a tradesman who lied to try hiding shitwork. And he could spot a mushy bid. This talent for raising a building out of the ground had become second nature after years pulling weekend construction details. The pay from these details became a down payment to build a few houses on spec. And by the time he'd earned a gold detective's shield, Nick's own home was free and clear, with a second one paid off to rent out.

However Nick's comfort zone was the chaos of police

work. The slamming doors at headquarters. The parade of characters, constantly coming and going. But in the quiet of these past three days, making preparations to move out of his house, he'd become lonesome.

"Drop by for a little lunch," he told the chief. "You can help me pack boxes. Then I can tell you **no** to your face."

"Sorry, I'm dieting. But you know, *you* could stand to drop a few. . ."

Nick saw it coming, "Listen to your inner detective, Chief: Never trust a thin chef."

CHAPTER 6

For the rest of that day, The Illuminator worked in her improvised home clinic, dedicating her first surgical Subject's body to Truth.

She'd covered Allengri's eyes during the facial surgeries. But dental procedures today would require full anterior view. So she improvised.

At the drug store she bought a single festive balloon. One of the Mylar type, silver, with words in pink and gold that spelled all over, "Happy Birthday!"

Then from the Home Center she'd picked up a workman's face shield. Like a welder's mask, but transparent.

Later at her garage workbench she'd sliced the balloon open with a razor knife, used a heat gun to laminate the Mylar upon the face shield's plastic lens.

Looking at her reflection, the mirror returned the mask's cheery greeting. Anonymity, with a twist.

Throughout the remaining daylight hours she hovered, adding final touches to Allengri's *true* look – his fangs. Performing this dental work, enjoying the precision, The Illuminator's breast bursted with Light.

Meticulously she applied etching solution to his upper incisors. First the left side, waiting patiently for the chemical to scar the enamel so the cosmetic bonding would adhere. Then she brushed on acrylic resin, wielding the ultraviolet gun to cure each layer beneath its soft blue light.

Then The Illuminator worked to build up her patient's top right incisor, working like a sculptor on a rough clay form.

Once she'd elongated these two teeth, she took up an electric hobby grinder to refine their curve.

She couldn't wait to grasp the full effect.

Allengri's facial surgeries had healed sufficiently. So she decided to remove the bandages. Although he remained in paralysis under the hypnotic drug Succinycholine, to be safe she applied the Velcro hand restraints.

To view The Work, even through the slight blur of the improvised facemask, was magnificent. Simon Allengri, product of a lucid mind.

She stretched. Worked out a kink in her shoulder. And dropped the bandages in the metal basin.

Red on gauze.

Cassandra had trained herself not to shuttle, present to past. But this moment she indulged. A temptation she tried to justify. Reward for hard work. Her work in meat and gristle, a sort of carpentry. To fix a man like Allengri was also to repair a past.

The pilot, dead.

The Colombian Andes, a world of white ice.

Young Cassandra's only medical text, a biography of her hero Clara Barton, founder of the American Red Cross. No way to stop Father's internal bleeding. Mother's compound fractures. Messy infections. Her parents. ***Her brother's*** parents. No provisions. Both would be orphaned. Nothing she could do. Brother back in Goddard. And she, stranded between peaks on a jagged, frozen, knife-edge.

Standing over Simon Allengri, resuming with the grinder, its whine dropped sharply in pitch the moment whirling abrasive met tooth – to make her parents' final words, "Take care of your brother," stop echoing in her ears. In the wisp of smoke from stone spinning hot on enamel – the sharp burnt-hair whiff – those late-teen recollections came undone, spilling.

She steeled herself.

Only in surgery could she staunch the memory.

Now she remembered the progression of misfortune. The seeds of Brother's death.

In her early teens, she'd strived with every fiber to convince her parents to take her to their Mission in Colombia.

She practiced cleanliness. Godliness. Appearances. Ironed her skirt pleats daily to make the right impression at Church school. To perfect her Palmer Penmanship had not been enough. So in order to prove to them she was Devout, she'd learned the art of calligraphy. Pure, she wanted to please them with *all* her writings. Even began to *think* in Capitals, to Magnify all things remotely leading to the Graces.

She would appeal to their Missionary work. Still in high school, she learned the names of the major Religious painters. During one of her parents' brief turn-around trips home to Goddard, she'd begged they take her to Boston's Museum of Fine Arts and the Gardner. Proved to them she could identify each painting at a glance. She even took Saturday art classes, practicing in private to copy every Sacred image.

Then she surprised them by learning Spanish.

The Mission, her parents told her on that exciting night they had said, "yes," was in the process of building a new school on the northern edge of the Colombian department of Cundinamarca, Spanish for Condor's Nest. By 1965 a hot zone controlled by FARC.

They'd left Cassandra in good care, in the convent to the north in Boyacá – just outside the Chibcha village there. Then hopscotched in on a single-engine plane.

For years, Cassandra had relished her parent's endless descriptions of indigenous medical curiosities of the Chibcha tribe – their tales of wondrous cures administered by a rural healer known as the Curandera Rosario.

So while they were away to deliver supplies, she had ventured off convent grounds. A rare occasion, she'd disobeyed. Pulled, it had seemed to her at the time, by the curandera's Ways.

Then her parents had come back three days shy of their planned two weeks. Found out. Unloading gear, her father had told the bush pilot, "Tomorrow we could fit in another run."

Cassandra had noticed a jump seat in the tail of the plane. Had climbed in and bounced a few times.

Her father had looked at her mother. "What do you think?"

The Colombian pilot had complained about the additional weight. The gear and all.

Her father would pay extra.

The crash had to have been her fault. The sudden downdraft. Like the hand of God. Engines whining, the plane had strained to overcome that icy ridge.

No provisions. Throwing snow chunks at the condors.

"Take care of your brother," her parents had repeated.

She'd tried to Nurse them. And when she couldn't, her eyes pulled at the text in her biography of Clara Barton – attempting to will instruction from those pages so Sacred in the history of helping.

There was no controlling their infections. "Learn to do The Work. Be a kind nurse," her mother had murmured.

"Or a skillful *doctor*," her father, delirious, had gasped.

The condors had already stripped the pilot to bones, beginning with his face. *Take care of your brother.* Her parents repeating the phrase in failing breath.

A nurse.

*Or a **doctor**.*

Wedged in a rock crevice to save herself from the snow squall that took them, she had been unable to stop thinking of her brother back in Goddard. His two weeks of summer camp ended by now, his return to their empty house. And no way to contact him.

She'd cut her hands up digging through snow crust to find flat, but rounded stones to cover her parents' eyes. Then packed granular snow to cover their faces, and tipped slabs of crust to shield their heads before leaving.

She knew, picking her way down the cliffs, starving and half-frozen, that the condors would soon come for them, too. Same way they had for the pilot.

Descending toward safety, she'd craned her neck to stare past ledges, up into that clear blue sky to see the condors flocking about that ridge, blotting out the sun.

At first she'd wailed, clawed the rock, unaware she'd torn out the fingernails; then beat fists against the mountain, grating skin away. But by second day she barely looked up

at that flock, arriving above her with the dawn, the dark out-
lines by day's end merged with purple dusk.

By the third day, level ground was all that mattered.

The peasant farmer, after discovering Cassandra collapsed in the weeds, had returned her to the Convent once
she'd regained sufficient strength to utter its name. There she
would build herself back up in the days that followed. And
without knowing it at the time, there she would lay the foundation for The Work.

Cassandra would learn nothing of what had become of
her brother, until weeks later back home in Goddard.

The farmer knew nothing of any plane crash. A walking
Miracle, he would say of *la nina que viene de la montane,* "the
girl who came down from the mountain."

The day the farmer had shown up at the convent with this
shattered girl, the pragmatic Mother Superior sent a rider on
horseback for the Curandera Rosario. A physician from the
Mission clinic could have been flown in easily. But the girl
would undergo further trauma in the linking: the Mission
clinic; her injuries of body; mind; and soul – and the loss of
her parents. This girl Cassandra would need different healing
than a Mission *empirico* could administer.

Cassandra had persevered in building herself back up.
Obsessed, some would say. One of the Blessed, would say
others.

After, it was as if an agreement had been struck between
the curandera and the Convent. Though these two worlds
had never exchanged words.

When Cassandra had learned a certain amount about
rural farming and herbal medicines from Rosario, the curandera would report the need to travel, or feign much to do
and send the girl back to the Convent. There she worked. To

keep her hands in service was to quiet the mind. Copying the Religious painters from books she refined imitation of their styles. Then she'd taken on the Supreme challenge. Pushed herself to learn the full art of Illumination. Like a physical form of prayer, requiring the most disciplined hand.

Amidst these accomplishments, more stints with the curandera.

She grew strong in the care of the Convent and the curandera. Vowed to fulfill her parent's last request, "take care of your brother."

Weeks before, on the same day Cassandra and her parents had left for Colombia, her brother had packed off for three weeks at summer camp with his Youth Camper troop.

Throughout her convalescence at the convent, so that Cassandra could make long distance calls to check on him, the sisters pooled their allotted phone time. All was well, she was told. Members of the Mission back home had made sure her brother was being cared for.

Yet whenever Cassandra had mentioned her brother to the curandera, a cloud of concern crossed the woman's sun-creased face.

The truth would not come to Cassandra until much later. While Cassandra had been surviving the frozen Andes, and then afterward rebuilding herself back at Camp Quiet in Massachusetts her brother had earned badges; had learned how to paddle a canoe; swam a mile; and memorized countless knots. All under the tutelage of a prep school teacher who during summer recess gave his time in the role of Assistant Campmaster – and who, hearing of Brian's parents' awful death, had volunteered to take the boy under his wing until members of The Mission could take things over.

The Assistant Campmaster's name was Simon Allengri,

whose fangs now glistened under The Illuminator's finishing touch.

She sprayed a fine water mist on Allengri's new dental work and gently moved his head to collect the rinse. Lowered the Versa-bed. Turned him as she had twice daily in avoidance of bedsores.

Then she would attend to her own body, in rigorous Capoeira exercises to strengthen and sharpen reflexes. It helped her dodge the old memories, a clash of past and present that she knew would be inevitable before The Work in this little town would be complete.

But first, before beginning her workout, she hung a freshly pressed tuxedo in the clinic – in full view of her patient – where upon awakening, Allengri would see the costume for his release very soon, back into his predatory wild.

For the dedication ceremony at Goddard's new police headquarters she chose austere femininity. An emerald sheath, black hose and heels. Bobbed auburn wig, mascara, eyeliner. She used rouge to suggest fine cheekbones, then brought blush to blur with a wedge of sponge and create a face easy to forget. Some cheap orbicular sun glasses to hide the irises, although to put them on brought a slight guilt, for covering the face that kept Brother alive for her.

She would take a taxi and have it wait. Only long enough to watch Nick a few minutes. Develop more of a feel for him while he worked in his native element.

Soon he'd be heading out. So Cassandra left the vanity table for her workroom, where she clicked on the web cam she'd trained on the old detective's house.

She shivered with delight. Found the new surveillance cam intriguing, as she swiveled it this way and that with the joy stick, panning the front of Nick's house.

His front door swung open. Dignified in his Neapolitan greatcoat and dress blues, he crossed the driveway. When he paused at the rear of his car, Cassandra zoomed in for a close-up. She said softly, "Turn into the light."

Unlocking his car, Nick felt he was being watched. Felt a quick, cold gust. Heard the newly hung **For Sale** sign across the lane creak on its bits of chain. He raised his chin slightly when he turned to glance at it.

"There." Cassandra clicked the mouse to capture a still she could use. When the image popped up on her screen as a photo, The Illuminator registered deep satisfaction within.

A certain oil painting project she was planning, to create a study of Accountability, would require this close shot of the old detective's face.

Outside she heard the taxi. At the last minute before leaving for the event she swapped the heels for flats.

CHAPTER 7

New police headquarters. Gleaming squad room. Buntings of red, white, and blue.

Nothing spared in the memory of fallen officer Jim Stevens. Not grieving nor guilt. The dress blues funeral with its snare drums. The clap of a thousand service oxfords on frozen pavement, marching Jim's remains toward the Church. The sound of the bagpipes had never left Nick's ears.

Today, the prickle of wool dress blues scratched and grabbed at the aging detective's neck and shoulders as he stepped to the polished oak podium to get a feel. He'd stood in this squad room dozens of times.

Ceiling fixtures reflected rivulets of light along the squad room's double-waxed floor. To look at the rows of shiny new desk-chairs, there it was, rolling in his mind again. Neither heads nor tails, like a coin still spinning after a toss: Which seat in this now immaculate place would be the first to go empty one morning at roll call? Which Goddard policeman next to die?

Nick brought out his key ring and grasped that second chrome handcuff key, his only memento of his protégé. The scrape, tick, and click of Jim Stevens' key had become a soundtrack to these worries for the two years since that fatal wreck. Now he used the key to trace the lectern's varnished wood grain and scrape across it, anticipating today's speech, and the uncertainty of retirement.

Nick had been a champion Goddard High School wrestler. That, and thirty-five years as Goddard P.D's first and only detective, had earned him the town's respect. Whether steering lost kids, or questioning crooks, Nick knew how to size and present. He conveyed paternal empathy with brushy eyebrows and coal-shiny, gray-streaked hair. Could soften his eyes into deep receptive pools, or flare those peepers into steely black pellets. With wordless curl of lip, or subtle shift of his thick frame, in that instant Nick's interlocutor saw wisdom in baring the soul. And like any true master, the detective applied his powers of craft judiciously.

Yet what long haunted some part of him lay deep, would never give itself up so easily.

Nick now set his key chain on the podium and reached into a breast pocket to locate his speech – a page from a yellow legal pad, penciled heavily and worn through at the folds. In the past weeks he'd scrawled the page in fits of inspiration, made the strike-throughs of doubt – so that what he *now* wanted to say spilled well into the margins. Unfolding the tired page, he was unsure if the speech would even fly.

Nick was torn from these thoughts as the media entered, mounting cameras, stringing cable, and placing mikes.

Lost reporters called to one another in the hallways. Distant rattling to test virgin holding cells. A swarm, bumbling about a new hive box.

Earlier this morning, from this very same lectern, Chief Robertson had made it clear to the detail of officers while readying: "I want this ceremony crisp and simple, with the dignity of a trifold flag."

Now Robertson strode into the squad room, sights set on Nick, carrying a dossier in one hand.

When the detective saw the case file he shook his head "no" and held out his palm as if to stop an oncoming bus.

Before the chief got to him there came a shout from the foyer. And there, appeared Braxton "Brax" Jewell, Chairman of Goddard's Board of Selectman. When Jewell called out again to Robertson, the chief turned on a heel and sprang to greet him.

When they entered the squad room Braxton Jewell's eyes met Nick's, yet neither man acknowledged the other. The undertaker's head a blonde permanent helmet of calamistrum curls. And that ever-approving smile, rows of tiny cigarette-yellowed teeth Jewell used to bite off sentences.

A man who would cheat the dead, Nick thought. Jewell had started his Goddard real estate empire by filling in a marsh to create Hillside Cemetery, where Patrolman Stevens lay at rest.

Now the chief was ushering the Chairman and his wife toward seats in the squad room. Bunny Jewell was an attractive woman, taller than average and with a figure most men would call striking. Her hair was the shifting blue-black of a crow's wing. Today she wore it up in a gleaming knot, pinned with silver combs, accentuating delicate and sweeping planes of cheek and a pair of dark eyes the shape of almonds that gave her a Moorish look – all to make her mid-forties seem ageless.

People who'd lived in Goddard a while would remember that at one time, Bunny Jewell made the daily commute to Boston to do the weather on TV. They had likely given up wondering what had ended such a promising career, so prematurely.

Jewell was saying to the chief, "Once I park my wife I'll do a walk-through on camera with the press. . . "

After the two headed off, Nick stepped to greet Mrs. Jewell. She looked more subdued than usual, around her eyes and mouth new lines of worry.

Her husband had jockeyed fundraising for the new headquarters, had gotten the lot donated from an investor in the Goddard Mall. Now acted like he owned the police station and everyone in it, since the project had catapulted him from a member of the small town's Board of Selectman to its Chairman.

The very next day he'd spent twelve hundred dollars on a bullmastiff – of champion bloodlines yet poorly trained – which he named Maximus. "You know," Jewell had taken the chief aside to clue him, "a bullmastiff's more or less a Senator's dog."

From the podium Nick kept his eye on the chief. After seeing to the Chairman's needs, Robertson careened to greet Jim Stevens' mother, Mary, who he led to a reserved chair, toward which Nick stepped to take her coat.

Back at the podium, the soon-retiring detective watched townspeople stream in. Gawking, wrongside a police station's inner doors.

He noticed where guests had tracked in grit – the sand broadcast on every New England road to provide traction – its grit a presence each winter, indoors and out. He'd known most of these people since they'd been teens. Now they carried babies or led grandchildren. Wherever guests turned a heel, Nick could see milky swirls that shown dull against the new floor's gleaming wax job.

A cluster of fresh-faced patrolmen arrived and filled the reserved rows.

The squad room was almost full. When Nick glanced toward the foyer he caught sight of immensity. Relieved to see the hulking form and dark countenance of Lou Civitelli, known affectionately throughout the town as "Peanut." Goddard's premier concrete supplier and foundation contractor – his mix making up the police station's foundations – provided by Lou at far below cost.

Nick waved. He couldn't help smiling.

Taking this as permission, Peanut made his tentative entrance. Almost apologetic, as if aware his huge form subtracted space from the room. Passing Nick a sheepish, waist-level wave with his thick hand, he lowered his immense body onto a pair of metal folding chairs in the back row.

Taking in the man's gigantic, seated form, Nick recalled that every year since Jim's fateful drive, Lou had donated a significant percentage of his concrete business proceeds to the Goddard Police and Fireman's Association. Watching a now-seated Lou Civitelli, Nick got a startling sense of how quickly this facility and its policing capabilities would be outgrown.

Outside, The Illuminator was pulling up in a taxi, looking the part of anyone's next-door neighbor. It proved a guilty pleasure to leave her patient alone in the clinic. Now, with Nick, she'd work a project purely mental.

She paid the driver and had him wait.

Once inside Headquarters, Cassandra slipped into a row behind the patrolmen.

By then Nick faced a packed house. He cleared his throat, and leaned forward. Felt a sudden cool spot in the small of his back where sweat had collected. He breathed in and out.

When he lifted his chin the room fell silent, and he began.

Cassandra pricked up her ears.

Nick's speech was short. He kept it crisp. Duty. Honor. And Commitment.

To calibrate, The Illuminator would need a psychic map of this man. Wanted to measure his strengths, to plumb any canyons of despair, to chart each subsurface fault and fissure.

So while he spoke, she remained keen – to a slightest flinch when Nick uttered words in reference to Patrolman Jim Stevens such as *sacrifice* and *loss*. Listened for any catch in his voice when he delivered words like *hope* or *potential*. Watched to see if his shoulders sagged, almost imperceptibly, to recount that Jim's path to the police force had been through Nick's very own high school Police Cadets program. She even gauged the color of the old detective's skin for its slightest tinge of gray as he described Jim's outstanding performance in Police Academy training.

Then, somber and square-shouldered, Nick invited the hero's mother to the podium in order to read a letter from the Academy's Commandant.

And as Mary Stevens read about Jim's superior performance, how in daily ten-mile runs he had consistently led the pack, dropping back to encourage stragglers, but finishing first every time, The Illuminator kept her eyes on Nick, sizing up his response.

And while Jim's mother read that letter, Nick fought off the sense he was being watched, inventoried.

The Illuminator saw a man burdened by guilt and used to carrying it. As the detective relived Jim Steven's loss only nine months into the job by way of Mary Stevens' reading voice, The Illuminator saw him shrink slightly, and then with dignity, spring back.

The moment Mary finished reading the audience erupted into standing ovation.

Nick guided her to her seat and then returned to the podium. Scanning the audience he caught a glimpse of Brax Jewell, lolling in a folding chair, ankle on knee, hand in his hair, toying with his own styled blond feathers.

Police Chief Phil Robertson had by then taken the podium. He introduced Forensic Specialist Chris Bailey, a powerful new addition to Goddard's law enforcement team. As lead officer in a new, state of the art Cyber Crime Lab, this addition to the force would support every police officer on the street. Calling Bailey "Goddard's secret weapon," the chief asked him to stand, which brought more applause.

Next Chief Robertson motioned to Nick. They stepped in unison to the waiting tripod and then drew away the blue satin shroud covering it, revealing a bronze relief in the likeness of Patrolman Jim Stevens.

Proudly Nick announced the dedication of the Goddard Police Station to Jim's memory. And the three: Nick, Robertson and Mary Stevens made their procession to the stations' foyer with the plaque. There they placed the bronze within a glass display case in full view of all who entered.

Moments later Nick stood by the doors wishing guests farewell. There were compliments on the new building, and best wishes for retirement.

He then walked Mary Stevens to a waiting squad car that would get her home, the street grit, born on the December wind hitting his skin sharp as pinpoints.

As Nick finished with goodbyes to Mary Stevens, his friend Lou Civitelli brushed by, leaving the detective feeling dwarfed by the concrete worker's sheer mass and bulk.

Lou had been a contemporary of Jim's through elementary and high school, the Rookie's fishing buddy later on, and few but Nick knew that the mason's donations had been instrumental in making sure the patrolman's mother was kept comfortable the past two years.

Now to Nick, the concrete contractor was saying quietly, in that low growl, "Next time you need mix, I'll take care of you." And even though Civitelli had poured the foundation for this station, and had lived in Goddard longer than Nick, and was surely aware of the detective's retirement beginning this very day, at a loss for other words he shoved his business card into Nick's hand:

CIVITELLI CONCRETE

WE POUR, YOU SNORE.

"Thanks Lou." Nick said. He pocketed the card. "But I hope I won't need this where I'm going." Then on his shoulder he felt Peanut's palm, gently set, but going all the heft and girth of a brisket.

When he looked up, Nick asked, "Yeah Peanut. What's on your mind?"

"Nick. Your speech about Jim Stevens was…was…. It was —." Lou's deep, resonant, yet hesitant speech was thick with something deeply heartfelt, and his eyebrows, heavy like rolled up wolves' pelts, gathered toward the center of brow above the great slab of the towering man's face.

But for the life of him, Nick could not understand what Lou was striving so hard to convey.

"What do you want to *tell* me, Lou? What *is* it, little guy?" He saw a tear forming.

"I only wanna say . . . " Lou searched for correct words "Your speech, about Jim Stevens, Nick, was . . . was very . . .. Very *pungent*."

Moments later this last guest was gone. With the media packing up, Nick stood alone, facing the bronze plaque of his protégé Jim.

For a moral man, the question mark is the shepherd's crook. And now questions too vague to identify tugged at him, told him his course of his life would veer. And silently he accepted it.

Because the answer Nick now fought off was distinct, more than a hunch, in fact solid as ice. Instead of putting the tragedy of Jim's loss to rest, he was now only beginning to glimpse the pith of it. And he knew what was coming was going to be a haul. In thirty-five years on the job, instincts like this one had never lied. No, Nick understood as he looked upon Goddard's bronze hero. This was beyond hunches, or instincts. It was about Knowledge.

From behind him he heard the chief speak. "Listen, there's always a desk here if you get homesick."

Nick turned and replied: "You know both my houses are already sold." Behind the chief he could see Braxton Jewell emerge from the squad room, waltzing toward where they stood.

As Nick watched Robertson shifting on his feet, the chief was thinking about his talk the night before with The Headmaster. And about his twin grand daughters. As Jewell drew nearer, the chief said to Nick, "Maybe then. . . You remember Braxton went to Pinecrest Academy. . .I'll call you for a *short look* at that missing persons thing. . . ."

That rasp again in Robertson's voice.

And yet the chief understood what he saw, the tired detective staring at his protégé, transformed into bronze. Now Goddard Police Department's perpetual protector.

By then Chairman Jewell had come up beside them, brimming with impatience, looking toward the chief with vital questions in his eyes. "I'm third-generation Pinecrest Alumni," the Chairman was saying.

Nick shot back, "You forgot to mention that a few thousand times, Brax."

The Chairman only glared and sucked air through his smile.

This time it was the chief's turn to raise a hand and halt traffic. "Enough for one day."

Nick was sliding a hand into his jacket pocket for his key ring. For Jim's key. But felt the hard edges of his revolver and then his shield, and beneath them the soft, folded speech he had prepared these past weeks: feathered, frayed, torn, and finally today – delivered. Gently he placed his service revolver and gold shield into the chief's hand.

Without another word Nick Giaccone turned, fully retired, and walked out into the brisk November air.

CHAPTER 8

The New England Weather Service had been keeping tabs on a Nor'easter brewing.

Cassandra remained unconcerned. In Pinecrest Academy's hundred-plus years there had never been a cancellation of Autumn Follies.

So while student newspaper reporters readied about Pinecrest's campus, The Illuminator bathed and clothed Simon Allengri for his debut.

Some schools hold bonfires to chase away the blues of shortening days, and dissipate new-kid nerves. Pinecrest's famous fall ritual was Autumn Follies, celebrated in the last half of the first semester, a time for both students and faculty to share in a day's absurdity.

Dress for the event had never been optional. Students competed as if with blood thirst, drawing lots to select the best attire. Each costume carried a heritage, prized by the school, and stored carefully throughout the year in a cold vault beneath the library.

Traditional costumes at Autumn Follies, such as the Musketeers, Merlin, Brer Rabbit, and the Three Blind Mice, traced back to the Founder – and were and worn with pride each December – in keeping with his philosophy: "With all of us so capable of tomfoolery, why not get on with the learning?"

Further Academy tradition held for wealthy alumni to sponsor new costumes, their unveiling a major spectacle of the event's kick-off. Donations accompanying the disguises swelled scholarship funds and buttressed endowments, while adding to a school's set of quirks believed to invite better minds.

Follies tradition, it was widely known throughout the town of Goddard, held for Category prizes to be awarded each Academy residence house: Best Traditional; Cleverest Use of Technology; Ugliest; Most Fearsome; or Most Lovely – from Frankenstein to Santa Claus, to Bluebeard and Astronauts, Father Time and the Fairy Tale figures of the Brothers Grimm.

Individual student awards came in the form of scholarships or preferred lodging. From day one of September classes, until that special early December afternoon, students were rush and hurry, earning advantage to win their pick of the finest masquerade.

Because to *draw*, and then *wear* many of the disguises brought its own honor, in light of the costume's provenance and the status of its First Wearer.

Scoring went according to two criteria and always had: a student's dumb luck in pulling a costume to suit, and the way one *wears* what has been drawn.

It had even been whispered for years in the halls of the Academy that if a student does not make best use of, or else *overcome*, the way he is seen at the Follies of his freshman year, he might well be regarded that way throughout life.

Cassandra chose to dress in pristine Vintage, choosing an outfit she'd stored in mothballs in her brother's attic: traditional winged white cap with red piping and matching white dress, hemmed below the knee. White opaque hose and nurse's oxfords. Then she brought her parent's old motor home around front to load Allengri, blindfolded but now fierce in black tie and tails.

She rolled the breathtaking Illuminated manuscript, then slid the scroll into a capped protective brass tube. Playbill for Allengri's debut.

Before leaving she checked on the birds.

Driving the motor home through the gates of Pinecrest Academy at the turn of dusk, Cassandra could see the breathtaking Follies Promenade, under way. Hundreds of students and faculty, a collection of the ghastly and the goofy, snaking through each campus building, the lead of the line just short of the Red Carpet that stretched like a tongue from Scutherly Hall's arched entry.

An ambulance stood by, parked near the auditorium as with all major Academy events. She parked in one of the outer lots and seated Allengri in a wheel chair.

Spotting the EMTs from a distance, Cassandra took a short cut behind the gym building to maintain it, timing her progress to emerge a short distance ahead of the procession, near to the auditorium, striding evenly, pacing herself to stay well ahead. Looked the dutiful guardian of an esteemed advanced-age alum, back at the academy for a day's play.

Cassandra had researched the event's format, and once inside the auditorium seated her dead ringer for Dracula accordingly. He would be first to get the spotlight, first to stand and bow, first to call out his character.

If he got through it. Because upon Allengri's lap she'd left a gilt-framed mirror.

The brass cylinder within his vest would gleam visible when the spotlight hit it.

The procession entered. Draperies drawn. Lights down, and music up.

The Illuminator dropped back, blending with the crowd to watch.

Now three Switzer Pikesmen adorned in varicolored stripe march down the auditorium's middle aisle to take their place before the orchestra pit: right, left, and center.

When the Halberdiers snap to attention the lights go down to blackness.

Thunder when their lances come down hard on the oakwood floor.

The eerie strains of the Theramin choir. Then a drum roll.

Behind the guards the stage lights up.

"Let the Follies begin!" calls The Headmaster, appearing dressed as a chef.

Spot light stutters from one creature to the next – the audience releasing oooohs, aaaahs and erupting chuckles – until the light comes to rest upon the First Follier.

The spot light has lit on Simon Allengri.

He's groggy. His withdrawal from the narcotics carefully timed.

A nearby first-year takes note, helps this Dracula to his feet.

Feeling bright heat of light, thousands of eyes upon him, Allengri gropes his face.

He tests point of fang, contorts his mouth, and releases a howl.

A gasp from watching students fills the red-tongued hall as if the auditorium itself craves breath.

Blinded by the spotlight, Count Dracula raises the gold-framed mirror, looped to his wrist on a length of braided chord.

He delivers a long and mournful cry, staggers toward the window, and yanks at the drapery's linings. After another look he crashes the mirror though the glass.

Entangled in gold chord, glass, and gossamer, Mortified by his truer self, Simon Allengri clutches his breast, writhes.

Gold chord cut on glass, the sound of the mirror hitting the ground below.

The teacher's knees fail. He leaks a plaintive whimper as his body accordions toward the floor.

Watching from a doorway, The Illuminator swoons.

CHAPTER 9

Center stage, squinting through the spotlight, The Headmaster ran swift mental calculations. One teacher gone missing, now going down in flames. . . . And the hundreds of students in this auditorium, each embarking on a future.

Deftly, in a play to counter panic, he joked, "That bloodsucker's part of the act." With quick thinking he added, "And you first-years thought *you* felt claustrophobic?"

He knew it had worked when there erupted roars of laughter.

Toward the two campus security guards who now stared at him seeking direction, The Headmaster then threw a rapid sideways slicing gesture of a finger.

He had managed to pass it off.

Introducing Costume Judging, the Follies' next phase, The Headmaster was able to steal a glance at stricken faces once the security guards reached Allengri and then spoke into a handheld radio. Moments later a stretcher was in the room, Dracula loaded, and then gone.

In an adjacent classroom as he loosened Allengri's shirt, the first responder peeled off his latex glove. He needed a better feel, looking for some kind of seam between the skin of the teacher's neck and what had to be an elaborate mask.

"This is no disguise," the ambulance man whispered to his partner.

The Follies in full swing, The Headmaster now appeared. Circling up every medic and campus security guard, he said, "I have no intention of alarming my students, with so much invested in their Pinecrest education. Until we get this figured out, Allengri's was a staged performance. Got that?"

It made perfect sense. There were nods all around. Without a hiccup in Autumn Follies, The Headmaster walked back stage to call the chief.

CHAPTER 10

A few minutes later the chief called Nick. "They found Simon Allengri."

"Back for the Follies. . .?"

"And dead," said the chief. That coarse quality again in his voice.

To hear it itched Nick's ear canal. "Dead how?"

"Bastard looked in a mirror."

Nick had given much thought to the twins' hopes for Pinecrest. He said, "Guy dies in the only place I'm not about to tell you no."

"Meet me at Scutherly Hall. Off the main auditorium there's a classroom for the Drama Department."

Nick switched off the call and went for his great coat.

On the way to the Academy, the detective drove past week-old remnants of Halloween: rain-sogged bundled corn stocks, sheet ghosts frozen stiff in a front yard oak. Smashed jack-o-lanterns still slicked the streets.

In the heavy lifting of cleaning house Nick had pulled a shoulder muscle. Heading toward what might throw retirement to the winds, he felt his neck muscles playing Twister.

Uniformed policemen strung yellow tape to secure the now-vacant auditorium. Next door in the small classroom, plainclothesmen took statements from an astonished pair of EMTs.

The security guards who first got to Allengri crowded about the now-lifeless body with the Chief and Headmaster. Chairman Jewell had arrived a few steps ahead of Nick and was making a beeline for them. Engrossed, The Headmaster seemed not to recognize Chairman Jewell. The Chairman stood expectantly, eavesdropping, craning his neck – appearing, in Nick's eye, like an underfed ferret.

Then a word from The Headmaster, and the chief made a sign to a uniformed policeman to escort the Chairman outside the official perimeter.

A veteran detective always notices something – this time the tint of the Chairman's skin when he grimaced. Nick stared so he could see more of the color as the man rolled back his shirt cuff. A new in-public habit of Jewell's was showing off his Rolex, pronouncing the name of the timepiece *Perpetual Oyster* through those tiny teeth, and then adding a lascivious wink.

"Hey Brax," Nick greeted the Chairman. "Ghouls night out, eh?"

When the Chairman didn't extend a hand to shake, neither did Nick.

Instead Jewell brushed Bullmastiff hair from his slacks. Yes, definitely bright orange was Jewell's skin, going all the way up the arm. Looking right in place in a room festooned for late-autumn festivities.

"Looks like Mister Chairman's been napping in the tanning booth," Nick quipped. "I'm trying to decide if you've gone orange, or just yellow."

The skin surrounding Jewell's eyes still shone white – like an owl's. *Eye covers*, Nick figured.

Jewell sneered. "You always come out with such clever words. Your wife Nora must've died laughing."

"With words like that I could never be you, Brax." When Nick turned to meet the chief and Headmaster he mentioned nothing about the coloration of the Chairman's tan. But a lingering image in his mind's eye made Nick wonder. In his entirety, might Brax Jewell resemble a pumpkin?

"Allengri bit the dust in an auditorium full of students so they moved him here," the chief was saying. "Coroner's on his way."

"Autumn Follies is all over the evening news. Why no footage of Dracula?"

"Standard procedure not to scare off kids trying to earn a diploma," The Headmaster answered dryly, but without fully answering the question.

Nick let it go. "Any idea how they grabbed him?"

"No clue." The two Plainclothesmen vying to become Nick's replacement, the chief explained, had already dusted Allengri's house for prints and processed for trace. The place had been wiped.

They found two things. Candy bars. The big ones kids sell door-to-door to raise money for sports."

"Trick or treat. . ." Nick mused. ". . . I think trick: Kid selling little-league candy turns perverted faculty member into Count Chocula."

"The trace they found in Allengri's house was some kind of hummingbird dander."

Nick had already said too much. Now he chose not to roll his eyes in the company of a school official.

"Allengri appeared to be heavily drugged," The Headmaster put in, and described the teacher's violent reaction to his own reflection, then collapse.

Nick crouched for a look at this paper-white Count Dracula. To look for needle tracks he used the stub of a pencil, probed the tuxedo's collar, the pant legs, and then shirt cuffs. At the left wrist he caught sight and told the chief, "Get a camera over here."

He gloved up, then removed the left cuff link, and drew up Allengri's shirtsleeve.

There on the skin appeared to be embroidery, in blue, like sutures. Nick could make no sense of the words,

CONTRAPASSO
Canto XXVIII: 141-2

"A specific reference," The Headmaster whispered over Nick's shoulder.

"To what?"

"Weapons-grade poetry."

Slightly turning the body he caught the gleam of something in Allengri's tuxedo breast pocket. A capped tube, made of polished brass.

Could be wired to something, Nick thought. Carefully he felt inside the pocket for any trip wire. In a single smooth motion he slid the tube free. Then unscrewed the cap and shook.

Inside he found a document. Ancient, by the look.

Seeping into Nick's mind was the inkling – this message might be aimed at him.

Camera flash blinded Nick when the plainclothesman photographed the left hand's sutured embroidery.

Spots before the detective's eyes retreating, he began to read,

He'd never laid eyes on such a page. Antique, yet so brilliant. Like the work of an ancient scribe or some rare and secret Church document.

The page emanated seduction, by sheer brilliance.

Nick couldn't help running a finger over the message's cracked surface, a mottled amber and pomegranate in color.

Then suddenly, reading the three lines, he felt himself growing protective – a sense that the characters inked in black might threaten to rob the other filigreed letters in crimson, green, and gold of their brilliance.

Nick closed his eyes a moment and then tried again to make some sense of this.

Flowering vines filled the page's burnished gold margins.

Among these vines three hummingbirds hovered at blossoms, each bird distinct and individual in color and attitude.

As if at play with these birds a moment, the detective's tired eyes now darted about to take in the page's every detail.

Some poetic cocktail.

To look upon the stunning Illumination, Nick's every certainty now seemed like a joke: a solid brick headquarters that now stood for Jim's loss . . . the detective's own retirement . . . name it.

Yet one thing was certain. The past had come back to haunt. As the detective hunched over this Dracula going stiff, neck muscles a contorted yoke, it was clear that the corpse before him was no ghost.

"Nick. . ."

The chief's voice now sounded like from miles away.

Deep in thought now about the first time he'd heard Allengri's name. And in those same months the things a high school-aged Jim had let slip. . .

The chief almost shouted. **"NICK!"**

Nick dizzied as he stood. Straightening, with pain signals shooting through neck and shoulders he found himself facing The Headmaster. The chief right beside him. Both staring.

The Headmaster read the manuscript in Nick's hand. The cloud of gray across his face betrayed cautious recognition. Then the official glanced away, toward the classroom door.

Again glancing at the Illuminated text still in hand, Nick realized he was still spellbound – by a mix of outrage and deep regret – forced to the surface by this document – a combination that could seduce and captivate.

Unsure *why*, Nick suddenly *had* to have this case, his plans for the future now shadows.

It was a sheer act of will for Detective Giaccone to restore the scroll to its brass sleeve.

He mentioned none of this, cleared his head, and could hear an edge of bitterness in his own voice that he didn't much care for when he asked The Headmaster who might've written all this.

"Talk to Canon Nailor at Brauser College." The Headmaster was preoccupied, now, with an entering knot of Pinecrest officials.

"I know of Nailor." Everyone did. As founder of the FBI Forensics Lab for Text, Notes, and Manifestos, the professor had put Goddard on the map.

Nick felt at all his pockets and came up with his key ring. For the moment, the small handcuff key in hand soothed with its tangible familiarity. With a glance toward the doorway he noted the small cloud of reporters that had slipped through. Until Pinecrest security guards held them off.

"Those dogs'll want a bone," Nick warned The Headmaster. "Chief Robertson has instructed me to do all I can to help .... Pinecrest's a great school."

The Headmaster's opinion of the newly departed became clear when he indicated the remains and then drew Nick nearer to whisper, "Things could have been far worse, Detective Giaccone. Allengri had tenure."

Holding up the brass cylinder, Nick added, "I'll need to work fast. By now the perp will be out hunting '*the man who is his own nemesis*.'"

"Whatever it takes to clean house."

The comment left Nick guessing as The Headmaster vanished with his entourage through another doorway across the room that the detective hadn't even noticed before, where more campus security entered to fend the press. In the crush Nick felt someone thrust a thin folder into his hand. When he opened the cover he found a professionally prepared dossier. Allengri's background, habits, phone, financial ,and Internet records. And what looked to be a house key taped inside the folder's cover.

Suddenly Nick felt a chill, glanced toward the door and thought: *The Coroner must've been mixed with that incoming bunch.* People joked that the man had been appointed to the job because he was sure to cut county morgue expenses. Because every room he entered dropped a full twenty degrees in temperature.

Now Nick watched the Coroner's approach. Chambers Fogg, M.D., a gray wisp of a man whose little moustache worked when he spoke as if to tidy his tweedy precision.

At the current line of sight, the brim of the Coroner's bowler hat, only elbow high to most and always pulled hard to the man's brow, prevented eye contact. Which was fine for Nick. The man's eyes impossible to forget, the bleached-out hue of a mourning dove made their irises almost indistinct from the whites. So at normal speaking distance Fogg's gaze was a milky translucence that bulged like a pair of small boiled onions.

The chief summed up the dilemma as Fogg removed his coat and pulled on examination gloves, leaving his hat squarely in place. "Meet Simon Allengri. Murder or self-inflicted. Jury's still out."

The rumors about Fogg had to be right, Nick thought. *This chill now can't be coincidence. Maybe the reason in twenty years, I've never seen Fogg remove that bowler.* Out loud, Nick added to the chief's summary that to look in a mirror had caused severe chest pain that led to Allengri's collapse. "I'd say heart attack."

Too fascinated by the corpse to heed Nick and the chief, the Coroner was already down on a knee. He spoke into a voice recorder but trained his attention on this Dracula as if addressing it. The Coroner began, "Showy work," his silken voice a lullaby to a presence beyond the grave.

Nick felt a prickle at his scalp. To distract he asked, "Who are we looking for? An M.D. parent getting even? Must be talent like *that* at an uppercrust school like Pinecrest."

The Coroner almost whispered, his tone as an apology, "The work is rough." His gloved hand received Allengri's chin almost like a caring stroke as he once again addressed the dead, "You've had a quick-change, Mister Allengri. Judging from this. . . if your last encounter *was* a physician," he gently sang, "he was surely no facelift man. The surgery is best described as. . ." the coroner pronounced it with a lilt, a poet birthing words, "*Augmentation Rhinoplasty.*"

He ran two fingers along Allengri's nose and again spoke into his recording device as if it were the only live thing in the room, "Quite hurried though . . . instead of grafting carti-lage, our cutter built up the tip of the nose and upper laterals by injection. Note to extract sample for lab tests – could be household silicone caulk."

When Dr. Fogg looked up at them Nick could not avoid the man's eyes. Their lack of pigment no ailment, caused by low melanin levels from time of birth; the condition affect-ed eye and skin coloration, which explained why Fogg was known to avoid sunlight.

It was equally known that Chambers Fogg M.D. gave his time freely in the County cadaver program to the benefit of nearby Brauser College Medical School. And because of such exposure, at times like this, Nick would speculate whether Fogg's bleached-out eye color was the result of seeing so much. To save himself from the sight, the detective prompted the Coroner, "Have a gander at its fangs. . ."

Fogg turned back to his work, hooked a latex-clad digit inside the Dracula's lip and pulled the cold mouth open. He ignited a penlight, then probed the sharpened teeth with a pointed metal implement with a crook in it. His voice was still a lullaby. "Fang dentistry, amateur – but dental-quality: our cutter used acrylic resin bonding to build up the incisors. Possible use of a hobbyist's grinder to shape them into curves."

Nauseated, Nick swallowed hard. A spinning Dremel grinding live, human teeth. Hummingbirds whipping about.

When he held out the brass tube and asked, "Want to see the message we found on the body?" the Coroner only sniffed and then twitched his tiny moustache.

The chief asked, "So, a homicide? Or something else?"

The Coroner didn't reply. Stripping off gloves and replacing the recorder in his jacket pocket, Dr. Fogg smoothed his moustache, plucked his upper lip, and then, reaching within his tweeds produced the Death Certificate. Filling in a few last facts, he said, "I'm stating cause of mortality as Death by Reflection, with contributing condition of Sociopathology . . . In view of Mr. Allengri's taste for the student body."

Very soon Fogg's ghastly gaze would again rise from beneath the brim of his hat.

The Coroner's next gesture was the only reason Nick and Chief Robertson didn't look away. Folding the Death Certificate in two, the little man held it like a library volume, but remained silent. Thoughtful ambassador to the cold side of the dirt.

Dr. Fogg lifted his chin and turned the onions on them. "There's no judging any book by its cover. I'll know more once I read the full cavity. The County hearse is on its way. . ."

The Coroner's swift motion of tearing the chief's copy from the three-part form seemed uncharacteristic in its violence.

Gently folding away his own copy of the paperwork, Dr. Fogg then lowered those goggled eyes to rest upon the dead,

"For now, Allengri, adieu," turned and slipped on his coat and departed, bowler hat still squarely in place.

Nick massaged his face in his hands and rubbed his eyes. They'd taken in much today. The pedophile Dracula. The breathtaking Illuminated manuscript. Fogg.

He looked at the chief, who seemed at odds as well.

Snapping to his senses, Nick shouted a few instructions to the uniformed policemen and plainclothesman. "Everyone but Forensics out." Some action might chase the chill from the room. He pointed to the dead Count. "I want every fiber of this bleeder's clothes processed for trace before the Coroner's boys pick him up for autopsy."

"You all right?" the chief asked as the officers sprung to work.

"Mutant!" Nick muttered gruffly.

"Fogg's eyes *are* a treat."

"I'm talking about Count Dracula here, Chief! Guys at a school like this can have a thousand victims. Gotta admit the genius of that surgery. No kid's going hang out with someone who obviously looks like a monster."

"Incoming," the chief warned. With the police barrier coming down, Chairman Jewell was sliding toward the dead body and taking a camera from his pocket.

"Crime scene, Ed," Nick shouted before the Chairman could get any nearer.

"My hands are tied," the chief added. "Headmaster's rules. Sorry Ed."

As they watched the bulk of Chairman Jewell ebb backward like a malignant tide, Nick mused, "Jewell must have a new scam going as a Paparazzi for Mortuary Monthly."

"This is big time crime for Goddard," the Chief said warily. "If we're not careful Brax'll insert himself in the case for the exposure."

"*We*." Nick narrowed his eyes at Roberson. "If I do decide to take this case. And that's **if**. . . .Chief."

"If," Robertson repeated. "You know, Nick. I wasn't going to say anything. But during our investigation of Allengri's missing persons status, Forensic Specialist Bailey came across some old legwork on Simon Allengri. Had your name attached to it." The chief gave Nick a long look, overacting the stern expression, as if trying to cause the simmering of a fish.

An old game. Nick stared back. Chased a small bump inside his cheek with his tongue. He caught it and bit. Was thinking about the teacher's frightful end: *No way I'm going to talk about that old legwork on Allengri now . . .*

He dipped his eyelids and made it clear to his old friend the chief: "Look. I want your grand daughters to get a shot at Pinecrest much as you." He held out the brass tube containing the surgeon-messenger's manuscript. "And besides, if this thing's accurate, somebody else is about to get snagged and facelifted."

"Keep your voice down!" The chief lowered his own, and said, "Jewell. He'll do anything to make hay with the honchos at Pinecrest if he thinks it'll give his run for office a boost."

Nick decided to come clean. Almost. Quietly, he replied, "Look, Chief. A long time ago I took a look at Allengri. For Jim Stevens when he was a Police Cadet. A teen-ager. I did an asset search. Stevens said it was for a personal injury claim."

Enough said. Something akin to dread crossed the chief's face. But he wasn't saying what it was. "Shh…," Robertson again warned, even though Nick had been whispering. "Jewell must have a mole at Headquarters. He already knows about your legwork. And he's not above using it against you to make points."

Rather than face Nick as he spoke, Robertson had turned partly away, as if to take in their surroundings. When he spoke it was as if to suggest the conversation were not officially taking place, "To force you to take this case to preen for Pinecrest, Brax will claim you misused police resources. Everybody will know its bullshit. But I don't have to tell you, Brax will do anything to make himself look better . . . He might even try to tie up your pension if it would boost his own stock. An excuse to dig up more shit if he's in the mood for the smell of it. If it happens to muck up Italy for you, he'll claim he's taking a hard line . . ."

"Twerp." Nick closed his mouth and thought a moment, now side by side with the chief. "So. For *your* sake. And the twins. I'll take a look at this. But we agree up front. If I *do* take the case – it's the last time I put off retirement. And whether or not I crack it, we do what we have to in order to shut Jewell up. And I'm gone January the first."

The chief was nodding. Almost smiling.

"And as a going away present I'll toss in a bonus," Nick muttered. "I'll find a way to take Braxton Jewell off your ass for good. Even though he got land to build a new Headquarters donated free 'n clear, if he stays around you'll pay for it the rest of your life."

Now Chief Robertson was smiling. "How?"

"You let me worry about that. I'll dig up something that'll stick."

The bloom now across Robertson's face told Nick he couldn't have been happier to agree. But now Nick could also see something else pulling at his old friend.

For the chief it was a combination. The dead Dracula-pedoslimer thing going stiff on the floor at their feet. And Nick's taking this case so easily, so close to getting out. The eyes of Dr. Fogg never made a murder case too cheery. But in thirty-five years working together, Chief Robertson had never seen Nick Giaccone like this. Especially at a crime scene. The plodding old detective so on fire. Primed to go for broke.

He asked Nick, "The Headmaster tell you to talk to Professor Nailor?"

Nick turned to nod.

"Good." The chief still evaded, observing the workings of the room. The two of them could have been watching a Little League game. Chief Robertson muttered, "I hear Nailor has an open hour tomorrow – toward the end of his nine o'clock lecture. You might want to show up a few minutes early." When Robertson turned his head very briefly toward Nick, it was to observe the detective with circumspection, "I see you have a dossier there."

"With a key taped inside. Any idea what it fits?"

"Allengri's house should still be sealed." The chief was muttering, then turning very slightly toward Nick, slipping a hand into a coat pocket and bringing it up under the dossier Nick held against his buttoned great coat.

"That's where I'm headed next," Nick was saying.

As Robertson stepped closer, he reached to draw the dossier in Nick's hand and conceal what he now held out. "These might come in handy."

When Nick lifted a corner of the dossier, in the chief's hand he saw his own gold detective's shield and snub-nosed .38 revolver.

The chief couldn't resist, "Nice to have you back, Nick."

"I'm not . . . *back!*" Nick deftly pocketed his gold shield and was gone.

The revolver he left behind in the chief's still-outstretched hand.

CHAPTER 11

Safely back at her brother's house, The Illuminator jotted notes. "To improve The Work..." she began, and thought back on Allengri's case. She had bruised him, necessarily. But only slightly, and not in places where it had shown. That cold winter's day she had sprinkled the drug into hot soup she'd brought along to visit him. Unfortunately he'd tasted it. So she'd Tazed him.

Next time, she now told herself, *use a flavorless knockout drug. Something to make them go down quick.*

Rophypnol, she wrote.

Dragging Allengri wrapped in a blanket. . . so sloppy and cumbersome. Unrefined, she thought. *A wheel chair and . . .*

Install electric wheel chair lift on the motor home, she dashed on the page, and then set the notebook aside.

Next – while the Coroner's men loaded the body of Simon Allengri for transport to the Count morgue for autopsy – Cassandra would attend to this teacher's Soul. A final step in treating any Subject.

For this ritual, The Illuminator works in darkness, save for a host of lit votive candles.

She puts on a CD recording of Scarlatti's Keyboard Sonata in F Minor – a troubled and troubling melody that tottered back and forth between advance and retreat – a pattern found in Nature, she reckoned – elegant and self-balanced as the come-and-go darting of her three beloved hummingbirds.

Now she summoned Sacred recollections. Before making a mark she presses her eyes closed. Easily in her mind she returns to that flash, the moment she'd shown Allengri the sketch of his new face.

She can see the panic rising in his eyes – then his Soul flailing to escape, craven, trapped, and frustrated – a burst of light. Proof he was human. Its tiny weak flicker evidence of his scant humanity.

Cassandra had stored that flash in her mind, in all its color. Now she set to work to render it.

She uncapped the inks.

By now The Illuminator had a strict technique in place. Lay on dark colors. Then lighter, upon the dark. And lighter still in layers.

That morning as dawn's Supplication, she'd dyed a single vellum leaf a special Midnight Blue. Now it waited before her.

Over the blue she applies a silvery wash and waits for this to dry.

Then, she applies mineral inks. Time passes. Upon those colors, to bring light into the piece, she applies a thousand points of gold leaf.

Some of the votives have burned down by now. Like small silent witnesses. Innocent, they flicker. Some go out.

Her last step, beneath the image she's created to match his Soul, she writes the Subject's name. Simon Allengri.

Now she has him in her page. The part of him, at least, that might have otherwise stolen into the Beyond.

Allengri's soul – *semblance* of a soul – she thought, has now been trapped – with all the artfulness Simon Allengri had used to ensnare boys like her brother, and Jim Stevens. And how many others at Pinecrest Academy? How many others?

Most of the votives have by now gone dark. Wicks pluming smoke.

She opens a drawer and removes a small bag made of satin, its damask design from the second Unicorn Tapestry. Loosening its tasseled cord she slips out the Book. Roughly the size of a Breviary.

The Book is growing thicker. Its heft reassuring.

The Book of Souls. One page for each: Pimps. Traffickers. Child predators like Simon Allengri. Bullies.

The images making up this compendium seem abstract, resembling photos from the Hubbell telescope. Dying stars. Exploding gas clouds. The Crab Nebula. Each color burst a final desperate attempt to seduce.

Cassandra can hear the wind outside. It shrieks. The Nor'easter's running late.

Threading a needle with light gauge catgut, she sews Allengri's leaf into this book in progress.

The Scarlatti keyboard sonata makes its runs and arpeggios. With it she feels a jazz and flutter tingling through her fingers.

It's begun again. Her Mystic powers growing stronger, as with each page added to the Book of Souls before this one. She feels it riffle though the muscles of her upper arms and into her neck now.

As always, on her very next surgical Subject, she will test this Book's new powers.

To complete this Ritual she remembers: the day she'd begun The Work.

She opens the Book of Souls to recall her first. Reads his name out loud to the empty house.

It was only weeks after she'd signed up to volunteer. A change of scenery following a full three years of Viet Nam bloodgush. And a place, she'd hoped, to reconcile past tragedies. Colombia. She'd proven highly skilled as nurse at the Mission clinic founded by her parents: finally, a means of continuing their work.

Maybe she'd been Guided: a girl of eight years had wandered into the clinic, complaining of stomachache.

Cassandra had the immediate sense there was more to it.

Minutes later the "Viejo Machista" showed up looking for the girl. A barrel-chested retired military officer who'd gotten used to having things done *his* way. Especially where the female gender was involved.

He was also a *menteriosa malla,* a lousy liar. How worried he'd been at the girl's disappearance from "the camp." All that was needed, he insisted, was a purgative.

There had been something about the way the *nina* moved, the moment the man had neared her.

Think quick, Cassandra had told herself. Then forged an order for an x-ray. First time ever breaking rules.

The girl's relief showed immediately, as if liberated from a captor.

The x-ray proved Cassandra right.

Probably trial run, the lead surgeon had said viewing the x-ray film, pointing out a huddle of oval ghosts that bulged the sack of the stomach. He'd seen it before. Someone was preparing to use the eight year old as *una mula,* a mule to smuggle drugs.

Then the surgeon insisted on admitting the girl.

The military man threatened. Had offered a wad of money. But the lead doctor turned him away.

Nothing could be done, Cassandra had then explained to the old military officer, who she now viewed as the young girl's handler.

Cassandra had marveled at what had risen, then, within her.

In the course of training to volunteer in this clinic, she'd been advised to keep an eye peeled. She'd heard descriptions of human trafficking that would pale the average American. Once or twice since her training, she thought she'd caught a glimpse. Always from a distance. It kept her up nights.

This time, Cassandra knelt. Sought Guidance. Then was sure. Felt the cure within.

She acted fast.

Walking the *mercenario* to the door once the young girl was in safety, Cassandra threw the man a quick wink. In quiet Spanish said she'd see what could be done. "Come back next morning," she'd told him. They would *make business.*

That night she'd asked around about the old battler. An officer, deserter, hired on now to command *ninas* for the upland drug lord named El Ponderoso.

His job was to prepare the children – who each month, through a straw adoption agency, made transit into Miami. With bellyfulls of latex pellets containing the purest cocaine.

Once Cassandra learned this, the rest had been easy. She had thought of her brother. The experiences of her life, she then realized, had converged to make this moment. Preparing her to "treat" the old military man.

It had to be Divine Providence.

The way Cassandra, as a mobile army hospital surgical nurse in Viet Nam, had been assigned to work under the unit's best surgeon. Unfortunately, but not unique due to easy access to heroin then in Southeast Asia, the surgeon fed a secret but serious addiction. The first time Cassandra assisted in one of his operations, the Army doctor had been impressed with her focus, speed, and steadiness of hand. A rock-solid hand she'd developed learning the art of Religious Illumination.

The deal had been struck mostly without words. Not perfect, but with few alternatives:

Cassandra became the Army surgeon's hands, applied his bulls-eye acumen, his motor skills eroding like wet chalk with each pushed plunger of the syringe. Within months she was a crackerjack in treating burns, grafting skin, and reconstructive surgeries. A set of hands, by the time of discharge, to rival the best of Army surgeons.

She'd become the curandera. The healer.

Then, with both hands inside a patient in the Mobile Army Hospital O.R. – she had fantasized. The horrors of her childhood, through medicine, might be transformed. Guiltily, removing shrapnel, her fantasies bloomed: *think of how the ones who harmed Brother could be made never to trick another – on a table like this.* Yet afterward she'd chastised herself for such thoughts, with gruesome private penances of fasting and purgation.

With Honorable Discharge after three tours, hopeful to dispel such impulses, Cassandra vowed to learn the depths of Rosario's healing ways – and then devote herself to Latin America's rural Mission clinics.

The Curandera Rosario's methods were simpler, at times appearing cruder, than in a nursing school or the military hospital. Her clinical goals, at times Mystical, at others Moral, seemed more civilized than any other Cassandra had encountered – given their root objective – to heal the world, as much as any given patient.

Without realizing, Cassandra had been Prepared – to become The Illuminator: for the day the *Viejo Machista* and the girl with a belly full of cocaine pellets walked into her clinic.

That day, in a spilt second while the girl had stood shaking, Cassandra's mind had flashed past ethical niceties and Mission care guidelines.

In that flash Cassandra saw Curandera Rosario one sunny afternoon, in the act of dispatching a rooster that had been wearing down the flock. Her mentor's disimpassioned stroke of axe. Afterward, the delicious *caldo* – broth.

But Cassandra never, in that split second's remembrance, forgot about the little girl.

And in the days after the case of the *Viejo Machista*, she'd ask herself how she'd known *exactly* what to do.

When the barrel-chested warlord returned for the *niña*, Cassandra was joyful. Made him comfortable. Yes, she reassured, they might be able to deal. The girl, Cassandra told him with a sly look, would be ready to go early afternoon, provided the man offer a small *propino*, or tip. To cover lunch, she said, smiling.

They ate at Cassandra's villa. The *Viejo Machista* had passed her a greasy roll of bills. She fed him a fresh-killed roast rooster, fried plantains, a nice flan, and poured him cold *agua panella* – a traditional drink made from ice-cold well water infused with raw sugar from cane. She had laced the drink with Phenobarbital and *Aguardiente,* a colorless Colombian liquor of one hundred-eighty proof – and then watched the man fall unconscious.

And that evening when the clinic closed, she'd worked late. With a quarter-inch incision between the sacrum and first vertebrae, she used four-inch *Tenotomy* scissors to clip the sciatic root. After that a quick slice into the hamstrings: she would harness the major calf and thigh muscles. Crude but effective, she'd then looped heavy gut suture through the Llitiotibial Tracts, out and through the Gastrocnemius Heads in a switchback.

In minutes she was drawing the heavy gut tight.

To her mind, while tying and then clipping the length of gut, came a momentary vision of Curandera Rosario: working with Cassandra years ago to allay fear of harnessing a horse.

The *machista* would be on his knees until The Forever – unable to stand or to sit, even in a wheel chair. Quick glottal snips with a pair of long-snooted Metzenbaum scissors had silenced the bastard's voice.

Cassandra then bribed an ambulance driver to help lug the now-silent child-handler to Bogotá's *Catedral Nacionale.* There, she parked him in a confessional.

The crude surgery kept the machista kneeling, in a position of perpetual Penitence. But when the time came to ask it, the man just couldn't tell the priest what Delivered him.

Always happy to serve the Soul – inspired by Sacred surroundings – as final touch Cassandra had calligraphed a cryptic message on parchment from fragments of Bible verse, and left it in her Subject's breast pocket.

The next day's news sheets told of the corrupt army officer's traffic in children and narcotics for the drug lord *el*

Ponderoso, of police attempts to nab them, of what had been found inside the church, all at the hand of one "Illuminador."

The chief surgeon that day invited Cassandra to his office. And when she arrived, only looked up at her, a question on his lips. But after a moment, simply told her how much he appreciated the work she was doing.

Authorities in the region never investigated that crime.

CHAPTER 12

A windborne trashcan lid spun toward Nick's windshield as he turned into Simon Allengri's street. He swerved, missed it, putting him dead-on course to crush the barrel.

In the rearview Nick could see the container's skewed mouth spewing white plastic grocery bags that shot upward in his wake like ghosts.

Walking from the driveway to the house an airborne newspaper wrapped Nick's face. He clawed it off.

Most of Allengri's place was concealed by hedges that the wind now whipped against its walls. Nick thought it strange – the teacher's house all glass and steel – amidst more staid faculty residences atop Cornish Hill.

For compass bearings the detective glanced up at the heavens. Curious, the home's exposure to the north. Other faculty in this neighborhood basked in southwest orientation. *Allengri wasn't much for sunlight*, Nick thought.

Circling the place . . . between wind shrieks through the bare sugar maples . . . he could hear crusted snow crunch beneath his shoes . . . discovered traveled footpaths to connect the back yard to Pinecrest's campus.

No sign of break, either front or back door. If the surgeon-messenger had grabbed Allengri here, he had to have first opened up.

Nick removed the yellow plastic police tape and read the label plastered across the door and jamb: "CRIME SCENE . . ."

Muttered, "Can say that again," shoving the key into the lock. Twisting, he pushed the door and broke the Sheriff's seal.

Inside, he sensed a malignant atmosphere. Chrome and stainless. White tile kitchen floor. The carpet a velvet plush in the same white, and as spotless.

Everything in place. Except for a candy wrapper atop the kitchen island. *Odd. . . rest of the place so immaculate.* Next to the candy wrapper on the black granite stood a shallow cardboard carrier. Promotional chocolate bars, the kind youth sports teams sell to raise cash. Its label read *Fundraiser Kit*

Nick stretched on exam gloves and turned the cardboard carrier. He saw a space. One bar missing.

What about the empty wrapper?

Sliced clean? Most rip it open. The perp had used a very shape blade. *Where's . . . the cut-off piece?*

Sliced open someplace else, Nick figured, turning the wrapper on end and peering inside, judging its size. *Could conceal a small weapon.*

In resuscitation attempts on Allengri the EMTs had seen marks to match a Taser. The wounds had been mostly healed. *The abductor must've zapped him.*

Next Nick stepped through each room of the house, opened every door, drawer and closet.

After a few minutes he'd seen enough of Allengri's house and bedroom to figure out The Illuminator's "candy" pun.

And it turned Nick's stomach. Allengri, living so close to campus. Teaching. Leading student trips abroad.

Bastard had keys to the candy store.

And what else?

Scum like this were chameleons, slipping into well-intentioned youth groups, the way terrorists camouflage and infiltrate.

Returning to the kitchen it came to Nick.

Candy bars . . . If the abductor had posed as somebody selling sports team candy. . .Could be a kid . . . A kid wouldn't have alarmed the teacher. . . maybe working with an adult accomplice. Because these days, cautious parents usually accompany their kids in any kind of door-to-door . . . .

Nick looked inside the hollow wrapper. Its measurements would accommodate a smaller model, one of those "personal Tasers."

That day, Allengri's "candy" had come with a kick.

He saw a single mug in the sink, washed clean. Heard a small crunch when his next step hit the floor. Nick directed his flashlight under the cabinet toe kick and saw shards. Kneeling, when he brushed a hand to sweep a sample, through his latex glove, the bits of porcelain felt sharp. Then, by aiming his light obliquely, Nick saw a dried film on the floor tile, very faint.

He grumbled, "Plainclothes men need new eyeballs."

Next thing, he was pawing through the trashcan beneath the sink. Inside, a sharp edge. He took out part of a broken mug. Next, food. He grabbed a cold and soggy handful. White and starchy and bits of vegetables. He bagged it.

The abductor had cleaned up. But only enough to cause a seasoned detective to look further. And find this.

Outside the fast frozen air cut his face and burned his sinuses. The pain of it helped clear his head.

Two mugs. Allengri knew the abductor. Or wanted to. Served something hot. The abductor's Taser comes out, hidden inside the candy wrapper. So, what went wrong? Nick could bet the farm those shards and bits of food would test positive for some kind of knockout drug.

He knew he had something solid. However he did not, as usual with violent criminals, feel contempt toward whoever made *this* house call.

He noted the distinction and put it in check.

Nick couldn't help wondering, dreading the thought, whether Allengri had harmed Patrolman Stevens as a kid. And he thought back on that ancient legwork that Robertson had brought up tonight.

On the way home he stopped off to give Bailey's lab the food sample from Allengri's garbage. When he pulled up at Headquarters his headlights lit the bronze relief. Jim Stevens' face gazing at him. And it hit him. Again:

My fault; I brought the Rookie into the job.

Driving home Nick went through it: *the body, the manuscript, the candy wrapper . . .*

The night's icy winds screamed. With it, Nick's instincts: **the facts are coming too easily**.

He wasn't sure what was worse. . . the surgeon-messenger out hunting to create *the man who is his own nemesis*. Or that – through whatever had taken place years ago with Jim Stevens – the old detective and the surgeon-messenger were in some way linked.

CHAPTER 13

Driving home, Nick had to dodge blown-down limbs that now crisscrossed the side streets.

Before heading inside his house he got Bailey on the phone to have him run an M.O. search against Interpol. Key words describing the surgeon-messenger's methods run through the database would turn up any corresponding crimes that had been reported around the globe. Nick also asked the Specialist to contact the distributor for a list of anyone local who'd purchased kits of those big candy bars sold by sports teams. "Send everything to my computer," he told Bailey and switched off.

Unlocking his house Nick heard a crash above his head when a windborne limb took out the entry light.

Immediately inside, his neck hair bristled so stiff the follicles itched. The place looked the usual. But he knew. *Someone's been in.*

He set the dossier and brass tube on his kitchen counter.

A sawed-off twelve gauge hung on mounts behind the china hutch. Nick led with the muzzle, stepping over packing boxes and around furniture wrapped in moving pads. He checked every room, door, and window. Even the basement. All clear.

Maybe he'd been mistaken. Never, before, had a case so gotten his blood up.

His night ritual was, without fail, a fresh-cooked meal and to tick off items on the day's to-do list. But tonight Nick went about the house switching on lamps. A lot more lights than usual, as if burning fuel into glow might protect his peace.

Then he hung his great coat, stowed the double barrel, and prepared for an all-nighter.

Microwaved leftovers would have to do. Fettuccine with gorgonzola sauce. Peas and pancetta. A couple thick slices of tomato, and a few pepperoncini. He sloshed some of the pepper juice over the tomatoes, and then shook out a layer of pepper and salt.

The lights flickered once as Nick walked his dinner into the paneled study. Switched on the old electric space heater beneath his desk, and began to eat. A soothing, rhythmic, ticking sound rose from the heater's coils that glowed a cozy red. Then he turned on the portable Magnavox black and white above his desk.

A trusted TV, he had watched the first moon landing on it. Its sound had failed long ago. But the voiceless activity substituted for company.

As he ate it washed over him: ever since dedicating Goddard's new Police Headquarters, Nick had been plagued. The day had left a chip, a crack in that seal between himself and the past.

Then, at the oddest times since hearing that Allengri had gone missing and student complaints of misconduct, Nick found himself wondering about that cardboard carton he'd come across while packing. Legal records, belonging to the deceased patrolman Jim Stevens. Each time encountering the box, he'd stifled that curiosity. Moved it aside.

Then he'd found it odd, packing and moving boxes. Each time he turned around, it seemed – there was that small carton again. During the two years the box had been in his possession he'd rarely laid eyes on it, nor given it a thought. Now it was unavoidable.

Chief Robertson had been right. Nick *had* done legwork on Jim's behalf a good while ago. When Jim had asked him to run a quick asset search on some guy named Simon Allengri, he'd obliged. Not exactly an illegal use of police intelligence. More within professional discretion. What, then, would the contents of that box tell him tonight?

Then two years ago, clearing the recently deceased Rookie's apartment, that box had been the final piece. "This'll only wind up in the landfill," Jim's mother Mary had sighed. When the attorney for Jim's case had passed, his executors had sent former clients their files in accordance with best practices. In passing the carton to Nick, Jims' mother had suggested in a way the detective had found troubling: "Whatever's in this box, keep it private. My son's a hero now."

Wordlessly he'd accepted the small carton, one more gesture of support for Mary Stevens. Even "closure," if such a thing even exists.

And since that day, Nick had left Jim's records sealed, unmolested. He'd thought, as a measure of respect.

Now outside Nick heard a limb on the wind that banged and banged against his house like the past trying to break in.

He shrugged it off and speared a tomato slice, gathered some pasta, and bit – contemplating tonight's crime scene. *This took precision, preparation, and facilities.* With the back of his hand Nick wiped away juices that had run down his chin. *What kind of person would risk a lucrative medical career to do this?*

When he laid a hand on the dossier marked Allengri, it was cold to the touch.

Outside, the wind's yowl. A sharp crack, and the banging stopped. The limb had parted the tree.

"Get on with it," he muttered, trying to convince himself that the old Allengri legwork for Jim would prove a mere co-incidence.

He moved to the closet doorway at the far end of the room, where a small porcelain Holy water font still hung on a nail beside its door. Years ago the small font had been his wife Nora's gift on his first day as a Goddard patrolman. When the job involved little more than a nightstick and a radio.

He looked at the Font now, the design above its cup depicting St. Christopher crossing a rushing river, carrying the Divine Child to safety on broad shoulders. Nora had always kept the font filled so Nick could dip his fingers and bless himself each morning before leaving for duty. Now its cup was dry.

Again the house lights flickered.

Nick's heart jumped when he opened the closet door and saw the carton's cardboard flaps – now spread wide. Yesterday the box had been sealed. He'd seen it. Now a clean slice that looked fresh through the mailing label across its flaps:

Hissing,
Maxilla,
Mandible
& Poole,
Attorneys at Law

Send to:

James Stevens,
34 Winslow Road,
Goddard, MA 01911

C O N F I D E N T I A L

Yes, Nick thought, his house had been violated.

Jim's privacy as well.

Call the chief. Get a team to process . . .

As much as these measures were correct, Nick knew he wouldn't be able bear the shame of reporting the intrusion. He thought of Bailey's men, twirling feathered fingerprint brushes on every surface of his place. In all their eyes the same unspoken accusation:

A seasoned detective, burgled. First day into retirement.

Then, what stared up at Nick from inside the box made him forget all this.

Bold face, it spelled everything he'd tried to force from his mind.

"Unholy Acts."

Nick carried the box to his desk and sat.

"Unholy Acts," read the yellowed magazine article by Paul Wilkes, apparently clipped from a *New Yorker* magazine. It told of a priest nailed for sex crimes and defrocked. His victims, countless boys who'd been members of Church recreation groups the priest had founded.

Brief notations jotted in the margins of these pages indicated that Father Provost, the subject of the *New Yorker* article, had been chaplain at Camp Quiet. Where Jim Steven's Youth Camper troop had spent summers.

Jesus. Please. Not Jim . . .

Beneath the magazine article, scads of legal papers. Nick set these atop his desk. In his mind a tug of war.

Don't let this be. . .vs. . . I want to understand.

Further down in the box he found a spiral notebook labeled **Exhibit A.** *Journal, Jim Stevens.*

The moment he opened the journal Nick felt his neck muscles double up in knots. Jim's tangled handwriting – fragments – suggested hesitance — and the raw courage to commit such powerful memories to paper. Atrocities committed by leaders of Jim's Youth Camper troop. Stories the star policeman had been unable to tell in life:

"I was afraid tell anyone. Not even the therapist I made an appointment with. I never went to the appointment and felt shitty. So on Cape Cod last weekend I told it to an osprey, above me on a piling. I was hung over. I remember that low tide smell on the flats like sulfur. The remembering. I couldn't stop. Pressure and I had to tell it. Going crazy I thought. Surrounded in spartina grass talking with this osprey. That bird listened and stood up there on the piling. I talked to it an hour. Can't even write that part yet."

To read it Nick felt as if he'd pulled up to a smoking wreck only moments too late.

Chock full of scattered bursts of writing, there was no underestimating the heft of such a journal in proving a case of abuse. Just like a school bullying victim Nick had read about last week, whose notes like these had brought swift justice.

Next in Jim's carton he found two books, <u>Scouts Honor,</u> <u>Sexual Abuse in the Boy Scouts of America</u> by Patrick Boyle. And a dog-eared copy of <u>Victims No Longer</u>, by Mike Lew. From Special Victims training, Nick recognized this title – a men's bible of recovery.

He gently set these books on his desk – wishing, still, a prayer on his lips, that this couldn't be so.

God. Please. God . . . don't let all this be about Jim.

The next document in the carton told Nick this prayer was not to be answered. It was the Complaint, which he recognized as a lawsuit's headline document, a summary of the injury claim to include names of who's at fault, causes of injury, charges and laws broken, and monetary reparations demanded.

Jim had been abused at the hand of Camper troop leaders.

Named as Institutional Defendants answerable to this lawsuit: The Youth Campers of America, and the greater Boston area Diocese of The Church. The summary explained that the Youth Campers had met in the basement of the Church sponsoring the troop in which Jim had been active.

However, under the heading: "*Individual* Defendants answerable to this lawsuit," the names had been sliced out – with a scalpel, by the looks – except for one name: **Simon Allengri.**

The detective's mind reeled – from Jim's suffering – to what might motivate this break-in – into a *policeman's* house – to slice out parts of the past.

At Pinecrest tonight, Nick had noticed something shifty. Was this some cover-up work in the wake of Count Dracula hitting the red carpet at Autumn Follies?

He didn't think so. The Headmaster wouldn't order a housecleaning if he'd wanted something else.

One thing was sure: the surgeon-messenger was playing a game of guess-who's-next. The striking message in Allengri's tux an invite for Nick to join the fun: *Prepare to soon meet the man who is his own nemesis.*

To look at the perforations on the Complaint document, Nick knew he was being shown a group portrait of guilty parties with the faces sliced out. To simply be told of these men's role in destroying a fellow policeman would've made it all too easy. To make him work for it would be to ensure it would never happen again.

"... *the man who is his own nemesis.*"

If Allengri was Dracula, the next victim would be some other well-known monster. Nick wondered: *What monster is 'his own nemesis?'*

And what about the sutured embroidery? The Headmaster had coyly termed it, "weapons-grade poetry."

Maybe tomorrow, Professor Nailor would shed some light.

Smart, Nick thought. *I'm kept here shuffling papers while the surgeon-messenger's out on safari.*

Rifling through Jim's private papers Nick felt like an interloper. But he came up with what he needed – marked **Transmittal** – the detailed inventory of documents a standard procedure in sending legal documents or evidence through the mail.

Using this list Nick carefully tallied each book and paper inside the box, down to Jim's journal. It took a while. And Nick took his time, methodically accounting for each document listed, in the process developing a sense of the attorney's method of referencing.

With a vague sense of righting things he stood, ready to replace every book and document in the box in the same order in which he'd discovered them.

But then saw that he'd missed something. At the very bottom of the box. Something that wasn't on the list.

A small message. Closely resembling the ornate Illumination discovered in Allengri's tux. Like an ancient church document. In that striking calligraphy. On that same antique writing stock. Its mottled coloration amber and pomegranate.

The simple message read:

> You will comprehend Jim Stevens' suffering after you have peered into the depths of the font.

It almost stopped Nick's breathing.

Singled out. Nick felt his face and neck flush in shame.

Beyond doubt now, the surgeon-messenger *had* breached Nick's house.

And Jim's private past.

Now it was clear to Nick: "Offenders."

An afternoon five years ago. A high-school aged Jim Stevens has joined the Police Cadets. It's their first meeting. So Nick is going around the room, asking each young visitor to say a few words about why each one wants to become a policeman. Without hesitation Jim replies, "To nail offenders."

The response takes Nick aback.

Sitting now in his study, reckoning with these facts, Nick tried to convince himself that Hell – in those days – nobody talked about these things. It was thought rude, back then, to "pry." *Because if you pried about **this** in those days, the shame would be pushed back on you . . . and the predators relied on that.*

That afternoon, Jim had been talking in code about Simon Allengri and the others – whose names had now been sliced out.

Now Nick remembered how he'd let it slide, by making a joke.

He'd uncomfortably replied to Jim, but brought the seated row of other potential Police Cadets into the joke as well, "You're in the right place, Mr. Stevens. Last week we ordered a whole keg of offender nails." He'd even amended the gag by making the motion of sizing a fish, and had said. "Big bastards!"

A tight laugh had followed through the group. A nervous laugh that said everyone in the room got it: what Jim had brought up wasn't funny.

After that, now and then, there had been more jokes about this subject from Jim. Testing jokes. Jokes that weren't jokes. Even into the days Jim came on the force. Like a lot of cops.

In the same way, Nick had avoided.

Handling this cryptic message about The Font – struggling with these memories concerning Jim – Nick was unaware how prepared The Illuminator had made herself for a next.

Focus. Nick told himself. He checked his watch. Nine hours till he'd meet with Professor Nailor over at Brauser college. To figure out the *first* message – the one discovered on Allengri.

He replaced everything in the carton. Except Jim's journal.

He needed to know. Maybe because of guilt for not listening more closely. Or for ignoring what he *had* heard.

And there was something else from Nick's own past. Faceless. Formless.

He thought: *Someone is going to be abducted.* But wondered if by focusing on duty, he might be avoiding the subject of Jim's suffering . . .or avoiding something yet darker . . .

Slow down, Nick told himself. He opened the journal to study every mark for what the Rookie might now, *finally*, be able to tell him.

Kid had a habit of hand-numbering pages, Nick thought, flipping through.

Then a page came loose in Nick's hand. He held it up to his desk lamp. *Sliced . . .*

He flipped back, checking page numbers.

A skip in sequence. Pages indeed sliced out. And by a very sharp blade. It had cut though, scoring the pages beneath. Leafing forward, Nick found more gaps in page sequence. Same clean slice.

A blade that left wavers in the cut. The way a short, bellied scalpel blade designed to slice skin might drag cutting paper. Perforations in the sheets below, Nick guessed, were due to manual pressure necessarily applied to make the full cut, from one edge of the page to the other using an edge designed to glide through human tissue.

To be certain, Nick would have to stop by Goddard Hospital to try a few scalpels on notebook stock similar to Jim's diary, and then compare the cuts.

How would the surgeon-messenger know to come to my house? Nick asked himself. The avenger shared intimate knowledge of Jim's past. Had to be connected to the lawsuit. By using the Dracula setup at Autumn Follies the motive seemed clear: to expose Allengri. And maybe some others.

So why, then, steal *these* pages, and cut the names of other predators in the Complaint document.

After demonstrating respect for Jim's private papers for so long, he now needed to find out what Jim had scrawled on those purloined pages.

He tried taking a step back from the questions.

Could this surgeon-messenger be someone who'd been harmed – the way Jim had?

Not likely, Nick thought. Despite myths, the research showed that the majority of guys who've experienced physical or sexual violence abhor it – to the extent of building their recovery outside the therapist's office around the prevention of similar suffering by women and children.

So then, why break in to show me an open box?

For the next few hours Nick scoured every last sheet of paper.

By three A.M. he'd read through the pile, and found a first name not attached to anything else: Gary. It was a quick note, tossed off on a scrap of legal pad. The note had been stapled through, but had pulled out, perhaps in the course of shuffling.

But stapled to what, and why? Nick had already read every document, and now in cross-reference the name didn't jive.

Then he found another scrawl, the name *Boother*, followed by several question marks. Near this scribbling was a pair of staple holes.

Matching it up Nick vaguely put it together: Gary Boother had been "witness #2," another victim of Allengri, possibly to testify in the event Jim's case reached a courtroom. Later on, it appeared, Jim's attorney had been thorough in separating the stapled name from the deposition, in order to protect that witness's privacy.

Nick sat back in his desk chair, still unable to fathom all he'd witnessed tonight at Pinecrest. Thinking about Simon

Allengri, the now-cold Dracula in the context of this new mass of facts, the old detective had to wonder: who was the *real* victim here?

He logged onto his computer. Forensic Specialist Bailey had already emailed all the crime scene photos. Nick replied, requesting to dig up Gary Boother's home address.

The dossier mysteriously handed him at Pinecrest contained pictures of Allengri *before* the surgeries. Now Nick printed the "after" shots that Bailey had emailed as attachments.

Placing the photos side by side on his desk Nick felt his stomach clench.

In the *before* Nick saw a distinguished looking man in his sixties, mustache and hair dyed black, a refined trace of silver at the temples.

He could still recognize some of Allengri's features from the first pictures – the eyes, the bridge of the nose – but the face in these pictures was altogether different. The hairline that had previously run in a gentle curve now arched into a severe widow's peak. The slender eyebrows were bushier, pointing downward toward the center. The nose was thinner, protruding over flared nostrils like a beak. The eyes looked narrower. And the ears had been trained to a sharp point. The hair was raven black. The lips blood red; two long, pointed incisors overhanging.

Bailey had sent the Coroner's blood analyses as well. They'd found Succinolcoline.

Nick Googled the pharmaceutical – a drug capable of sustaining total dissociative paralysis – potentially used as anesthesia for surgery or as a form of chemical restraint.

Dissociative paralysis?

Nick looked up that term as well. Drugged with Succinolcoline, Allengri had been unable to move a muscle. But he would see everything, his mind alert and conscious – witnessing every step of surgery being performed on him yet unable to intervene.

Nick saw the dead match. Child victims of men like Allengri endure the mirror image: holding still, aware of what's being done to them, the brain locked: *this **definitely** shouldn't be happening* versus a heart-pounding *keep still and pretend it's not.* Its dissociation and paralysis. The victim counting seconds that take a year. Hovering in that void. Till it's over . . . until the adult does this to them again. Or the victim instills the fear of God in the perpetrator's heart by declaring **no more**.

Another email hit Nick's in-box.

Tests were back on the food found at Allengri's house.

A mixture. Carrot. Chicken stock. Celery. Some starch. Probably pasta or egg noodle.

Nick knew the recipe for chicken soup.

But to abduct Allengri there'd been an additional, secret ingredient: Phenobarbital.

Nick dialed Headquarters and asked for Bailey. Robertson had handled the hire, and they'd only met briefly at the dedication. Now together they began to hash out a theory. The abductor had posed as a kid, maybe, selling door to door that night. Something went wrong with the soup doctored with Phenobarb. The drug carries a bitter taste, Bailey told Nick. The Taser had been Plan B. The surgeon messenger was either disorganized – and thus did not follow a strictly-configured M.O. Or else, more frighteningly – liked to spice things up – so these serial crimes would follow some kind of experimental arc, maybe to satisfy the delusion of achieving some perfection of craft.

Nick finally asked the Specialist, "Why drug chicken

soup as a knock-out?   Why not just ram a needle into Allengri's neck?"

"A needle's not quick enough," Bailey replied. "No injected drug works instantly, like on TV. While it travels blood to brain there's a lag. They'll put up a fight. Maybe turn the needle on the attacker. Our guy likes to schmooze the victim. Get 'em groggy on an oral narcotic. Then probably needles them up with something hard core to the bloodstream, to keep 'em down for transit."

Nick asked whether hummingbird dander had been detected on Allengri's tux and Bailey's answer was yes. They agreed to order a DNA test. To identify species of such an exotic animal might narrow geographic origin, and as such, reveal the surgeon-messenger's travel patterns.

When Nick hung up a curious sensation came over him. Maybe it was the late hour. Or the fact he hadn't eaten much.

Then he was back standing in Allengri's kitchen, felt that crunch of porcelain beneath his heel, and the detective saw it unfold as shapes. Imagined the surgeon-messenger presenting at the door. Selling candy. Nick could see a smaller build, but no face. A boy? Maybe a disguise. Now Allengri, in an attitude of licking his chops. Besides the candy bars the visitor carries a Thermos. Something to ward off the chill. The teacher produces two mugs. Then the faceless "boy" adding the drug. Allengri gets wise to it. A struggle. One cup hitting the floor. The Taser comes out.

Nick realized this was the second time tonight he'd found himself entranced. First time, at Pinecrest, with that odd document.

Hocus pocus had always been fine for praying. This was police work. A detective a man of facts, reasoning, and judgment.

Raising his head to lose the horrid kinks in his neck, Nick found himself looking at the framed picture of Patrolman Jim Stevens above his desk.

Glancing away, he encountered Allengri's before and after photos, imagined terror in those eyes at Autumn Follies, once this faculty member had seen himself in that mirror. With the realization, mysteriously, the old detective felt eased by an unwinding, the windlass of knots in his neck magically relaxed.

Chicken soup, he thought enjoying sudden ease, for the first time all night moving his head and neck freely. *Cure all.*

It was five A.M. when Nick again set Jim's history neatly back inside the carton. To have his desk clear now added further to his relief.

"So neat," Nick said out loud to himself. Several times tonight he'd remembered a morning two years ago – the one of Jim's fatal squad car wreck.

Around three A.M. the night before, the Rookie had responded to a rape call. First ever. Jim had sped. The girl had fought. Had even caught a piece of the guy, Jim had told Nick later on at the station. She'd been aspirating the bastard's ear lobe when the Rookie had pulled up to the scene.

Jim had blamed himself. Shook up. Irrational. Unable to prevent the assault – even though he'd been dispatched minutes *after* the rape had been perpetrated – believed he'd failed the victim – and because of that had failed as a policeman.

Nick had tried to explain to Jim that night that this kind of dedication – this kind of concern for victims of violent crime – made him in every way a top Goddard cop.

In all his years, Nick had never seen an officer so bad off. Now, looking at the box of evidence stacked so neat, he understood what had been echoing within Jim – from his adolescence up till seeing externally – very graphically – the result of sexual violence on that young girl.

Jim had gotten her to the hospital.

And after that had erupted the Rookie's bone-shuddering grief.

Then, hours later at sunrise, Jim hit a patch of black ice that took his car spinning into that fatal phone pole. Driving way too fast for a routine call.

Now the reason for Jim's crash was clear.

The vehicle the patrolman had been chasing on that final call matched the description of the vehicle driven by the rapist. So in his mind, Jim had been racing to catch the young girl's assailant. Also in his mind, he'd been racing to rescue himself from maggots of his past. Like Simon Allengri.

Planning the next steps of his investigation – alone in his study – the silent old TV flickering black and white – these inklings writhed and rasped in Nick's skull like a basket of snakes. A man of duty, precise and diligent, he ignored the sound of those serpents trying to choke his focus, the rasp of their dry scales crackling like dead leaves in a fist.

With dawn breaking, he prepared a metal Thermos of coffee and a pair of sandwiches at his kitchen counter. Beside these waited the mysterious brass-ensconced message, the dossier on Allengri, and facts and photos he planned to discuss with Professor Nailor.

After that Nick would question Gary Boother. Specialist Bailey had dug up an address.

Nick would want to talk to every student victim at Pinecrest who'd lodged complaints against the teacher, but that would be impossible. For the present, victim's names were protected.

The detective walked back into his small study, where the old portable TV on the shelf above the desk still flickered black and white. Smiling newscasters on screen were giving silent morning reports. To look at the old television now, he wondered why he'd kept the damned thing so long. A piece of junk that could make no sound.

All Nick could think was that Jim had found no ears to hear *his* pain. No one to go to bat for him. And all of a sudden, Nick hated that TV for its silence.

Still sitting on his desk, the box itself was Nick's proof – of his own failure to read clues, fed him by the high-school Police Cadet who in shame hid an ongoing Hell. Any Detective worth his salt should ask what lies behind such clues.

A plodding old detective who, other than wisecracks, had never rocked the boat.

Grabbing with both hands Nick raised the set over his head. Putting all his weight behind it, he drove the TV down upon the box of history with a crash.

Candy bars and chicken soup. The surgeon-messenger's deadly puns had engaged him.

CHAPTER 1

Daybreak, windless and crisp.

Scraping ice from his windshield Nick remembered, in the course of the post-crash investigation, the State Police psychologist's report had factored in Jim Stevens's call sheet and driving speed in pursuing the "gray van" matching that of the rapist.

Police protocol held that response speed to any radio call be strictly according to level of risk. So to rescue bystanders hit by gunfire during a bank heist, a policeman would drive at high speed. However when heading for a "routine with no endangerment to life or property," like the call Jim had been answering at the time of his death, a patrolmen would drive at posted speed limit.

A sticky point in post-crash investigations following Jim Stevens' death had been the psychologist's questions of *why* the Rookie had accelerated to 120 MPH. More than three times protocol.

Clear as Nick's freshly-scraped windshield, Jim's trauma as a teenager had come back to haunt.

Sweet, the detective thought, *now I'm supposed to take down whoever punished Allengri.*

When Nick's cell phone sounded it was the chief. "Parents of twelve boys attending Pinecrest Academy have filed liens against Allengri's estate. And lawsuits are piling up against the school."

"What are the chances of getting names?"

"Still sealed."

Nick couldn't hide his interest. "They have a case?"

"I'd say! Family psychologists are all over the radio saying that this – *surgical display* – or whatever you want to call it – is actually *of help* to these kids in dealing with the trauma. Helping them to not blame themselves."

"No kidding." Nick wondered how a guy like Allengri could have operated for such a long time at a place with the reputation of Pinecrest.

"Allengri's autopsy?" Nick asked.

"There was a directive. His lawyers blocked it."

"And billing his estate. *That's* what I call service." Nick saw a hole and went for it, "So, this a Homicide or not?" Hoping he'd somehow get off the hook.

The chief let out a little grunt, then explained, "Somebody woke up a judge." An injunction had been issued.

After that, under direction of Dr. Fogg, the teacher Allengri had gone to pieces for an eager team of first-year medical students, whose able hands had parted the cadaver's every bone, muscle, and joint. Inventoried and then weighed each of the predator's organs: spleen, liver, heart, and brain. They even pulled his teeth.

The brain they froze with liquid nitrogen. Then used a rotary Microtome, like a precision cold cut slicer, to shave the cryogenic tissue into thin slices to perform tests beneath high magnification.

Each student, on the surface, had ardently labored to uncover any anomaly that might elucidate, further, the cause of death. Yet what had privately fueled each student working through the night was the drive to find a reason, the minutest evidence, the tiniest hint – why a man like Simon Allengri might choose such a path in life.

Attempts throughout that same night by Chief Robertson to contact each of Allengri's living relatives had been frustrated. No one would accept the body. Two had hung up on the chief outright. Another had screamed into the phone, "Can't you people leave me alone?" obviously hounded by the press.

Receiving news of this, Dr. Fogg had seen to Allengri's final-willed wish for cremation by firing the County morgue's kiln. By first light of day remaining flesh met flame. The predator's clay foreverafter ash, unto dust.

The chief concluded, "In the end Fogg stayed with the same 'cause' on the death certificate. Once Allengri saw himself for what he was, his heart stopped."

As he listened to the chief, Nick was leaning forward in the seat of his parked car so far that his chest pressed up against the steering wheel. "In words I can understand, Chief. Do we call this Homicide or not?"

"Closest Fogg would get to *that* question was to call Allengri's death an Act of God."

"Act of *who*?"

"I know where you're headed with this and I'm sorry," the chief said coldly. "To pull you off the case now would send the wrong message. The note on Dracula's body says 'Prepare to soon meet the man who is his own nemesis.' So I suggest you do."

"I get it."

Damn, Nick thought, and fell back against the seat.

The chief asked, "You get a look at today's paper?"

Nick had. The front page of *The Goddard Morning Sun* beside him on the seat featured a photograph of The Headmaster standing over an unconscious Allengri, engrossed in reading the striking manuscript.

ILLUMINATOR STRIKES IN GODDARD, read the headline.

The story told of "Illumina<u>dor</u>," in Latin America, who over the years had been elevated to the status of a folk hero through a series of unsolved crimes. Each had taken place in small villages. Thought to be an advocate of the poor and weak, Illuminador was said to be a Divinely Inspired master of disguise, entry and escape, exacting "surgical vengeance" from evildoers of all kinds.

The legendary figure, it was believed, had mastered the Mystical arts of the curanderas, indigenous healers who for centuries had practiced a fusion of Spiritual, herbal, and surgical medicine and shamanism.

Each of Illumina*dor's* victims had been released in public places as a warning to anyone else who might be considering the darker sins – and left with a calligraphed Illuminated manuscript. Each victim turned into a monstrous grotesque. In every case the surgeries had been performed without pain, each victim suffering massive trauma upon viewing their own reflection. Consequent investigation found these "special patients" to be, without exception, criminals of the lowest degree.

Nick did a quick Google search on "Illuminador" and found the *Morning Sun* reporter had done his diligence. He had been planning to provide Chief Robertson a summary of

Jim Steven's legal history. But to read about this South American Illuminador now, something held him back.

Getting off the phone he tried to convince himself it was duty. A way to maintain distance between this investigation and his personal feelings. Besides, to say anything to the chief about Jim *now* would raise questions he couldn't yet answer.

Even for Nick, there seemed no bottom to the well of questions.

First, talk to that witness, Gary Boother. Get something conclusive.

Today's news story sounded more like legend than fact. Even so, *Illuminador's* M.O. was an uncanny match to Allengri's abductor and facial remodeler.

Maybe the teacher had been done up by copycat. A serial copycat, it appeared from the message. Yet if a *second* monster showed up – and if that one also proved to be a predator – well, this *was* Boston – damned fertile soil for cultivating The Illuminator as legend and folk hero.

At the gates of Brauser College the detective flashed his shield and asked for the location of Professor Nailor's nine o'clock lecture. The guard marked the building and classroom number on a campus map.

Entering Slater Hall, home of Brauser's English Department, Nick carried Allengri's dossier, grown thicker now. The breast pocket of his great coat concealed the polished brass tube containing the extraordinary manuscript. With every step the cylinder touched his sternum – a pistol-barrel presence, knocking at his heart.

Nick thought of the morning's headlines. **Illuminator Strikes in Goddard**. *Progress?* Word was out. The Illuminador. The Illuminator. Whether in Spanish or English, at least his quarry had a name now.

Press like this could play both ways. Could pump up a psychopath like The Illuminator's sense of importance, to escalate the abductions and grisly surgeries. Same time, a news story might warn potential victims and save lives. But Nick knew this might not apply here – because even though men of Allengri's stripe were pure cowards once confronted about their behavior by the victim – they were also devoid of a sense of wrongdoing and thus unlikely to heed the warning a news story might offer.

Realizing this, Nick shut out a guilty inkling – a slippery waltz toward resignation – that either way, and despite his best detective work, with The Illuminator in town the men who'd harmed Jim would receive what the Lord intended.

BOOK II

CHAPTER 2

Nick waited outside the professor's classroom while Brauser undergrads greeted the day groggily with Mountain Dew and poetry.

Professor Canon Nailor's immense height and agility were impressive. Wearing canvas pants and Pendleton shirt in a Black Watch plaid, the man resembled an adventurer and phrased his insights like a soothsayer. Square-jawed and in thick beard trimmed with subtlety, in speaking he showed rows of thick, strong teeth.

Nick watched the six-foot-five inch scholar, launching from the balls of his feet, gliding from desk rows to chalkboard in order to dash a word. With immediacy he lay down a monologue on his way to the rear of the classroom. And then back toward the chalkboard, to record another key term, drawing students' questions in his wake.

Nailor's kinetics whipped a pulse throughout the classroom, a surge and pull of his teaching, sure to infuse learners with a kind of blood and oxygen that it seemed, from Nailor's delivery, might one day mean life or death.

He lectured:

"In *Beowulf*, we meet our first of three monsters: Grendel, a savage made incarnate as punishment for Cain's misdeed."

Canon Nailor nodded toward a student in the middle row, "Greg, read aloud if you will. Begin with, 'Spurned and joyless. . .'"

The student began . . .

"– Spurned and joyless, he journeyed on ahead and arrived

at the dawn. . . . Flame more than light, flared from his eyes.

He saw many men in the mansion, sleeping

. . . he would rip life from limb and devour them,

Feed on their flesh . . ."

Professor Nailor interrupted to ask the class: "Why is *Beowulf*, the oldest known piece of English literature, also one of the most violent?"

Question hanging in the air, he came back at it: "A story passed from mouth to ear during the Middle Ages when few could read or write. Consider purposes such a tale might serve, scattered amidst shadows of peasantry and ignorance."

Nailor then hardened his gaze and turned to the blackboard.

"MONSTER," he wrote large in hurried strokes.

Chalk scraped and cracked.

"From the middle English 'MONSTRE.'"

He dashed the word boldly.

"From Latin, MONSTRUM," he underscored.

"Meaning PORTENT, or, OMEN."

"From 'MONERE' – to warn." And he underlined the word's root.

The Professor ominously turned toward the class, facing them squarely. With a glance toward where Nick stood waiting at the classroom door, Nailor menacingly pronounced:

"Monster as message."

The lesson was over. And Nick knew he was beholding a master.

Words couldn't better fit the file he now clasped in hand. He was confronted by a chilling thought, recalling Robertson's words the night before at the crime scene, "You might want to show up a few minutes early." Nick wondered: Could this lecture have been for his benefit?

Once close enough to shake hands, he noticed Nailor's brooding gaze. Could recognize weary circles a law man acquires witnessing fates that forever after chafe, wither and with seasons replenish, as crisp leaves collect against the stone markers of graves.

"I'm a bit under the gun, Detective Giaccone. . ." the scholar apologized. "If you could walk with me . . ."

Nick had trouble keeping up with his strides.

The Laboratory for Textual Forensics occupied a warren of offices beneath the Brauser College library, the larger spaces interconnected by a series of arched brick tunnels, like catacombs. The Founder, a distiller by trade, had built the college during the heyday of prohibition. Nathaniel Brauser, legend had it, had built ample catacombs beneath the book stacks to hide hooch.

Inside the text laboratory, student assistants fed high-capacity scanners from various document storage boxes that lined every wall and hallway, stacked floor-to-ceiling. Immediately Nailor sprang to the aid of one of his assistants to save a sheaf of stapled pages from jamming a document feeder.

The professor instructed, "I usually ask clients to drop their material at the loading dock. By the number of cartons, I find a fit in our schedule."

Nick reached into his suit jacket for the brass tube containing The Illuminator's scroll. "I have one document. My chief said. . ."

"I only received word that a Goddard detective was to call on me." The literary sleuth indicated a towering stack of cartons marked **Quantico**, each stamped with a case number, "That load has to be processed for a midnight deadline. Eighteen cartons of writings – to ID an anonymous ransom note consisting of a mere *five* lines."

Nick wasn't giving up. He shook out the brass cylinder's contents. "Only three lines here. But it's beautiful."

"I wish I still had time for 'beautiful,' Detective. Three lines. Unless you have enough of your suspects' writings to fill a small database, to allow me to analyze comparisons . . ." but from the distance Nailor paused a beat and his eyes narrowed to regard the gleaming manuscript tube Nick held out, "you offer nothing for me to work with."

He again indicated the tower of cases from Quantico. "This is a hostage situation."

Nick was thinking about the next surgical victim. And Jim's box of papers, sitting at home on his desk. He persisted, "Can't you just take a moment to analyze the handwriting or whatever?"

He watched Nailor's face become that of a man who can't believe he's even involved in such a conversation. "Handwriting analysis is **not** a thing we do here." His voice had become strenuously polite.

Nick felt an undergrad twinge. From this professor, about

half his age. "Maybe with a quick look you'll get a hunch about whoever wrote it?"

"I'm sorry, but I don't do 'quick looks,' nor do I 'get hunches.' You might consult a profiler. I can recommend several."

Nick had expected that by showing up he'd at least be told what all the calligraphy meant. He needed to get Nailor to bite. "Look, all I know's *shoe-leather* forensics. Even so, you'd be a lot more help than a profiler. Your article in *Collar* magazine said current Literary Criticism employs Psychotherapeutic theory, Jung, and everything in between. You called it a doorway to the mind that swings both in and out – and you wrote that a "text" can be any type of evidence we can 'read.'

Nick had spent part of the previous night cramming and now quoted from memory, "'paintings, sculpture, music, motion pictures, or any combination of media.' I think three lines falls in there somewhere." Then the old detective gestured with the manuscript. "This job's for your colleagues. For Pinecrest Academy. And there could be more victims."

Nailor regarded Nick as someone for whom doing the reading was not nearly sufficient.

Desperate, the veteran detective opened the dossier and held out a photo of the embroidery on Allengri's left hand.

He saw a split-second bloom of interest pass the professor's face. Then gone. "There'll *always* be more victims. . ."

"Surely you'll. . ."

"Surely I'll what? Tell Quantico their hostages should wait? Because the local prep school rolled out the Autumn Follies red carpet and found it infested?"

Nick lay a hand on the doorknob, feeling beat. And then he thought about Jim Stevens. And then the "man who is his own nemesis." Wondering how many more surgeries after that. He turned back, wearing a face of determination.

Raising a hand, Nailor pleaded in the way of a man who already knew what he'd hear next, "Please. . . don't beg."

Beneath the professor's layers of polish, Nick saw horse sense and the camber of spine.

Nailor squatted to heft a carton and turned to head for the Reading Room. Over his shoulder he called out, "I was promised two more assistants this semester, and wound up with . . . well, you can see."

When Nick opened the door into the cold he thought about retirement in Positano, Italy – evermore distant and quickly fading. Frozen.

Desperate, the old detective thought back on what he'd learned the night before. About the Rookie's suffering. He called out to the professor, "This case involves Jim Stevens. The downed policeman here in Goddard. His death is likely related to what that Count Dracula at the Academy did to him as an innocent teen-aged kid. Which makes Simon Allengri a cop killer."

Canon Nailor turned in his tracks, set down the box resting on his shoulder, and approached.

"I have two boys myself." The scholar regarded the manuscript in Nick's hand. "And these are the surgeon's word-works. . ."

A single blast of winter air through the open doorway made the Textual Forensics Laboratory a flurry of documents.

"I want to take a look," said Canon Nailor.

Another icy gust.

The professor shivered. "But please, Detective, shut that damned door!"

CHAPTER 3

The professor led the way down one of the tunnels till they hit a dead end. There the word-sleuth bumped his fist against a brick, and a panel silently slid to allow entry. "The college installed this last spring to help me keep an eye on student assistants."

They tramped up a spiral stair that led to Nailor's office, a glass Victorian conservatory built against the eastern wall of the library's Special Collections wing. The airy structure overlooked a tiered garden, and beyond that, the campus pond. Even in winter, the pair of French doors that opened out to a balcony framed the campus like a painting.

Nick took in the furnishings. "Not bad."

"Brauser accommodates. That billiard table once belonged to Mark Twain. On loan during restorations of the author's home in Connecticut."

Even though desperate, Nick felt skeptical of Textual Forensics, of entrusting cut bodies to the arrangements of words on paper. Why had these doubts surfaced now, he worried. Standing here in a professor's office reminded him he didn't like school. "I'd never close a case with a pool table in my office," Nick said, realizing, now, that it showed.

"I don't play the game nearly as much as I'd like," Nailor replied coolly, and leveled his eyes at Nick. "Somehow I close enough cases that Brauser allows me to stay. Sit, Detective."

Don't screw this up with wisecracks, Nick reminded himself. He *did* breathe easier to have Nailor engaged. But would've been far more comfortable knocking on doors and questioning potential suspects.

"What did you study in college, Detective?" Nailor was asking, "In the way of getting to know you." On the professor's desk were letters and documents bearing foil Federal seals. Scrolls and missives in a dozen languages. On one corner, a handful of passports, all from different countries.

"Criminology. In night school, after Viet Nam." Seated before the professor's desk, he felt like a beginner.

"Hasty scholarship is my greatest fear," Nailor began. "And police work is nothing hasty scholarship. So here I suffer."

Whatever that means, Nick thought.

"Pass me that manuscript."

When Nailor unfurled the document his eyes widened. "Wow!"

"Wow?" Nick repeated. "English Professors really say that?"

"When a document such as this turns up? Yes!"

While Nailor studied the manuscript, Nick scanned the certificates, honors, and some awards for field archery covering the office walls. When Nailor looked up, Nick was caught staring.

The expert explained, "I'm a butcher's son blessed with a prep school education from Essex and a doctorate from Oxford. But I learned what I know about saving lives and police precision handling a boning knife, cutting meat every

Now two years later, pulling into the diner to wait for Gary Boother, Nick wished he could find a way to fully grasp all he'd discovered these past twenty-four hours.

The Flying Yankee. The diner's sign displayed a blinking neon rocket that orbited a nameless, burned-out planet. A waitress named Tippi brought Nick's coffee, eggs, and double sausage and called him "hunny."

As good a place as any for the detective to hear another piece of Jim's life.

Nick kept the dossier and morning newspaper on the table. A vague sense of obligation and he again read a document from Jim's case.

The Charges for which Jim's counsel had sought damages leaped off the page:

Negligent Entrustment

Conspiracy to Commit Sexual Abuse

Negligent Failure to Warn

Negligent Supervision

Negligent Infliction of Emotional Distress

Negligent Entrustment

Breach of Fiduciary Duty

Negligent Infliction of Emotional Distress

Intentional Infliction of Emotional Distress

These were charges Nick didn't even know existed, despite his years in law enforcement. Still, he'd gathered few details about what Jim went through.

Thinking about the victim he was soon to meet, Nick

summer for my Dad."

The celebrated Canon Nailor was trying to make Nick
Giaccone feel comfortable. It was working. . . Nick leaned
back a little and relayed everything he knew about Allengri's
tie-in to the Youth Campers. Jim's old lawsuit. How for the
sake of decency he'd keep Jim's personal privacy a professional priority.

Nailor knitted his fingers together and made a little
steeple, which he pressed against his lips. To start off, perhaps
the detective would like to receive a "crash course in Textual
Forensics."

Nick shook his head. "I read up. Your methods made
Brauser College famous."

Professor Nailor hadn't the foggiest idea that he'd begun
saving lives during that Christmas break, a few years back.
He'd merely been tinkering with his son's early-vintage home
computer, to prove a point raised in dinner conversation –
that every writer's word and punctuation patterns are distinct. Uniquely individual. Even a writer's reliance on rhyme
or the consonant stop. It was like a code.

Soon after, testing this discovery, Nailor had recovered a
lost Shakespeare poem, backed up by empirical findings to
refute academic naysayers from Oxford to Berkley. Scotland
Yard had then dubbed Nailor's textual findings, "Fingerprints
on a wine stem."

Hearing about this, the FBI wore a path to the professor's
door. Brauser College built him a lab. Since then Nailor had
parsed everything from ransom notes to full-blown terrorist
manifestos.

"Have a look at these," Nick lay his dossier upon the professor's desk and turned each photo. "Allengri's left hand. It's
embroidered in catgut sutures."

Contrapasso

Canto XXVIII: 141-2

"The Headmaster called this, 'Weapons-grade poetry,'" recounted Nick.

The professor came to his feet, "At the very least." He un-shelved a single book. "Dante. Canto twenty-eight. A passage from <u>Inferno</u>." Nailor found the page and read the Italian aloud. "Cosi osserva I me lo contrapasso."

"Your Italian is excellent," Nick said. For his own sake he repeated Nailor's words in Italian. Then in English.

Nailor beamed, replying, "And yours is *fluent*."

"It means: 'In me you see the perfect contrapasso.'" Nick shrugged, but he felt a small rise of pride. "As a kid I spent summers with grandparents in southern Italy. But **contra-passo?**" he admitted, "I've never encountered the word."

"Directly translated, it means 'counter-step.' The idea of it became Church Law after the renaissance poet Dante demonstrated the concept so thoroughly in <u>Inferno</u>, where *Contrapasso* depicts punishments custom-tailored to the sin committed."

"What comes around goes around?"

"In the most particular ways," Nailor cautioned. "<u>Inferno,</u> shows us politicians and clergy of all types being tortured in Hell for their corruption. This torture is a reflection of each sinner's crime in life. Or sometimes it's a mirror image." The literary sleuth leaned back comfortably in his chair, which somehow made Nick feel even more at ease.

He ventured: "The flip side of Free Will."

"Exactly. To sin is to also to choose the inevitable Divine counter-measure. Thus: *Contra . . .passo.*" With an air of utter informality, Nailor continued as if he might be bringing Nick in on a juicy piece of scuttlebutt, "Dante had this one character, Count Ugolino, condemned in the Hell of his long poem <u>Inferno</u>," the professor's tone now fully informal. "For some reason in life, one of old Ugolino's enemies got him locked up in a tower along with his two sons. Pretty soon Ugolino got hungry. The man ate his own boys."

Nick gulped.

Nailor waved the book <u>Inferno</u>, "So in this poem we get a Hell created by Dante. And there, the Count Ugolino is shown serving his 'Contrapasso' through eternity."

"Which is?"

"Ugolino forever gnawing at the skull of the political foe who'd had him locked up in the first place. But Ugolino's appetite is never satisfied." The professor showed the ghost of a smirk and added. "I'm sure I couldn't imagine gnawing an arch-enemy's noggin."

Nick couldn't either. Although he thought of Braxton Jewell.

The professor added, "Few realize that the phrase 'let the punishment fit the crime,' which you know is the basis of our penal system, came straight from Dante's Law of Contrapasso."

"How does <u>Inferno</u> end?"

Nailor paused a moment to size up Nick in the way of a new and promising student. "Dante, in the deepest circle of Hell, must climb up Satan's back in order to rejoin the world of the living."

"Now there's a fine jungle gym!" exclaimed Nick, again glancing at Allengri's photos.

His eye went to a framed Conte crayon study of two human skulls on the professor's wall behind the desk, one skull drawn at an oblique angle to the other, as if to invite speculation as to the slightest distinctions among the class of mind that had inhabited each of these shells.

Nick decided to try again, "*Illuminated* manuscript," he repeated with care. "Why *Illuminated*?"

"'Illumination' refers to the colors and the gilding in certain religious documents, thought to be the vehicle of prayer and spirituality. Each step – the calligraphy, decorating the margins, even the process of gold leafing to bring glow to the letters beginning each line – corresponds to a different stage of the Creation." Nailor produced a magnifying glass and examined further. "Very elegant, this page. On true animal skin vellum, and very old. But dyed purple. I've read of that technique but have never seen it first hand."

Nick jotted the word "vellum."

"Its significant that this message is on real skin. Animal, that is," Nailor added. "Given Allengri's misdeeds and the laws of Contrapasso."

Turning back to the manuscript, Nailor warned, "Unfortunately my own 'methods,' as you call them, won't be enough for us to fully appreciate this piece of work. We should consult Jorge Graham, a leading expert on the physical characteristics of Illuminated documents. He keeps an antiquities shop on Boston's Newbury Street." Nailor kept his eyes on the manuscript as he spoke, quite obviously rapt in viewing the piece.

Nick wondered if the professor, like he the first time, would become mesmerized.

When the professor looked up, Nick saw the clear and stable gaze of a man well versed in the charms of letters. "Graham's an expert on inks, design, materials – even state of the art testing methods. For example, he'll be able to decode what the three hummingbirds pictured among the vines within these margins can tell us about the mind that penned this. But for now, why don't we see what the *words* might tell us."

Nick nodded. He felt awkward. When he tried to spread the message on the professor's desk it kept curling. It surprised him when Canon Nailor unlocked a desk drawer, retrieved a clip, and then weighted each of the message's four corners with a .45 automatic pistol cartridge.

Nailor squinted. "Your Illuminated manuscript is comprised of snippets."

"Snippets. Sounds painful."

"In other words a sort of Frankenstein document," Nailor observed. "The Illuminator butchered different texts and reordered each. Very violent to unhome literature from its context."

"Not to mention Allengri."

"I was speaking in a literary sense. This is an unnatural

text. In my work I analyze how a given writer patterns words and punctuation. This message is only three lines, all three from a different source."

Nick was impressed. "You see that first glance?"

"I'm afraid I do." Nailor looked at the message, then up at Nick, "Always start by looking for signposts. So let's focus on this first, lone word 'Cotansuca' and consider it a title."

Nailor ran a computer search on the word. "According to the FBI Dead Languages Database," he explained, "'Cotansuca' translates to "uprising." From the ancient Chibcha tribe, still alive and well in South America. Jorge Graham will shed additional light. He's traveled there to study and write about the ancient ways."

Words and syllables, while someone's out hunting to make another monster, Nick was suddenly thinking. Felt his head might explode, to splatter the professor's desk with parts of speech. He wanted to reach for Jim's handcuff key, but instead sat motionless.

Nailor had worked with scads of town detectives. Had learned by now to spot their restlessness. Knew they'd rather bang on a hundred doors than sit still for an hour to dice up a document. The professor recognized these signs in Nick. From this point on, he somehow made it look easy. And to Nick, what came out of the next five minutes sounded like a profile from a top caliber Forensic Psychologist.

Step by step the professor shared his findings and patiently explained how he'd arrived at them. He compared The Illuminator's message to a museum exhibition. The exhibition of this "uprising" – would accord to classic themes like Dante's Law of Contrapasso. To avenge. With acts of vengeance tailored to the subject's crime.

The professor ran another search, on a part of the document's first line, "Chamber of Horrors" and came up with a million hits in the database. None of them from classic books. "I suggest for the moment, we take it that the Chamber of Horrors is where the exhibition is located," the professor suggested. "Face value, so to speak." He added, "Let's also not rule out a figurative interpretation of the line "Welcome to my Chamber of Horrors." He mused, "The way someone might say, "welcome to my world."

"So the exhibition you're talking about could be The Illuminator's set of personal horrors."

"I would think. Now – I recognize the entire next line. From Bram Stoker's <u>Dracula</u>," said the professor. Reciting the line 'Water sleeps but enemy is sleepless,' he stood, and from his shelves retrieved the dog-eared paperback. In a moment he had opened to the line and explained, "In citing this The Illuminator issues a warning." Then Nailor picked up a photo of the remodeled Allengri. "That the line comes from the book entitled <u>Dracula</u> is fairly obvious. Its a direct reference to the departed." He thought a moment. "Like labeling a piece of evidence for the court."

Nick added, "So Allengri, as Count Dracula, is the first object to be displayed in the exhibition."

"So to move on to the next line, the next object to go on display will be this 'the man who' is his own nemesis?'"

"Quite sharp," replied the professor. "The question is, of course, who 'the man who' might be." Canon Nailor thought a moment. He said, "The reference might be broad, or quite specific, since," the professor spread his arms, "all of us in the human condition have capacity to work against ourselves."

"Our own nemesis."

"However The Illuminator speaks to us in the language of books. First, the embroidered skin that refers to *Contra-*

passo from the Dante. And then the book character Count Dracula, from Bram Stoker." The professor narrowed his eyes and speculated, "But I fear that to look at figures from the world of books doesn't take us near as we'd like. Because the best stories illustrate ways even the hero can work against himself."

"The human condition again."

"Precisely. Our capacity to act as our own nemesis. Along with the Free Will you mention, not to work against ourselves. But still – this fits a thousand book characters."

This gave Nick a sinking feeling. He asked, "How do we narrow it?"

"The simplest answer is usually best," replied Nailor. "The Illuminator strikes me as reaching out to the masses through easily-recognized types. Case in point: Count Dracula. So I wonder – if 'the man who is his own nemesis' might mean Mr. Hyde – counter-identity of the more genteel Dr. Jekyll."

"Besides – Robert Louis Stevenson's <u>Dr. Jekyll and Mr. Hyde</u> came out during the same historical period as <u>Dracula</u>. And like <u>Dracula</u>, the novel falls into the same category of Gothic literature. What we now call Horror."

Nick shrugged. "Makes good sense."

"I'll tell you what makes me think so," Nailor continued. "Both Dracula and Mr. Hyde are, in some sense, a form of Contrapasso. Dracula lives an eternity seeking blood, the fluid of life, from an innocent and virtuous character in that book. Yet the Count remains lifeless. Such a predicament would qualify as imprisonment. In <u>Dr. Jekyll and Mr. Hyde</u>, the monster Hyde is a sort of punishment for Dr. Jekyll's experimental toyings that go counter to the things of nature. Also amounting to a type of Contrapasso."

"Fits," Nick said as he again studied The Illuminator's message. "But a Hell of a lot of work to expose a dirtbag."

"Or two. Or three. . . and in the process, provoking thought within the community. So consider this: you mentioned a powerful drug The Illuminator uses to subdue these – ah – patients."

Nick went through the dossier and found his notes. He sounded out the word s u c c i n o l c o l i n e , and explained, "I'm told the drug causes dissociative paralysis. Meaning that Allengri would have been awake and aware of every stage of surgery. But physically in a state of paralysis and without physical pain."

"Exactly," the professor fired back. Enthralled, by the look of it.

But all this fidgety business with words still made Nick tense. He was thinking: *Could've spent the morning finding suspects. And still no closer to The Illuminator.* Until he heard Professor Nailor's next statement.

When Nailor lifted a photo of the transformed Count Dracula he said, "For young victims of men like Allengri, there's a lot of staying still and hoping what's happening actually isn't." He shook the photo, "To use that drug and perform this surgery would be the 'perfect Contrapasso.' The Illuminator exerts absolute control. Reshaping the outside to reflect inner corruption. The process is repeated in the manuscript's painstaking detail – ornate religious appearance on a vellum made of animal skin – The Illuminator is God reshaping Lucifer into a hissing Satan."

"And The Illuminator's out hunting up a next victim while I sit here playing Scrabble." The moment it flew out of his mouth Nick wished he could have called back his words. *What's gotten into me?* Felt sweat travel the hollow between his throat and jawbone. No idea why he'd spoken the way he had.

The scholar had paused. He said, tentatively, "You show great passion, Detective. And a depth of experience and integrity." A solid man himself, he saw another veteran detective trying to retire, trying to get off the job. A worn-out cop, mouthy-desperate to put the pieces right and still not knowing he'd already begun to.

"I'd be irate if I stood in your shoes," Nailor said. "To discover that a deceased Patrolman had been victimized. And then be forced to investigate the death of the criminal suspected of harming him. And in the course of it, to hear *him* referred to as the 'victim.'"

The textual sleuth brushed the bullets aside, rolled the Illuminated message, and pushed it back into its brass cylinder. He capped and handed it back to Nick.

Nailor stood. "Detective, parts of this message may not be visible to the naked eye. I still seriously recommend we make that trip to Jorge Graham's shop in Boston. I understand you want results, and rapidly."

He said **we,** *so I guess he's not throwing me out.* Politely, Nick asked, "Specifically how can Mr. Graham aid this investigation?"

"Documents like this one often contain other messages, hidden beneath the ancient vellum's surface. I can't go into technical details, but Graham's a top man for this. You see the document as a note. I see it as a manifesto. Graham will see it in a different dimension," Nailor said. Above the dark circles his eyes shone the gleam of scholarly intrigue. "He might give us a blueprint of The Illuminator's mind."

Ever since opening up Jim's history last night, Nick's entire being had been declaring a state of emergency. Now, much as he favored old-style detective work – to hear the words *us* and *together* uttered so kindly now – and from a sleuth of Cannon Nailor's stature – held infinite appeal. So he accepted. Nailor would make arrangements for them to go meet Graham tomorrow morning in Boston.

Before he turned to leave, Nick asked the professor, "With Mr. Hyde, that will make two 'exhibits.' Do you get a sense of how many? Where will this end?"

Nailor shook his head. "That I cannot tell."

Nick felt a wave of guilt. In the breast pocket of his great coat, protected within a legal-sized envelope, he still held the small note about The Font that The Illuminator had left for him in the bottom of the box.

He thought about mentioning it. But for the first time in thirty-five years' detective work he was paralyzed as to what to do.

Because to disclose this second note would be to admit to having been burglarized. Nick didn't understand why he couldn't do it. The whole thing made him feel privately ashamed.

According to his usual yardstick for an investigation, he still had Bupkes. No suspect. No identity for Mr. Hyde. To speak up about the break in, he'd by now convinced himself, wouldn't change a damned thing. *What's done is done.*

Outside, sitting in his car, waiting for his windows to defrost, Nick fought a wave of guilt for holding back.

He noticed a new voice mail and listened to a message from the real estate agent representing the buyer of his rental house. Closing scheduled in **two days**. *Finally! Some decent news.* If the closing went off he'd be a giant step closer to the old family home in Italy.

On the way across town he stopped at Mercy Hospital. Mere minutes experimenting with note paper and scalpels proved his theory about the pages cut from Jim's journal. Definite scalpel work.

Surgical instrument in hand, he thought of The Illuminator out there. Hunting.

Now Nick reached into his great coat, opened the envelope and read,

You WILL COMPREHEND JIM STEVENS' SUFFERING AFTER YOU HAVE PEERED INTO THE DEPTHS OF THE FONT.

He had it in writing: *Whatever it The Font is, that's where all this will end.*

CHAPTER 4

As Nick drove the roads of West Goddard on his way to question Gary Boother, spikes of early sun through bare trees reminded him of that morning he'd received the news of Jim's wreck.

To distract he took in the subtle ingenuities that brought comfort whenever he was in the less fashionable parts of town. A marquee sign that blinked on and off:

RAE'S BEAUTY SHOP

in the shop's window a sheet of cardboard lettered in black marker:

WE SELL LIVE BAIT, TOO.

Nick turned into Hill Street and drove till he saw, beneath a weeping willow's winter-brittle mop, the battered mailbox that read: Boother.

The driveway proved a potholed distance. At the end was parked a station wagon bulls-eyed with rust. A dark brown house hunched from the hillside. The roof sag and strips of peeling paint gave the place a wearied, unshaven appearance.

A silence about the place, a sense of dislocation, cut off all around by a thick buffer of hemlocks. The only sound, Nick's shoes grinding grit as he ascended the cement stairway.

He'd expected an entry door at the top, now a rueful tinge of dislocation when he came to yet another walkway. *Strange hospitality, to make visitors walk the greatest possible distance to find a door.*

Finally, a porched entry. Then he heard the throaty snarl. Barking. When a window curtain moved Nick sighted black paws against the window pane. Heard the scrape of claws. Low growling. Another lunge.

A little further. Beside the door he read the scrawled spray paint: "Beware of Dog."

Then a sight in the back yard caused Nick's breath to catch.

At least twenty bird feeders filled with seed. A wire stretched from a corner of the house to a rusting short-wave radio tower. A blue jay, a starling, and a shiny blue-black grackle. Freshly shot. Dripping blood. Hung from the wire by lengths of monofilament. Nick felt the swirl of revulsion and put a hand against the house.

The dog had gone quiet.

He knocked once.

Inside, a vestibule door opening. Then: Thump! The dog up hard against the door.

"Fancy! Down!" a woman's' voice scolded. "Fancy!"

The same growling.

She opened a crack.

Nick felt his heart leap. Saw snapping jaws pushed toward him between the door and jam's chipped edge. Black, rubbery lips and gums. Spittle dashed from the clacking German Shepherd's fangs.

Nick took a quick half-step backward.

"Fancy!" At the base of the dog's neck a sinewy finger hooked the choke chain. But the hand's owner remained behind the door. The voice disembodied.

"Whutchu want?"

"I'm looking for the Boother residence."

The gnarled hand yanked backward and the dog was gone. But not that elongated, gargling growl.

Then, up higher, a woman's craggy face appeared through the crack. "I ain't buyin' no insurance!" Her eyes darted up and down, pecking at the suit Nick wore. "An I got God enough!"

"I'm a Goddard Police detective. Does a Gary Boother live here?"

"Well, Christ in a bar fight!" the woman said approvingly. "Shoulda said you was police!" But her eyes narrowed, as if pinching her next question down to size. "I'm Gary's mother. What's he done?"

"Nothing like that," Nick reassured.

She opened the door "a scooch wider," so Nick could see the German Shepherd's dull blue eyes, with a hideous veil over them that chilled his very marrow. "Only a few questions." When he made a gesture the dog lurched, snarled. Flash of tongue that sent out foamy specks.

"Down! Fancy!" Mrs. Boother yanked the dog to a quiet sit. "Don't mind this one! Mostly goes by smell." She added, "Shoulda' been a police dog. 'Though Fancy's as blind as midnight!"

"So I've noticed."

"See now?" she remarked curtly, "Sweet's can be."

"And Gary? Is he home?"

"Son works in the bag plant. Nights 'leven to seven, you see. But today he had the doctor to go to. Be home 'bout an hour."

"I can wait."

She peered at Nick. "There's a diner up the road."

"The Flying Yankee. I saw it." he replied. "Right next to the beauty salon that now sells live bait."

"Rae's always *did!*" the woman rasped conspiratorially. A secretive wink at Nick, waving him nearer, she gossiped, "Me? I calls it the *Worm and Perm.*"

Nick handed off his card. "My mobile number's on there."

"I'll *kill* Gary, he's in trouble."

"He's not in trouble," Nick turned toward the back yard, "but there's something I need to ask." What he saw there made him gulp with disgust.

The woman glowered suspicion. "Always cooperate with police."

Gesturing toward the back yard, Nick asked, "Why are three freshly-killed birds hanging back there?"

"Gary's father taught me shootin 'fore *he* went off." Mrs. Boother's face beamed with pride. "They eat food put out for the *good* birds."

"So. You shoot only the **bad** birds?"

"Only shoots a few. Example for t'others. That ainagainst the law."

"I suppose not," Nick replied.

As Nick drove to the diner to wait for Gary Boother he tried facing the idea – interviewing a man who, like Jim Stevens, had likely endured the acts of Simon Allengri. Yet unlike Jim, had lived with the memories a while.

In contrast to such concerns, today's snow-covered

morning seemed almost dreamy. To again carry Nick back to one like this two years ago that had ended in a nightmare. New Years, the morning of Jim's death.

It helps, Nick had reminded himself moments after he'd heard of Jim's wreck, for the family to see a squad car pull up in front of the house – for family members to register that pause, right before the driver steps out – a driver other than their son – as the news begins to sink in, telegraphed in a language that transcends words. Nick had set out for Mary Stevens' house. Prepared to be that person in the squad car. That messenger. Then, just before her street, he had detoured.

He'd wanted to make sure, unable to fathom words of the emergency room doctor who'd pronounced Jim dead, who had reassured him: "With the suddenness, that patch of ice, immediate impact with that utility pole, in his blunt-trauma death Jim Stevens had probably felt nothing. He was lucky." How bizarre, using Jim Stevens, lucky and death all in the same sentence.

Nick had easily spotted the accident scene. That Goddard Water Authority backhoe, rocking and banging in war against permafrost to dig up the ruptured water main that had caused the ice, the backhoe's yellow paint job a warning way too late.

Rolling to a stop he'd seen the glitter, points of morning light through shattered windshield particles, lovely as a diamond runway across the surface of a larger, darker glass. He'd gotten out to place a hand on the cold wood of that fatal phone pole.

A sound went out of him. His legs hinged. And Nick felt the sparkling fragments sting his kneecaps. Then he was numbed by the sight of circular skid-marks that vanished like serpents back into the mirror of black ice. An ice that rejected the first rays of that new-minted year.

wondered what effect the time might have had on the guy, if any.

He fretted whether Boother would even talk. And if the answer was yes, how it would come out.

Keep this simple, honest, and straightforward, Nick thought. *Put yourself in Boother's shoes. And play fair.* What would it be like, to carry unwanted memories? To as a grown man, read about The Illuminator crimes over your morning corn flakes? To then get a call from a detective? To sit across from him answering questions? In a public place?

Grim reality was, to rule out Boother as a suspect he'd need to apply pressure. To eliminate him quickly would be to do a favor, Nick reminded himself. Like ripping off a Band-Aid.

However if Boother spooked he'd back off, reassure, and come back later.

After a short wait he called.

In preparation Nick moved from the lunch counter to sit at a booth – waiting – turning Jim's silver key on his ring. He thought to fold the newspaper, to put the headline and photos of Allengri well out of sight.

Nick waved to Gary Boother as he came through the door. Without smiling the man returned the wave, stopped at the front counter to order a Bud Light, waited, and then walked it to Nick's table.

His hair was cropped short, uncombed and molded by long hours wearing a cap. Maybe six foot two, looking a bit bloated in gray coveralls, Boother inhabited his body like it was all corners.

The detective introduced himself. "I used to work with Jim Stevens. Retired now, sort of."

The hands jangled lighting up and Boother shot smoke

through his nostrils while still inhaling, glancing at Nick's key ring. "If you're retired, what are you still doing with a handcuff key?"

"It was Jim's. I carry it to remember him," Nick explained. "Hell – maybe underneath it all, I'm afraid I'll get locked up."

Boother's lips tried to pry a smile but remained tight. His eyes picked about the room. Avoided Nick's. ""This about Jim? Or *me?*"

"Distantly related." Nick kept it vague in case Boother proved talkative. "I understand you provided information in a lawsuit Stevens launched. So, let's talk about you, first."

The man only shrugged and bobbed his head.

"What do you do for work?"

"Shift supervisor," Boother replied obediently. "Doubles every other week. Off every other week in between. We make plastic bags for Wal-mart."

Nick raised his eyebrows, "You'll never have a work shortage." Boother had time on his hands. Nick turned his eyes slightly harder. "How do you spend your time during off-weeks?"

A small sweat had broke on Boother's lip. "Winter's coming. So been cutting wood for the stove."

Nick nodded. "And your contributions to Jim's case?"

Boother slid his hands back and forth along the edge of the Formica table. "That was weird," he said, his voice tentative. "The Youth Camper sex abuse thing."

A truck driver sitting nearby trained his eyes at the floor, listening.

"It must bother you," Nick began.

"What? All that was years ago." Now the hands danced the table edge like birds on a wire. Boother's sleeves had crept up to reveal small burn marks. His knuckles showed homemade tattoos. The hands, calloused. Fingertips too. *A guitar player.*

"When did you join the troop?"

"After my father left for Viet Nam in '74. When he came back after Saigon Fell, my folks got separated." Boother chuckled.

"What's funny?"

"My mother made me join the Youth Campers so I'd stay out of trouble."

"Looks to me you did a decent job of it," Nick said, looking up. "Your deposition says several men had inappropriate contact with you."

"Inappropriate? That was the seventies." He tried to make a joke, "Campmaster Roache was always quoting that bumper sticker, 'If it feels good, do it.'" Gary Boother stared off for a moment.

"Campmaster Roache. What was his full name?"

"George Roache."

Nick wrote it on his pad, wondering if the number of letters in the name would fit one of the slice-outs in the Complaint document.

"Roache had this way with people. Like some kind of a god. But he could make you feel like a sub-loser with a glance. Or some little comment. And he had this wine cellar in his basement. Every week he invited some of us Campers to go over there and make wine. Even school nights. Our parents thought we were working on badges. He let us drink on campouts. Once the camp work was all done. He pushed us on that."

He'd used the wine to lure, Nick thought. A step into the forbidden. Trap the teens in a minor vice. And then escalate the scale.

But the Campmaster often showed a stricter side, Boother was saying. In private he was your best friend one moment,

"Then in front of everyone he'd say something really mean in front of other campers to embarrass you about what went on in private."

"To demonstrate the power to shame. A warning shot to keep kids from talking."

Boother only shrugged. "You never knew when Roache's mood would switch."

Nick held still and summed up, "Sounds like a Dr. Jekyll & Mr. Hyde situation."

Boother's eyes lit up.

Nick hadn't even gotten to ask about Allengri. And already Exhibit B, Campmaster George Roache. Normally he would have stood up, reached for his handcuffs, and brought Boother in to sweat him.

But face to face, every fiber of Nick's being registered that the man sitting before him was harmless. Someone, in fact, who would likely take on far more than his share of maltreatment to avoid a fuss. Definitely not the avenger type. And in no way a suspect.

Suddenly it was as if a steam valve had been cracked and Boother was trying to cool the jet by explaining away the Campmaster's acts as harmless, "But Roache put together amazing trips." Hitting on his beer between gulps of breath. . . "Hell, our *parents* weren't going to be able to take us on the kind of trips Roache set up. Every one of us wanted to stay on his good side."

"A real Svengali. . ."

Boother showed distrust for the word. "Huh?" The guardedness then melted to innocence and need for release in now telling it. "There was this time at Mount Katahdin, down Maine. You'd come around a turn in the trail, and all of a sudden you're standing at the edge of a forty-acre boulder field flooded with water so clear you could see the giant boulders beneath the surface. Katahdin's five peaks mirrored on the water over the top of them. Maybe a big bull moose a few feet from shore ducking under and coming up chomping mouthfuls of water weeds. Four or five red-tails circling, starlings diving.

"One time this happened and I was about to bolt. Just then Roache came up behind me on the trail and put his hand on my elbow, inched me forward till both of us were like five feet from this moose that weighed better than a ton." When Boother looked up from his cigarette drag at Nick, a youthful wonder had found a way between memory and now, to replace the tensions of a well-guarded face. "My heartbeat was gonna blow though my chest."

Boother smoked again, spreading his hands to indicate remembered surroundings. "Roache pointed to that moose and said: 'There's never been hunting in Baxter State Park. You could get close enough to ride him.' He'd say: 'Try finding one of those in Goddard. Try finding that in a book.' Like some kind of magician. All us Youth Campers even called him Gandalf." Boother took another hard drag. Then he drank.

"Did you kids love this magician?" Nick asked, "Or fear him? Like a cult leader."

The innocence in Boother's face became a knot of mixed emotion. "He had that moody side. Like with that bull moose in Maine. He accused me, 'You're too much of a big sissy to get on it.' Somehow five minutes later, Roache'd have me bathing naked in the same flooded boulder field."

"Taking pictures?"

Boother nodded half-sideways and waved the cigarette hand. "Then after the weekend, I'd be back in Goddard trying to get by with my mother, with no child support from my father. . ."

"In the course of your Youth Camper, ah . . . experiences.
. ." Nick tried to euphemize, not knowing where Boother was
in terms of any understanding of this as abuse, "have you also
spent time with Simon Allengri?"

Gary's eyes shifted to a backing big rig outside in the lot.
Blue-black smoke clapped from its pipes.

Nick gave it a full minute. Then, "Gary?"

"Ho. Yeah." He took a quick drag and continued. "Sorry.
I went off."

"You're doing fine."

"What was it you asked me?"

Clearly Boother had yet to connect emotionally with
these events. "Allengri. Did you . . . ah . . ." Nick knew he
wasn't saying this right, " . . . stay with him – like Roache?"

Boother's words were unexpectedly sharp. "I said all that
back when Jim's lawyers interviewed me!"

The waitress stopped by asking if the two needed anything else.

Boother handed off the empty. "One more."

"Have you recently contacted these men or anyone
else from the Camper troop or Jim's law suit?" Bailey had
already checked it out, but Nick asked it anyway, to measure
the response.

"I wouldn't know where to look. Like I say, I just work at
my job and play guitar. Mind my own business."

"Any names other than Roache?"

Boother's eyes grew wide. He shook his head and spit out:
"I don't remember."

"Gary, I need you to tell me," he watched the eyes. "Are
you angry at any of the men who did those things to you?"

"Angry?" The pupils held. "Why *would* I be? I mean, I
sort of did it *with* them. Together, I mean. And it was just
for a couple years." Unexpectedly, Gary Boother told Nick

some details the detective had trouble even jotting on his note pad. A prolonged silence. Then Boother dismissed the silence with, "After that I got a girl friend. Nobody chased me down."

"But you were a **kid**. You didn't *do* anything with them. They *did it* to you. It was **abuse**. Why didn't you join Stevens in the law suit?"

Boother flinched. "You kidding? It's embarrassing! And besides, like I said, it was just a thing that happened, like an understanding between us."

"How old were you?"

"Fourteen. When it started."

"You don't think they took advantage of you? Not even a little?"

Boother stiffened. "Look. Simon Allengri paid for my guitar lessons. George Roache threw a party for my High School graduation. More than I can say for my father." A tear had formed in the corner of one eye.

"Okay. So let me ask you this. Do you ever think about. . . it?"

Boother drew, released a cloud, then followed up with the beer. "Sometimes, but I try to leave it – in the past."

Nick had not looked forward to this part. But he knew Boother's reaction would tell him all he wanted to know.

Taking a breath, the detective opened his dossier. Nick said, "Since you worked all last night, you probably haven't read the newspaper." One by one he added more . . . sliding photos in a row on the table in front of Boother. The pictures made the tiniest hiss sliding across the Formica table top. Nick continued, "Yesterday evening Simon Allengri hit the red carpet at Pinecrest's Autumn Follies transformed into this. Surgically." The very last photo was Allengri, the Dracula, on a morgue slab. "One look in a mirror and his heart stopped." Then Nick unfolded the newspaper to make the headlines unavoidable.

Boother's eyes popped. When he set his beer on the table he gripped the bottle it as if its twelve ounces might prevent his two hundred fifty-plus pound body from taking flight. But he couldn't keep himself from glancing back at the dead Allengri, a disturbed and questioning look spreading across his face.

"What do you think of this?"

Gary quickly lit another cigarette.

Nick held up the one already burning in the ashtray.

Glancing at it all laid out before him on the table, Gary said, "That's some sick shit," his voice catching. He made work of stubbing the extra butt.

Nick recited the dates of Allengri's disappearances, pegging the time-frame against Boother's work schedule. "Can you provide a whereabouts for those nights?" he asked.

Boother's face showed shadows of an innocent but frightened man.

Waiting for the rest of the answer, a stray ribbon of Boother's smoke dud found Nick's nostril. His eyes watered, and for a split second he was an addict again. He drew a quick sniff to clear his head and slipped the photos back into the dossier.

Boother said, "I was moonlighting every day off work," digging through his wallet. "I landed this gig. Working all around the state. So I was on the road then installing sneeze guards on the soup and salad bars at all the Seven-11s." He handed Nick a worn business card, "That's the contractor," rewarding himself with another deep drag, followed by another hard pull on the beer, "Go ahead and call 'im."

Boother looked ready to either shut down or walk out. Nick handed back the card but jotted the name and number. "I believe you." With this he decided to tap a softer line of questions; sooner or later all roads lead in the same direction. "You mentioned guitar."

Boother visibly relaxed, relieved by the topic shift. "I play – when I'm not working. Back then in the Youth Campers, me and another guy played pretty often on campouts. After that we got together once in a while."

"That's nice," Nick said, trying hard to sound harmless, "What kind of music?"

"Back then? John Denver. Simon & Garfunkle."

"'Hello darkness my old friend,'" Nick repeated from memory. "Who besides Simon & Garfunkel could make a phrase like that sound soothing? What was your buddy's name?"

"Brian. Brian Shockly."

"Your best friend?"

"I always pretty much keep to myself."

"Was Shockly a Youth Camper?"

"Roache was big on showmanship. Every year the troop did a variety show to raise cash for trips, reading out plays or poetry. Songs. One year in the show Brian Shockly backed me up on guitar. After that Roache invited him to join our troop. Roache was always adopting in kids like that."

"Adopting in?"

"Into the troop. Or at least the wine making at his house. He invited Brian along to Mt. Katahdin on Labor Day. It grew from there."

"And later initiated physical contact?"

Boother ducked his head slightly. "Pretty much I think. It was just something you knew. Then one time I walked in . . ."

"And saw it was true. They were doing it to Brian. So no more pretending they weren't doing it to you."

Boother's eyes became blue wells. "Yeah. After that we decided to get out of Goddard. We both quit high school and made a plan to drive cross-country in some old Winnebago. You know, just pack clothes, guitars . . .. Climb mountains and play music. Nobody to fuck with you." He described it like a remembered dream he wasn't sure he'd even dreamed.

"Adventure," Nick said. "For me back in the nineteen seventies the adventure was Viet Nam. But I can sure understand wanting to see a world beyond Goddard, Mass," Nick assured. "How was the trip?"

"Never happened."

From his wallet Boother handed Nick the worn photo: Boother and Shockly in front of a tourist cavern, both holding guitars. Shockly's long hair and beard and seventies-style jacket of draped animal skins made it difficult for Nick to get much of an impression. But the eyes. . .. Had he seen them before?

Nick returned the photo. "Where was this taken?"

"The troop used to go spelunking in Wiggins Caverns. Later on me 'n Brian partied there. I hear some developer's turning the Caverns into a kind of fun park."

"Supposed to open next spring." Nick had seen the billboards. "Isn't spelunking risky?"

"It got my mind off things."

Then when Boother spoke it seemed as if to paint over gray memory: "Brian wanted to get involved as a co-plaintiff in Jim's suit. But it didn't go so hot. First year at B. U. he had a breakdown and bailed on college."

"Shockly ever show any resentment toward those men?"

"About eight months ago, we were partying." Boother began sheepishly, hiding his face behind a shaky drag on his Marlboro. "The Caverns. Off-season we'd sneak in and play guitar and party. The locks weren't so hot . . . if you know what I mean."

Nick caught the drift, spread his palms upward on the

table, "Look. I'm retired, I'm not going to bust you."

"The place had a great sound . . it echoed like crazy. We made a fire and opened a bottle of Wild Turkey. Talking, catching a buzz 'n shit. You know. But Brian started getting crazy. Not just crazy. Like he quit giving a fuck. Told me all what happened with Roache and Allengri and some other guys. I thought *I* had been in the weird shit!"

"The other guys,'" Nick repeated, "Did he mention names?"

"No."

"But Shockly was really upset about what had happened."

Boother dumped it like a mouthful of hot porridge. "He wanted to blow 'em all away."

"Blow them away?"

Boother looked Nick hard in the eye and brought a hand over his mouth with the cigarette, left the hand there even after drawing, parsing a decision, his hand blocking the words, then shooting blue blades of smoke out between the fingers. When the hand finally came away from his face, Boother confessed: "We did blotter acid that night. It hit us different. I was half asleep, 'cause I drank more. But all the talk got Shockly's blood up.

"He left the Cavern to get a deer rifle out of the trunk of his car. Started working the bolt, and telling me he could take'em out easy. Told me: 'I could dress up in camo and sit in the woods till nighttime outside the house, hollow out a potato and make a silencer. Allengri won't know what the fuck hit him.' Then he slapped in a clip and fired three shots into a tree." Boother took a long, introspective drag. Blew out. "That shit's not my thing."

Pay dirt. A potentially violent suspect who had motive, opportunity . . . and a rifle. But Nick had to smile: to use a silencer like that, Shockly would have ended up with a lap full of potato salad, a bullet flying wildly, and anyone within a mile calling the cops once they heard the rifle's unmuffled report. Even so, he asked, "Where's Brian these days?"

"I called only once after that and got his answering machine. Left a message. But he never called me back. That was it. Like I say, that night spooked me. I'm into guitars, not guns."

"Shockly married?"

"Had a girlfriend. Tiffany something. She caught him with someone and kicked him out. Tiffany Test. Lives over in Charlton, I'm pretty sure. Couple miles from here."

Nick jotted the name. "She know about Brian's thoughts of Homicide?"

"You'd have to ask her."

Firearms, Nick thought. It didn't fit The Illuminator's profile. Too quick and final. Lacked the drama, the slow precision of the victim-witnessed surgery, dramatic skin embroidery, and Illuminated penwork. *But. A guy floating out there somewhere with a gun.* Nick asked, "Why would Shockly target Allengri? Why not Roache, or others?"

"Oh, he talked about doing 'em up."

"And you have no idea of Shockly's whereabouts?"

"Nope. Probably better off."

Nick had all he came for.

"Have you ever married?"

"Didn't last."

"Sorry to hear that." Nick leaned slightly forward.

"You have any other family besides your mother? Close friends?"

"I *was* friends with Brian Shockly," Boother said, suddenly closing his mouth as if he'd been too off-guard.

Nick put one hand on the other upon the table and nodded, feeling the gulf of sadness that spread between them in the moment. With a finger he pointed to the tattoos on Boother's knuckles. "Prison tats?"

"Hell no. Me and Brain Shockly did these."

"Must've hurt," Nick replied.

"I can take it. But Brian could always take more pain than me." Boother started getting up. "I gotta go. I have my mother to help."

"Yes. I met your mother," said Nick. "She's a crack shot on the starlings and blue jays."

Standing to go, Boother replied, "I guess it serves them right for stealing."

Nick was relieved to cross Boother off the list. Guy had had enough trouble. If only to add another name – Brian Shockly.

At least on his own home front things were progressing: with the sale closing a couple days from now he'd be down one house, and up the first half of his nest egg.

Outside the diner a snow was falling. Some men were stringing Christmas lights. Another man spreading salt on the lot's icy patches. When they tested the lights the colors looked unreal against a sky like slate.

With The Illuminator's surgical plan to sculpt a Mr. Hyde now fully on the books, Nick knew he had to work fast.

But right now he'd have to run down this trigger-happy Brian Shockly.

He called Bailey for addresses and phone numbers for a Brian Shockly and a Tiffany Test. Bailey came back one for two – with Ms. Test.

Maybe Shockly had decided to make the trip out west on his own, Nick thought. Test might be able to tell him. And she lived two miles from the diner.

"I ran a few queries against the name, " Bailey was saying. "Single mom. Works as an EMT, ambulance driver. New face in town so she works the Hell shift."

Ambulance driver, Nick thought. A jolt. "There's your medical connection. Might even be our Illuminator." While Bailey filled him in Nick headed for the girlfriend's house. She'd moved to Goddard two years ago from El Passo, where she was arrested for drunk and disorderly. Pled to a misdemeanor and remanded to twelve-step meetings.

"Newly sober," Bailey read off.

"Maybe," Nick countered.

"Apparently a day care Social Worker over at Mercy Hospital Pediatrics observed alcohol abuse and dug up what happened in Texas. Probably still attending AA meetings to maintain custody of her child."

"She's running threadbare," Nick replied. "With those medical contacts, she could be getting even for the ex-boyfriend."

"*Or* working *with* him. Listen to this," Bailey said. "She was cited last month for Road Rage over in Charlton. By a motorcycle cop. Sergeant the name of Ron Geister. Know him?"

Of course Nick recognized the name. Nicknamed "The Rooster," Sergeant Geister headed up the motorcycle squad in the bordering town. He'd made a name for himself by writing speeding tickets at three times the usual rate. Then boosted to sergeant after engaging the Department of Transportation in a study to show that more that sixty percent of those ticketed for speeding more than once annually also engaged in other compulsive behaviors such as smoking, or hard-core gambling. And that to seek help for one usually helps solve the other, with the result of cutting down highway deaths – and turning lives around.

Nick asked Bailey, "Know why everybody calls him The Rooster?"

"Because of the complaints," Bailey came back. "Every time Geister hands off a traffic ticket, he tells the driver to wake the Hell up."

"Bailey," Nick said. "See if you can get Geister on his radio, and patch him though to my cell phone."

Within moments The Rooster was on the line. Nick asked the sergeant what he remembered about the incident with Test.

"You don't forget'em like *that* one," said the sergeant, recounting a few details. Finishing up, Nick asked about violent tendencies.

The Rooster replied, "Got issues. . . " and filled him in.

Nick found himself shaking his head.

He put in another call to Bailey, and asked for a search on the name Gary Boother had given him. "George Roache. Used to be Campmaster for the Youth Camper troop here in Goddard."

Nick caught himself. He'd almost said, 'Back when Jim Stevens was a member of the troop.' But he wasn't going to spill that to Bailey till he'd had a chance to cover it with the chief.

CHAPTER 5

Pulling up to the residence Nick saw Tiffany Test outside in her driveway, headed somewhere by the look, unlocking a faded El Camino and placing an overnight tote bag inside.

Crossing the snow-covered front yard, Nick flashed his shield and asked, "Ms. Test?"

"I go by Tiff." A swag, in the way she eyed him. Physical, as well, hooking both thumbs in her belt line, and then, the jut of a hip.

Nick couldn't miss the hefty waft of perfume and remainder of a deep Texas accent. She wore EMT uniform pants. And on top, a shimmery gold blouse beneath her uniform jacket. Makeup maybe a bit heavy around the eyes.

"I have to ask a few questions, Ma'am."

"I'm not your 'Ma'am,'" she started. Irritable. Exhausted by the look.

"This'll only take a minute."

"I just got off ten days straight and headed in again. I'm running late."

Nick took out his notebook. Asked for her whereabouts

going back to the day Allengri had gone missing – until he hit the red carpet at Autumn Follies.

She offered an alibi. "We were in Texas. Visiting my *ma'am*. Can prove it, too."

"We?" Nick hoped her next words would be "with Brian." But it was not to be.

Me and my daughter. We flew Delta. Go check. I'm moving back there with my mother once this damn thing is over."

"What *damn thing*?"

"Social services is filing to take away Platinum. That's my daughter."

"Brian's daughter?" Nick asked, jotting a note.

"What'z*hat* matter," she shot back. "Since Brian's not paying."

"Does Social Services know you were cited for Road Rage last week?"

Tiff Test rolled her eyes. "I only flipped off another driver. Who motioned to pull over and duke it. So I obliged him."

"With your daughter still sitting in her car seat?" Nick asked flatly.

A sharp retort. "Not like I told *her* to fight. Anyway, the other driver phoned in my plate number. Claimed I had made a 'threatening gesture.' Probably saw my EMT uniform and thought I was police."

Nick knew a little R & R can do wonders. No scale for Road Rage. Flipping someone off, or ramming them with a pickup truck, either one could apply the label and stigma for life.

"The cop started lecturing all about "professional de-meanor," the woman went on. "So to get Officer Horntoad to hop along I told him, 'Just write my damned ticket so I can go home and get some sleep. Then you can go write up more first responders.'"

She showed Nick a vinegary smirk, "That's when he wrote down *road rage*. The Court assigned me to anger management class."

Nick kept up the pressure. "When the officer frisked you he found a Microtek Halo strapped to your forearm beneath your uniform."

"That's right. . ."

"Automatic blade tactical knife," Nick said. "How'd you come by a weapon like that?"

"Christmas present from my old boy friend."

"How romantic. Any chance your boyfriend's named Brian Shockly?"

"This is about Brian?"

"Depends. You ever see him violent?"

"Opposite. After the scare he got all obsessed with personal protection. Had me on the range every Saturday. Handguns. Skeet. Learning the nun chucks and cage fighting moves at night. At first it was kind of cool, but then . . .I couldn't brush my teeth without Brian doing a safety check. Like crazy."

She looked up at Nick, "But you know what's really scary? That cop who wrote me up missed the nine millimeter I had stashed beneath my kid's car seat."

Nick looked at her. "You said '*after the scare*?' What's '*the scare*?'"

"Look." She dug in her purse and passed Nick an ID card. "My concealed weapon permit. Driving ambulance I don't choose the addresses. My partner got clubbed in the head with a hockey stick for lugging a stretcher into a meth lab.

You could hear her right eyeball pop when it hit the fucking window pane. *That* was 'the scare.' My partner's still in a coma. You wanna go question her too?"

Nick pressed his lips together and let that last bit go. He said, "I need to talk to Brian next. . . ."

"Talk to freaking Brian?" She scoffs at this pea brain detective she's talking to. "Brian put a gun in his mouth. 'Bout couple months ago."

Nick closed his eyes. Then, "I'm so sorry."

"Sorry? Deer rifle we used to shoot target together. At least not here at my house. His neighbor called it in. Freakin' mess, I heard. Good thing his parents left behind a cemetery plot and insurance enough to burn and bury him. *That's* fore-thought."

"Parents? Where can I . . .?"

Nick heard a 'plunnngg,' as a text message hit her cell phone. Tiff Test glanced at it. "Look. I need to drive a guy to my AA meeting and then pick up my daughter from day care and take her to the sitter. Then I'm back on duty at three-thir-ty. So . . . "

"Another moment. Brian's parents . . .?"

"Died when he was thirteen. Besides that I couldn't pry a thing about his past. Brian's' *only* rule. . . Besides 'keep your weapon oiled.'"

"Did he get help? For his abuse? Counseling?"

"Abuse? Now you're shitting me. Right?" She shakes her head. Looks at her watch. "My mother told me I shouldn't stay involved…"

Nick interrupted, "Your breakup. I understand Brian was unfaithful. . ."

Suddenly indignant. When Tiff put a hand on her hip, her head seemed almost to slide backward an inch or two on rails, then abruptly stop, her eyes half a click narrower, not to miss this fool detective who she now repeats, *"Brian* was un-faithful?" She jiggled her hips. "Anybody who could've told you *that* would also know *I* beat Brian at the cheating game, *two* to *one."* She let out an acid laugh, "Those combat moves of his worked like Pilates."

When her cell phone chimed she glanced at it, took the call, "Hey…a ba-by."

Nick looked at the overnight tote in the woman's car beside the child's car seat.

She looked at Nick. Whispered into the phone, "Gimme a minute," then crudely to Nick, "So Baretta, we good now? Like, can I *go?"*

Nick reminded himself that in a few more weeks he wouldn't have to do this any more. But right now, this woman had possible motive, to avenge her ex-boyfriends' suicide. And something else. A case not long ago in nearby Boston of an ambulance driver using access to the Emergency Room to get hold of powerful narcotics – of the class The Illuminator had been using. Nick didn't see this woman's style match-ing The Illuminator's. But what if The Illuminator wasn't working alone?

When he reached his car he called Bailey and told him to monitor her activities – phone calls, email. "Also, see if you can get a GPS location report from her cell carrier for the last thirty days."

"I don't think she's the Dante and Dracula type. But for now I'm not ruling her out. And Bailey, I need you to verify these travel dates. Delta airlines. For a Tiffany and a Platinum Test." Nick read off the specifics.

Moments later Bailey called back. The air travel checked out. And that there was indeed a Myrtle Test who lived in

El Paso. Likely the mother.

"Okay, but keep the watch on her till I tell you otherwise."

"And Nick," Bailey said, "I have the whereabouts of George Roache. The Campmaster."

Had one of the plainclothes do some checking. Roache was quietly asked to leave his leadership in the Youth Campers a few years ago. His marriage of twenty-five years fell apart and he moved to Boston. Let me see, to Dorchester." Bailey read off the suburban Boston address and Nick jotted it on his pad. "Thanks, Bailey."

CHAPTER 6

Nick tapped **chief** in his phone contacts and brought Robertson up to date on what he'd learned about the Illuminated document during his meet with Nailor.

"The professor wants a second set of eyes by his old mentor, Jorge Graham," he explained. "He's an expert on finding old designs beneath an Illumination's surface . . ."

"So go!" replied the chief.

A sinking feeling reminded Nick that sooner or later he'd need to come clean and give up the other short Illumination, about "The Font." And that he'd been burgled.

Yet for now he held off, relaying the goods on his meet with Gary Boother, including Brain Shockly's campfire games with the deer rifle. He explained about Tiff Test and the suicide: "Which puts Shockly off the list." They should focus now on the Campmaster, George Roache, a possible candidate for Mr. Hyde. With Father Provost a close second, who according to Nick's own attempts to locate him via the Internet had apparently fallen off the planet. "I'd better warn Roache," Nick said, noting that his creeping contempt for the man had graduated to utter loathing.

He thought now of sharing what he'd learned about Jim Stevens' suffering at the hands of these men. But considering such a conversation brought a stabbing pain to Nick's forehead – the pain searing the moment he opened his mouth. So he closed it, telling himself that for now, with so much already in the mix, he'd do better to spare his old friend Robertson this news. "What about on your end?" he asked.

"The whole town of Goddard's gone crazy with this," the chief complained. "One of my grand daughters was sent home from school for talking about this Pinecrest thing in class."

"Kim or Kylie?"

"Kylie."

"The firecracker."

"Dissecting a snake in school Biology class she said something about men like Allengri."

"Teacher should have set the damned snake aside and held the discussion. How else kids going to avoid ending up victims?"

"This is rich," the chief chuckled. "A couple days ago all Nick Giaccone cared about retirement. Now you're carrying a banner for Allengri's victims."

Nick hadn't been planning it. But now he dropped the bomb. "As a teenager, Jim Stevens *was* one of Allengri's victims! It factored into his death."

The chief cried out like a body part had been yanked from him, "*OUR JIM?*"

Then Nick began to explain. "That was the 'Personal Injury' case when Jim asked for me to dig up a few things . . ."

But Robertson was not to get it all just then. On the chief's end of the line Nick heard background conversation.

Then he heard: "Hang on . . ." Robertson's voice that acid rasp again, making the inside of Nick's ear itch. More commotion. Then Robertson's hurried, unintelligible muffled talk.

"Something wrong? Chief? You okay?"

The chief barked into the phone, "Bunny Jewell's gone missing!"

Meeting Nick on the street out front of the house, the chief told him, as if answering the question that hung in the sleety rain now falling on them: "At least no fundraiser candy bars left behind."

Relieving news. But still not enough to rule out another Illuminator abduction. Immediately Nick noted Braxton's own new Cadillac, midnight blue, parked in the driveway. The freezing rain had started at dusk. All three garage doors stood closed. And Jewell's car under a rough crust of ice; he'd been home a while before reporting Bunny's disappearance.

"State police and locals are on alert," Robertson told Nick as they walked the driveway.

Only months before, Jewell had moved his wife out of their apartment above the funeral home that stood in front of Hillside Cemetery. They'd built new in a better section on Prospect Hill, the spacious hip roof Colonial that Nick and the chief now approached overlooking the reservoir. Boasting its three-car garage, and widow's walk on top, Jewell liked to tell visitors that on a clear night he and Bunny could make out the Worcester skyline.

The man Nick and the chief encountered that night was not the same blitzing Braxton Jewell they'd come to expect around Headquarters. Yet he was far from sheepish.

"I knew I should've paid the damned OnStar," he complained. "We'd at least have the Caddy back by now." He paced the front porch, biting down to make his jaw muscled flex.

His wife Bunny had been missing a good seven hours now. When he'd gotten home her car had been gone, but not her cell phone – a sign she'd return shortly. She had left no note. Jewell had checked some other things. No purchases against her credit cards during her absence.

Nick noticed jitters, and asked, "How many rooms in this house?"

Like a first-time father Jewell replied, "Four bedrooms. Living room. Den. Exercise and tanning room. Kitchen. And home theater."

Signaling admiration, the detective added, "Plus that three car garage." Dipping his lids, he asked, "Why a three-car. There's your car. Bunny's Caddy. What's behind door number three?"

"My cargo van," the Chairman explained tersely. A convenience. In the event of a late-night call Jewell could avoid driving down to the funeral home to get his hearse in order to go pick up a corpse.

The old detective and chief soberly exchanged nods. Nick suggested, "We should get a crew started inside the house."

"Right now," the chief added.

Jewell spat out, "I don't want a bunch of cops here. . . You're not going to find any of that hummingbird dust in *my* house. . ."

In official tones the chief told Nick, "This *is* the Chairman's *residence*. Maybe for now let's you and me handle this."

The momentary look on Jewell's face was that of the patriarch who'd seen things brought 'round right.

With due cordiality and barely a glance toward Robertson, the old detective suggested Jewell walk him through the day's events. The chief excused himself to go inside to call off the team.

The Chairman had said goodbye to his wife that morning around nine A.M., before heading to the cemetery office. After that he had driven to check on some of his properties around town. Bunny'd had errands to do. And would use her Cadillac. The gold one.

Nick asked, innocently, "Any known enemies, Brax?"

"Of course I have enemies," Jewell seemed to be enjoying the attention. "A town father's going to have. . ."

"Fair enough," Nick interrupted. "Any solid threats though? Phone calls? Emails?"

"Not a one." Jewell joked lamely. "Guess they know ole' Brax Jewell carries policemen in his pockets."

To both ignore, and question this man, was like riding a hybrid of camel and jackass. Nick asked, "Anything missing?"

"We were going to have people over for drinks. So yesterday I had Bunny pick up vodka and a bottle of peach schnapps. The schnapps is gone."

Nick knew Bunny Jewell had always been a teetotaler. The daughter of an optician, she'd gone to Pinecrest, where she'd met Braxton Jewel. They had dated through high school, but not steadily. Bunny went on to Brauser College. While Braxton had left Goddard to attend mortuary school in Cincinnati.

Braxton Jewell had learned the funeral home business at the side of his own father, where he'd mastered the lucrative arts of charming the poor in spirit. Far past a time when Bunny's father might have seen it otherwise, she and Braxton had wed. Nick knew Jewell's wife as an overly polite woman who had tried hard to make a good home.

"The schnapps tells me this could be just a lark," Nick said, to gage Jewell's reaction. He suggested, "Maybe she's gone to a friend's. You know, girls night out."

"Bunny doesn't touch a drop. She was supposed to. . ."

Jewell was getting more anxious. As opposed to concerned or worried, Nick thought.

"Supposed to, what?" he asked.

"She had errands."

"Understand, Brax," Nick tried to sound reassuring. "Hell – you're an insider. . . . As a sworn law enforcement officer, I'm obligated to ask this next question: Has your wife been down lately? Any concern about her hurting herself?"

Jewell shook his head. Began tapping his foot.

"Like I said, I had to ask that one, Brax. Its obvious things are on the ups going for you two." The way Jewell had been telling it these past months, he and Bunny were Goddard's rising stars – at a time when everything from the stock market, to crooked home mortgages, to foreclosures, and unemployment – had competed for daily headlines. Only a month ago in fact, Jewell had leaked plans of making a bid for the State House next year. A few days afterward the news had hit *The Goddard Morning Sun*, along with Jewell's announcement of his purchase of a Hyannis Port condominium – a measure, Nick had thought reading the news piece, for Jewell to appear more candidate-like.

"We'll find your wife," Nick said conclusively. "There's an all points bulletin on your wife's car with the locals, and State Police. Homeland Security has been advised should she appear at an airport, train station, bus terminal or border. From here on it's a waiting game. I'll go inside and find the chief." Nick watched the Chairman's eye travel to the garage doors.

Again the car parked outside the triple doors interested Nick. Unlike Jewell to let that car see a speck of rain. In fact, since first showing off his Caddy last August, more than once after a downpour Nick had seen Braxton getting after it with a chamois.

Nick asked, "Anyone you might suspect of kidnapping

for purpose of blackmail? Or ransom?" But from Jewell received the same negative.

Then Nick asked, "Tell me, how's business?"

"In a slump." Jewell returned. "People aren't dying like they should be."

To think of that Pinecrest teacher's 'final blaze' last night as Dracula, Nick had to wonder. Yet the slough in Jewell's income stream intrigued him more. In a display of humility, the detective indicated the new luxury coupe still in the driveway, and offered, "I'm concerned, Brax. Your new Caddy will be icing up all night."

Jewell's face momentarily clamped down upon itself.

Nick laid a friendly hand on his shoulder. "Give me the keys and I'll garage it."

A worried look and Jewell yanked away his shoulder and with contempt snapped. "Stop playing valet and go find my *other* car . . . and my wife."

"Okay," Nick agreed obediently. "I will, Brax." The Chairman had gotten the order of things to be found all wrong. ". . .my *other* car . . . and my wife. . ." Nick headed back inside the house, leaving Braxton Jewell to go on pacing his new front porch.

Inside, Chief Robertson sat at Brax's kitchen table. He looked up at Nick, "Get it?"

"Follow me," Nick replied and led the way. "There's a reason he's parking his car in the driveway."

Opening the door into the garage they encountered the bullmastiff Maximus, guarding the stacks of coffins.

BOOK II

CHAPTER 8

Sipping juice in her kitchen that morning, The Illuminator read the headlines on her laptop. The Work was gaining national attention.

By the time Nick had reached Professor Nailor's classroom that morning to absorb the lecture, The Illuminator had been seated at her worktable, gently smoothing the pages she had slit from Jim Stevens' journal.

Her quick visit inside Nick's house had gone swimmingly.

And today was to be a busy day.

Filled with preparations.

In fact by late morning – by the time Nick had sat down in the Professor's office – Cassandra had already finished sterilizing her surgical instruments and had scrubbed the home clinic top to bottom. Then inventoried and replenished supplies of pain drugs and bandaging.

Next stage of The Work she'd turned her attention to equipment upgrades.

Driving Brian's old pickup to a local freight forwarding company, she'd picked up a mail-ordered electric wheelchair lift. After that, she drove to the Home Center to purchase lengths of foam pipe insulation, several tubes of construction adhesive, and a caulking gun she'd use to apply it. She additionally bought a Milwalkee Sawzall reciprocating saw and a package of demolition blades; an electric drill; a set of high-speed bits; and steel bolts for mounting the wheel chair lift to the I-beam chassis of the motor home. Also a few threaded eyebolts. And some snap-guard mounts of the type used to affix emergency fire extinguishers or pressurized canisters to an emergence vehicle's bulkhead.

By the time Nick took his first cup of coffee at the Flying Yankee Diner in the wait to interview Gary Boother, The Illuminator had returned home to her brother's house and begun to transform the motor home into an ambulance in disguise.

Despite temperatures falling to the teens, Cassandra wielded the Sawzall, wrangling its it's long, thin chattering blade to cut away the motor home's every interior bulkhead. Then, to cover rough edges, she cemented the foam pipe insulation in place. The extra padding would protect her next Subject from stray bruises or contusions.

She screwed the fire extinguisher mounts into place and used these to secure tanks containing Oxygen and Entonox. Then connected the necessary tubing and plastic masks, and installed pieces of hardware on the wall above the canisters to keep the delivery devices at ready.

After that she moved her work to the vehicle's exterior, mounting the electric lift beneath its side door.

By using a wheel chair door-to-door, there would be no more lugging of drugged Subjects. Anything to prevent the slightest bruise. Now every mark would be according to Design.

Back inside her mobile unit Cassandra drilled holes through the floor to install the eyebolts. With these fasten points installed, the wheelchair and its occupant would travel with more stability now, secured to the eyebolts by ratchet-type webbing straps.

Then she was back inside the house, in warmth the remainder of that afternoon, where she rewarded her efforts by working with the hummingbirds. Through a series of exercises and rewards, she reinforced trust and affection for the remainder of the day. Distracting her from thoughts of her brother, she found the training rituals quite soothing. She looked forward, though, to resuming The Work.

By dusk, she decided the pick-up of her next Subject had waited long enough.

When she played back the past few hours' video, the web-cam she'd trained on her next Subject's home told her everything. Early this morning he'd come out on his front stoop for the newspaper. Had paused, eyes searching the street as if suspicious.

Gathering Intel on a new Subject was to store up an anointing, clean-burning oil. Fuel that would soon kindle The Light.

With the click of a mouse she had captured a still of him. Immediately she pasted the image into the "Goddard_ Nemesis" file of her new MorphAesthetica. The cosmetic design program enabled cosmetic surgeons to electronically model enhancements to prospective patients' features – marketed as a sure closer in making the sale.

Cassandra had learned quickly these past days. Working the sequence from start to finish, she'd gotten all the details just right. The hours slipped away in the making of minor adjustments; forgetting time and space, replaying and adjusting the morph, again and again until the result was near perfect.

She'd even forgotten that her body required food, or sleep. And for some moments, forgot her brother, proving this work a Salvation, precisely because it helped her forget. Those emergency calls back to the States, her brother's abrupt hospitalizations, his desperate pleas for cash, often when her own money had been in short supply. His weakening. Failures to find the right treatment.

He'd refused the standard therapies.

She had sustained her younger brother in every way she could, each time she could, in a world that seemed devoid of sure solutions. And even now that he was gone, part of her still nursed him. Kept him alive. This was The Work. Some people whittled. Others knitted or shaped clay to make useful objects. Cassandra worked in a more delicate medium, more vital, redesigning the predator's faces, exposing their hidden truths to The Light.

Into her small black medical satchel The Illuminator now placed the special drugs and an expensive bottle of red wine. Also in the medical kit she placed her Book of Souls, ensconced in its tasseled silken sack. She had sensed a new power coming to her while sewing in the page upon which she'd captured Allengri's soul. And in abducting her next Subject for surgery, she would put this raw new power to the test.

Walking to her bedroom she removed her blouse and brassiere. Stood a moment before the mirror, cupping her breasts, releasing them, and making mental calculations.

She took a pair of spandex biking shorts from a dresser drawer. With scissors from her vanity table she cut out the crotch and legs, changing the garment into a kind of binder. She pulled the split crotch over her head, and fit her arms through what had been leg spaces. Stretched tightly across her chest, the spandex restrained her breasts with remarkable effectiveness. "Flat as a choirboy," she said aloud, regarding herself in the mirror.

A Red Sox t-shirt rendered her profile effectively masculine. But just in case, she stepped into a pair of denim overalls. As a final touch, she pushed a wadded sock down into the crotch of her panties. "The bait," she said, patting the spot. She removed the Taser from the top dresser drawer and hid it in a pocket of her overalls. She'd planned a light touch for this evening, but she never forgot: be prepared.

Driving the motor home toward the Subject's residence, The Illuminator imagined herself at the wheel of a mobile M*A*S*H unit, dispatched from Above to intervene in a still-active Emergency of Evil.

As she drove, The Illuminator silently recited a prayer she had composed while performing surgery, then had dubbed the Scientific Truths of Righteousness:

We, Children of God are composed of 75% hydrogen and oxygen (water), 18% carbon (soot), the remaining 7% of other elements (salts and minerals of Earth). And the stories we share to heal the World.

Gusts of icy wind hit the motor home broadside, making it sway, and she rides it out.

BOOK II

CHAPTER 9

She breathed an air of new beginnings.

By this hour, the three hummingbirds roosted in the empty clinic and waited, within a house steeped in silence. A single lamp washed light across the Versa-bed: clean and fresh.

There's no describing the bursts of Light while setting up for a next Subject.

The Capoeira most often kept that in check, evened the flow.

She swings the motor home into a street entering the Subject's neighborhood. Anticipates new powers, now, from within the Book of Souls. Hopes for luck.

Spying the correct street, her eyelids momentarily flutter with delight. She eases the steering wheel through the turn and then slows.

In the distance recognizes the surveillance cam she'd mounted atop a utility pole, opposite her target's house. Had doped a lineman and then donned his chaps, spurs, climbing belt, and hardhat – looking the part – and then climbed the pole to set a camera. Next time, she'd hijack a cherry picker.

As she drove past the Subject's house she saw a shape move past one lighted window. Her plan required she park close.

She suddenly stops short when a group of arm-in-arm adolescent partygoers stumble off the curb, making their way across the street, five in all, staggering and passing a joint.

They halt. Look up in fear, she notices, when her motor home lurches to a stop.

"In the name of The Work," she pleads in a soft voice.

Almost immediately the revelers split up and load into two cars, parked one behind the other, then drive off. This allows her to ease the motor home into the large parking space left behind – two doors down from the Subject's house.

She logs onto her laptop in the now-parked motor home to review the target's recent activities.

The five who'd just driven off had been his visitors. The Subject would be tidying.

The Rise of Light blossomed within Cassandra's breast, as she is fully inhabited by The Illuminator. She opened her medical kit, snapped a heavy-gauge needle of medium length onto a syringe, and drew from a vial of Rophypnol in solution.

With the needle she pierced the wine bottle's foil seal near its edge, guiding steel against the green glass neck, till the needle's tip emerged from the bottom side of the cork. Red wine would render the sedative's telltale blue-green tinge undetectable. With a push she added the date-rape drug.

Then, using a second syringe, she drew from a different vial, marked Romazicon, and injected herself in the thigh.

With this antagonist in her blood, she'd be immune to the Rophypnol. The spiked wine, meantime, would knock her prey silly.

Another Subject. Another Act in the comedy.

She grasped the silken sack containing the Book of Souls and wondered how its gift, as new powers, would present. *Remain open*, she told herself. *Receive.*

Before the rear-view mirror she practiced her best tipsy boy act. Then she was out, carrying the bottle of spiked wine in one hand. In her other hand, on tasseled chord swung her hand-sewn, silk-protected Book. A Sacred record of physical graffiti.

CHAPTER 10

Fragments of ancient TV he'd missed sweeping his home office floor reminded Nick that never had he displayed such outrage. To see the black plastic chips now unsettled him.

Last thing he'd expected on his first day retired was to spend a night re-reading the Complaint and legal briefs for Jim's lawsuit.

Stories that clawed at his heart.

One common element: wine. According to Boother, the Scoutmaster Roache had the kids stomping grapes in their underwear down in his basement to make it. Underage drinking on every camping trip. There were other things. Unspeakable.

Nick would've preferred to question every past troop member. Each *potentially* had motive. But far more likely, these survivors would hold *themselves* hostage. Their principle instrument of torture: self-blame.

Bailey had tried. But the local Pequod Counsel of the Youth Campers of America had claimed that no records of these troop members existed. Although he strongly suspected this to be a line, the detective hadn't been a bit surprised hearing it.

Gary Boother, when Nick had asked, had said he could no longer remember names of others in the Camper troop. Scared. And understandably. Nick knew if he'd pushed harder, it would've been the last he'd see of the man.

At least, Nick thought, victims' tales surfacing in the news now, detailing their courageous survival of Allengri's acts, might help Gary Boother and others to comprehend that these were *serial crimes,* committed by an *adult,* rather than the *fault* of any *boy.*

Nick couldn't help regretting that Jim had never had such an opportunity to shed shame.

Hard to believe. A gleaming new Headquarters dedicated to the star cop's memory only yesterday.

Since then, the whole world had changed.

For what he *now* understood of Jim's courage and bravery, Nick thought they should have built the Rookie a skyscraper.

Retirement? Nick thought. *Yep.* This investigation *could* delay it. *But not forever.* In a moment of positive thinking, he'd contacted the tenants in the Positano house to inform them they'd better head back to Monte Carlo.

Even so for Nick, crowding his dreams of Italy was a nightmare: of himself – encamped in a Goddard outskirts roadside motel with both homes sold and a suitcase filled with cash – yet chasing The Illuminator well into his eighties.

After their meeting at Jewell's, Nick had done his best, had tried to help Chief Robertson get a handle on the atrocities endured by Jim Stevens. Had explained his theory of how the Rookie's trauma might have hit home that final shift – to end in a fatal wreck. Yet inability to console the chief had left Nick feeling incompetent and spent.

Even so, during the drive home from Baxton Jewell's house he'd called Bailey to ask for everything on the man's finances – from the funeral home and cemetery – to real estate deals and holdings – to what he spent at home on food, utilities, and gasoline.

Nine o'clock now, and according to Dispatch, still no sightings of Bunny's car.

Since her disappearance showed no signs of an Illuminator-style abduction, Nick had to suspect the husband. Yet the particular rotten waft of *how* the man was involved was still to reveal itself. Maybe a life insurance scam in the making .. . or a rigged kidnapping . . .

Unusual that Nick could arrive at nothing.

Bunny, he knew, would never play along with hard crime, *per se.* Braxton was an all-out shit, and she allowed him too many of their decisions, many that might involve shady dealings – dealings that a wife of a man like Braxton had better only half-know about, and be looking the other way for the other half.

Logging onto his computer Nick saw that Bailey had already scraped up a small pile on the couple.

He bulldozed through the data.

Bank accounts drained over the past few months. Securities sold off, both Braxton's and his wife's. Every one of Jewell's real estate holdings for sale, but like everywhere now, none selling. Every one of them a financial drain.

For all his show and talk of bids for the State House, it appeared Jewell teetered on insolvency.

What's this? From the Cadillac dealer. An email: "To surrender wife's vehicle. . ." Jewell had fallen behind on payments on both new cars. When Nick read back several emails in the string, he determined that a compromise had been negotiated: voluntary repossession of *one* of the cars, in order to save the *other*.

Nick recalled his meeting with Jewell earlier that evening. The itinerary Brax had given for the day.

Nick got the number and called the dealer at home. It had been set up for today with the rep from GMAC Finance.

Not only had Braxton volunteered his *wife's* car to go, but he'd sent her to return it.

Coward!

But according to the dealer, the car had not yet been returned.

Nick felt a brief wave of relief. Because this meant Bunny Jewell might be out there joy riding. Showing up at an old friend's with a bottle of liquor.

Unless she was in the hands of The Illuminator.

But to punish what? Nick thought, *The Mortal sin of being married to an asshole?*

Some other information Bailey had sent provided Nick a sense of how the woman spent her time. Mrs. Jewell made use of her time mostly in mid-level society work. A marathon to benefit breast cancer research. Another project to acquire laptop computers for a literacy project to benefit lower-income neighborhoods in Worcester. Here and there, the usual luncheons.

And this?

It jumped off the screen: **Patron of Mercy Hospital.** As such, Mrs. Braxton Jewell was a member of a small group planning to underwrite a new cancer clinic, which was still in early stages of architectural design.

Nick was astonished. Emails between Bunny Jewell and the hospital's Development Office indicated that she'd been a help in preparing press kits for the program, for a media launch on the schedule for early spring.

Explains why there's been nothing about the new clinic in the papers, thought Nick. *Or their gift, for that matter. But Patron? With Jewell's finances what they are? Patron means big dollars.*

Nick went online to check out the hospital's giving program. Designation of Patron, he discovered, was reserved for donors of six figures.

It didn't add up.

What *did* add up – at least toward his investigation of The Illuminator crimes – was the potential of a big donor to cultivate *medical* favors.

Nick's mind was reeling. Sensed: not a lot of time till The Illuminator would make a first cut on the man who was his own nemesis.

Take it easy, Nick told himself. The motives for Braxton Jewell to be involved in something like The Illuminator crimes was limited to only one thing he could think of: The creation of a crisis with the Allengri incident, and then being on record for somehow cleaning it all up. Farfetched. Brax Jewell wasn't that smart. But a charade like that would buy votes – and influence with Pinecrest Alumni.

What about Bunny? If she'd been used as a pawn to gain medical access, maybe she'd stumbled upon something. And her disappearance part of a cover up. Which would cancel out the two possible explanations Nick had thought of earlier: an insurance scam, or a rigged kidnapping. The detective's mind even went to a case he'd heard of in which members of a terror cell had used donations to gain access to one hospital, and then robbed one of its labs of radioactive isotopes.

In another minute he was rifling back through the

spreadsheets and financial data. Then again scoured every email Bailey had forwarded.

He found something on his second read through: Bunny and Braxton Jewell had been put down by Mercy Hospital for a "Planned Gift" of one hundred twenty thousand dollars. The date, late last summer. To be paid within one year. *He'll probably renege on the gift once he's elected.*

This commitment only a few days after Jewell's appointment as Chairman of Goddard's Board of Selectman. Then he'd bought the Rolex and that slobbering mutt Maximus. All the talk of a bid for the State House. Then the Hyannisport condo.

Jewell is banking on some big score to buy his way into the State House . . . its gotta be rotten.

But what could be more rotten than all The Illuminator had been digging up?

Turned out as Nick sifted facts, the stacks of brand new caskets discovered in Jewell's garage had been tip of the iceberg. Veneer knock-offs shipped from the Far East that the undertaker advertised on his mortuary's web site as "locally crafted," and "hand hewn." Which tapped out to a hefty four hundred percent markup.

Specialist Bailey had been the one to figure that one out, after coming across an invoice for a gross of brass marker plates engraved with the words "Made in U.S.A." Fraud, certainly. Arrestible offense, maybe.

It was late when Detective Giaccone sat back in his desk chair, thinking. *Remortgaging Bunny's family homestead turned funeral parlor, Braxton Jewell's bet the farm on a bumper crop of corpses.*

He certainly had enough on Jewell to put Braxton in a room. Find out anything he'd held back about Bunny.

But to do that would clue the bastard in. He thought, *Never corner a rat.*

Nick had to focus on The Illuminator, presumably out on the hunt. Besides, if he came down hard without something major, Jewell would only play his trump card. He'd insist the Chief intervene. And Nick wasn't about to put his friend Robertson on the spot. Especially now.

Most important, Nick tried reminding himself, it was impossible for Jewell to be both an idiot *and* a sophisticated murderer – at least of the surgeon-messenger's caliber. And Bunny's disappearance didn't carry The Illuminator's scent.

He decided to let this fish swim. Because whatever Jewell was into next, it would be a far larger score than from peddling caskets.

Question now was: *what?* and *when?*

Per usual Nick had kept track of his thought processes. Reviewing emails or other evidence, he had always jotted his questions, how he'd answered them, and consequent ideas or follow-up tasks – in a shorthand only he could comprehend.

Ticking down the list now on the sheet beside his keyboard, his eye lit on the note: "voluntary repossession." The return of Mrs. Jewell's Cadillac, which in her absence had not been fulfilled. *Hell,* Nick thought, *might've been reason for her absence. Maybe she did get tired of the bastard.*

From present evidence there was no telling.

Thinking back to Allengri's hideous cadaver, Nick wondered if this trail on Jewell was a waste of precious time – so far afield of cut bodies and Illuminated manuscripts. Even so he tried reasoning it out:

Possible the repo had been a glitch...a mistake. Given Jewell's propensity to show off, for his wife to be without the car . . . the one he'd just bragged about buying her would bear explaining . . . and blow the whole "someday-Senator" act he'd been trying to sell around town. So to keep that car on the road . . . with his wife behind the wheel . . . and the car out of the repo-man's hands would be top priority in keeping up appearances. . . the mortician's forte.

Something had caught Brax by surprise. The big payoff was late in coming – and the miscalculation had stretched him thin enough that he'd come up short and lost the car.

Nick knew: all he had to do was keep close tabs on the Chairman.

The only question was: for how long? So to narrow it, he backtracked. The election for State Senate didn't get under way until April. But he knew that candidates had to register by February before they could build a campaign. By February Jewell would need a payday.

The theory hung together. But it didn't fully explain Braxton's hovering around the grisly scene at Pinecrest the other night. To see the Chairman on any crime scene had seemed odd to Nick. What had been his intent? *Maybe Jewell will tag along and use The Illuminator case to gain free publicity.*

That part added up. Braxton could make hay either way – whether Nick nailed The Illuminator – or not. Given the news coverage, as high in profile as Goddard had *ever* seen, the Chairman would cling. Lurk in the shadows. Then get on camera. Given access to the chief, he'd no doubt use that to bill himself as key player in the investigation.

BRAXTON JEWELL: CLEANING UP CRIME. A headline or single sound bite like that could boost votes to win an election.

Still – first – where would the money come from for Braxton Jewell to run?

Nick swiveled in his desk chair. This was about blood, skin, and bone.

Prepare to soon meet the man who is his own nemesis.

Some kind of protection would have to be arranged for anyone identified as The Illuminator's future victim.

Victims. Nice word for it.

Leafing through notes on the meeting with Gary Boother, Nick came back to the name of the Campmaster. George Roache.

He'd already ruled out the priest, Father Provost. With the *New Yorker* article in Jim's box of evidence, the media had already had its feast. And he'd already served time. Besides, even Bailey had attempted to find the ex-priest's whereabouts and come up empty.

So much for registering offenders.

More and more, the surgeries seemed the alluring alternative.

Monsters The Illuminator carved out served to *expose*, to warn *society* – as much as punish *individuals* or *institutions* at fault.

Nailor had said it himself in pegging The Illuminator's motive. That to even the score so spectacularly, for all the world to see, might be a stand-in for countless victims' day in court.

By Bailey's report, Campmaster Roache had moved out of Goddard, but now lived a short distance away in Dorchester. A man of shifting moods by all reports. *A regular Jekyll & Hyde.*

As a sworn supervising officer, the law dictated that Nick warn the old pervert.

He did the math. The Campmaster would be nearing his eighties. Tapping in the phone number, Nick wondered what old Campmaster Roache would sound like at this time of night, to be warned that he might meet the same a surgical sentencing as his old pal and accomplice Simon Allengri.

It was almost midnight when Nick's phone call woke him up. Neither of them had any idea at that time that The Illuminator was in full disguise, parked in her motor home on Roache's street, drugged bottle of wine at the ready, Book of Souls in hand, prepared now to go bear him Witness.

"Campmaster Roache," Nick began.

"Nobody's called me that in years. Who *is* this?"

"This is your past calling," Nick answered abruptly. "I'm a police detective. Don't hang up if you know what's good for you."

"What do you want?"

Crisply, Nick replied, "I'm a friend of Jim Stevens, one of your Youth Campers." He thought about saying Gary Boother's name as well, but had vowed to protect any such witness's privacy. He said, "I'm sure you remember Jim Stevens . . ." and then decided he'd not hold back, " . . because you had a hand in his death. But that's not why I called. Your life might be in danger."

"Jim Stevens? Hand in his death? Who *is* this? I remember nothing of any *Jim Stevens!* How did you get this number?"

Duty bound to make this call, Nick had planned to issue only a basic warning. But now, to hear Roache's voice so devoid of conscience, he spoke impulsively, deploying a term Boother had explained off record. Nick said, ever so politely, "So 'The Dance of a Thousand Fingers,' which I wager you recall performing on young Jim Stevens and a number of other Campers in your tent – means nothing?"

On the other end of the line, only silence. Then the brusque reply: "Don't knock it till you tried it!"

Nick said, "You appointed Simon Allengri, your so-called *Assistant Campmaster* to an honorarium you invented known as 'Order of the Bull.' Tell me, how many others did you anoint to prey on kids?"

From the other end of the line came a breathy mix of snort and giggle.

And then the old Campmaster's voice was filled with pomp and impatience. "Have you nothing better to do with your time?"

"I certainly do," said Nick. "So you should thank God I called to warn you. Beware of visitors selling chocolate."

Roache returned a quick and haughty response: "The affairs of my visitors are none of your affair. The complaint department is closed. Twelve midnight you call me with this! And now I've got someone ringing my door bell!"

There was a click, then a dial tone.

"Due diligence complete," Nick said, and spent the rest of the night preparing for his meeting next morning in Boston, with Professor Nailor's mentor Jorge Graham, the authority on what might lie beneath the stunning manuscript's skin.

CHAPTER 11

Retired Campmaster George Roache lived in a restored three-story Dorchester Victorian, giving every appearance of upstanding propriety.

He answered his door gruffly, still irked by the phone call. Some crackpot detective wanting to spoil things.

But Roache's mood lifted the instant he beheld this boy at his threshold, who carried a bottle of wine. This boy who looked to have a glow on. With a face so closely resembling... *What **was** that one's name?* One Youth Camper he'd groomed over a period of months, and then shared with Allengri and the rest. But there'd been so many. "Pray, what is your name, young man?"

"I'm Collin." The Illuminator had used the name last week in a chat room. "You and I meet Online sometimes. Remember?"

"Please. Come inside." Her brother's old Campmaster almost couldn't contain his glee. To see this boy, who now stumbled across his threshold.

The boy who called himself Collin giggled and held out the expensive looking bottle. "Told you I liked wine!"

"Delightful." George Roache was by all descriptions quite ordinary. Maybe a bit stalky, balding, and with a full, round face. He could have been a next-door neighbor. Or choir director. Or the man who bags your groceries. His eyes, like a tiny pair of polished stones seemed to sparkle when he took in Cassandra, who looked fully convincing in her boy disguise.

Roache leaned forward ever so slightly as he absorbed her, his gaze designed to flatter – but a tincture of suspicion showing itself. He asked, "How did you find my house?"

"You have a friend. Like we chatted about. He told me only drop by. Like a present to you. I promised not to give his name."

As he heard this Roache nodded approval, grinned in satisfaction. From an already open bottle of wine on the end table, probably opened for those prior guests, he poured two glasses and offered one to this boy. "I have many friends." Roache then sipped from his own glass. He asked, "How old are you, Master Collin?"

"Sixteen. I just got my drivers license!" The boy Collin who was The Illuminator now stroked the rough silk of the sack that enshrouded the Book of Souls. Felt a power rising from the small Book. Filling her. *Play along,* she told herself.

She let loose another giggle. The open bottle of wine, she noticed, had the sort of label that an armature wine maker might make on a computer and then proudly apply to each bottle of his vintage. It read *Chateau Roache.*

George Roache reached to move a wisp of hair on the boy's forehead.

As he did this, The Illuminator had to take strength from the Book in her hand.

Roache seemed the sort of man who didn't miss a tick. Drawn by the silken parcel The Illuminator clutched, he was saying, "That small bag. . .What is it you have there?"

"A little art project is all. It goes along with. This . . . kind of play . . . " The Illuminator made herself smile, noticed the old Campmaster's goblet almost empty. She looked at the still-sealed bottle on the table that she'd spiked with Rophypnol. Her plan had been to play the role of Collin, get Roache to open the bottle and drink, and then once he was knocked out, to use the wheel chair and electric lift to load him.

However the first rule of a special forces op, she'd read, is to adjust the plan once you get inside. So as The Illuminator looked around Roache's house, an improved plan began to crystallize.

Holding up the silk-wrapped parcel, she added, "This is a little book of special Designs I make. I do one for each of the men I have been with. . . To show all the colors. . ."

By the look of George Roache now, curiosity was devouring him.

The Power she'd felt trickling into her from the Book of Souls was now a constant flow. She would test it.

Planning each step of what would come next, The Illuminator looked at the open wine bottle and measured it contents by eye. Less than one glass remained. This would pose a challenge. She decided not to open the mickeyed wine – yet. But she'd need to move things along.

She took her special Book from its wrappings and asked, "Would you like to see what's inside?" She sat on the sofa.

Roache sat right beside her.

As she slowly paged through, the man leaned close, admiring her Designs.

"Exquisite," Roache was saying. "I've never seen anything like this." He reached and pulled greedily.

Cassandra was not about to let this predator take hold of her Book. Instead, to gain this con man's confidence, moved it with care, allowing her hands to move with it, onto his lap.

To play such a dangerous game she had to tap all the power, from deep within herself – the surviving part of her – which she'd first encountered as a child, coming down from the frozen mountains in the three days following her parents' death by plane crash. Once she had discovered that power, each day since she had strengthened it.

Now, like so many times in the past, the Book of Souls called to that reserve of strength. Awakening it and joining forces. The Book, now, would neutralize Roache. Make him putty in her hands.

With no doubt she was thus Guided, she told him, "I have much *experience*."

Roache then became breathless. Still as a statue. Then one of the Campmaster's hands came up to find to her chin, lifting it to make her eyes meet his. His other hand had found the sock, bunched and wadded beneath the clothing at her crotch. With this advance the man grinned, as if granting himself some obscure permission.

For a *real* boy of Collin's age to encounter contact such as this in the company of a man like Roache would be reason to flee that house fast as possible, making as much noise as possible, then call the police, and then report the whole thing to as many trusted adults as possible.

But in the past The Illuminator had subdued men far more powerful than George Roache.

Highly trained in the martial art Capoeira, a Taser in her pocket, a Divine plan in her head. And in her hands a Mystical Book.

She calculated her next few moves. Told him in the most innocent way, "This art helps me remember all of those other men. . ."

Turning the pages of this Book, she tossed him more bait, "See here Mr. Roache? . . .I put their name at the bottom. Each colorful page represents a man just like you. Afterward I record what I see in their eyes. . .when . . ."

The Illuminator gasped when she saw his response. It had to be an Intervention of the Book: the retired Campmaster's hands left her lap, fell to his sides, and hung limply.

And when she again looked up at his face, she saw that Roache's eyes had glazed over in a dull bluish film.

His features had been ardent, but his face now wore a certain sag. His rigid posture had melted into a slouch.

Roache had become mesmerized by her Designs.

Without another word she turned the page. Felt more of the Book's powers shimmer into her limbs.

Watching him carefully she saw that the more pages she turned for him to see, the more docile Roache became. Like charming a snake from a basket with a flute.

She paused. Sipped the last of her wine, and looked directly at Roache to ask him, "Would you like me to make a Design just for you? . . . Once we have. . .finished?"

Hungrily the Campmaster nodded. His eyes shone in raw, addled appetite.

The Illuminator smiled to herself. The hunter had become the hunted. George Roache was all but hers.

With care she returned the Book to safety, protected within its silken sheath. She told him, "Show me your wine cellar."

Roache was fully cogent, but his will had been sapped. He nodded and led the way. Through a door. Down some steps.

She wanted to see. Her brother had used to make wine with Roache. Now she stared at endless wooden racks of bottles. Row upon row. She asked him, "You make all this with the help of Youth Campers?"

When Roache nodded she saw the sickening glare of euphoric recall in his eye. He said, "I had a bigger cellar when I was Campmaster in Goddard."

"Where do you keep all your pictures?" she asked. She'd had him under surveillance since her brother's death. Roache not only filmed and photographed his and other mens' acts with young victims. He sold the images as well.

Suddenly a brief look of confusion passed across the Campmaster's now-dumb face. Then, the flash of irritation. A flicker of disdain. Pomp. The mark of a dangerous man.

A moment she'd been working toward. To witness that *other* side of Campmaster George Roache that her brother had described so well. It was certain – this indeed was, "The man who is his own nemesis."

Such men prize control. Cowards when directly confronted. Yet vindictive in the aftermath.

She took care not to break the spell the Book of Souls had cast over him.

Demurely she tilted her head to one side and looked at Roache. Then lifted the covered Book and held it above his head.

Further disarmed by the gesture, Roache looked this curious boy Collin up and down. If the man's cruel side had surfaced, it had slid now back out of sight into some writhing nest within him.

Roache obediently mumbled, "Videos. . . " and led the way. Up two flights. Down a hallway. "There."

He pointed to the first door they came to.

It might've once served as a bedroom. Roughly twelve by eight. But now every inch of the walls and window had been covered with shelving. Every inch of the shelving at capacity: DVDs, VHS cassettes, even a section for Super 8 – home movie films in gray metal tins. Also a small desk for the postal meter and variety of shipping envelops.

Roache indicated his wares.

The Illuminator again raised the small Book, like a promise, and asked, "Where do you make these movies?" It took all she had to fake a smile. "We still have a full bottle of wine downstairs."

With a sillied grin, the Campmaster beckoned.

Further down the hall. This room much bigger than the last.

She figured he must have knocked down a wall to combine two rooms in order to accommodate what was for all purposes, a small sound stage.

Roache muttered, "I call it Boy-llywood." Despite his complacency he looked drunk with anticipation.

There were Klieg movie lights. A pair of studio-quality cameras professionally mounted on motorized wheeled bases. A large bed. On a table a number of hand-held digital cameras.

Beside that was what appeared a kind of waiting area. Like one might see at the day care. A low child's play table and chairs with Lego blocks. A toy car racing set. And beyond, an area obviously meant for adolescent guests with sofa and TV. A stereo system with racks of CDs. Video games. A counter with sweets and snacks. Even a bowl filled with shiny jack knives.

Without a beat The Illuminator picked up one of the hand-held cameras. She said, "I have an idea!" And took Roache by the hand. "Come along."

He seemed perfectly pleased, now, to be led. Down the hall. Down the stairs. And back to the parlor. Their two empty glasses waited on the table beside the sofa.

Beside them the bottle of drug-spiked red wine.

She said, "The man who sent me said you at one time liked to camp. That's why I have a surprise outside. Its a motor home." She held up the camera. "Would you like to make a camping film?"

Roache's nod and smile conveyed a mix of intrigue and complacency.

The Illuminator moved across the room. She held up the bottle of spiked wine. "First, this. . ." And she took out a pocket corkscrew.

"Let's make a game of it," this boy Collin made it all sound like play, pulling hard to unstopper the bottle. "I'll pour us each a glass. But promise – we don't drink until you see my surprise. Okay?"

Her quarry nodded compliance.

"Remember. You have to promise!"

"Promise," Roache mumbled.

And they were out the door and across the street.

She carried both glasses in one hand, her book in the other.

Before opening the motor home door, she handed Roache his glass, smiled and raised her own said, "Okay now. Bottoms up." And she drained it. "You too now. . ."

She waited until Roache did the same.

Now The Illuminator held the Book of Souls high above the man's head. "Step inside." She swung open the door.

Roache stepped up and was in.

She followed.

Her quarry looked about, troubled by the unit's gutted interior, swaying on his feet. Tilting his head to look at a wheel chair strapped in place dead center.

The drug had obviously begun taking affect. George Roache absorbed these surroundings, trying to make sense of them. Along one wall, a row of bottled medical gasses. The black doctor's satchel.

Her brother's Campmaster began to collapse.

The Illuminator reached to catch his glass. Gently she guided George Roache's slumping form into the wheel chair.

She used nylon straps and some zip ties to secure him for the trip.

Started him on the I.V. with Paralytic drip. As she inserted the needle in the Campmaster's vein, The Illuminator thought of her brother and told Roache in a soft voice, "I'm going to make you a star."

But before she drove off, The Illuminator went into her medical satchel. She took out a single chocolate bar that she had earlier removed from her Fundraiser Kit. Used a scalpel and forceps to avoid leaving prints in slicing the wrapper.

Making a last trip inside Roache's house she wiped away her prints and planted the signature candy wrapper clue next to the half-full bottle of drugged wine.

Then she drove back toward Goddard to set the stage for a new, improved Jekyll & Hyde. Goddard's first Campmaster to premier, publicly, a double-feature face.

CHAPTER 12

The peninsula of Cape Cod, home to beaches of fine golden sands, awaits two hours' drive from Goddard.

Meteorologically, it's a world away.

In any season the Cape is a fog-haunted place, where winding back roads and mists gathering through the night have left more than their share of cars nose-down in a bog or marsh.

Even now, in winter, moist sea air warmed by the Gulf Stream miles to the south, silently drift toward ashore.

Not far offshore the electronic sensor on a channel buoy has been tripped by this warmed water vapor. Now the buoy sounds, a lonely horn, to warn of what's slipped by.

The fog bank is already ashore. A thick, obscuring curtain that hugs cooling sands and the saw grass edges of the black mud clam-flats.

Creeping onward, the mist consumes the low pine scrub growth within its cottony shroud.

Cape Cod's back roads, built up on sand berms to keep them well-above tideline, twist in obedience of salt marshes

scholarly warfare throughout a previously close-knit research community.

The result was that the scholar was now described by
many of his most esteemed colleagues as a genius – and by
as many of his closest friends as a madman.

The main reason, Nick had been able to make out from
his Online reading, had been the turn-around in Graham's
most fundamental beliefs. Living among tribes throughout
South America, witnessing their indigenous medicine and
dealings with workings of the mind, he'd come to believe,
and at times rumored to practice, in what amounted to White
Magic. In private circles of the highest minds, he was believed to have mastered the Unknown. A modern-day Mystic.

Nick hadn't slept in two days. But Graham's strange
resume had fired something inside him that he couldn't quite
describe. A curiosity of the uncharted he'd have rejected
outright, before witnessing Professor Nailor's softer science
first hand.

So for the rest of the evening he went back through everything Specialist Bailey had dug up on the Latin American folk hero "Illuminador." A legend of Colombia's back
country rumored to have harnessed the evil arts known as
maléficio – in order to do good.

Rural practice held for a curandera to prepare a deceased
corpse for burial. The payment for such services food from
the garden or perhaps a couple of hens. Yet very few of these
shaman could be bought. However, the occasional corrupt
Curandera would accept a bribe, from an enemy of the
departed – to make *maléficio* – as vendetta. The common
method, to secretly sew up a reptile or small mammal within
the corpse's breast on the night prior to burial, in order to set
revenge upon the soul.

Illuminador, Nick read in one anthropological journal,

and estuaries that decide landscapes.

There, the elements of sand and water mean an abundance of low-lying cranberry bogs, dotted between vacation villas, and some of the northeast's finest golf courses. The surface of these vast open spaces lays five to six feet below surrounding lands, their appearance in winter like barren, sunken football fields. And the roads that cross these empty domains sit high above them as straight, unguardrailed causeways.

Flat and colorless, any winter bog would look stable enough to walk on. But beneath this shallow plant-carpet lies a flooded trap, joined only by submerged roots. Tended by day labor in season, the unlighted expanses tonight appear as wastelands.

Open water ditches crisscross these plantations, and surround their perimeters like moats; the perimeter ditch separates the floating carpet of plants from insects and the intrusive weeds of summer. In winter, water in these open ditches helps slow temperature drop to ward off killing frosts. And since saturated airborne water cannot make frost, it hovers, trapped as fog, to either side of the elevated bog road.

Suddenly, a big, pillowy flake of the cold vapor breaks loose and drifts into the road.

Whites out vision.

Bunny Jewell swerves to miss the ghostlike shape. Heart hammers. Her right foot dabs at the accelerator. Her left foot jams the brake, then letting off, so the car lurches into the mist.

Disgusted with every particle of this existence. *Away from him. . .* a mantra by every inch of her since dusk, when she'd celebrated crossing the canal bridge to Cape Cod. Now she castigates herself for drinking the sweet peach liquor.

This morning she'd stood up to him like never before. "Why you making a big deal. . . . Its only till things get lined up . . ." Braxton had cajoled. "Besides, he'd told her, the new models were coming out, "In a month I'll have you in a better Cadillac. . ."

A few minutes after two, that afternoon, she'd been headed for the dealership. Her directional blinking, and every intention to turn into the lot. To return the car, like she'd finally agreed. She'd *always* finally agreed . . . But this time, at the last possible moment, she'd straightened the wheel and sped off.

At first, to not obey Braxton frightened her. But before she'd gotten a hundred yards down the road from the dealership the fear had dissipated.

Then she'd suddenly felt like one of those long winter warm fronts that could pop open apple blossoms in December.

She had sped back home to pack a change of clothes and some underwear. At last minute, without understanding why, she'd taken the bottle of schnapps.

Then she found the Interstate and set out for Hyannisport. Cape Cod. The new condo.

Bunny had never fully learned to drive, in the sense of choosing a route, planning a long trip, and navigating the distance on her own. She would've learned the route, she now told herself, had her husband let her drive once or twice on the summer weekends they'd escaped Goddard to the new place. Once or twice she had even asked him about making the trip alone since he'd bought her the car, the first she could call her own in twenty years' marriage.

But with each request, Brax Jewell would have none of it. Bunny's learning to drive, for him, had only been in order to save the cost of a hearse driver. However she'd always shown up late at the funeral, claiming trouble with traffic, or difficulty with the route. With more attempts, Jewell finally accepted that his wife would not double as his hearseman. And after that, over drinks with friends at the country club, Jewell had made jokes at her expense that in this professional capacity, his wife had been unable to overcome her fear of a sudden backseat driver.

She had never objected to this cruelty, instead telling herself that at least they were dining at the country club.

The road from Goddard to Hyannisport is a very long one. Rare were the days the trip could be completed in the allotted time. Like tonight. Freezing drizzle had slowed the weekday commuters to a crawl along the Interstate, from the time she left Goddard.

Despite this evening's delays, Bunny counted milestones: the first leg from Goddard, then crossing the Cape Cod canal, and then on to the city of Hyannis. After she'd driven across the canal bridge, the peach liquor began to go down easier.

She'd stopped off at the Hyannis mall and wandered. The drizzle had let off, the air warmer as always nearer the coast. She'd swayed as she walked. People had stared.

So she had staggered back to the car to make the last few miles to the condo in West Hyannisport.

There came her troubles. She knew the name of the street. Would recognize the condominium complex if she could only find it. Told herself she might need a few tries.

Now she struggled to follow the narrow bog road. Tufts of snow-white vapor drifted into her path and as quickly – dissipate.

Suddenly in a thick bank of it.

Again a flinch, and Bunny came down hard on the brakes.

Lurching to a stop she heard the empty schnapps bottle roll along the car's floorboards. Thought about turning around – about going back. She would need a wider road to turn the car. Braxton would be irate. But after a few days, things would return to normal. *Braxton's normal.*

These bogs are endless. She thought how she had said yes – years ago had stood by and let Braxton convert the family home she'd inherited. He'd had political ambitions since she'd met him at Pinecrest. In high school it had been Student Council. Then Braxton made the trip to the State House in Boston on Junior Government Day. Later, after they married, he had promised the funeral home to be only a stepping-stone – a sure bet – given all these aging baby boomers.

So he'd sold off the mortuary his father had built. Then renovated Bunny's family home to make it a first-class mortuary. Arguing that it was in a better part of town. And they'd lived upstairs. Temporarily, he'd promised. With a constant flow of what amounted to houseguests in dire despair.

And then, another "stepping stone." Braxton had begun filling in the marshy lands behind the place. As a child Bunny had walked these lands with her father, learning the names of each plant and bird. Had vowed to donate the large parcel to the town of Goddard as a sanctuary after he passed.

But through a million small compromises made in ten years' marriage, she'd made Braxton's political ambitions her own. Still, she regretted having converted the land, to what was now Hillside Cemetery, in order to fund them.

She got the feeling now. She was nearing the condo. First time, by her own choice, she would spend a night away from him.

The narrow black asphalt out front of her car in a straight black line could have been a road to Heaven. On each side the low-lying fog lay pillowy gray-white.   To keep the car on the narrow asphalt felt like trying to trot across a balance beam.

Bunny Jewell had always loved weather. At Brauser College majored in Meteorology and Atmospheric Science, and had taken every course she could in the sister science of Oceanography. Her senior thesis had been a study of the way solid and liquid materials can be held aloft within gasses as Colloidal Suspensions.

Bunny Jewell knew her fog. Taking early walks on the beach while her husband snored in the condo, listening to the early horns, she liked to wander barefoot and on her skin feel the moist, warm air, drifting off the ocean and then over the Cape. Breathe its warm musk of salt and sulfur during outgone tides. She thought it enchanting – to think how, above the scouring sands the soft moist air hovered, until the water molecules within these warmed currents cooled too. Became attracted. And then joined.

To combine – make air into more that it was – that could inspire the buoy-horn's lonely solo note, or halt a steel-hulled freight ship.

She'd always silently wished her marriage had been more like that. Had tried to console herself on those misty mornings – with it beading on her skin – that natural attraction *did* exist in the world – the transience of ocean fog her only hard evidence that to want that for herself was no illusion.

By now, as she slowly drove, all air outside Bunny's car has gone white. The Cadillac's hood ornament no longer visible. With no orientation of left or right, up or down, she could be piloting an airliner destined for far-off lands. Or heaven.

Driving, for a moment, she becomes engrossed in these wonders. *Had* to be across the bogs by now. The black road should be curving. Just ahead. It's enveloped in such cottony puffs. She thinks it's by instinct, to now dreamily turn the wheel.

When the car left the road a loud **THWUMP!** reverberated upward from its chassis. Bunny pitched back hard in the seat. Watched the bright cones of both headlights climb clouds. Then fast, the nose of the car pitching downward. All air knocked out of her by the steering plunging into her chest. The air bag, white, like fog inside the car to consume her. Within her breast, before going unconscious, she heard the sound of something crack.

CHAPTER 13

Nick's personal vehicle was a Ford Crown Victoria P-71 Police Special, but this morning he borrowed a squad car from Headquarters in order to make use of the flashers. Properly lit up, he and Nailor made their destination in under thirty minutes.

Most cases in the detective's career had come down to *how, when* and *where*. The real nightmares amounted to *why*, and this one was showing all the signs.

Nick had spent part of the night reading up on Nailor's mentor Jorge Graham. Bachelor of Arts in Religious Studies from Columbia University. Graduate studies in Rare Books at the Sorbonne, and then Perugia. And a post-doctorate fellowship under the Vatican Library's chief reliquarist. After that at Harvard, young Graham had been a rising star, a tenured professor at twenty-six and three years later made full professor.

Years later came his fall. After living among indigenous peoples to explore Latin American Mysticism, his renunciation of academic convention. The articles he'd published during that period had cut the field in two. Ignited all-out had combined tenets of shady *maléficio* with those of up-standing indigenous healing, as well as modern medical-surgical techniques. Harnessed strengths and powers to heal and rescue in the most unorthodox ways.

More hocus-pocus, Nick had thought initially. Normally he wouldn't have wasted time reading such tripe. Yet there had been odd sensations. First, when he had examined that Illuminated manuscript: some powerful, entrancing influence. Then a second instance at home in his study after he'd walked through Allengri's house — the same trance-like state, in his mind he'd mysteriously been able to replay each step of Allengri's abduction.

Strange occurrences? Nick wanted hard facts now more than anything. But to have met Professor Nailor – the man seemed able to coax real detective work from words – not quite from thin air – but from a book. And now Nick was determined he'd force himself, if need be, to work these two worlds together – both the smoke and the substance.

The front window of Graham's shop was marked by a singular gold-leaf design of an open book with elegant typeface below that read:

DAYSTAR RARE BOOKS AND ANTIQUITIES

Nailor pressed the door buzzer.

A blotchy-haired Sussex spaniel lay still upon the wood floor just inside the window, as if soaking in a wan pool of sunlight.

Flattening a hand against the glass, Nick surveyed the inside walls. Painted the color of butternut squash, the room emitted a glow that almost burned off winter's haze. He saw stacks of ancient volumes. Rich tapestry fragments hung from the walls. Flickering at the extreme rear of the shop he could see an arrangement of seven gold candlesticks that footed towering ivory candles, six of them alight with flame.

He squinted and cocked his head, trying to decide whether the motionless dog curled up on the floor was sleeping, or indeed stuffed.

A pint-sized man wearing a pale olive cardigan bustled past the shop's several library tables, his hands fluttering like park pigeons to convey "just a moment."

Nailor whispered to Nick, "My mentor Graham's become a bit of a recluse. But whatever happens today, hear him out and then give it time to add up."

A warning, too late.

Inside the shop they could see the old man stop at an oaken table festooned with cracked leather volumes. The moment he reached beneath the table, the entry door buzzed.

Upon entering Nick was struck by the waft of attics and kindled beeswax.

And keen blue eyes. A fidgety manner. Swift sharpness of mind, the detective could see. And perhaps a budget of days to share it.

There was also no ignoring the old scholar's head, large for the body, and the liquid motion of patting his hair – a few silvery threads arched over a shiny scalp.

Graham blinked and blinked as if there was too much light in the world.

Nailor handled the introductions.

Throughout, Nick maintained an almost scientific interest in the fact that the ratty-pelted dog had still not changed position.

Graham had stopped blinking. He brought Nick into his eye, it seemed, "You are the intelligencer from Goddard,

Professor Nailor tells me." Then he busied himself taking the detective's greatcoat.

Nick had never before been called an *intelligencer.* "I'm a small town detect–" he began.

Graham held up a finger, and like a medium, proclaimed, "The *small* town will make a poet of the policeman!"

Then the little man turned an expectant gaze toward his former student, the now-famous literary sleuth: "And Professor Canon Nailor?   Catching any miscreants?" Graham blinked away, his eyelashes fanning this forge till it would hammer out an answer.

"I'm barely able to police myself," the professor apologized.

Graham turned back toward Nick, dipped his papery lids, and then pronounced in grim summary, "Vexed by fatal book fragments."

Strangely when Nick next inhaled, it was to be calmed by the warm honey-dusk of the shop's lighted beeswax candles. Without realizing the result of this breath, he was drifting into a state of relaxation. He had guessed the shopkeeper's age to be in the late eighties, and now felt transparent to the man, and as such, firmly accepted.

Graham's fluttering eyelids even caused Nick to consider something he normally would never have given a thought: what it might be like to live in a world that still flickered in separate frames. It was the kind of thought that caused Nick to momentarily consider his stage in life, leading into retirement. The individual events of his *own* thirty-five years' work had become a single stream of fact. In the scent of beeswax candles, the collections of ornately framed Illuminated texts in Latin, Nick slipped back to the Masses that he had savored as a teen.

Next, reasons for his work today clearer than ever, Nick felt new energy. He uncapped the brass cylinder and began to remove the scroll.

"Before you do that . . ." Graham opened a drawer and handed Nick a pair of white preservationist's gloves. "Use these."

He guided the detective to a worktable and set out a clean, acid-free matte. "Here. . . Gently." Then Graham placed sand weights to keep the piece from curling.

"First – let us explore the physical text." Graham reached for a large magnifying glass mounted on a metal armature and swung it into focus above the manuscript.

"Your surgeon-poet is a true devotee of the Black Arts. Solid calligraphic hand. Painstaking detail. Skilled application of the gold-leaf. Elegant." He paused.

When Graham moved the magnifier to peer up at Nick, its lens became the scholar's colossal blue eye, "The gold leaf you see adheres to the surface of the document the moment the calligrapher gently breathes on it." He blinked once at Nick, "Each step of this ancient process corresponds to Scripture. So in a sense the physical craft of Illumination would serve as a form of prayer – I find it interesting how The Illuminator has applied this in surgery."

Graham lowered his lens.

Then without another word he pricked at the document's corner with a stainless steel dental probe, until a tiny raw patch was revealed beneath the message's purpled surface. "The writing material is very old vellum. Likely fifteenth century."

"Vellum?" Nick repeated. "Like construction blueprints?"

"That would be *rag* vellum. From cotton. *Your* scribe used *animal* vellum. From a fetal lamb or calf."

"Fetal?" Nick couldn't believe his ears. "As in *aborted*?"

"For Bibles and liturgical texts, absolutely. To produce a lasting text."

Nick asked, "So from, say, a cow, could you do a whole Bible?"

"Truckloads of livestock would be required to skin a *proper* Holy book," the scholar replied. He continued to work at the document with his pick, and said, "Vellum of this vintage is a golden color. This purple . . . *this* ancient piece of vellum was dyed. Quite recently."

"Why purple?" Professor Nailor asked.

"A technique called Chiaroscuro used by Religious painters during the Renaissance. The dark colors are applied first, with a succession of lighter colors over them for dramatic contrast. In the discipline of Illumination, the technique was reserved for only the most important of Church documents."

Graham then surprised Nick when he said, "I would be interested to see *inside* this manuscript."

"Inside?"

"I believe this to be a *palimpsest*. What's inside might be a clue."

"Palimp - what?" Nick asked.

"Palimpsest, detective. Blank sheets of fifteenth-century vellum simply don't exist, even for recording a salvo to such spectacular crimes." Graham moved the magnifier to a different area of the document. "Ancient scribes in need of a new leaf would use pumice to scrape away text or images from less important Illuminated manuscripts. And then start over."

"A delete."

"Which is what The Illuminator must have done. This practice allowed a fifteenth-century scribe to record new prayers over old texts. Yet since inks of the era contained iron, the original Illuminated text or image can be recovered through the use of Magnetic Resonance Imaging."

"MRI. . . So you're saying this man-

uscript needs a trip to the hospital . . ."
Graham's eyes shone. "Detective . . . I suppose I am!"

Nick understood. "If we can recover the original design, we can trace it. Maybe, then, to The Illuminator's purchase of the piece from a dealer or collector." *At last*, Nick thought. *A way to turn this mush into evidence.*

Graham had swung away the magnifier, but kept his eyes on the manuscript. Finally, he intoned, "Let's talk about the source of this message, Detective. I trust you have read the newspapers about 'Illumina**dor**.'"

"A little far-fetched, don't you think?" Nick asked, "All that supernatural business about magical healing."

Graham frowned. "Believe what you will." From a nearby shelf he produced a modern volume. He opened the book to a picture of an ebony-skinned Saint with a group of small animals gathered at his feet. Nick thought it curious that the figure held a broom in hand.

Graham said of the picture, "Meet Saint Martin de Porres. Among the first Saints of the Americas beatified. He is still believed by many to be able to move through walls, Detective. And bilocate. In order to heal people. Note that de Porres is always depicted carrying a broom."

"Gotta love a Saint who cleans his own house," Nick said.

The philologist indicated the document's first word, "Co-tansuca" – and thus pronounced, his voice carried it like a spell. "The moment I saw this I recognized it from the Chibcha. The pre-Colombian language."

"It means uprising, Professor Nailor told me."

Graham looked soberly at Nailor, and then back at Nick. "To **lift** up or uprise, to become furious." Then the man's face drooped sadly, "An agricultural culture. The Chibcha were not warriors. They became victims of Spanish conquerors.

But managed, miraculously, to hold onto their language and culture."

Graham continued, "A lover of animals, De Porres showed compassion for even the lowest vermin. . . It may be that The Illuminator you are pursuing works under the delusion of imitating this Saint."

Turning once again to the evidence before them, Graham's professional distance became almost clinical. "This message is a Discecta membra."

Nick looked at him questioningly.

"By using the Church medium of Illumination and Gothic book fragments, it's like dressing an act of vengeance in Vestments." Graham cleared his throat. "Look at these vines that run up and down the document's margins – Passion Vines, it looks like. And rampant. I interpret the vines as a touch of fanaticism."

Stepping to a nearby computer Graham chanted a poem:

> Oh, cut me reeds to blow upon,
> or gather me a star,
> but leave the sultry passionflowers
> Growing where they are.
>
> I fear their sombre yellow deeps;
> their whirling fringe of black,
> and he who gives a passionflower
> always asks it back.

The verse brought Nick a chill. "Always asks it back," he repeated. "Sounds shady."

Graham beamed. "Like Illumina**dor**, the passion vine originates from Latin America." He moved to a computer and struck a few keys, "I'll consult a web site to identify the iconography of flower types."

After clicking a search hit, Graham read aloud: "An Augustan friar of Mexican extraction had carried sketches of the plant to the Vatican. There, the blossoms' very shape had been declared a Miracle."

"Called the flower of the five wounds." Graham read, "The five petals and five sepals were believed to signify ten apostles – only ten – leaving out Judas the betrayer. The purple flower is surrounded by seventy-two tiny filaments – believed to be the number of thorns in Jesus' crown." The old scholar pressed his eyes closed.

The report he would later send Nick would contain much more. That the flower's three-pistil stigmas are believed to signify nails. The five stamens the number of Jesus' wounds. The vine's leaf to represent the spear that cut the wound in Jesus' side – the dark spots under the leaves the thirty-three pieces of silver paid to Judas. That the Incas had referred to the species as the Vine of Souls, which housed ancestral spirits. The Mayans, meanwhile, associated the buds of the vine with severed human heads. . . .

Graham left off his reading, indicated the manuscript, then looked at Nick and the professor, "Every drop of ink and bit of gold leaf on this document corresponds to a different aspect of this criminal's deteriorating mental state."

"Which is?"

"The ultimate Contrapasso," Graham said. "To use religious artifact and ritual to combat what so many see as ungodly."

Nick asked, "In that case, what of the hummingbirds in the margins? We found dander at the abduction scene and on Allengri's tuxedo. It all points to the Illumina**dor** from South

America as being the same as *The Illuminator* in Goddard."

"The three birds pictured might prove significant," Graham purred. "But nothing on this document suggests why. That they are depicted as taking nourishment from the blossoms of these tangled vines makes me wonder what exactly is being nurtured."

"Flowers, hummingbird dander, all of it." Nailor continued the thread, "Every slice and surgical stitch on The Illuminator's victims writes another line in this story."

"Meaning, as investigators, we're playing catch-up," Nick said.

"As a humble student of these tribes, I *do* know *this*," Graham indicated the glass-encased antiquities surrounding them, and continued, "That *Illuminador* – who we think is also The Illuminator – has studied under the Curanderas . . . healers who for hundreds of years have known what twentieth-century medicine calls the placebo effect."

"That the cure will succeed only when there is *belief* in the cure," Nick replied.

"There's more to it: seeing is believing." A patient with a broken leg, Graham explained, might not fully get the message until he sees the cracked bone on an x-ray film. Seeing it, something clicks inside the mind. The result is a shift that ensures he will avail himself of proper care.

"So to see Allengri as Dracula is to see the broken bone and appreciate the injury for its full impact."

"Or to put this in terms akin to sapped emotional strength, a chance to stop the bleeding. . . in the psychic sense," Graham replied to Nick. "For victims of men like Simon Allengri, I imagine that the predator's image looms in the unconscious like a Goliath. To bring that monster from shadow to full *golem* we get a Dracula, publicly declared a predator, frightened to death by the light of his own reflection, and then his substance turned to dust. A way back to believe . . ."

"In oneself," Nailor finished.

"Genius," said Nick.

"Medical necessity, to be precise," Jorge Graham corrected. "Its unfortunate – given the human mind's first response: '*This can't be. . .*' The best place to hide a live dinosaur fished out of Loch Ness would be to release the leviathan at your twelve-year-old's soccer game. The Illuminator's craft, transmogrifying men like Allengri, reaches deep into the unconscious and alarms Mission Control to unsilence its belfry."

"What's this got to do with The Illuminator crimes in Goddard," Nick asked, impatient with Graham's run of psychojargon.

"It's all related. A way to understand motive," Nailor stepped in to explain. "If Illumina**dor** and The Illumina**tor** *are* the same, this person might have also faced great trauma, maybe loss. Maybe some crisis in Belief. Something to cause the psychotic break – a psychic lock down to their *known* world. In this case a chamber of horrors."

"Sufficient to split the personality and divide the identity," Graham added grimly. "A rebel on the one hand. But on the other hand applying the ancient Religious form: Illumination. Divine retribution. The most Fundamental notions of morality."

"And uses the language of Belief to close gaps in the system. As if the substitute will repair a brutal past."

Nailor said, "Its uncanny that anyone in this condition could function very long."

Nick was shaking his head, incredulous. "And yet, The Illuminator functions smooth as a surgeon."

Graham's face was now stern. "Delusional or otherwise –. Do not underestimate this criminal. Think of the frail, aged woman who lifts the car to save the infant."

The old scholar's face hardened even more, eyebrows like frost above eyes of glacier-blue. "I warn you. Rule out nothing of Heaven or Earth when it comes to one who has studied Curanderismo."

To now look at Graham's posture Nick could see that the scholar had finished. For now; he would retain the manuscript to make arrangements to "see through it," to original iron-based inks using Magnetic Resonance Imaging. He had a friend in the lab at the Boston Public Library who was traveling that afternoon to Baltimore, and would be pleased to stop it off at Johns Hopkins. The chance of deciphering the document's original text seemed excellent.

Nick went for his key ring. Enthralled. Worried – about parting with his only scrap of evidence. "How long will the manuscript be tied up? Peoples' lives might be at stake."

Graham held up a finger. "Or, at least, their *looks*."

It would be a matter of a day. Maybe two. Graham put his hands together as in prayer, his brow lined slightly. "We hope."

Suddenly, to Nick, the old man looked troubled. "Is there something else?" he asked.

Graham raised crystal-blue eyes, "Still, I pray, Detective . . . that our 'Illumina**dor**' storied in today's news is not one-in-the-same with the poet-surgeon Illumina**tor** you seek to apprehend in your small town of Goddard."

"*Why*?" Nick heard himself ask the nightmare question.

Between blinks, Graham's penetrating blue eyes coldly pried away at Nick's defenses. He said. "If they *are* one and the same, I believe The Illuminator will elude you."

CHAPTER 14

A languorous morning, as always after capturing a new Subject.

The birds perched in the clinic, Campmaster Roache suspended on a paralytic cloud. The ventilator puffed to supply his each breath, hissed to draw off the exhale.

The CD playing in her work room was a Scarlatti Piano Sonata in D Minor played by Horowitz. The Illuminator sat sketching the Campmaster's new visage, from a partial bust she'd modeled in clay during the small hours of the night. She reached to rotate the piece, leaned back, then adjusted her work light to chase a shadow from its face.

Pausing, she thought about Light. How the great minds have tried to trick it to do their bidding: Fiber optics. Prisms. Relativity. Lasers. Quantum physics. New shined shoes. Or Church.

Light, fuel of the world. And she, Chosen Agent in the brilliance of The Work.

Empedocles the Greek philosopher himself had postulated it. Had justified the myth that Chronus had cut off Uranus'

genitals and thrown them into the sea to allow the birth of
Aphrodite – who was later to light the fire in the human eye
– making possible sight itself.

The Illuminator would become such legend, had sought
Guidance to make it so, would have faced the same Treatment herself if she'd landed in her brother's abusers' moral
position.

That's the rub, though. Men like Campmaster Roache
can't see. The Treatment awaits, but they can't partake. Won't
stop. Don't. A Cosmic dropped stitch.

So to patients special as these, she'd devoted every speck
of herself. A sole practitioner, had developed a medical specialty of one.

Her charcoal stick made an abrasive sound as she added
texture. Then in soft pencil she configured a very specific,
poetic feature that she would create surgically around the
Campmaster's left eye.

When she saw the effect, her body filled with the delicious Flow of Knowing and she breathed deep and felt the
fizz of it.

Entering the makeshift clinic, The Illuminator stepped
behind the head of the Versa-bed and placed the drawing
before George Roache. Looking up at the monitor she gauged
his response: A delay. Then in the eyes, that little beam.

Called and answered. A soul. Pinned to the cornea.
Writhing. Seeking a lip or split to squeeze through. Still too
stiffly secured to the body. Its shell. *To dislodge this one will
take some doing.*

She reaches past his head to retrieve the sketch, considers
the drawing. It's a tough racket, convincing some Subjects.

Like shucking oysters, she thinks; *some pop right open; with others, you can bloody your hands and still get nowhere.*

Curandera Rosario had taught her: a patient's Belief in the cure is key. The remedy depends on it as much as any herb or surgery.

A Tax Collector had come to the Chibcha village once each year to collect from the rural farmers. He'd rushed to Rosario's home one day, seeking relief from stomach pains. The Curandera told him the reason. "A bleeding animal lives within you."

The man had brusquely turned away.

Arrogant sort. Rosario knew no remedy could succeed until she had first unearthed his Belief.

"Let me prove it, before you go die alone on the road," the healer told the man. She then crushed the dried leaf of the *perro* tree beneath his nostrils, and immediately his nose began to bleed. Then, reaching into her pocket for another piece of this leaf, prepared in a different way, when she crushed this beneath his nostrils, the bleeding came to a halt.

The man then pleaded. He would pay anything for her cure.

She'd accepted no money for her services, and explained that to share one's gifts is the way of the world: "The animal inside you is greed."

In the end the Curandara did not actually operate on the man; she put him under and created a shallow mock incision and stitched it to create a healing scar. When the Tax Collector came to, he plaintively asked Rosario, "Is it out?"

"And destroyed." She had held out a palmful of ash.

Thus relieved, the taxpayer gave back to the village all he had taken twentyfold, thanked Rosario and went on his way, a new and lighter man.

The Illuminator knew the case of Campmaster Roache called for medicines this strong. The seeding part of the surgery would go quickly. With only a couple days to bloom into full aesthetic effect. A very special ingredient would be necessary to cultivate such Contagion below his left eye.

Treatment plan in place, she couldn't wait to go collect this key material.

The cemetery was only a short drive. Nick would be busy on the chase. So she needn't bother disguising her brother's face. The sun was shining. She could be herself. Drive his old pickup.

At Hillside cemetery she stands before her brother's grave, marveling at the new headstone, its towering magnificence. And it takes her back to Colombia only ten weeks ago, the day realized she had lost him. Five hours on her feet in the O.R., closing for the Mission clinic surgeon when she'd sensed it.

The shock had immediately registered in her body. A swift, sharp pain that stabbed from the roof of her mouth to the back of her head. Then dull. Silence. In her ears the sound of blood. She had heard the rifle shot as if she'd been in the same room with him. Then she knew. Sewing, stitching up her patient with rattled hands, she slowed herself enough to finish the job, before racing off to a phone. Only to confirm what she already knew.

She steps toward her brother's grave now. From her pocket retrieves a trowel and digs a slug of frozen earth from the marker's base and slips it into a small glass container.

CHAPTER 15

W alking away from Graham's shop Nick felt exposed, haunted. Felt the need to shake it off.

Back at the car he told Nailor about a lead on an illegal trafficker in Boston. Thin. Though it might prove a link to the hummingbird dander.

"Shoe-leather forensics?" the professor asked brightly. "Count me in."

Nick punched up the squad car's beacons and they headed for Harvard Square.

Down a side street, the detective pointed, "Urban Bird."

"This isn't optional," the teen minding the shop door said through a set of lip piercings, then reached for each of the investigator's hands and pumped antiseptic gel on their palms. She explained, "There are other pet stores on this street. Customers handle reptiles, then spread salmonella to our birds."

Inside, the barrage of a thousand sounds. Bright hot colors and warm earthy smells stopped the two detectives in their tracks. Tangled tree branches lined the ceiling. Macaws, Amazons, Caiques, Conures, and African Grey Parrots perched everywhere. Some munched seeds, the empty hulls raining to the floor. A pair of Hyacinth Macaws' strong beaks made short work of blocks of 2x4, dyed in bright colors and strung on lengths of dog chain.

Suddenly.

A haunting, gravelly voice. Like from beyond the grave. Calling: "I won! I won! I won!"

Nick looked around, eager to identify the voice's source.

"I won! I won! I won!" Over and over and over. It sounded like the devil.

He traced the voice to a caged black mynah bird.

"Where's the owner?" Nick asked the employee brandishing the gel. He was out of jurisdiction, but anyway flashed the gold.

She pointed to a door at the rear of the store.

The bony little man seemed to blend with the back room's bundles of perch branches.

"I'm Detective Nick Giaccone," explained Nick to the store owner. "And this is my . . . partner, Canon Nailor. FBI consultant on this case."

The man extended a thin, shaking extremity that both Nick and Nailor chose to pass up.

"We'd appreciate some information on hummingbirds."

"What sort?" the man asked guiltily. "We should talk out front." He tried inching them.

Nick pointed at the passage from which the man had emerged. ""Why not in there? Where we can talk about illegal trafficking."

Nailor shot the detective a questioning look.

The shop owner's lower lip started quivering. "I – I don't know anything about h-hummingbirds. I breed and sell parrots."

"Then maybe you want to explain to the U.S. Fish and

Wildlife Service the reason you're breeding fruit flies."

Professor Nailor looked even more perplexed as Nick crossed the room to the shelves of glass beakers, each topped with an inverted plastic funnel – the small end of each funnel plugged with a tiny cork.

From late night Web surfs, he knew exactly what he was looking at. He took an empty test tube from a rack, then popped the cork atop the funnel that capped one of the beakers. Then held the test tube, inverted, above the spout.

A small, dark cloud of fruit flies bumbled upward to fill the tube.

Nick covered the top of it with his thumb and then held it below the panicked man's nose.

"Fruit flies. . ." Lifting his thumb he released the small cloud of the insects into the air.

It made the man sneeze.

"Old school hummingbird food, once pureed," Nick explained to Nailor. "Imported hummingbirds are very illegal in this country. If you order Neck-tar, the food used in zoos, sooner or later somebody might find out you're buying and start asking questions," Nick said. "So dealers in illegals raise fruit flies and grind them up to make a high-protein food. Delicious, eh?"

Nailor arched his eyebrows as the detective again faced the storeowner, who now rattled bodily. "What's your name? How long have you been you trafficking in hummers?"

"Kraus. Sigmund Kraus. It all – it began as an experiment. I took in some birds from a man who came into my shop. I don't even know his name. A few birds survived. Then it became a thing –."

"Everything becomes a thing," Nick scowled. "How many birds here?"

"Seven."

"Let me see them."

Kraus didn't argue. He drew a key and unlocked a narrow door designed to blend with the wall and then stepped into darkness.

When he switched on a light they could see the aviary. Colorful blurs that zipped. Some hung, mid-air. Others darted to the mesh barrier, then retreated. Three sat on perches, chittering.

Nick's voice was harsh. "I could close this store!"

"Where would all my birds go to live?" moaned Kraus, shrinking at the threat. "I shouldn't be doing this – I think it all the time. But these species are becoming extinct in the wild."

"What happened after your guy brought the first ones?"

"I started getting calls. Customers," the man said, fidgeting with his hands. "He set the whole thing up. I was the hotel: food, water, shelter. More every month. Customers started coming – I guess word-of-mouth. I have some important customers," said Kraus.

"What did you do to *them*?" Nailor asked, pointing to the perched specimens. "They're not moving. Are they sick?"

"Most people think hummingbirds have to keep moving to survive. That's a myth. They spend seventy percent of their time sitting and sunning and singing."

"How peaceful. . ." Nailor almost looked amused.

"Oh no!" Kraus protested. "If they sense an intruder they fight like street urchins."

"Thanks for the colloquium." Nailor glared at Kraus. "Did you ever have a customer from Goddard?"

Nick pulled out and flipped through a notepad for the names turned up by DNA tests of the dander. "My suspect keeps three species. Let's see: Purple-backed Thornbill, Copper-headed Emerald, and Velvet-purple Coronet."

"Those couldn't be mine," the man said. His eyes betrayed great relief. "Those are South-American birds. Andes hummers. Mine come from Mexico, down in the Yucatan. The birds you're talking about are endangered. I don't traffic in endangered. Only rare."

"Rare but not endangered . . ." Nailor mused on this distinction.

Nick's voice was sarcastic, "So at heart, he's saving the species."

"How their feathers glow," Nailor suddenly remarked at the birds flitting about the secret aviary.

"Structured like prisms." Kraus had now almost stopped shaking. "That's why people pay so much."

"Pay so much. . ." Nailor turned his frown toward Nick and lamented, "He'd seemed so earnest."

Nick then made a call, to see if Fish & Game would come for the birds. "Is that so," he replied to the warden, and folded his phone. "Fish & Game doesn't do hummingbirds. I'll need to think about you, Kraus. In the meantime, don't leave town." He turned to Nailor. "Let's get out of here. . ."

"You were good in there," Nick said to the professor walking out. "Maybe you should have been a detective."

"Exactly. But what was that you told Kraus? *This is my* . . . *partner. FBI consultant on this case.*" Nailor intoned, "A slippery dodge, your being way out of Goddard jurisdiction. With such a gift for unearthing horseshit, you might have been a college professor."

Nick heard himself let go of a chuckle, glad to be back to his old self.

As the two men walked past a newsstand on the way to the car, he spied the headline:

PINECREST ACADEMY MONSTER MASH:
WHO'S SORRY NOW?

He tossed a dollar on the counter and took a copy.

The photo showed Braxton Jewell and the Chief standing side by side in front of Goddard's new Headquarters. Nick read the caption, "Warrior for State House gets tough on crime in Goddard."

CHAPTER 16

The Illuminator stands over Campmaster Roache as he lies in the clinic *Versa-bed*.

She recalls the triage math she'd learned in a Viet Nam surgical unit: cases of little hope set aside, so the many could be saved.

That logic had become a precept to The Work: to sacrifice her own single soul in order to sanitize the world of men like Roache. In so doing, to protect unnumbered Innocents.

Now she thinks about speeding things up.

She could whip through The Work on Roache. And while that heals, go catch the next and get him started growing skin. To create *that* monster, she knows, she'll need yards of it.

While the next one lay soaking up nutrients and manufacturing the most prized of commodities, she could drop off Roache on his own special Red Carpet. Then harvest the third man's derma and finish him.

Do what it takes. She had learned that much from her parents.

She deliberates. Remembers in the past greater work-
loads had been a breeze: care for twenty-five soldiers in a
combat unit from prep, to surgery, post-op, through to rehab.

In the years after, as volunteer in the Latin American
clinics, a caseload of six or more patients throughout the
cycle of reconstructive surgeries had been a snap.

Now, the more she performed The Work, the more she
wanted to.

But in Goddard, for her brother's sake, she would deliver
her finest.

Don't rush. She told herself.

Roache stirs, as if her thoughts had telegraphed.

Only in performing surgery could she calm such jitter-
bug thoughts.

An array of surgical utensils beside the Campmaster's
bed winked back the new halogen work lights.

CHAPTER 17

Outside it had begun to snow.

The Illuminator is gloved and gowned. Anonymous behind her scrub mask, she wears newly purchased micro-surgery goggles, each lens outfitted with a high-powered loupe.

"Goddard, Massachusetts, shrouded in white . . ." she rhymed in whisper, ". . . prepared this moment, to bring The Light," and injects the air lock of Roache's I.V. with another dose of liquid hypnotic to ensure no physical pain.

Then, with a felt tip she traces upon his face, working the left side only, to mark intersections of the major neurons, Roache's seductive pathways. She's planning a traffic jam.

She positions the scalpel's obsidian tip above the first inked guideline and makes the almost invisible cut. Clamps and draws back the dermal layer. She snips a neuron. Then repeats the procedure on the next intersection. Another. So many.

With that part done she needed to move, rotate her neck and shake her hands to loosen muscles.

The next stage will be more tedious. One at a time.

She uses a cored biopsy needle to remove the tiny plugs of cheek tissue surrounding the left eye, taking great care to keep the network of small tunnels shallow. With a glass pipette she dribbles into each recess a clear fluid. She had concocted the serum from anticoagulants and enzymes. It would mimic, with perfection, the ill effect of a female mosquito's saliva – reducing platelet count, suppressing autoimmune responses, such as the production of interferon and t-cells. To dribble the liquid into each pocket of Roache's flesh will ensure the itch of a thousand mosquito bites.

The Illuminator had tailored the surgical procedure she now administered to fit Roache's crime in life. The page from Jim Stevens' journal that described the campmaster's cruelty against his Youth Camper troop – including her own brother – waited on her writing table, weighted by a lump of Andean coal. In Jim's tangled handwriting, it read:

> I was thirteen, at summer camp. The usual campfire and skits. The whole troop half-smashed on that red wine Campmaster Roache made with us at his house and always brought. After lights out Campmaster Roache caught us playing cards.

> He called us out of the tent all pissed off. Then Roache made us strip down and made us stand at attention at the edge of the frog pond. Then he put a lit Coleman lantern at our feet. To attract the mosquitoes, he said. He rubbed bug repellent on himself. He kept us at attention thirty minutes. He was drinking wine from a cup as he watched us. We were getting eaten alive.

If anybody slapped a mosquito, Roache added another five minutes to our sentence. He used his
flash camera. Campmaster Roache. Permissive one
minute. Sadistic the next. A real Jekyll & Hyde.

The Illuminator, by this point, has readied each insertion
point on the Campmaster's face to receive seeds of Roache's
evil. With Adson forceps she inserts into each wee facial
grotto a granule she had collected earlier that day from her
brother's grave. Sterile. She'd autoclaved them.
But their edges would abrade.
Magnified by the loupes she wears, the tiny stones remind
her of meteorites.

Healing of the surface skin will be quick.
But the granules will cause pustules, clusters of them, pink
like champagne grapes. At his debut she will back Roache off
the cortisone. Then, with the particles to irritate – plus the
serum's chemical equivalent of mosquito saliva – he will be
consumed by unbearable itch.
Then he'll reach for the mirror she plans to leave
with him.
Roache's aftercare will be a scratch.

A good Church education. A higher purpose. A solid,
steady hand. Who could blame her for evolving justice
quicker than the law? Who could fault her, recognizing that
statutes of limitation sag and bag and need an eyelift?
The Red Carpet for Roache only a day away, The Illuminator worked rapidly. Neatness counts. Cleanliness. Godliness. Appearances. Daily ironing of pleats and starched white
collars. Brother had it easier. Until.
Until coming home this last time to watch the last of his
life drain from him. And then, to find out how it had ended,

too, for Patrolman Jim Stevens. To remember, then, that her brother had tried to become part of Jim's brave battle against the perpetrators who had harmed them both.

The Light is once again bubbling throughout her trunk and limbs.

As she places the particles, points of red rise to the pink-white edges of Roache's flesh. The halogen work lights feel warm on her skin and triggers the recall of a sunlit day, picking *moras,* blackberries, on Curandera Rosario's subsistence farm near Boyacá.

Cassandra, at fifteen, pulling away the vine, her skin raised in pink scratches, a few broken through. Tiny blood drops beading.

Unnoticed, watching through breaks in the vine, Curandera Rosario had marveled that the girl knew instinctually how to break open a comb and smear a small amount of honey to disinfect and seal out bacteria.

A day later the healer pointed out the completed healing to Cassandra, recognizing that the young girl had *Los Regalos,* The Gifts, and would become a special kind of healer.

Rather than tell Cassandra of this yet, Rosario praised the rapid healing and advised the girl to always listen to the Wisdom she carried in her body. She had advised, "Never be afraid to be the first to use a cure that your heart tells you will heal."

The next day Rosario went alone to the market place to see a young wife who was carrying her husband's child, and had the day before begged for help. The curandera told the woman to bring her worries to Cassandra.

Rosario had relayed nothing of this to her apprentice. Instead she stayed hidden and watched as the woman cried and told Cassandra her fears about her husband. The girl had taken a moment, then told the woman only to go home and that night to lay beside her husband. To mention before they slept that night, that they would each dream the same dream about the snake under the bed. Cassandra had told the woman to come back the next day, and to bring her husband. "Remember, I will dream this dream also and bring healing. Do not be afraid."

The next day, the Curandera pretended to be busy grinding corn but watched and listened. When the woman arrived with her husband, young Cassandra spoke confidently to them and said, "Did you go home last night and go to sleep?"

"*Si*, as you said."

Cassandra looked at the woman, and then at the husband, and told them, "Yesterday I told you to go home and sleep and that we would dream the same dream. And what was that dream?"

The young wife looked at Cassandra, then at her husband, and after a slight pause, replied, "It was the dream of a snake under our bed."

"Good," answered Cassandra. She noticed that at the mention, the husband grew uncomfortable and made the sign of the cross on himself. "And the rest of this dream?"

Cassandra turned to face the husband and explained, "We dreamed of a snake that was under your bed. And that you, Senor, took the brave action and killed this *culebra* – this snake."

Cassandra took the hands of the wife in hers, and then gathered those of the husband as well. "The dreams tell us what is true. You are a husband and a wife and you have much love for one another. *Senor*, you have been brave. For the killing of this snake saves you both from being bitten in the dream, where it is surely fatal for your body and spirit, and for the well being of the child your wife carries inside her. Live well now!"

She let their hands fall free, and they all walked into the *choza* for cakes made of white corn and a drink of water from the curandera's well. The man blessed himself one more time. A sweat had broken on his forehead.

Days later the husband and wife came with gifts from their garden. The woman was smiling. Not long after, the curandera delivered their child and they all, Cassandra, the husband and wife, and the curandera Rosario – became friends.

After Cassandra grew more in the skills she learned from the curandera to read people's coffee. And, how to counsel. That it was possible to change one's life, should the audience of the coffee not favor the cup's result.

By nightfall, George Roache lay resting, his face lightly bandaged. To promote a sense of well being, Cassandra released the birds in the clinic and played music: a Scarlatti Keyboard Sonata in A Major.

With Roache's debut so close, she turned her attention to the journal page waiting in the library. The Illuminated message that the improved George Roache would carry to his debut would tell the story about the boys, the Campmaster, and the mosquitoes.

For a moment before sitting for the task of calligraphy, The Illuminator lingered in the clinic to watch the birds, listening to the music. The runs and arpeggios seemed almost synchronized to the hummingbirds' flutter and buzz.

Little engines, those hummers – the only creatures who understood her precision – her mental capabilities – her sense of purpose, stamina, and agility in the symphony of making things right.

CHAPTER 18

Another abduction, in Boston, had lit up the wires.

"Candy wrapper and everything." The chief called the moment after Nick had dropped Nailor at Brauser College. "The guy missing's a George Roache, taken from his home in Dorchester."

"Jim Steven's old Campmaster." As he drove Nick set his cell on hands-free and brought the chief up to date – how he'd warned Roache the night before. Then how Canon Nailor had predicted this monster to be a rendition of Mr. Hyde.

Nick then relayed how well the professor's theory jived with Gary Boother's description: Roache's sudden swings from permissive party host to outright cruelty. As such, the Campmaster filled the bill for: "The man who is his own nemesis." Lastly Nick relayed all he'd learned about The Illuminator's manuscript during his visit to Jorge Graham. And his decision to leave the piece of evidence with the old scholar for testing.

"We found Bunny Jewell," Robertson interrupted. "She's in Hyannis Hospital with broken ribs."

"And you already locked up Braxton, I hope."

"He didn't do it. Directly. . . While fleeing to Hyannis-port, Bunny drove into a cranberry bog."

"So then why's her husband giving interviews for the newspaper?" Nick knew enough not to mention the chief's presence in today's news photo. "Jerk should be in Hyannis caring for his wife."

"I suppose that's the *big* news. . ." replied the chief, "She refuses to see him."

"Its about time."

Nick would be free to satisfy a morbid curiosity for a walk through Roache's house. Despite contempt, he felt he wanted to know more about the type of person who might attract The Illuminator's healing gifts, or damage Jim as a young boy. So he kept the squad car and sped off to get a look at the abduction scene.

When he showed up with sandwiches and coffee for the Boston P.D. patrolman who stood in the sleet outside the Dorchester shingle-style, it got him five minutes inside.

That same malignant atmosphere as Allengri's place. Roache's house sported a wine cellar. And upstairs, the studio. All that footage.

He thought: *Somebody should burn this place.*

Getting home late that night Nick boiled chicken stock in a saucepan. *Who's the cutter?* Heated a quarter-inch of olive oil in a large skillet, and sliced a yellow onion and sautéed its thin ringlets.

In a race before the onion went transparent he grated a half-cup of asiago. Then crushed a handful of dried porcinis and added them to the broth. Their dust brought to mind pulverized oak gall, a main ingredient, he'd read, in inks made from scratch for Illumination.

When the sautéed onion turned golden, the color of antique vellum, he added the cupful of pearlescent Arborio rice, stirring to get it hot enough to absorb the stock. The skillet billowed a thick cloud of steam with the first ladleful of the boiling liquid. Its vapors made his nose run. A slight headiness with clearing sinuses.

Nick worked the risotto, ruminating while he stirred. As the kernels absorbed broth, the billows of steam slowed his racing thoughts, taming those images so he might stare them down, watch them vaporize. He added more broth when the wooden spoon dragged.

Who could – would – perform the painstaking surgery necessary to transform these men's faces into such grotesque masks? Another ladleful. Another cloud of thick steam.

And how to sit anonymously – without the victim ever seeing the perpetrator's face? A perp smart as this – to risk publicly in displaying the fruits of such labors – would also take utmost precautions. It would all require incredible discipline, planning, and a facility to perform the surgery.

Nick alternated: ladles of boiling broth – with pushing the wooden spatula in a circle against the bottom of the stainless skillet revealing silvery circles.

He watched the risotto take shape – the rice drinking in the mushroom flavor – no longer rice now, but something else growing in body. Nick could only wish for the ability to absorb so well all he'd been dealt. First to lose Nora. Then Jim. *Now this . . .*

All the broth had been absorbed. He cut the gas, dumped in the asiago, and the risotto came to a creamy halt.

Helping himself to a steamy bowl, Nick went to his little office and switched on the space heater. He sat with his dinner, scanning deposition transcripts from Jim Steven's carton. When he blinked, imagined versions of Roache's gruesome visage flashed across his consciousness, then Allengri's.

Multiple monsters, Nailor had suggested. Not the average act of revenge.

If he could figure out the *how* and *when* The Illuminator would hunt up a next victim, he might save a life. And in the process Nick might also get the big collar on record for his friend the chief. An errand worth showing up late for retirement.

Hoping for something new from Nailor or Boston P.D., Nick checked email.

One subject line caught his eye: Contrapasso: A Season of Consequence. There was no sender's name. Only the email address: Illuminator@hotmail.com. His fork clattered to the floor.

The attached video clip was only moments in length. It showed a patient lying in a hospital bed, prepped for facial surgery with scrub cloths covering all but the left side of the Campmaster's face. Aged, it looked like, beyond the photos Bailey had dug up.

The video had been shot using a special filter to achieve a lens flare effect. It made the foreground array of surgical knives, clamps, and probes twinkle like stars. A gloved hand reached for an unusual looking scalpel that bore a glimmering black stone tip. And then the screen went dark. A single word faded on-screen and sparkled in gold: **captivated?**

Nick played it back a second time. And a third. Through the latex gloves he noticed the build of the surgeon's hand, small, with fine joints. In the background, when the camera panned, Nick thought he caught the corner of a window, and outside – sky, and part of an arch made of steel.

Nick forwarded the clip to Bailey in Cyber Forensics and requested an ID on the arched structure outside the window in the video. It might give them a geographic fix so he could find The Illuminator. Get this over with.

He called Chief Robertson.

The chief bleated, "Now The Illuminator wants to get in *your* face. He's looking for affirmation."

"Might be a her," Nick said.

"*A woman?*"

"Take a look at the video. The hand."

"Maybe some kid," Robertson said. His voice, to Nick, seemed dismissive. "Kids do all kinds of shit now. Viruses. Identity theft. Remember the little-league candy? Why the Hell not this?"

"Bit of difference between selling bogus candy and severing facial tissue." Nick was getting frustrated. He couldn't understand why he was so suddenly so fully pissed off. He'd felt defensive, impotent, ever since the theft of Jim Steven's journal pages. Now he felt self-righteous, like he alone had been left holding the bag, the only one who really gave a shit, or any thought, to what had been done to Jim. And it bothered him deeply to be alone with it.

Nick said, "Guess I'll say goodbye for now," still seething, yet in a tone carefully modulated, before laying down the telephone on its cradle.

Sweating at the collar, all he'd seen at Roache's house flooding back. . .

Fix this.

Who am I to fix anything? he thought. *I broke it missing Jim's cues . . .*

Nick sat for a moment to cool.

Why's this cutting into me so deep?

Then came the call from the buyer's agent. The closing to sell Nick's rental house had been delayed.

"I can keep their down payment!" Nick barked.

"Actually, Mr. Giaccone, you cannot," the agent snapped. "The contract included a financing contingency. My buyer wants to wait a few more days for an earnings report before liquidating stock. That falls into the category of financing."

That falls into the category of a crock, Nick thought. *A financing contingency means approval for a mortgage.* But with housing prices falling and the word "foreclosure" more common every day, he said, "You told me you had a cash buyer. I'm going to keep showing the house."

"And I still think it *will* be a cash buyer. C'mon, we've waited *this* long."

Next came a call from Bailey that had Nick speeding to Headquarters.

"I wanted you to see this for yourself," Bailey explained, walking Nick into the Forensics Lab. He brought the video footage up on his monitor. "Watch the play back." With a keystroke he displayed it on a large, wall-mounted screen.

Nick recognized the delicate hand. Part of the face prepped for surgery. The black-tipped scalpel. Then the camera's pan and pull back.

Bailey paused the video. "Look beyond the bed in this frame."

On the other side of the bed in the shot appeared to be a window. Blue sky outside. Some steel arches.

"I identified those arches as the Tobin Bridge," Bailey told him, and with a mouse click, displayed an image of the bridge.

With a few more clicks the Specialist got rid of the bridge, and returned to the video. "But no way this'll give us geographic fix," he explained.

"Why not?"

"Because the window beyond the bed in the video isn't a window."

Not something Nick enjoyed hearing. "Looks like a window . . ."

"Right now the video is still. Watch what happens." Bailey placed the cursor on a small black form in the upper left corner of the frame. "That shape up in the sky above the bridge? See it?"

"And?"

"I'll go in close." When he pulled in closer Nick saw a dark and irregular blur.

"Now I'll enhance it."

Nick brought both arms across his chest and with one hand gripped his chin.

Bailey hit buttons that sharpened the image.

"Now you can make out the wings. See?"

"It's a pigeon in flight."

"But see . . . when I advance the video, its wings stay still."

"Meaning the window behind the bed's a decoy. A picture pinned up for the sake of the video."

"So we would think this was videoed in a room overlooking the Tobin Bridge."

"And then discover the exact opposite," Nick scoffed. "With a pigeon – stuck – high above the river."

"Detective Giaccone," Bailey said. "I think The Illuminator has a thing for you."

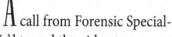

CHAPTER 19

A call from Forensic Specialist Bailey woke Nick at four A.M. He'd traced the video to a proxy server in Afghanistan, relayed half a dozen times – originating from a coffee shop in Chelsea where computer work stations were let out free with the purchase of a latte. The chief had already sent Plainclothes men to check out the coffee shop.

Nick only shook his head; it's a law enforcement officer's sworn obligation to check out every lead, even when it's anticipated to produce little more than pastries.

During his shave that morning, recognizing more traces of his father's jaw and brow than he could welcome, Nick arrested the razor at his Adam's apple, guessing. By now the avenger with an edge would be very close to the third subject.

It forced the detective to wonder: how many more before The Illuminator's poetic justice would be complete. Given what he'd learned these few days, the potential seemed endless.

He wiped steam from the mirror.
The realtor called.

Closing was back on. Today at four. "I'm telling you Nick, the craziness of these buyers never ends. . . . But they just *love* your little house. . .."

"In that case make sure they bring all cash."

Nick walked outside in his robe and sweatpants. He stood on the front porch scanning *The Boston Bugle*.

His eyes lighted on a story by the Associated Press. It told of a boa constrictor that had gotten loose in Miami, which brought a chuckle. The snake had entered through a hole in the backyard fence. Then silently crushed and swallowed a family's Irish setter while kids played noisily in the above-ground pool. The boa was only discovered because it could no longer fit back through the hole in the fence.

No headlines about The Illuminator, or the abduction of Campmaster George Roache.

Nick felt warm sun on his cheeks and forehead and looked up. A melting day.

Too quiet for a Saturday.

CHAPTER 20

Sunlit and lazy, quicksilver snowdrops pattered into a gully of snow-melt below the eaves. An occasional ice chunk slid from the roof and broke into the puddle of slush below.

Cassandra sprinted across the driveway to the motor home to back the rig close to the house so Roache's transfer would go unseen by neighbors. On her way back she pushed the wheelchair she'd need for the Campmaster's debut.

Before going back inside her brother's house, she paused for a time on the stoop – closing her eyes – letting the sunshine warm her face – *like Colombian sunshine* – between two worlds. Opening, her eye spied a droplet hanging from the eaves – the world upside down within it – swelling, about to burst.

It falls, and she catches it on her tongue.

With a hip she propped open the screen door, pushed the wheelchair inside and let the door bump closed.

A crust of snow slides from the eave, crashing into the puddle below.

She had dressing of her own to do before costuming Roache in his leader's uniform.

Brian's green Camper shirt and yellow neckerchief fit her tightly, but once she was bound would be perfect. His nylon snowmobile pants, she thought – a convincing cover for the bottom.

After all, she would be setting up Roache at a sled race.

CHAPTER 21

Every day since Robertson had called about Simon Allengri to bring him into this case, whenever Nick had walked into his own house, it had felt like he'd parachuted, half-amnesiac, back into his half-finished moving project.

Partly-packed boxes sat gaping, accusing him of sloth. Nora's old things, out of closets, reminded him that three years hadn't been enough to part with them.

So, with the closing to transfer ownership of his second home only hours away, Nick turned to, energized to be back at it.

He'd have money today from the house sale. And with January was less than two weeks off, he could have this place empty on time.

Today he was ruthless, dispatching his own unfinished projects to the trash.

Encountering some items of Nora's that he'd promised to her family members, he had to face now that they'd never come collect them. So he made arrangements to have these shipped.

By two o'clock Nick had sealed every last box. His skive shirt was soaked through. It all felt right.

Then he moved to the basement, hauling derelicts of the past upstairs, making a heap in one bay of the garage. He'd hire a junk hauler.

The physical work helped distract him. But as the day wore on, those missing journal pages kept creeping to mind. How he hated The Illuminator for the intrusion! Carrying a barrel of junk up the basement stairs he tasted acid in his throat.

By four, near exhausted, at the kitchen sink he downed two tall glass of water, took another into his study, then tried Jorge Graham's number to see about results on the palimpsest, but no answer. So he cleaned up, put on a fresh undershirt, underwear and trousers, and headed off to the closing, a prayer on his lips it would go smoothly.

Two hours later he was back home with a cashiers check for a little over two hundred thousand. Good as cash.

After hanging his great coat in the hall closet Nick brought up his dukes, bobbed right and left, and threw a quick combination of celebratory shadow punches – left, right, jab.

Retirement within reach. From memory he could smell the lemon blossoms that perfume the family house in Positano each spring.

BOOK II

CHAPTER 22

Scissors in hand, Cassandra stepped up behind her patient and all three birds scattered from where they'd lighted upon the plastic tube going into Campmaster Roache.

Snipping away bandages about his head she admired her work on the monitor. Good, but not Perfect. Sufficient for The Purpose. She shaved him, applied a moisturizer, blindfolded and then wrangled his still half-drugged body into the wheel chair.

According to the schedule Online, festivities of Camp Quite's five-mile Midnight Sun Sled Race would be winding down. Campfire skits at five.

The challenge was to balance the Subject, keep them in the air, but not too groggy. Not animated, either. That would sap manageability. A risky enterprise, but key to Sublime Presentation. So The Illuminator had measured tolerance, tapered the drugs, and let them wear thin just before Delivering the old Campmaster.

Cassandra drove the motor home through Camp Quiet where Youth Campers wearily lugged their tundra sleds, in the place of dogs that would normally pull such vehicles, this race an exercise of obedience and stamina. Campers and leaders alike spent their last energy winching some sledges onto trailers and the beds of pickups.

TV crews had covered the day's events live. And Cassandra had put in a call before leaving, to drop a tip to the press – about spectacular events to come after the race.

She parked the motor home beside the newly constructed dining shelter, the words "The Grub Shrub" burned into a distressed plank above the door.

Roache looked almost cheery in his oversized green leader's uniform. Head, wrapped in warm scarves, heavyset body snuggly propped in his wheelchair. She had tapered him from the Cortisone, so his facial pustules had already begun to send signals, soon to overwhelm as mosquito itch. To keep his hands still for this, she'd applied zip tie wrist restraints, covered now by blanket.

She pressed a button and heard the lift's descending electric whine lowering the man in the wheel chair to the frozen ground.

A ski mask protected her own identity.

Wheeling him across the parking lot she caught a rut and Roache lurched forward. Cassandra was quick to catch him by the shoulder. One polite Campmaster held the shelter door.

"Got an old-timer here!" Cassandra said in her best boy-voice.

Roache grunted.

At the building's center stood a large stone fire pit, above it a welded sheet-metal flue. Clearly, The Grub Shrub represented the winter heart of Youth Camper activity, where the Pequod Council fire circle burned through every squall and snow. Yet a joke had been perpetuated among Campers and Campmasters alike – that the building's drafty construction and oversized, open flue fire-pit upheld the physics of gas re-frigeration – to burn a flame and yet wind up freezing.

Cassandra parked Roache beside this crackling fire. It was almost five. A little ahead of schedule.

She reached over his shoulder to place a hand mirror on his lap. She had tied a string lanyard to the mirror's handle, which she now looped over his wrist. Roache would not miss witnessing his own debut.

After that, she slipped the brass tube containing the Mos-quito Pond manuscript into the shirt pocket of his Camp-master uniform.

Throughout these final preparations she could see outside: Media groups with cameras, Campers and leaders. All now plodded toward the building for final scoring of the day's race.

She removed Roache's scarves and with the scissors up her sleeve, snipped his wrist restraints.

The Illuminator hissed, "It's sssshowtime." She saluted him with three fingers, backed into the crowd of Campers, and was gone.

CHAPTER 23

Next morning the *Boston Bugle* carried a color picture of a two-faced Roache, sold to the Media by one of the Youth Campers, snapped only a moment before Campmaster Roache had begun to claw his itch.

The article explained that the great pink clusters of contagion The Illuminator had created upon Roache's face represented fruits of the Campmaster's debased labors in using wine to lower young Camper's defenses. Beneath the eyes, a surgical scrambling of facial cues referred to the man's Jekyll & Hyde personality.

The news headline shouted, IN VINO VERITAS: ILLUMINATOR'S VICTIM #2 USED WINE TO SEDUCE YOUTH CAMPERS.

According to several sources, Roache had played the winemaking scam on kids from every walk of life and from all over. Not only Youth Campers.

The TV crews at Camp Quiet had splashed the story live. So in stiff competition for coverage, *The Bugle* had been held to hit the late-night presses. Multiple victims of Roache had promised the paper to go on record with allegations later in the week. Many of them grown men with families.

The headline of another story, below the fold asked: **Who's Old Scout?**

The accompanying color photo displayed The Illuminator's latest manuscript. Dyed purple like the first, yet less ornate.

The message found in Roache's pocket, like the page found on the vampire at Pinecrest, was divided into three distinct sections. Although the first segment ran several lines.

It read:

~ from Old Scout's Journal

I was thirteen, at summer camp. The usual campfire and skits. The whole troop half-smashed on that red wine Campmaster Roache made with us at his house and always brought. After lights out Campmaster Roache caught us playing cards.

He called us out of the tent all pissed off. Then Roache made us strip down and made us stand at attention at the edge of the frog pond. Then he put a lit Coleman lantern at our feet. To attract the mosquitoes, he said. He rubbed bug repellent on himself. He kept us at attention thirty minutes. He was drinking wine from a cup as he watched us. We were getting eaten alive.

If anybody slapped a mosquito, Roache added five minutes to our sentence. He used his flash camera. Campmaster Roache. Permissive one minute. Sadistic the next. A real Jekyll & Hyde.

To read this . . . *from Jim's journal. . .*Nick had trouble holding still.

Section two of the document was more brief:
Even as good shown upon the countenance of one, Evil was written broadly and plainly upon the face of the other.

And the third section contained a warning, presumably describing the next victim:
Prepare to soon meet the Basilisk.

> **FROM OLD SCOUT'S JOURNAL**
>
> I WAS THIRTEEN, AT SUMMER CAMP. THE USUAL CAMPFIRE AND SKITS. THE WHOLE TROOP HALF-SMASHED ON THAT RED WINE CAMPMASTER ROACHE MADE WITH US AT HIS HOUSE AND ALWAYS BROUGHT. AFTER LIGHTS OUT CAMPMASTER ROACHE CAUGHT US PLAYING CARDS.
>
> HE CALLED US OUT OF THE TENT ALL PISSED OFF. THEN ROACHE MADE US STRIP DOWN AND MADE US STAND AT ATTENTION AT THE EDGE OF THE FROG POND. THEN HE PUT A LIT COLEMAN LANTERN AT OUR FEET. TO ATTRACT THE MOSQUITOES, HE SAID. HE RUBBED BUG REPELLENT ON HIMSELF. HE KEPT US AT ATTENTION THIRTY MINUTES. HE WAS DRINKING WINE FROM A CUP AS HE WATCHED US. WE WERE GETTING EATEN ALIVE. IF ANYBODY SLAPPED A MOSQUITO, ROACHE ADDED FIVE MINUTES TO OUR SENTENCE. HE USED HIS FLASH CAMERA, CAMPMASTER ROACHE. PERMISSIVE ONE MINUTE. SADISTIC THE NEXT. A REAL JEKYLL & HYDE.
>
> EVEN AS GOOD SHOWN UPON THE COUNTENANCE OF ONE, EVIL WAS WRITTEN BROADLY AND PLAINLY UPON THE FACE OF THE OTHER.
>
> PREPARE TO SOON MEET THE BASILISK.

Re-reading the first passage – about Roache, the boys, the lanterns and the mosquitoes, Nick had to sit. When he read it over a third time a lump like a sizzling golf ball had formed in his throat.
Hold it together. . .
He decided to apply Nailor's methods in rough form, so

carried the newspaper into his study. There he turned pages in Jim's journal at random, comparing the phrasing. Even with the huge contrast between The Illuminator's lovely calligraphy and Jim's hurried strokes, the detective found the writing style to be a match. That same hesitation – choppy usage.

It was beyond doubt. To create a diploma for George Roache's transmogrification, The Illuminator had taken a page from Jim's book.

Nick couldn't help wonder: how would reading news like this affect Gary Boother?

The phone rang. Robertson. The news channels were still all over the Roache story. "We'll need statements from every victim coming forward."

"Then you better appoint some detectives. I'm headed to Mass General to question Roache. The last one didn't last."

"I'll pick you up. . . ."

"Better for Nailor to have a look," Nick countered. "He might catch a detail that'll tie in with the manuscript. You send out the plainclothes men. Start with the adult survivors and see if their alibis are solid."

CHAPTER 24

Nick wasn't sure he'd even be able to reach Nailor, given the professor's high-priority hostage situation. Yet the scholar was pleased to be consulted on this recent Roache development. He'd already closed the other case with the full kit. Enough to seal away another bad guy for a lot of years.

When Nick offered to pick him up for the trip to Boston Mass General where Roache had been admitted, Nailor replied, "I have a faster way."

The McLaren F1 sat ready in one of the tunnels beneath the Brauser library. A hands-down favorite of supercars, its twelve-cylinders delivered 627 horsepower to produce a top speed of 240 miles per hour.

So deep was the catacomb beneath the library that the car's engine, roaring to life, would cause a tinkling of chandelier prisms high above the main Reading Room. First-year students commenting to staff and faculty about the anomaly were advised, simply: "blame the dragon."

Such occurrences were not uncommon during Canon Nailor's busiest months.

The particular catacomb that made up the sleuth's car park ran all the way across campus, and then exited thorough carriage house doors in a dugout fieldstone wall in an off-limits area behind the Chemistry Building. Motion sensors rigged in succession throughout the tunnel gauged the McLaren's speed, relayed to trigger the pair of double doors to open, just long enough for the car to exit. So like a bullet leaving the barrel, the textual sleuth's only concern in heading off campus was acceleration.

When Nailor pulled up outside Nick's house, the old detective stood dumbstruck.

"Were you expecting the book mobile?" Nailor asked.

"Machine guns and oil slicks?"

"Better," Nailor explained, the mid-engine design left plenty of room under the hood for informatics. Auto scanning, printing, data storage, and full-text disambiguation connectivity to every literature and language database in the world and outfitted for up or download via satellite – with access from the cockpit and at any speed.

Painted no-luster black lacquer with wheels of matching midnight, Nailor's speedy reading machine was the ultimate statement in scholarly black ops.

Now carrying untraceable plates, the McLaren had been confiscated from a pickup man in Miami employed by a Mexican drug cartel. "The car was bright yellow when DEA grabbed it."

"Bright yellow, huh?" Bending low enough to slide in to the passenger seat, Nick groaned, "Can't understand how the genius got caught."

Ramping onto the Massachusetts Turnpike, Nailor told

him, "I've always wanted to open this thing up."

While the car hurtled toward Boston only inches above the pavement, Nick noticed a calm that had come over the professor as he worked the paddle shifters.

He shook his head when they passed the billboard, wondering if the town of Goddard really needed to be frightened any further.

A chamber of horrors . . . Nick thought.

Snowflakes the size of small hands started falling. With them, monstrous images began to drift into Nick's mind of the real-life Jekyll and Hyde that awaited in a Boston hospital bed. Then, like the big snowflakes against the warm windshield, they vanished.

Still accelerating, Nailor glanced over and saw Nick's stricken face and offered, "No worries about the snow. It's all-wheel drive."

Then he buried the needle, causing Nick to think back over twenty-five years without a drink.

Above the engine's growl, roar, and whine, the two detectives shouted to catch up on pieces of the case.

"The Illuminator's M.O. is evolving. Streamlining," Nailor began. "This 'Old Scout' manuscript looks to be on new vellum . . .which means, at least for the moment, no more palimpsests. . . The pattern of three sections of text is a match to the Allengri case. Two out of the three textual elements in this manuscript quotations – both related to Mr. Hyde."

"Who we'll meet today in Boston."

"And same as before, the document's third section hints of the next monster to be sculpted – a Basilisk."

"Whatever *that* is."

"The nastiest of mythical creatures. Said to descended from the Medusa, it kills with its stare. In form the Basilisk combines the beaked head of a bird, the body of a serpent, and wings."

Nick said, "Yet the Illuminator uses common language this time – from Old Scout."

"No. Quoting Old Scout is *not* common language. In fact to quote Roache's victim directly, is on par with the first Cotansuca manuscript."

"Expert testimony."

"Why else would The Illuminator give voice to Old Scout?"

"The court of public Opinion."

"If we can determine the identity of Old Scout, we'll know who's being avenged. Which could lead us straight to The Illuminator."

Thing is, Nick thought, *I already know the identity of Old Scout. . . and it's only leading to more monsters. . .*

Pulling into the Massachusetts General Hospital parking garage, Nick was damned glad the ride was over.

The Intensive Care nurse checked their credentials and explained that Roache would take time to stabilize, "after that look in the mirror." When Nick engaged her, he found the patient would very soon be moved to a room. The son, George Roache Jr., was inside with him now. Early that morning he had driven from down south.

Nick hadn't known about any son, and hoped he'd be able to get a statement. So he scrawled a note and asked the desk nurse to relay it.

She then instructed Nick and Nailor to go up to the floor and wait. There they found a pair of Boston patrolmen, at ready to guard the room.

When a white-coated doctor of considerable build and shoulder-length white hair approached, one of the uniforms whispered, "That's Dr. John Bacon, Boston Medical Examiner."

"Have you seen Mr. Roache?" asked the Examiner. A slight, pleasant drawl in the voice.

Nick glanced toward the room. "Not yet. But I can't wait."

"You see things in Boston . . ." The Medical Examiner's voice seemed a honeyed melody of sun and shade-trees, and in his eye, Nick noticed, a durable beam capable of burning off the most horrid of conjured memories. "In my residency I performed a post-mortem on a corpse hauled up in a fishing trawl off of Georges Bank. Once we got him onto the table I could hear – a sound – like crinkling cellophane. I couldn't understand it, till we opened him up."

Bacon gestured toward the room reserved for Roache. That glimmer again. "I have to say . . . The four-foot Conga eel living in that poor man's windpipe was not as gruesome as the creature now on his way to occupy *that* room." Although the doctor's eyes remained bright, his huge frame shuddered.

Nailor remained composed. He asked, "You think our cutter's a plastic surgeon?"

"*Plastic* surgeons correct form and restore function."

"*A cosmetic* surgeon, then?"

"*Punitive surgery* might describe this – if such a specialty was ever founded," in Bacon's eyes remained the sparkle. "I recognize s*ome* command of facial surgery. Hardly *expertise*. Yet there's something captivating about this work on Mr. Roache. Fine cuts. The clean heal. The absence of scarring indicates an Obsidian scalpel – a simple tip of volcanic glass, mounted on a split wooden handle and then bound by wound thread, in the style of Paleolithic knives and spears. Both primitive and precise, the black glass is five hundred times sharper than any steel."

"This poetic choice of instrument," Nailor observed, "It adds up to more than mere cutting tools."

Reminded of the Dremel grinder that had shaped Allengri's fangs, Nick unconsciously ran his tongue up over his front teeth.

Rushing toward them in the hallway, a medical team wheeled a gurney, followed by a full police guard, their radios squawking to shatter all hospital quiet. "This would be Campmaster Roache," Dr. Bacon announced.

Patient's face covered by a cloth, the entourage pushed past and disappeared into the room.

The extra guards came out and spoke briefly to the policemen to each side of the door. Next a stern-faced nurse came out and took Bacon aside, showing him a report and whispering something that brought gray pallor to the physician's cheeks.

With a nod toward Nick and Nailor, Dr. Bacon managed, "Go ahead."

Inside the hospital room, winter window light cast a pale

blue through the pleated privacy curtain. The shadow of yet another nurse moved behind it. She flapped the drape open, disposed of a spent syringe, and headed for the door.

"Wait," Nick said suddenly, near panicked to stand so close to the still-live predator. "Please, if you don't mind waiting." He thought he detected tears starting to well in the nurse's eyes, but the hard lines around her mouth showed no evidence of sympathy for the man in her care.

"Mr. Roache is suffering addiction to Stadol and too weak to kick." Slowly she drew back the privacy drape. "So make it quick."

A stalky man dressed in an oversized green Campmaster's uniform lay before them. He faced away, toward the window, puffing oxygen through a tube in short, catching breaths. As if the act of breathing poisoned as much as delivered life.

The baggy costume threw Roache's body out of scale, tilting the sense of reality about and within the room.

A little dizzy, Nick stepped closer. "Campmaster Roache," he began.

The figure turned its head. At the sight, both men shrank back and raised hands before their eyes.

Then Nick forced himself to study the face. The left side of Roache's mouth stretched taut into a predative smile, a ghoulish grimace that showed teeth and bulging gums. Left eye wide open, brow in an arch. The eye drooped heavily with clusters of fleshy sacs beneath, torn now due to Roache's un-abating itch – clawed by his own hand where skin met fluids the color *vin rose* – an unclean marriage that stirred utter nausea and disgust. Rather than empathy, the sight of the face, with its detestable features, provoked a festering sense of hatred.

Nick pulled back his gaze, had to focus out the window at the parked cars below, now coated white. He had seen the face of a fiend. And from beneath the awful surface thought he'd even caught sight of the Campmaster's arrogance, a deeply buried self-disgust, and yet a total absence of remorse.

He again faced this perpetrator. "My name's Giaccone. The detective who spoke to you on the phone the night of your abduction."

"I told you, Scouty –," Roache puffed, too warped by the drugs, apparently, to distinguish this detective from figures haunting his thoughts. He convulsed arms and legs against the restraints.

"Nurse," Nick asked, "did you find any kind of a note on this . . . on Mr. Roache's body?"

"The left hand," she replied precisely, bending over Roache and moving sheets to uncover it, "Here, the embroidery."

"Ah – the maker's – maaark . . ." Roache puffed.

A shade closer, Nick was spellbound to see The Illuminator's handiwork so up close and personal, examining the blue-sutured embroidery:

The Argument

Book X

"More weapons-grade literature. . ."

"Weapon-*ized*. This time from John Milton's poem, <u>Paradise Lost</u>," replied Canon Nailor.

While Nick jotted on his note pad the professor explained: "The famous passage known as 'The Argument' portrays God turning his right hand man Lucifer into Satan to account for wicked designs – the archangel's body transmogrified by the Creator into that of a hissing serpent."

Nailor brought out a digital camera and begun snapping pictures.

A curl of contempt crossed Roache's lips when he saw it.

"Did your surgeries cause pain?" Nick asked, while the professor snapped shots from various angles.

"Numb. Drugs – only the mirror . . . makes pain . . ." He gathered breath and then rattled the bed with his restrained, embroidered left hand, grunting, **"Monster. Now!"**

"Complaints of rain by the spider who built in the spout," Nailor muttered dryly.

They found Dr. Bacon waiting at the nurse's station.

"We could use a list of equipment, drugs, and supplies a surgeon would need to carry out something like this. Like that scalpel you mentioned."

Bacon nodded. "You might also be interested in the message your surgeon was writing upon Roache's face with it."

"Writing?" said Nailor, "I'm all ears."

Dr. Bacon traced an index finger along his neck and explained, "The facial nerve exits the skull just below the ear and divides, like a road map, to control the seventeen muscles of facial expression. All this orchestrates our non-verbal communication."

"And seduction," observed Nailor.

"That awful grimace your surgeon caused is actually the reverse-procedure for correcting a palsy."

"So the cutter knew exactly which nerves to sever," said Nick.

The glint in Dr. Bacon's eye grew brighter. "Whoever did this *also* performed a Transconjunctival Blepharoplasty . . . *also* in reverse."

"What's a reverse Transconjuncti –."

"Those pus-pockets around the eye," Bacon explained. "To create such magnificent infectious blooms, the surgeon would have to implant some substance beneath the surface of the face."

Nailor asked, "How many doctors are capable of such a thing?"

"Plenty *could*," replied Dr. Bacon. "Although I can't imagine one of them *doing* it."

"So we talk to these doctors. Maybe their assistants."

"Assuming personnel rosters for the operating rooms are still on file," Bacon cautioned, "Which I doubt."

"How long will Roache last?"

"Not long, Detective. He's been confined to bed. Opiate withdrawals, and cardio atrophy – both put him at high risk." Dr. Bacon narrowed his eyes. "I'm curious as to the material embedded to cause controlled infection around the left eye. It could lead to something. In fact, I almost look forward to Roache's autopsy."

"*If* the predator dies," Nick said.

"They always do, eventually," replied Bacon flatly.

Nick made a motion of shaking his head, but wondered if he might persuade Bacon to give him the read on the Allengri photos, which he now held out to the doctor. "We believe this to be a related case."

With a glance the man shut his eyes and reached to push the cover of the dossier closed. "I've already seen these head shots," Bacon said, his face grave and unyielding. "The same history with the kids, I remember."

Nick nodded.

"I have a son," the light in Bacon's eyes losing warmth now. He gestured at Roache's door, shaking his white locks. "What they do to their victims. This is like an infection, like a ghost that enters through the body, but can leave only through the mind as the magic of language."

Dr. Bacon asked if he could examine Allengri. To compare

cuts and heals.

Nick shook his head and said. "He didn't last." Then presented a newspaper picture of The Illuminator's most recent message. "Our surgeon is escalating. The next science project will be a Basilisk. It's a. . ."

"I know of the Basilisk." Dr. Bacon's demeanor changed from curious assessment to cold resignation. Handing back the photo he drawled, "Skin grafts will be required to create the wings. . . But for this serpentine body. . . They'll have to flay the leg bones. The foot bones. The genitals they'll have to tuck or cut."

CHAPTER 25

Tuned into the "Nick Giaccone" web cam, Cassandra had watched as the detective and professor had sped off to Boston. Tidy duo they'd been forming.

That afternoon she spent with brushes before an easel, making final touches to enhance a fine copy or a painting she had ordered online. An oil on canvas of a Religious classic.

By dusk she dabbed and blended final strokes. Had seamlessly painted over the face of St. Peter, replacing his visage with Nick's.

The afternoon of artwork had been to reward herself.

Her clinic again scrubbed now, sanitized, all ready for a third Goddard subject. The linen on the bed smelled of fresh lavender. She'd even left a light on.

TV reporters were still asking "Who's Old Scout?" about the Illuminated manuscript.

And then came the news of George Roache's fatal stroke.

By nightfall Cassandra was seated at her worktable with a single leaf of new vellum. Pens at the ready. Her Book of Souls awaiting another page.

The ritual required full darkness, save for lit candles. She meditatively drew the drapes, sat, and pressed her eyes closed. She needed to return to that morning she had first shown Roache the drawing: panic in his eyes like a foxhole prayer.

Now she remembers placing the sketch. Envisions Roache's eyes the way she had seen them up on the monitor. And then, from deep in his eyes, the faintest light. *How it had tried to bolt!*

She had recognized, then, that the design on her trophy page for Roache would be composed in cold colors. Coldest of all Designs within the Book of Souls.

To begin she applied a wash of Prussian Blue to the small page before her. Then mixed a little Flake White with Red Cadmium. She spread this with the edge of a pallet knife.

The result on the vellum page gave the impression of light bands. A snare of colors against the blue background that made it look stark and bankrupt.

Unlike other pages created for her book, Roache's page would bear no gold leaf. The metallic she would apply to *his* page would be silver foil, dulled in an acid bath.

While the colors dry, she opens the silk tasseled bag and retrieves her little reliquary. The Book of Souls. Flipping through each page, she seeks a page with colors near as cold as today's.

She finds only one.

Another anomaly.

A Subject she had altered yet let live. But only after she had tinkered with the inner valves and glands of his chemistry.

The Medellin drug lord was named El Ponderoso.

El Ponderoso had been boss of that first Subject, the old

military man she'd made Penitent, foreverafter to kneel. The man she only thought of now as *el Viejo Machista* of the trafficking trade.

Turned out, the eight-year-old girl that the old *Machista* had brought to her clinic had required abdominal surgery to remove the burden. The girl was saved, but told Cassandra about another.

About the boss El Ponderoso, who maintained the nasty habit of sampling his own wares – orphans – before their departure to Miami – their bellies heavy with latex pellets containing product.

After that Cassandra had sought him.

In El Ponderoso she had found the mouth of a poisonous river. So impassioned, Cassandra had not concerned herself with Aesthetics. Decided instead to *dis-able* the man in a sexual way. Amazing what the removal of a few small glands can do to reign in the Tastes and Drives.

El Ponderoso, she now read the name at the base of a page in her Book of Souls.

El Ponderoso of the revving impulses.

To look upon this cold design, she thought back on surgeries she'd performed on the man. Parts of his plumbing all gone now.

Lord El Ponderoso, evermore down a quart.

To *live*, for such a famed and showy drug lord, would be so much greater punishment than death. The man's noggin so chocked with memories he'll wish he'd be able to erase. Memories for which the rest of him no longer mixes the necessary Chemicals.

He could no longer bother those Orphans. Those Innocents.

Money, now, is the only thing El Ponderoso can get off on. She had let him keep the mansions. The Italian shoes. The fashion models and cars. Now all for show – since the man could no longer perform.

The Illuminator held no illusions. She let him keep his lucrative coke ops too; another would only step into his place.

And ever since that day, she'd siphoned from the drug lord's offshore holdings. Never would he recall spilling account numbers and laundering routes while under the drugs she'd injected.

The money now infused her Goddard operations.

Cold colors of the Book page she'd devoted to him told it plainly. Ultimately, El Ponderoso had bored her. Altogether uninspiring. So thoroughly unredeemable. *Ta ta to that one!*

Into the Book she sewed Campmaster Roache's completed leaf, wondering what new powers the page would lend her in bringing The Work.

BOOK II

CHAPTER 26

They'll have to flay the leg bones. The foot bones . . . Bacon's words had transported Nick three thousand miles from Goddard, and several decades back in time:

For that split-second back in combat, dug into a hillside in a downpour – pinned by rockets and gunfire, holding down his best friend Jason Aquilla who cried out and thrashed in a slurry of mud. The two had signed their names and then gone on a bender that ended reporting for duty – mere kids turned U.S. Marines in a single drunken escapade.

Weeks later, Nick had to use his every bit of strength to restrain Jason, ignoring the man's screams while a Corpsman picked away splinters of his femur, tibia, and fibula with the tip of Nick's K-bar. The medic had run out of bandaging, had torn the back panels of Nick's field jacket in order to bind the remaining flesh left like a tenderloin.

Now, rattling downward in an elevator on the retreat from Campmaster's hospital room, a fluorescent light overhead stuttered with the car's every buck and rattle as Nick worked to clear his mind of this recall. He hoped his distress had gone unnoticed to the professor standing silently at his side.

Shaken, exiting Mass General hospital, Nick received the return call from the son of that Campmaster they'd just witnessed.

What do you say to a guy whose father's recently been transmogrified, Nick wondered as he took the call.

Now in his late forties, George Roache Jr. would be happy to share his story. He explained briefly to Nick that at the time of Jim's legal dealings, George Roache Jr. had offered to testify against his own father, who had handed off his only son to a friend known to victimize boys.

They settled on a nearby café as meeting place.

Nailor offered to sit this one out. He sympathized, "I don't envy you this interview, detective."

But entering the restaurant, Nick was pleasantly surprised to discover George Roache Jr.'s ease and openness, his tousled order. Reassured by the firm but careful handshake. The way the man gently pressed a friendly, bandaged, right hand on the detective's shoulder.

"What happened to the hand?" Nick asked instinctively about the wound.

"Nail gun accident. I'm a home builder."

Nick winced. But he had to ask, "I guess these days, what carpenter worth his salt *hasn't* had nails through his palms?"

"Bread?" George Jr. offered, passing a basket of warm rolls.

Nick split the bread and reached for butter – trying to figure where to start. "I can't imagine how hard this must be. Coming here," he began, spreading, watching butter disappear into the bread's softness.

"You kidding?" George Jr. poured chilled water for himself. "You, detective?"

Nick nodded and passed his glass. "You're not – mortified or, ah–."

"I know you're here on business, so I'll get to it. The mental pictured I've carried of my father was pretty much what I saw at the hospital this morning," George Jr. said lightly, buttering a roll of his own with a small silver knife. "In fact, to see his nature drawn so accurately by that vigilante was like medicine to me."

"So you liked the surgery." Again Nick eyed George Jr.'s bandaged hand.

George Jr. noticed the glance and rolled his eyes. "Look. The only surgery I do is on old houses."

"In college you were premed."

"And collapsed while dissecting a monkey. Squeamish."

"You had access –."

For a split second George Jr.'s eyes flashed like gas jets. "*My father* made up my mind about this *for* me –."

"How old are you?"

"I'll be forty-seven in March. When I was fourteen, my father told me we were going fishing. I had never been, before. We ended up at a pond near the home of what he called "a special friend," a cardiologist named Dr. Gorgalo. While my father waited on shore, Dr. Gorgalo raped me in a row boat."

Nodding, Nick found himself closing his eyes. Then he took out his pad and made a note of the name.

"Some fishing trip," George Jr. continued, describing how that day he had felt "evicted" from his body, and how afterward had placed his personality back together over time, surviving by reading books his wife Jill had found him: Gandhi, Civil Rights history, Holocaust literature, Feminists. How later, at last, a self-help book came out for men.

"Thirty years ago nobody talked about battered women and there were zero resources. Now almost every church sponsors a women's shelter." He ended with "If therapists gave out frequent flyer miles, I'd be taking my vacations on the sun."

Nick had to smile.

Yet from last count, some of Jim's journal pages were still at large. And it nagged him. He asked if George Jr. had ever read or heard about a journal Jim Stevens used to keep about what took place.

"Never," George Jr. told him. "Jim was a big hunter and fisherman. . . I wouldn't have taken him for the journal type of guy."

A server began setting out antipasti.

"Somehow I found Grace." George Jr. smiled. "When my wife Jill gave birth to our first daughter. Now I sleep at night. My kids are my ending. My beginning. And I get to have the pleasure of building things." He took some of the appetizers and passed the plate to Nick.

"But your father – the Campmaster? Did you find Grace for *him*?"

George Jr. lifted an eyebrow. "There's a limit." He chewed calamari and then washed it down. "The best I could do was to sign a waiver so the hospital can keep giving him whatever drug The Illuminator got him hooked on."

He served himself another small helping. "In my opinion, my father needed somebody to transmogrify him every day of his life."

"Did you exchange words?"

"My father was a coward. When I told him I would testify against him for Jim Stevens, he got his lawyer to try cutting a deal. In exchange for his own immunity he offered evidence and testimony on Simon Allengri and Dr. Gorgalo. Jim joined up after my time, so I wasn't a Youth Camper when he was in the troop. But Jim and some others told me how my father,

Allengri, and Gorgalo had built an extensive network."

"A ring."

"With members from Maine to Massachusetts showing up at almost every Youth Camper trip claiming the title "Assistant Campmaster." None of the Campers had ever met most of those guys before. It was a feeding frenzy."

Nick decided rather than add insult to injury, he would hold back from George Jr. what he'd learned about his father's more recent kid-porn business. He asked, "What about a Father Provost?"

"I remember *him*. The chaplain at Camp Quiet."

"And he was part of the ring?" Nick had been famished coming here, but now no longer felt hungry. "There was a New Yorker article about that priest mixed in with Jim's old papers."

George Jr. nodded. "To discover a full-page picture of Provost's face in that magazine was what woke Jim up to his abuse. He wanted to make sure those guys wouldn't hurt more kids."

So, Nick thought… a toss up: either Dr. Gorgalo or Father Provost will be a Basilisk. To narrow it down, he asked, "Was Provost named in the suit?"

"No. Only my father, Gorgalo, and Allengri. And the Youth Campers and the Church."

For the moment Nick would lay his bets it wouldn't be Father Provost. He asked, "Its obvious why Jim went after the Youth Campers. But why the Church?"

"Good question." George Jr. seemed to be thinking of a simple way to tell it while he finished chewing. Then he rocked back in his chair and explained, "The troop meetings were held in the Church basement. Things started getting around. Like for instance, my father's ritual of inviting certain Campers to his tent and exchanging massages with them. He had a way of making it unfashionable for scouts to wear any clothes when inside a sleeping bag. Bits of this circulated. Later a group of Campers' parents started scouting around, asking questions. Then they met with leaders who ran that Church to complain."

"And that ended your father's leadership of the troop?"

George Jr. scoffed, "They didn't do a damned thing. Which allowed my father and his sick friends to keep up their bullshit. Until about a year later, when Jim Stevens leveled his lawsuit."

In such pleasant surroundings, to see George Jr. so unruffled and matter-of-fact, Nick still had difficulty taking all this in. Backtracking, he asked, "I have a name. Another of your father's and Allengri's victims I think. Does the name Brian Shockly mean anything?"

Grief now shadowed George Jr.'s face. "That was a big reason I came forward to testify. Brian was sort of a double-victim. In the beginning he was to be the co-plaintiff, and his case was just as strong as Jim's. In the end they didn't even depose him. Jim's lawyer said he didn't trust a jury with him."

"Imagine, a lawyer with trust issues."

"The prejudice ruined it."

"What kind of prejudice?"

"Brian was all over the place. Sexually. How did that lawyer put it to Jim? Oh yeah, 'Shockly likes to take walks in the park at night, but he isn't exactly walking his dog.'"

Nick held off mentioning Shockly's suicide. Yet it seemed both men had already acknowledged its ghost. It hung between them.

"So how did Jim's lawsuit end? I've been trying to find court documents. . ."

"You won't. Once I came forward to testify, it was over,"

George Jr. Said. "The parties ponied up before a suit was even recorded at the courthouse."

Nick felt a weight lifted. To meet a guy brave enough to take the stand. And against his own father! To learn that somebody had stood up for the Rookie when he'd needed it. And now Nick had it. Front to back. What had been done to Jim. How he'd fought back. And who'd come in as back up.

He had everything except a suspect.

Unsure how to end this meeting, he asked George Jr., "How did you end it with your father today?"

"He was pretty far gone on the drugs. So the words I said over him were more of an epitaph: 'Here lies George Roache. The only thing that held his house up his whole life was that the termites were all holding hands.'"

CHAPTER 27

Nick found an expectant Canon Nailor at the espresso counter in the hospital lobby. He gave Nick the update, "Graham called. The manuscript you found on Allengri carries a secret beneath its skin."

Minutes later they were across town, pressing Jorge Graham's door buzzer.

Inside the shop Nick saw the scholar working at one of the shop's tables beneath a single light. When he came to the door the old man seemed less animated than before, his face grave, while his eyes still shuttered the dim evening light.

On the table he'd laid a series of three document images in full color.

The first one Nick recognized. The original Cotansuca manuscript.

Nick easily placed the second image in line as well. It was the Illuminated manuscript that had been left with Campmaster Roache.

"So what do you see in all this?" he asked the scholar.

Graham brought the two images, of manuscripts found on Roache and Allengri, side by side. "Notice," he said, "Each of these contains three distinct pieces of text. The Illuminator exhibits a curious preoccupation with the number three. Let me explain. . ."

Graham then moved these aside to focus on the third piece of evidence on the table.

The picture made Nick think about the days of palaces and dragons.

It showed three wealthily dressed princes emerging from a castle – met by three skeletons rising from graves in grass just outside. Nearby, at the mouth of a cave, was a man dressed as a monk.

Nick couldn't take his eyes off it.

"This palimpsest image, discovered beneath the first Illuminated manuscript. . ." Graham indicated the image of the three dandies, three skeletons and the monk, ". . . underscore The Illuminator's preoccupation with the number three. Let us not forget," he cautioned, " those three humming-birds pictured within the margins of the message overlaying this one..."

Then he explained the meaning of the latent image he'd discovered: a theme recurrent in European artwork of the 1400s. It was called The Three Living and the Three Dead. "The story goes that three fancily-dressed nobles out for a days enjoyment are confronted by three skeletons who warn them: 'one day you will be as we are now.' An invitation to repent and reform corrupt ways."

Nick then indicated the part of the image that showed the Holy man in robes, "I suppose that explains the monk."

"Close!" Graham raised a digit skyward and replied. "I was able to locate this very same image in an old auction catalog. It had been sold to an anonymous bidder. According to that catalog, the Holy man is St. John the Baptist. In this picture he guards the cave where Mary hid with the Emmanuel to avoid Herod's murderous troops. The Church celebrates the miracle as *Childermas* – or Feast of the Innocents – the very first Christian martyrs. Celebrated December 28."

"Legend has it that at the moment St. John saw the Roman soldiers approaching, he used a leaf to scoop a spider from a tree and set the creature down at the cave's mouth. Immediately the spider set to spinning."

"When the soldiers arrived, their leader accosted the Saint, who for their purposes looked the vagrant. Yet the soldiers asked him, 'Has anyone had entered this cave?' Indicating the glimmering web, the Saint gave the answer, 'How could Herod's rival hide within?'"

"Meanwhile, inside the cave, Mary hushed The Babe to be still. And the soldiers moved on. Known, by many, as *The Spider Miracle*."

Nick nodded reverently.

"A tragic reality, however," added professor Nailor, "Was that many *other* infants were brutally murdered by Herod's soldiers that same day."

"Thus the *Feast of Innocents*, a day of remembrance," sighed Graham.

"Shame . . ." Nick lamented, ". . . nobody thought ahead to recruit more spiders."

CHAPTER 28

Early dusk. The Illuminator had parked the old pickup on a side street, then cut through the woods to Nick's house carrying the easel and finished canvas. She was inside in minutes flat.

First she arranged the artwork, and then installed the tiny surveillance cameras, placing the relay base behind shelved books in the detective's study. While installing a program on his computer from a flash drive, she heard an engine's roar.

Peeking from a front window she could just make out the black McLaren against the dusk. Its dark form hugged the ground like a supercharged ghost. Outside the driver's window stooped Nick's broad shape. She could hear parts of a conversation, unintelligible above the roadster's throaty idle.

Ever since Dr. Bacon had shared those gruesome details describing the Basilisk surgery, Nailor had seemed uncharacteristically short on words.

When he cut the engine the silence was deafening. His brooding eyes settled on Nick's. "None of my business. But ever since you received that video clip of Roache in surgery, I've come to worry for your safety. It's all beginning to seem very personal. Even this Old Scout page makes me uncomfortable. Call it a hunch."

"You told me you didn't get hunches."

"I'm learning *shoe-leather forensics*. From the master. Fire me if you like. But consider yourself warned."

Nick didn't answer. The details about the Basilisk and fast driving had him rattled, and he'd hoped it hadn't shown. But now what Nailor had to say was a match for his own nagging thoughts.

In a tone of friendship the professor once again spoke, "You know in all contact sports, push eventually comes to shove. Goddard P.D. already has one officer down. And besides, it would be a shame for you to be – *late* – for your own retirement."

Before Nick could reply Nailor turned the key and blew away the silence.

The Illuminator had tried to escape via Nick's back door but through the pane could see it jammed by a blow-down limb. Then she'd tried the basement windows. Barred with steel. *Cop's house.*

She should have been frightened. But instead the risk was exhilarating.

Keeping low to get past the living room windows, she made her way into the garage.

Walking toward the house Nick kicked at the day's softened snow and watery ice melt.

A slurry he'd slip on frozen solid, next morning, walking out to his car. Decided he'd sand it.

A bucket in the Ford contained a mix of sand for traction

and salt to melt ice. He unlocked his trunk. Using a small VW hubcap kept in the bucket for spreading the stuff, he scooped a helping.

Peering through panel joints in the overhead door, The Illuminator watched the detective step about the driveway, sifting grit.

Soon the two were standing within inches of one another, separated only by the garage door's thin panels. Through the horizontal crack she could make out the hairs on his neck. A crust of dried shaving soap at the tip of one ear. The weather was cold enough for her to see his breath when he turned.

She heard a tiny buzzing and saw Nick take out his cell phone.

It was the chief.

The two Plainclothes had come up with nothing from the coffee shop. The phones at Goddard P.D., meanwhile, hadn't stopped lighting up. Every loose fastener in the state was beating a path to take credit for The Illuminator crimes.

"That's easy," Nick told him, "Just use knowledge of the second missing journal page to weed out the false confessions."

"What second journal page?" the chief demanded.

"I forgot to mention. . ."

The chief cut him off. "Doesn't matter. The Illuminator has become Jim's best advocate." Public sympathy for the Rookie's plight was by now a given. TV news had been showing clips of a victims' rights group all bundled up, camped out in the snow on Boston Common. They were singing songs and sewing a quilt for The Illuminator.

"I can picture it," Nick said, walking to his car. From the bucket he scooped again and then sifted more salt and grit along his front walk to make it safe.

To get out undetected, she'd have to time this. Beyond the discarded derelicts Nick had heaped, the garage had a side door. Given the layout of the place, she'd have to move with precision so he wouldn't see – to open the door and then bolt through the woods – at the exact moment Nick walked inside through his front door. Through the crack she watched him finish spreading grit, turn, and head back for the driveway.

"And get this," Robertson told him on the phone, "After what the Campmaster's son gave you on that cardiologist Gorgalo, I've been pushing to provide protection to save him from becoming a Basilisk. Get this: his attorney just called. They're refusing. Says if Gorgalo accepted protection in connection with the Roache and Allengri cases, someone might spin it as an admission of Gorgalo's wrongdoing. He threatened legal action if we push it. "

"So appearances are more important than physical safety. Guy almost deserves to be transmogrified."

"Trans-what?"

The Illuminator tried to make out Nick's words above the beating blood that thundered in her ears.

"Proves Gorgalo has something to hide."

"So who are we looking for?"

"Someone with a God complex," Nick answered, "Organized. Controlling."

She could hear Nick's shoes grind grit as he walked back to the Ford to toss the old hubcap into the trunk. He said, "Gotta be a guy," and slammed the lid.

"Don't assume so quick . . ." the chief countered, "Think about the artwork. The embroidery. The small fingers in that video. I'm betting a woman."

Key ring in hand, Nick headed for the front door. To the chief he speculated, "Complex and disciplined, educated in theater, literature, and calligraphy. And running a clinic below the radar."

He heard Chief Robertson sigh, "I've forgotten what I think about all this."

"Rescuing transmogs. Lends new meaning to *saving face*." Nick inserted his key in the lock.

"This latest Illumination is no bed-time story," the chief was saying. Next statement echoing Nailor's concern of 'push coming to shove,' the chief warned, "Better sign out your weapon for the next few nights."

"I keep a loaded shotgun in the house."

Ready to sprint, stealing peeks to chart Nick's every move, The Illuminator's heart pounded with lust for risk.

Great, Nick was thinking as he turned his key in the lock, *Now the chief's in a knot. And sooner or later Nailor's going to press me for reasons The Illuminator's got a game on me.*

When Nick opened his front door, he immediately had that feeling.

He said nothing to the chief.

When he turned in the direction of the living room the detective saw her tableau: an easel, a painting on its ledge, and at the apex, a patrolman's cap.

In disbelief Nick lowered the phone, but he heard the chief's voice come through thin and metallic, "Nick? . . . Hey!"

Nick brought the phone back to his lips, and whispered, "Somebody's been in my house," and then closed it.

He bladed his body as he moved room to room with the shotgun.

BANG!

From the garage.

He moved through the kitchen to the door. Flicked off the safety. Slowly he turned the knob, and again with care to blade his body he took a breath, focused, trigger finger weighing as he kicked the door open.

An empty garage. Its side door, caught by the breeze, again connected with the outside wall:

BANG!

But not a soul.

Outside, Nick found tracks. A small-sized lug sole.

Then he turned, mind wild now, thinking: *might've left a bomb.* He tore the place apart – couch cushions – closets – flipped his mattress – checking to make sure none of his moving boxes had been tampered – each drawer and cupboard. But every room was clear.

The old detective was left then standing in the living room, staring up at the painting on the easel, where his own face looked down at him guiltily.

He'd once seen the original, hanging in the Metropolitan Museum, years ago during a springtime trip to New York with Nora. So he easily recognized the canvas, Caravaggio's late masterpiece: *The Denial of St. Peter.*

The painting depicted Roman soldiers questioning the

Apostle at the moment he disavowed knowing Christ for the third time.

The Illuminator, Nick thought, looking at his own face superimposed upon that of the Saint.

Inches above the painting, hung from the easel's apex, the patrolman's bonnet made him think of Jim Stevens. But when he reached for it, the name tag inside the cap read: N. Giaccone – his very own. And then he saw – folded within its crown – notebook pages. And immediately recognized the handwriting.

Nick felt his face flush. His heart slamming in his chest while he read the Rookie's shaky hand:

I was thirteen, at summer camp. The usual campfire and skits. The whole troop half-smashed on that red wine Campmaster Roache made with us at his house and always brought. After lights out Campmaster Roache caught us playing cards.

He called us out of the tent all pissed off. Then Roache made us strip down and made us stand at attention at the edge of the frog pond. Then he put a lit Coleman lantern at our feet. To attract the mosquitoes, he said. He rubbed bug repellent on himself. He kept us at attention thirty minutes. He was drinking wine from a cup as he watched us. We were getting eaten alive.

If anybody slapped a mosquito, Roache added another five minutes to our sentence. He used his flash camera. Campmaster Roache. Permissive one minute. Sadistic the next. A real Jekyll & Hyde.

Only hours before, he had seen this text. Verbatim – to the letter here – but in highly decorated script on purple vellum – to match the Illuminated manuscript left in the uniform pocket of the transmogrified Campmaster Roache.

It had been signed

~from Old Scout's journal.

Now to hold these shaky pages in hand made the tragedy more real, rattled Nick's very foundations.

Jim is Old Scout.

It was irrefutable. This was the story of Mosquito Pond. Deployed a third time.

Nick thought about Graham's words: "A curious preoccupation with the number three."

And then moments ago, Nailor's warning about push coming to shove.

He thought about The Illuminator. Felt outraged, post-emptively protective for all he'd failed to do – that Jim was being dragged into this – whatever the Hell **this** was.

Nick didn't notice the tiny camera above his head, installed minutes before by The Illuminator.

Had no idea this was all being videoed.

CHAPTER 29

Brian's old pickup rattled and spat a final cough as Cassandra hurried inside to strip off her overalls then wrap snugly in a robe. Sitting at her computer she called up the cameras she'd installed above the customized Religious painting. In a moment she had Nick in her sights.

Using a disposable mobile phone, she dropped the tip to the press, complete with technical specifics to access this video feed, then turned on the TV set to see the beauty of The Work unfold.

At nightfall she ran through her Capoeira routine to quell the bursts of Light. Stories always helped. Tonight she recalls the legend of one *capoeirista* who could transform himself into a beetle to avoid capture by the police. The master had developed a *corpo fechado,* a "closed body," invulnerable to harm by any metal – including bullets. But his secret had one day been revealed; killed by an enemy with a knife carved from tucum wood.

Her own enemies would find no such vulnerabilities.

Cassandra showered, dried off, and with a razor trimmed hairs. Onto her skin she spread a thick layer of Vaseline – to her neck, collarbones, breasts and abdomen. Drew warm water into a basin and carried it to the living room. There awaited quick-setting gauze impregnated with quick-dry plaster – used to set broken bones.

She lay on a chaise, dipped a sponge into the luke-warm water, and dampened her trunk. Then draped the impregnated fabric layer-by-layer, beginning at the throat line, covering her clavicles, then to conform across the breasts. Taking care to alternate the strips herringbone fashion to follow the muscular contours along her rib lines. She lay striated slats diagonal to cover her abdomen and then parallel to contour into the spread of her thighs.

Then she waited, calmed by the curing plaster's heat. Its slight shrink pulled a little at her skin. It took only minutes for the shell to harden.

She popped the reverse-mold from her torso. Humble beginnings for The Illuminator's shining armor. Even so, she admired the form.

Onto the inside of this shell she brushed gesso, dried it with a heat gun, then applied a thick coat of carnauba wax as mold-release.

The two-part epoxy resin brushed thinly would stiffen the piece. These chemicals filled the house with a pungent, earthy smell, their catalytic workings once again generating warmth in the piece.

Once the coating hardened she could begin applying gold leaf. She set this fragile foil with a sable brush, carefully spinning its shaft between her fingers so with each circular swirl the gold foil beneath was transformed – appearing as yet another scale of a brave, golden dragon. She would engage battle with the detective so clothed, this armor she now created a cascade of brilliant coining.

Next, to bolster its integrity, she laid down alternating strips of carbon fiber, brushing on more fast-cure epoxy between layers. By dawn the structural base had set and she laid three layers of Kevlar – to create a barrier that would stop a sword or a bullet.

On another day she would accessorize – create the gauntlets, the armlets, and the anklets before finally fitting her warrior's breastplate with a comforting, close-shorn lining of shearling.

BOOK III

CHAPTER 1

Nick needed to confirm beyond doubt that these pages were Jim's.

From the carton on his desk he removed the journal. Placing the page edges against the sliced stubs, he recognized the perfect match.

He didn't need to call an authority on Textual Forensics to understand what The Illuminator wanted to communicate.

By superimposing his likeness onto *The Denial of St. Peter*, he'd obviously been cast in the role of the Saint. "You will deny Me," Christ had told the Apostle.

Pages in one hand, patrol cap in the other, it came to him.

In a sense: he and the chief had kept Jim's legal history from the press – out of respect for the Rookie's privacy – and now he was being taunted by The Illuminator for keeping Jim's business, "Under his hat."

But the revelation cut much deeper. Because it was clear – in a more particular way when he'd read about the Mosquito Pond atrocity in Jim's own hand – that years ago the kid had sorely needed to clue him in. To pass the message.

Tears came to the old detective's eyes. Either the kid's voice had been too scared or too quiet. Or else he simply hadn't been listening. But he knew that wasn't it either. He'd heard. But had avoided taking the necessary risk to dig in.

Nick sat. Paralyzed, his brain unable to process what he'd learned with all he knew.

BOOK III

CHAPTER 2

"You're standing in the crosshairs," the chief was telling Nick. "Question is, *why?*"

For the moment the detective kept his answers to himself. Still waiting for a right time, the right words – knowing that both had come and gone so many years ago. It would only make a mess of the investigation to explain it now, he wanted believe, but knew deep down he was avoiding.

The team brushing print powder on every hard surface of Nick's house seemed punishment enough. Made him feel like a stooge. It was pride. Or shame. He knew it: no veteran cop worth his salt would allow himself to get burglarized.

"Why," Nick repeated the chief's question, then tried making light of it: "As in *why me?*"

The chief looked the doctored painting up and down. "Obviously about denial. Maybe that nobody thought to ask Jim or some of the other Youth Campers about what was going on way back when."

"Do you think *I* was in denial about that?" Nick heard the defense in his own voice. "Jim hardly even let on to me."

"Jim **let on** to you?" Chief Robertson gave him a searching look. Nick wished he could say what magic words would go back and fix it all. His mind grabbed at the words but he couldn't find the right order to put them in.

The chief said, "We need The Illuminator's connection to you in all of this."

Nick kept his mouth shut and tried not to take it personally.

Robertson noticed that he was. Softening his gaze, he offered standard boilerplate, "When Police taunting is associated with serial crimes, its usually directed at the police in general. Everybody knows that, Nick."

It bugged him worse that the chief was the painting over the face of it now. In view of Old Scout's story, it was all so unacceptable.

It slammed inside him again and again. Years ago when Jim had hinted, Nick thought, he'd let it pass. Most people did back then. There was no way to tell, now, if he'd taken a different path, what difference he might have made in Jim's life.

Jim's life. If...

Unusual for Nick to become irritated by a Plainclothesman, now dogging him: "'Ja you get a look at the perp? I found footprints...'"

Nick shrugged. "Why not put an all points bulletin out on everybody wearing Vibram soles?"

Nick was about to apologize when Professor Nailor walked in. Once he looked over the tableau, sized up the message, and then took in the layout it seemed he, too, might be sparing this aging detective's feelings. He used all the right jargon: The Illuminator was delusional and speaking to the community, with Nick as intermediary. Seeking validation by placing the detective in the role of father figure.

Nick appreciated the intention, and even knew Nailor was *technically* right. And for that matter – to take this St.

Peter message at face value – so was The Illuminator. For the harm of boys like Jim to go unchecked it was a failure of the entire community.

All true.

Why then, Nick wondered, did it sting him so?

"Not a word of this leaves this house!" Now the chief was going extra miles to bolster him. Instructing the team: "No way do we give it to the media that The Illuminator's been inside a member of Goddard P.D.'s house. Especially Detective Giaccone's."

Nick tried not to feel irrelevant.

"Guys! Bailey's on the line from Headquarters. . ." exclaimed one of the Plainclothesmen, a mobile phone clasped to his ear, "Put on the TV, channel 5. Looks like somebody dropped a tip."

When Nick switched on the living room flat screen nobody could believe it.

He saw himself, on his own TV screen, standing in his own living room alongside Nailor, the chief, and the small swarm of policemen.

"It looks like we're live," the Plainclothes said.

"How do we stop. . .?" the chief was asking.

Nick waved his arm to test on-screen response. And immediately knew he was being ridiculed. Mocked by The Illuminator.

He snatched the plainclothesman's phone and asked the Specialist, "Can you ID the computer streaming these?"

"Yeah, Nick. Its yours."

One by one they found her cameras. Tiny cameras, each the size of a common pin. Moments later one of the Plainclothes disconnected the relay.

BOOK III

CHAPTER 1

By now every TV station carried the footage.

She was pleased. Even online, *The Boston Bugle* had posted all the right pictures.

One caption read, "Detective Nick Giaccone reads a page believed to have inspired The Illuminator's 'Old Scout' message..."

The page author's identity was still unknown.

Her brother's house felt, now, almost like a home.

The Illuminator switched on the alabaster lamp.

She stood and stepped to the mantel. Ran a finger along the tops of a grouping of newly framed drawings hung successively in a line. Drawings that depicted the progressive formation of a fetus' face in its crucial first weeks after conception, during the joining together of its several different elements, when there lay the risk that the process will not be quite completed.

The mantel and walls displayed other framed pictures, of children who through no fault of their own, had been born with severe facial deformities – and the 'after' shots, their smiles glowing, eyes bright, features corrected.

That *had* been her life's work. And it had fulfilled. Until the last time she'd come home to rescue him. The time when she had rushed the fastest, her brother's condition worsening far more rapidly. The time when she arrived feeling the most behind schedule and had lost the race. Afterward, the void. Then, the Work had become everything.

And she'd decided to take it on the road, to Goddard. To imprison his assailants' essences within her Book of Souls.

She remembered the rhyme she'd made the day of her arrival: *Here to heal the source of dear Brother's loss, to begin The Work in Goddard with the year's first killing frost.*

Cassandra went to the work table and with a scalpel sliced opened the overnight package from the medical supply, carefully removing its contents: tissue expanders, each wrapped in a transparent bluish plastic. The Illuminator had planned, memorized, even assigned numbers to each of the small incisions she would need to make: behind the armpits, above the triceps, and outside the scapulas. Had studied how she would insert the empty balloons. Would calibrate the daily injections of saline solution required to expand each sac, to promote skin growth. Water and salt and time, and to pump his system with protein, vitamin D, and special nutrients, would create ample material for shaping Gorgalo's flightless wings.

She carefully arranged the now-flat expanders on the stainless steel tray alongside the rest of the instruments for these procedures: a needle holder, bayonet forceps, mallet, Takahashi forceps, Siegel retractor, chisel, Converse retractor. Next she unfolded a sterile blue fabric cover and laid it carefully upon the table. Last she set the tray upon the fabric, then wrapped the setup, folded down the corners, and applied short strips of masking tape to close the surgical kit.

CHAPTER 4

That night Chief Robertson took Jim's journal home to read it.

"I have to take my hat off to the Rookie," he said next day when he saw Nick. "People should know about bravery like this. . ."

Robertson didn't press his friend for having held out about the burglary. In fact he'd remarked at the detective's restraint, dubbing it a savvy mix of caution and respect. Public knowledge of the journal pages would neither hurt nor help in nailing The Illuminator. And if Jewell had found out about all this earlier the mess would have been far greater.

What *did* matter, Robertson told him, was to take yesterday's hint.

Nick felt he was being schooled and didn't much like it.

The Illuminator would do whatever it took to put the Basilisk on public display on the *Feast of the Holy Innocents*, December 28 – the chief was saying, "Which probably means we need to take another look at protecting that Gorgalo pile of shit."

That the cardiologist's lawyer had protested didn't absolve Goddard P.D. of their obligation. The doctor's arrogance in having his attorney reject such protection wouldn't prevent the same attorney from filing a negligence claim should Gorgalo get snatched and go under the knife.

That, the chief told Nick, could *really* delay Italy.

When Nick and the chief looked at one another something passed between them. A lot of cops would have let the doctor get what's coming to them. It was not the first time either had rested belief in alternative forms of justice.

They'd played the game before. Nick already knew the solution. All he had to do was to make it the chief's idea.

So he mentioned that since Dr. Gorgalo lived in N. Carnan, N.H., evidence that The Illuminator was about to abduct the doctor would change the situation to Interstate – to warrant Federal intervention.

The chief replied it was a safe bet the Feds wouldn't get within a hundred feet of The Illuminator crimes – at least till time came to make the collar. The FBI would have no problem taking credit for *that.* And once the moment arrived, the Feds would make no bones in claiming jurisdiction.

Neither here nor there. At present, anyway.

Naturally Chief Robertson would want to make the collar on his own turf. Therefore he made the phone call.

He'd found it strange. But not outside his experience.

The Federal agent who answered had let Chief Robertson talk. Then swore up and down he didn't have the resources to commit.

Yet when he finished speaking, the FBI man facetiously remarked, "Maybe Dr. Gorgalo should hire some Youth Campers for security."

When the chief relayed this Nick had to smile, then watched as Robertson called New Hampshire State Police and asked to speak with an old boy he knew there. Once the call was connected, Robertson indicated for Nick to pick up on an extension, and then spoke to the long-timer the way old cops sometimes talk.

The old boy had heard the name Dr. Gorgalo before. He said this in a way that told the chief whatever he'd heard about the doctor could not have been good.

The New Hampshire State Trooper wasn't about to force a protective custody situation – if only to avoid riling Gorgalo's legal beagles. "And besides, there's appearances both ways. New Hampshire State Troopers can't go around being seen to furnish personal security . . . . 'specially for some people." That could get "sticky." The trooper used that word. "A State Police car up in these hills brings a lot of questions . . . But as you say there's a life at stake here. The rest of it goes to a Higher Court."

In the end the Trooper said he'd set it up all with N. Carnan P.D.. "Not much going on there." He'd see to it that the locals put a car at Gorgalo's. "Not on the property. But out front, on State pavement," he said.

"Put it this way," the Trooper summed up, "if Gorgalo's seen his two friends go to The Illuminator the way you say, he's going to be in some kind of sweat. And if he's the type you say, a 24-hour police presence at the end of his drive-way's bound to give him another kind of sweat. How does that suit you?"

"Shrewd to use locals," Nick said after the chief discon-nected the call. "Wanted to keep his own boys in the clear for when the shit hits the blades." For Nick a new respect for the chief and his deskwork was replacing a weary field-hand's contempt.

CHAPTER 5

On The Illuminator's writing table awaited the page to justify The Work on her next Subject. A fresh piece of vellum, ink bottles, quills, pigments, and nib-sharp styluses at the ready.

The final purloined journal page stood out white, a rebellion against utter darkness beneath a single lighted lamp.

Jim's handwriting read:

This time when Gorgalo took me camping, at the last minute when we were leaving, he said we had to pick up another kid Timmy–seven or eight years old. Timmy was a heart surgery patient, Gorgalo said, and it was follow-up support to visit this way, to camp out weekends with the doctor. I met his mother at their motel. The first night camping Gorgalo had me sleep in the tent. The second night it was Timmy in the tent, and I could hear, it was the same with him as Gorgalo did to me. Then the next day I saw the fresh scar on Timmy's chest when he changed the large dressing–I remember could see the small metal staple-stitches all in a row. He had the heart surgery three weeks before. He told me his mother didn't have money or insurance–Gorgalo was the hospital administrator. He operated for free. Gorgalo called those staples Timmy's 'zipper.'

Cassandra had purchased a specialty tool. The doctor's transformation would be closed in stainless stapling. Just like little Timmy's.

Before making the long trip to collect Gorgalo, The Illuminator couldn't help taking up her drawing pad and scratch final lines to complete the physician's new, true self.

Every strike of charcoal on paper was a testament to poetic surgical precision.

Sculpting a proper beak for Gorgalo from paste of crushed cartilage would be no more trouble than to build an ear from scratch, or to erase a toddler's cleft palate. She had scrubbed in as a volunteer for plenty of auricular reconstructions, with lesser tools, in cramped quarters, and in compromised sterile conditions.

The phase of transformation after that – to disarticulate Gorgalo's leg bones – would be a snap, compared to recomposing limbs from infantrymen's war-torn smithereens. And the process would leave enough remaining flesh to compose the Basilisk's slithy empennage.

If she was careful with the legs she'd have ample skin left over, would stitch these remnants to the new-grown material in constructing the wings.

She leaned back to admire the creation on her drawing pad, its tapered form seductively curvaceous. Winged, yet earthbound.

Fully warmed to her plan for Dr. Gorgalo's future, she made green tea. Then settled on the sofa with her laptop, a coverlet thrown cozily over her shoulders. Into her fingers came the slight vibe of the machine's memory waking up.

With a click she opened Morph-Aesthetica. She'd developed a feel for the tool, from countless hours teaching herself to properly render her charcoal sketch of the Basilisk in all three dimensions.

Now she updated the design with confidence. She fussed. Sipped tea. Reset some contours. And considered the results.

Warmed to The Work, Cassandra clicked through each step in the series of views she'd created to plan the autogenous cartilage harvest, here and there making fine adjustments. Next she opened the Multi-view Menu to run the facial changes in full progression. She selected the Editing Brush, and with a few cursor strokes subtly refined each stage till on playback it flowed seamlessly.

Selecting the Finishing Wand, she added skin texture and then balanced color tones. By configuring a list of settings and selecting the correct panels and views, she then scripted out an animation that depicted a culmination of the incremental surgeries.

She saved this animation under the name: "Gorgal_face_body.mrph," and saved the completed file conspicuously on her hard drive.

Easy for the detective to find. An enticement.

With a mouse-click she played the sequence. Before her eyes the subject's lips melted into nose. The fleshy shape elongated into a downward crook. She fixed the image in 3-D, clicked *rotate*, and came face to face with Dr. Gorgalo's eyes – staring at her over the jutting Basilisk's fleshy beak. She zoomed out, watching his lower parts lose their identities and transform.

Intoxicated, she felt a cool drop of sweat slide down the curved meeting place of her breast and armpit.

CHAPTER 6

With one house sold and payment received in full, Nick stole a few moments to check in with the agent handling the sale of his personal residence. Full commitment had been received in writing from the buyer's lender. Closing of the sale still on track for January 2.

Switching off his phone Nick thought, *If I survive past December 28 . . .*

He'd spent part of the night cleaning fingerprint dust from his walls. Then had gone online to buy his ticket to Rome.

The moment Nick clicked **PURCHASE,** he received the call from Dr. Bacon: the autopsy on Roache was complete – with findings of "mineral granules" embedded at the base of each "grape-like pustule" below Roaches' left eye.

Nick asked if he could send a patrolman for a sample. Bacon replied that he had already arranged transport for the goods. A unit from Boston P.D. was already halfway to Goddard.

Professor Nailor stood in his back yard under lights teaching his elder son subtleties of the compound bow when he received Nick's call. As with most novice archers, the teen would need to unlearn the reflexive urge to ease muscle tension upon the string's release, which would cause the weapon to imperceptibly dip – immediately before the arrow had fully left the bow. Only proper follow-through, Nailor patiently explained to the youth, would allow an arrow to meet its mark.

To demonstrate the principle he raised the lightweight bow, like a toy in his hands, drew back, and released. "See," he told his son, still holding fast, long after the arrow met the bull's eye. "And I'm positioned to draw another arrow." When he saw Nick's call come up on his mobile phone, the intelligencer handed off the bow and told his son, "Now, you try."

Once Nick relayed Dr. Bacon's findings, the professor remarked, "Mineral particles. Reminds one of sands through an hourglass."

"Time, slipping away," Nick heard himself mutter.

Politely, after a short pause, the professor offered the service of a colleague in the Geology Department who could test and possibly identify the substance. *If* a sample could be arranged.

Nick made another call, to ask if the police courier could take his sample straight to the college.

Inside of an hour the lab at Brauser was running tests.

"It's common Basalt," the Geologist told Nick. "Trap Rock, used in sauna stones because it holds the heat. And in tarmac."

Another message. . .

Nick had lived in Goddard long enough to remember the old trap rock quarry. And he also knew that Hillside Cemetery had started out as a marsh: cat tails and red-winged blackbirds – until Braxton Jewell had made a deal with the quarry owners, offering the marsh as a place to dump their spoils.

Once these wetlands had been filled, Jewell spread a thin skim of topsoil and brought in trees. Thus was born Hillside Cemetery.

On the newer graves, Nick had first noticed visiting Nora's resting place, the mineral had shown the tendency of working up through the recently disturbed earth, so with each spring rain, the grass became straw-colored to mark the outline of the concrete burial vault below.

Because of these bare spots, groundskeeper's bills had been a constant grim reminder of his beloved's loss.

Some people in town called it "the Hillside Curse." And at the rate Jewell's cemetery office billed for re-sodding, Nick had caught himself speculating more than once that Brax Jewell might've planned it all as a moneymaker.

"We need to ask Nailor. . .What's the meaning of Trap Rock?" The chief exclaimed when Nick called to fill him in. "We're talking cemetery here. . . The Illuminator could be planning a straight-up murder!"

Nick would rather focus on the surgical implications. He told the chief: "The trap rock granules would aggravate the itch each time Roache scratched. A self-propagating sentence – like the one the Campmaster had imposed on those kids that night beside Mosquito Pond."

The Illuminator, Nick thought as he hung up the phone, *Casting stones.*

He got his great coat and made for Hillside Cemetery.

BOOK III

CHAPTER 7

The Illuminator worked readying needles.

From vials stored in her refrigerator she drew one syringe for herself of Romazicon, and two of Ketamine to quiet her quarry once she nabbed him, a dose that would last the entire drive back to Goddard. The Rophypnol she would administer orally to abduct him.

She logged onto the web cams surrounding Gorgalo's house.

Fresh snow. New tire tracks. *And there. . .a police car out front on the street.* It would make an enthralling challenge.

She decided to dress for success. Overkill, she knew. With all the body work the doctor would need, a bruise or two wouldn't make or break *this* particular finished product. Given the distance of his house from the street, she could easily steal in through the woods behind the place, stroll inside, and hit him with the Taser.

But no. *Think festive.*

In her bedroom she removed her blouse and brassiere and got the modified spandex bike shorts that had been so trouble-free as a binder. "The bait," she said as always with the placement of the wadded sock between her legs, and then pulled on the flannel shirt and overalls.

At her vanity table she traced the impish lines of her face with a foundation, plus a blush of rouge to emphasize male youthfulness, and then brushed out the contrast. Lightly rolling a mascara brush across her upper lip and chin, she created an appearance of faint stubble. Like the Artful Dodger her brother had played in junior high school.

The cardboard boxes of wreaths and birch logs she'd made waited in the breezeway. The birch logs were her favorite, three inches in diameter, twelve inches long, each drilled with three inline holes to anchor the red candles, then decorated in stapled sprigs of hemlock, checkerberry, mountain laurel, and deer moss. She remembered how, before The Accident, she and Brother had sold simple decorations like this door-to-door after school every day throughout Advent, a "confidence-builder" their parents had said, and a sure source of money for holiday gifts.

Dr. Gorgalo would be a willing consumer. Maybe he'd invite her inside for hot chocolate.

Minutes later The Illuminator was off to make a house call, lumbering along the Interstate at the wheel of the motor home.

CHAPTER 8

Walking past the headstones at Hillside Cemetery, Nick could hear the occasional sound of plowed snow falling into slush. Could smell the warm, premature dirt-smell of spring rising from the melt that rung headstones warmed by a day's sun.

Approaching Jim Steven's grave, flashlight in hand, Nick kicked away snow till he could make out clearly the lines of turf died away. Kneeling, he pinched up some granules and by eye and saw it was a direct match for the Basalt that had been implanted upon the maw of Mr. Hyde.

Suddenly he heard a voice. In the distance. Beyond those graves and trees. . . Some song . . .or a chant. . .

No sidearm, thought Nick.

He tried to make out the words.

The singer grew nearer.

By instinct Nick went into a crouch and turned a lowered shoulder toward whoever was headed his way.

The voice sounded hollowed-out, as if from some sorrowful gulch. Closer.

In a moment Nick could at least make out the tune, "Hop Up My Ladies."

The words? Disturbingly different:

Oh the cow kicked Nelly in the belly in the barn . . .
but the doctor said it wouldn't do her any harm . . .
Oh the cow kicked Nelly in the belly in the barn . . .
but the doctor said it wouldn't do her any harm . . .
Oh the cow . . .

On and on and on until in the pitch black Nick could distinguish a figure among the graves loping toward him . . .

. . . but the doctor said it wouldn't do her any harm . . .
Oh the cow kicked Nell . . .

When detective switched on his flashlight, the lumbering figure halted, and let loose a sepulchral, "W h o o o ' s there?"

"Police!" Within the circle of the flashlight was a whisky-bulb nose and spider-veined face. Skeins of shoulder-length grey hair. Swallowing saliva the bulging Adams apple up and down the corded neck looked like a lawnmower piston.

The gravesman was a known quantity around Goddard. Squinting into the beam with red-webbed eyes, jaw clacking in the way of a leg-hold trap the man announced, "Its only me G i r a r d !" Loudly and stretching his vowels as if to reach the words toward the moon above.

Nick said, "And it's **me!**. . . First Detective Giaccone." He lowered the beam. Extremities poked outward against the man's clothes like hinged tomato stakes.

Regardless of countless visits to this cemetery, Girard, each time they met, showed zero recognition of Nick's name or face. In that same distant intonation the gravesman howled, half insistent, half in fright, "L i g h t your self."

"Christ Almighty! Look!" Losing patience, Nick brought the beam to bear upon his own his face. "I'm a cop." He flipped his shield so the beam caught it. "What are you doing here? After dark . . in a graveyard?"

Still, the groundskeeper showed no recognition. "Girard always checks a r o u n d , nights," he squelched, "Likely to see s o o o o m e t h i i i n g. Likely's n a w w t."

The circle of Nick's flashlight beam caught a ridge in the man's jacket below the armpit. He knew to read it to be a pint, not a pistol.

The gravesman glanced around nervously. Then suddenly, like dozens of times before, he began to jabber about dead grass in that loathsome tone. "Looking like you'll have to re-turf some areas, if it were up to old G i r a a a a r d." With twenty dollars, the work would be "cheaper than going official, through the cemetery o f f i i i c e." So the grave would look natural by spring, Girard explained he'd get it done "i m p e r a t i v e l y ." He applied the final word like it could scrub the frosted air of his whiskey breath and make the deal slide through.

Nick replied he'd hold off till spring.

When he turned, his flashlight caught something that warranted a double take. Sighting across three crucifixes, the beam lit an extraordinary tomb nearby that Nick had never seen before.

Girard said, "That one's brand n e e e e w – only one here Vermont White m a a a a r b l e."

The stone angel was stark white. Towering. Coldly magnificent. Face meditative and discerning. Its white marble set off an eerie, frosted glow amidst the surrounding, darker granite stones.

To stand before it, looking up at the white stone form tapped something deep within Nick. Despite the great angel's dour attitude, its tiptoes connected with the base stone only minimally, a marble weightlessness settling from flight upon the Grace of partstretched wings.

Girard murmured, "Fellow's been planted there since S e p t e m b e r . But then, last m o n t h , s o m e b o d y paid all this fancy work."

Nick turned his beam to read engravings on the pedestal.

Brain   Shockly

December 28, 1959 – October 24, 2007

Below the name and date, an image engraved as bas relief depicted a gruesome scene of infanticide that brought Nick a sudden shiver.

The epitaph haunted Nick even more:

> *This angel drifted groundward.*
>
> *Rise of Light whispered, "Night is lost,*
>
> *silver breath-lace crystallized:*
>
> *a new day's killing frost."*

Brian Shockly!

The detective snapped a picture of the bas relief with his cell phone and sent it to Professor Nailor, with the text message, "need to ID this."

Then he asked Girard, "Who paid for the Angel?"

Girard, kicking at a ball of slush with an untied brogan, looked up at Nick, his eyes wide, as if he'd just woken up, and his mouth parted into a grin. The man drew out the vowel sounds with the beyond-the-here quality of voice. He moaned, "I know YOU! You're that O l d   S c o u t   d e t e c t i v e !"

"That's me," Nick admitted.

The man had resumed his chanting in the slightest voice,

> *. . . the cow kicked Nelly in the belly in the barn . . .*
> *but the doctor said . . .*

"Speak up, Girard! Who paid for the Angel?"

Then, to Nick's surprise, he heard in that carved-out susurrate, "Girard was thinking to use a key 'n   o p e n   u p   t h e   o f f i c e   and check ledger books – but its too bad he was just goin' home when he saw you. Tomorrow you could talk to Mr. Jewell. He comes to the office noon time."

"You have a key?"

The gravesman nodded.

Nick bit part of his lip and took out his wallet. "If I were to pay you, say, in cash – for that little bit of re-sodding – you think you could throw in a look at the books?" He pushed three twenties into Girard's hand, spitting back the term the odd man had used earlier: "Imperatively?"

"Meet me at the front door," Girard mouthed, barely audible, and rushed off into the dark.

When the gravesman let him in Nick immediately caught sight of the back window still open. "A key. Right," he said, "Better shut that so Brax Jewell doesn't catch a sniffle tomorrow morning."

Then he instructed Girard, "Give me a few minutes. I've paid for it," and looking at the window thought, *I could've kept my sixty bucks.*

He then searched every file cabinet.

On a shelf he found the ledgers. Going back to the cemetery's first days.

Opening one of the older ones, a sheaf of papers slipped from inside its back cover. *Real estate appraisals,* Nick noticed, gathering the sheets from the floor. *And recent.*

He read through each one. *People refinance all the time these days. But Braxton's cemetery?*

Folded inside the cover of one of the other books he found survey plans. Nick examined them closely. From what he could tell, the land these so-called "lots" stood upon was one and the same as the graves throughout Hillside Cemetery. There were copies of financing application as well. Nick read all of it.

Pay dirt! Jewell's big score. Using an out of state lender who would never view the collateral first hand, Jewell Eternities had been approved for loans totaling over two million. Each of the loans would disburse to a series of shell companies after first of the year. What backed up the debt amounted to phony lots that encompassed graves.

Next minute, Nick had Bailey on the phone and explained the whole thing. Then with explicit instructions to the Forensic Specialist, he faxed Bailey every condemning document.

Meanwhile Girard could be heard outside,

. . Nelly in the belly in the barn . . .
but the doctor said it wouldn't do her any harm . . .
Oh the cow . . .

Nick flipped ledger pages indexed **S** till he found the page that carried entries for the internment of a Brian Shockly. And for the stone angel.

Between the facing pages was a hand-drawn charcoal sketch of the great grave maker.

Nick jumped when he heard Girard pronounce over his shoulder in that far-away voice, "That big angel ain't nothing compared to what they paid up front to keep f l o w – e r s . Enough for a hundred years of f l o w – e r s ."

Next moment the detective was busy chastising himself: hearing about Brian and the deer rifle he'd gotten in a hurry – even more so after learning about the kid's suicide. Causing him to overlook the possibility of family vendetta.

The ledger entries he now looked upon for Brian Shockly's internment showed cash payments by mail – from a payee marked "anonymous family member." And by the looks of the engraved scene of – what appeared to be infanticide at the base of the stone angel – the "anonymous family member" member was The Illuminator.

Half distracted, the detective looked up at Girard and asked, "What kind of flowers?"

The gravedigger ran his hand up across the lump beneath the armpit of his jacket, kept it there, said, "Passion vines," and then walked out, singing of Nelly, the barn, and the doctor beneath breath the flavor of whiskey.

CHAPTER 9

Once she'd snatched Dr. Gorgalo, The Illuminator would need to use a pay phone.

Fortunately her ramp off the Interstate teed at an intersection where she spotted Minute Mart. With the motor home parked behind the convenience store, she dropped a quarter in the pay station out front to make sure she'd be able to get a dial tone.

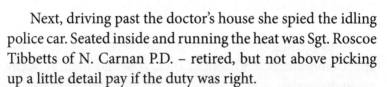

Next, driving past the doctor's house she spied the idling police car. Seated inside and running the heat was Sgt. Roscoe Tibbetts of N. Carnan P.D. – retired, but not above picking up a little detail pay if the duty was right.

He squinted into the headlights. Cautiously she'd braked and slowed into the slight curve in the road. So the sergeant gave a friendly wave as she continued past.

Close ahead Cassandra saw what appeared to be a school bus turn, recently plowed, and well out of the policeman's line of sight. She switched off her headlights and rolled to a halt.

Then yanked on a knitted stocking hat, brought her face before the mirror, and smiled congratulations to a reflection of Brian in his boyhood, at the moment looking rather Elvin in matching red and green wool hat and coat.

From her medical kit bag she tucked the vial of liquid Rophypnol into a breast pocket, then slipped the barrels of both syringes of the longer-lasting Ketamine into the pockets she had sewn into the collars of her shirt. Then she took a needle hard to her thigh, dosing herself with Romazicon. The Taser went into the bib pocket of her overalls.

From the back of the motor home she unloaded the six-foot toboggan. Also a large, green burlap Santa sack she'd sewn for the occasion. She filled the sack from her boxes of wreaths and decorated birch logs. A small box held tapered red candles to go with the festive logs. She secured everything on the toboggan with black rubber bungees.

To make the load appear extra festive she piled a few of her lovely wreaths on top.

She would carry the finest of the birch logs under her arm, set with three red candles as a sample of her wares.

Pulling on gloves, she took up the cord and tugged her burden toward the doctor's house along the snowy roadside, packed flat by school children's footprints.

Approaching the parked police car she could hear a radio sports announcer, and behind that, now and then, scratchy radio dispatch.

Inside the squad car Sergeant Tibbetts was listening to a hockey game and finishing up a can of sardines with soda crackers.

When The Illuminator pulled her toboggan up close to ask the old policeman if he would buy a Christmas wreath or centerpiece, Tibbetts did his best to return this boy's disarming smile, but replied no thank you. "But the feller in this house here is a doctor and he'll maybe buy a couple, the way *they* get paid."

The green bag on the toboggan bulged with good things.

Pulling the sled past a curve in the driveway she saw Gorgalo's house. A gray ribbon curled from the chimney and draped lazily, carousing with the few red sparks that popped and fizzled against the black and twinkling. A gibbous moon and the single carriage light out front bathed the yard, driveway, and one car in the nocturnal luminescence of White Mountain winters that casts and carries in diamond blue, from snow to snow, over rolling piles of firewood; the nearby chopping block, rung in footprints, tonsured with icing.

The Illuminator's breath caught with the simple beauty of it.

Drawing her burden closer his house she beheld a splitting axe, toe of its bit stuck in the chopping block. On the axe handle's end knob was a snow-tuft, melted and refrozen, tempered by daylight into an icy crown that glimmered in the pale light like a solitary wishing star.

From this axe her eye traveled the length of Dr. Gorgalo's house, climbed its rooftop blanketed in spun sugar, tested glowing panes that indicated life within. She noticed everything, including two propane tanks that hugged the side wall, their tops heaped with white. The red brick façade and wide, broad painted frieze of this New England Greek revival implied timeless integrity. Until she counted – along the broad white fascias to each side of the steep-raked front portico – where icicles shimmered starlight and reached toward the earth like ten obscene fingers.

She let the toboggan slide to a stop against Gorgalo's front steps.

Before going in, she looked back to check. Parked out there on the State road, the policeman lacked a clear sightline to the doctor's house.

Anyway, the hockey game was into overtime now and Tibbetts was almost into a piece of the Missus' mincemeat pie, put up just nice.

The Illuminator pressed the doorbell, glancing back at the chopping block, the splitting axe. At last moment she turned, grabbed the hickory handle at its curved belly and levered it out. Then waited by the door, throat of the axe tight in her left hand, concealed by a leg.

The door opened and Dr. Gorgalo ate her with his eyes. He stood short of stature, slight, the face nonetheless shedding a flicker of arrogance. "Hi there, little friend," he said, cocking his head sidelong. Then a squint, feigning studious familiarity. "I know you, don't I?" A little forward of his own stance, he inhabited his body too easily.

From behind her leg The Illuminator swung the axe in an arc, letting it drop to make the iron head clink against the bluestone stoop. "You left this outside," she said, making her voice a little husky. "I thought kids might get hurt."

Gorgalo held the smile. In the eye a tincture of fear, bridled by conceit.

Before the doctor could respond, Cassandra held her festive birch log toward him. "I'm selling these table centerpieces to earn some money for Christmas gifts." Hastily added, "I make everything myself. My mother and I just moved here. I'm Freddy." Leaned the axe against the house. Shy smile.

"Maybe I'll buy one. . ." Gorgalo braced the door with a leg, freeing a hand to take the log and admire it.

She handed him the sample, scuttled down the steps, and brought her toboggan into view. "I have lots of 'em."

"Only four dollars," said The Illuminator, touching her cheek with a gloved hand. "Ten if you buy three."

"Only four dollars each? Its cold out here!" Dr. Gorgalo gestured inside, "The wood stove is roaring. Come in! Come in! Freddy, you said? Come along!"

Once she was inside Gorgalo put a finger to his lips, "Say, little friend. I'm just about to make some hot mulled wine. With honey and nutmeg."

She said, showing reluctance, "My mother's coming back in an hour. I want to sell the rest of my logs before she gets back."

"An hour. . . " Gorgalo repeated, "I'll buy a few to give as gifts at the hospital. We'll work everything out." He added, with a wink, "No need to tell your mother about the hot wine. Come on into the kitchen," said the doctor. He planted a hand on the back of The Illuminator's shoulder, holding it there as they walked toward the kitchen. Then used a finger inside the back collar to test for fuzz on the skin of the neck. "Why not take this scarf off?"

Putting wonder in her voice, The Illuminator asked, "You work at a hospital?"

"Surgeon of the heart!" Gorgalo turned the stove knob so a blue gas flame burst and fanned beneath the saucepan. He added burgundy, orange juice, honey, cinnamon, and then grated fresh nutmeg.

With one hand inside her coat pocket Cassandra stroked the vial of Rophypnol.

Gorgalo filled two mugs, gave her one, then excused himself to retrieve his wallet.

She dosed his mug.

"Here we are," the doctor said, cheerfully laying a thick, black leather billfold on the counter. He took a seat at the table beside the boy selling decorations and laid a hand to her wrist, narrowed his eyes and then raised his hand to take a brief hold her chin, considering the face. A faint smile. Perhaps vague recognition. "Have we met?"

"We did just now."

Tantalized. Gorgalo dropped his hand and took a thorough drink, then opened his wallet and peered inside. "Tonight I have cash for two." He leered at her. "Come back Saturday. I'll buy a dozen."

The Illuminator could hear it. Gorgalo's tongue going thick.

When he blinked, the lids dipped too long. The head tottered.

"Wh-a-a-a –." The doctor's head fell to his chest. Shoulders sagged. Almost liquefied, the small of his back slid down the chair until he slumped to the floor.

"Sleigh ride time," she whispered.

There was a door leading from the kitchen into the living room, which she closed and sealed with the roll of duct tape from inside her jolly sack.

She next got a wrench from his garage and used it to disconnect the kitchen gas line.

Placing her fine birch log centerpiece on the table, she carefully straightened each candle and then lit all three.

Once she opened the valve, it would only be a matter of time for the gas, heavier than air and hugging the floor, to build in volume till it reached the three lit candle flames.

The burlap sack, filled with so many wreathes and birch-log candle holders, was far too heavy to lug inside. So there before the front door, she emptied it of its contents, and then carried her unsold wares inside his house. She brought the sack into the house as well.

Dr. Gorgalo fit nicely inside. This made it easy to drag him. But before she did, she laid sofa cushions upon the blue-stone steps to avoid any bruising of his skin. Precious skin.

Once outside she then loaded him onto the toboggan and bound the bundle with the rubber straps.

Before pulling her load up the snowy driveway, Cassandra went back in the house, opened the gas cock, and came out with a single wreath, which she placed atop the sack containing Gorgalo.

Then she took up the rope and gave the toboggan a tug, muttering as she drove the load forward, "And dash away. Dash away. Dash away all!"

Sergeant Tibbetts watched from his squad car as the boy tugged hard to move the toboggan over a hump left by snow plows where Gorgalo's driveway met the street. Straining at the rope, The Illuminator thought about the whispering gas now filling Gorgalo's kitchen.

"Let me lend a hand!" Sergeant Tibbetts called out his squad car window. In a moment's time the two had the toboggan past the hump.

"Mighty good load there," Tibbetts said, handing her the rope. He added, "I hope you sell all of 'em."

Cassandra thanked the policeman and rewarded him with a wreath.

"That'll please the Missus, if I don't mind," the sergeant said, placing the wreath in his trunk. "No problem anyway, the game's just got over."

Tugging the sled back to the motor home was downhill. In a few minutes Dr. Gorgalo was loaded, secured in the wheelchair with nylon straps, and dosed for the trip.

She looked at her watch. Enough time to start an IV for Heparin therapy to ensure the skin grafts would take.

On her way through town The Illuminator parked behind the Minute Mart and placed a call to 911. Acting panicked, she reported: "a gunman robbing the Minute Mart gas station in N. Carnan," and supplied a fictitious name.

Driving off, she could see the police cruiser in the rear view, beacons blazing, Sgt. Tibbetts bravely responding to this hard crime call. *Good.* He was in a safe place with a reasonable excuse for being off his post.

The sound of the kitchen's open gas line still filled her ears, like a mother's reassurance for a hurt, "S h h h h h h h h h h . . ."

From the Interstate's on ramp, above the thick pines, she could see the halo when Gorgalo's house became an exploding orange ball.

CHAPTER 10

Sergeant Tibbetts had called his chief. Who had called the New Hampshire State Police old boy. Who had called Goddard's own Chief Robertson. Who had called Nick to say that Gorgalo's house was in cinders. No body had been found.

The phone call also provided Nick opportunity to catch the chief up about the mineral bits found embedded in Roache's face – how the discovery of their origin had led straight to Brian Shockly's grave. Likely planned that way by The Illuminator. "It's an expensive monument. But I looked in the books and everything was handled through the mail. No names. In cash. Accompanied by a charcoal drawing for the angel."

"Has to be family." The chief said it first. "I'll have Bailey pull everything on Brian Shockly."

When Nick went to his study he found an email from Canon Nailor. He'd identified the bas relief on Shockly's grave. The engraving had been taken from a painting titled *Massacre of the Innocents* by the celebrated Religious painter Giotto.

Nailor had attached an image of the original. Nick clicked on the file and saw the painting to be the same as the engraving on Brian's headstone. It depicted the execution of multiple infants with King Herod looking on from a high tower.

Massacre of the Innocents, he thought. *Celebrated on Brian's date of birth, December 28. To celebrate the first Christian martyrs. Same theme as Graham's palimpsest.*

This made a second reference to the event.

"A curious preoccupation with the number three," Graham had said.

The Illuminator was putting everything in place for a *Grande finale.* The Basilisk, the most spectacular Contrapasso. Transmogrification number three.

There was no longer any question in the detective's mind why he'd been chosen, why his visage had been superimposed upon *The Denial of St. Peter.*

Christ had told St. Peter: "You will deny me three times before the cock crows. . ."

Never should have crossed Brian Shockly off the list, Nick lamented.

CHAPTER 11

Lying snug in clinic, Gorgalo's only job these nights was to heal from tiny incisions made for the insertion of tissue expanders between the scapulas and skin.

Sole item on The Illuminator's Christmas list: for the doctor to manufacture the commodity, in the same, patient way he'd once groomed boys like brother Brian to withstand the touch. Gorgalo now lay still, veins flooding with intravenous nutrients to further enable The Work.

She had bet on it that Nick would be no dummy, that by now he'd correctly read the granules in Roache's face. Had made the connection between the missing pages and what The Illuminator was teaching him about the way he'd handled Jim Steven's subtle cues about being abused by her Subjects. She even guessed Nick had already been to Brian's grave and seen the engraving, made the connection, and would soon be visiting this house.

To conclude that her conversation with Nick was a live one brought a burst of The Light.

The sun shone brightly that morning as The Illuminator combated holiday traffic, preparing to move locations, shuttling – back and forth from the house – to what would be the arena of Gorgalo's debut. She'd planned every click and detail. Pain drug supply. Rations. Made a stop to make sure she'd have sufficient coaxial cable for all the cameras. Another stop to buy more gauze, tape, and disinfectant.

Back at the house she moved fast, stowing her procedure trays and smaller surgical appliances in the motor home. The tailgate lift came in handy while loading weightier items: the portable respirator, tanks of medical gasses, and broadcast equipment.

At her computer she checked every remote surveillance cam, and then installed and tested a few more in and around her house.

The last of her computer work was crucial: to make sure the files that mattered would not be missed by a certain diligent but aging detective.

Like her own body, this house and its contents were transitory. But not The Illuminator's trophies. She removed her armor from its velvet wraps, carefully placing the silk-wrapped Book of Souls in the pocket she'd sewn into the interior of her breastplate. Then she re-wrapped everything in the velvet and laid the bundle on the motor home's passenger seat.

Before bringing her patient aboard to transport him, Cassandra checked the vehicle's every interior surface for anything that might snag skin and complicate the grafting. All was smooth and fair. Then she got the engine running and ran the heat.

With Gorgalo bound in the wheelchair and loaded, she ratcheted the nylon webbing straps tight to keep the wheel chair stable.

Then she went back to manage stagecraft. A garden hose and pressure washer awaited in the basement. With these she misted the house's every exterior surface. Then she moved to the yard and gardens. Soon every wall, shrub, and object on the property glimmered wet.

Anticipating prismed surfaces once it froze, she went inside one last time to say goodbye to her brother's house.

In the living room she took a framed photo from the mantelpiece to gaze at her brother, standing beside his friend Gary Boother at the caverns they had so often visited.

Although transitory, sadness filled her in the prospect of leaving this place. Since the endless hours spent with MorpAesthetica in designing Gorgalo's enhancements, had she begun to get comfortable, and after that Brian's house had become The Illuminator's home.

She set down her brother Brian's photo.

My brave little birds, she thought. They had one more role to play.

She went to the basement for Nek-tar, life's blood for her little assistants, which she'd been careful to order through third parties, using freight forwarders to relay each carton, so the purchases could not be traced.

She found her three birds perched in the surgical suite, still as porcelain. When she turned on the halogen work lights the false sunrise awakened the birds. Their hunger impulses as well. Each flitted in anticipation, advanced and retreated in defense of its glass feeder while she poured the sweet, red juice.

She knew the police profilers would now expect her, by this point, to be "disorganized." So with care not to alarm the birds she set the clinic in convincing disarray.

Then before leaving, she filled her mouth with the ruby syrup, choking back tears. Now, when she offered, all three

– Bolivar, Antonio Nariňo, and even Cortez – would whip
and whiz to take nectar directly from her lips. In the way of
goodbye, each one drank the sweet red fluid this way. "Gotta
fly," Cassandra said to her small, dear friends.

Her overnight bag and laptop waited by the door. Her
pocket contained a brass tube that contained the third and
last manuscript, telling of Dr. Gorgalo's extracurricular
surgery on the boy named Timmy. She also packed some
basic accessories – along with stage makeup and the bug-eye
sunglass she'd worn to the Dedication of Goddard's new
police headquarters. When Cassandra picked up the bag, set
to go, she shivered, chilled by the drafts now throughout her
brother's house.

Before driving off toward the caverns that would be the
stage for Gorgalo's Basilisk spectacle, Cassandra made a last
few swipes to wet the house with the pressure washer. After
stashing the equipment she returned to the motor home.
Removing her Book from its silk wrappings she felt new
power radiate from within the tiny volume. The strength of
it far greater since she had sewn in a page marked George
Roache.
As the motor home containing Gorgalo sat idling, she
faced her brother's house. Balancing the Book of Souls upon
her two palms, she raised it to the level of her mouth and
gently blew across its leather bindings.
Later, the newspapers would remark:
"Temperatures in Goddard that day were well above
freezing . . .the house, yard, and even the Cheyenne pickup
truck in the driveway were discovered mysteriously glazed
with a thick coat of ice that brought down the massive front-
yard oak in splinters. "

CHAPTER 12

The Forensics lab at Goddard Police Headquarters was a boiler room of moving staff, ringing phones, and squealing faxes.

By the time Nick got there that morning, Forensic Specialist Bailey had dug up a decent pile on Brian Shockly and his sister. Accounts. Travel. Everything Brian had owned, bought, or sold. The house in town his parents had left after their death. Even library loans.

Bailey explained to Nick, "The older sister Cassandra Shockly's been on and off the grid."

When Canon Nailor arrived, Forensic Specialist Bailey began launching the evidence to a data wall.

As Nick, Nailor, and the chief stood scanning these records, the Specialist provided soundtrack:

Cassandra Shockly, a.k.a., The Illuminator. Volunteer enlistment as a Licensed Registered Nurse in 1970. Joined the 30th Medical brigade and then assigned to the 67th Combat Support Hospital in Pleiku, where she's reported to have developed a solid hand assisting surgery. With an honorable discharge in 1973, Cassandra Shockly had been awarded a Meritorious Service Medal.

After that had been some moonlighting at local hospitals and clinics, mostly fill-in work for permanent staff that didn't last more than a month or two. Then volunteer assignments at a host of Missionary clinics throughout Latin America.

"Now to follow the money," Bailey said. He launched graphs and spreadsheets, showing a trail to her deceased brother's Brian's accounts that had stared last August, a month before he died. "Its some sort of reverse-laundering," Bailey said, tracing the money trail to a Medellin drug lord named El Ponderoso who had also been under investigation for human trafficking until a couple of years ago when that activity had abruptly stopped. "As of yesterday she zeroed every balance and the trial vanishes."

"With the help of Professor Nailor, we've dipped into Quantico's intel," Bailey further explained. "And since 2004 The Illuminator's used El Ponderoso's drug money to support her operations." To the screen the Specialist launched transaction after transaction for the purchase of medical machinery from small to large: surgical instruments; syringes and bandaging; electric hospital bed, an Autoclave; even a portable Ventilator. Cameras and broadcast equipment. Everything sent to a re-shipping service that had itself been under investigation for interstate transportation of firearms.

"Only thing keeping the doors open is a deal the proprietor cut with the FBI as informant on another case," Bailey explained. "Of course right now the Feds are only minimally cooperating. But once we catch a break they'll be knocking on Chief Robertson's door."

When Bailey cleared the screen the only thing that remained was a photograph. Cassandra Shockly. The Illuminator. It made Nick's stomach clench.

His face became that of somebody who had spoken to a dead man.

"You OK?" the chief was asking him.

The detective took a breath and explained. That day interviewing Boother he'd been shown a photo of a heavily bearded Brian Shockly. The face on Bailey's screen now was clearly that of a much younger Brian. A boy. It didn't make any sense.

The same – but . . .

This, Nick explained in astonishment, was also the face of the boy he'd helped install the **For Sale** sign across the street from his house the morning before he'd dedicated the new Headquarters.

Then Bailey clicked to display another photo of Cassandra Shockly wearing surgical scrubs, holding a small girl with bandaged face, furnished by a clinic she'd served in Latin America.

Nailor, the Chief, and Nick stared at the screen. Finally Bailey said, "Cosmetically, she's turned herself into her brother Brian."

"And financially," Nailor concluded.

"To relieve him in battles," added Nick. "She's coming in as backup . . . as the stone angel." From memory Nick recited a line he'd seen etched on Brian Shockly's headstone, "'Angel drifted groundward. . .'"

The chief now looked questioningly at Nick. "So then how do we explain The Illuminator's fascination with you?"

"All I know is that its got something to do with not protecting Jim Stevens as a kid – her brother Brian must've told her something. . ." Nick shook his head and explained. "She's holding me accountable – for Jim's death, or his abuse. Maybe both. I wanted to get Nailor's take on this. Maybe she's blaming the system, but sending the message through me."

"Because she knows it'll be delivered, Nick. Your reliability's well known," the chief's tone conciliatory.

"This should help." Nailor asked Bailey to call up a series of emails that Cassandra had exchanged with Brian.

Certain phrases in Cassandra's emails were highlighted, such as "**set things right**," and "**those bastards**." And the referent of the phrase "those bastards" were listed as well: Allengri, Roache, and Dr. Gorgalo.

"I performed some textual analysis," Professor Nailor explained, "Cassandra and her bother had a pact. Brian had made attempts on his own life. Cassandra held the perpetrators of his abuse accountable: Allengri, Roache and Roache. Their pact was that in the event of his death, whatever its cause, she would avenge him."

"Causing Brian to take his own life to speed up the revenge," the chief said.

"And a psychotic break for Cassandra." Nailor put in. "I've consulted with a Forensic Psychiatrist I often use to create profiles in the course of my textual sleuthing for the FBI. Facing trauma so profound, Cassandra Shockly created the parallel identity The Illuminator. She displays all the symptoms of Dissociative Identity Disorder, when a person displays multiple distinct identities – in this case, it seems from all the evidence, with Cassandra subservient to The Illuminator. Now The Illuminator fixates on Nick, through association with Jim Stevens," Nailor explained, adding, "That's the extent of any *rational* explanation."

The chief put in, "Almost as if Nick is next in line to take the heat."

Nailor explained, "The line Nick recited from Brian's epitaph, "*Angel drifted groundward . . .*" suggests the belief she's acting as messenger of God, returning to the scene of the crime to ensure that history won't repeat itself. That she chose Nick might be merely because, figuratively speaking, he was closest in his link to Officer Stevens. She believes she's passing a baton, of sorts, to Nick. Gambling he'd become sympathetic, on behalf of a fallen policeman."

As Nick thought of Jim's suffering at the hand of Allengri, Roache, and the cardiologist Dr. Gorgalo, he had trouble with the Professor's categorization of The Illuminator as psychotic. At the same time, he thought, to stick anything into another human being without their permission – a scalpel or otherwise – was the act of a first-class psycho. All he said was, "I need to finish this. How can I get a fix on her location?"

Nailor had tapped into his contacts with the State Department, the results of which Bailey now used to fill his data wall. He indicated a photo: "This is the clinic she last served, in Medellin. Gone since last August." He advanced the frame. "This one's her last known residence down there. Colombia's DAS Departamento Administrativo de Securidad has a team of agents on standby to go in at State Department say-so."

"Before we come to that – what's the media spin looking like?" the chief asked.

Bailey now clicked through video clips. "Here's what the world has to say." A daytime talk show doing a show called "Old Scouts We Know and Love." *Vanity Fair* wanting to interview the surgeon-messenger. A Hollywood director planning a movie called *The Illuminator*.

Nailor then stepped forward. Contacts at Homeland Security were tracking chatter related to any events for December 28. Nothing precise – but one set of filtrations had been interpreted to suggest that The Illuminator was planning to stream presentation of the Basilisk live on the Internet.

Nick was thinking about his talk with that survivor back at the Flying Yankee. "What about the brother? Brian?" Nick asked. "I interviewed another Youth Camper. A pal of Brian

Shockley's. Name Gary Boother. The two of them had been planning some kind of road trip – out west and back through Canada. Told me '*We had passports and everything.*'"

"Bailey," Nick remarked, "Get me passport activity for Brian Shockly."

In moments, the embarrassing news: a Brian Shockly who had resided at 8601 West in Goddard, Massachusetts, had entered the country through Boston Logan one week before Allengri had been abducted.

"Before offing himself, Brian must have mailed his passport to Cassandra," Nick said. "That pact."

U.S. Customs dates of entry for the passport bearer jived: the medical machinery purchases started two days later.

Nick pondered. *Has to be a place to store it all. A place to work.*

Chief Robertson told Nailor, "There's enough here for a go-ahead to DAS in Medellin. Nick, until this gets cleared up I'm posting a couple of uniforms at your house."

But when Professor Nailor and Chief Robertson looked around, Nick was already on his way across town.

CHAPTER 13

The vast expanses
of Wiggins Caverns echo with the sound of the breathing machine that keeps Dr. Gorgalo alive.

The Illuminator has crushed cartilage, then used
this pulp to form a Basilisk's beak. While that heals
she'll commence in building the tail.

Masked and scrubbed, Cassandra Shockly stood
over her Subject. Her skilled and sensitive hand gauged pressure applied to the scalpel to ensure proper depth of cut, as
she sliced along the line marked in felt tip along Gorgalo's
leg, toward the ball of the ankle, not lifting the scalpel's black
stone tip until finishing the cut at the extremity of his foot.

So sharp. Little blood rose to the incision's edge. She
clamped the dermal layer and stripped it back. Now she could
trace and then part each muscle and tendon that wrapped
the leg bones.

When finished, Gorgalo's hard parts would end at the
pelvis. Every leg bone would go. She'd leave the toenails attached and had even started a protein supplement to enhance
their growth to end the tail with a scaly, stegosaurian finish.

Now she hooked the gastrocnemius muscle with a
gloved finger and followed it, down along the tendon to its

termination on the bone. With the other hand she brought the scalpel. Made the cut.

Next the calcaneal tendon, his Achilles. Cut it. Next the solieus. Then the flexor digitorum longus. Cut. Cut. Wrap it all in skin to bind with catgut.

CHAPTER 14

A short crow bar concealed in his great coat, Nick parked in front of Brian Shockly's house. The palest remnants of sun lit a glaze that covered the house and its environs like a gold metallic glass. Including the shit-beat Chevy truck Nick had seen at the vacant lot across from his house the snowy morning installing that **For Sale** sign.

Thanks detective.

The completeness of the home's glassy surface – entrances sealed – the glazed-over pickup truck, Brian's truck – plus the wreckage of the ice-laden front yard oak tree – made it look as if some malevolent ice storm had swept in and frozen the place in time.

Carefully Nick made his way. Following small lug-sole tracks he now recognized, he found the pressure washer and water hose stashed in a trashcan.

Around back he found the walkout basement. Through a crack between jamb and door he could see the deadbolt had not been set. *Twenty-five years old at least. But still, a tract house is a tract house.* Nick laid a bet with himself that the jamb hadn't been shimmed properly.

When he slid the tip of the crow bar between the edge of the metal door and frame, the flimsy jamb flexed like rubber. A little more pressure on the bar and the bolt cleared the striker plate. Silently inside in less than thirty seconds.

The place had to be one of Jewell's early spec houses, Nick figured.

The basement was littered with empty shipping crates. Across the room he saw the Autoclave. Shelves of stainless sterilization trays. No dust on these surfaces.

Inside the Autoclave was dry and cool. Lined up on shelves he saw quart-sized plastic bottles filled with ruby-red fluid. Their labels read **Nek-Tar**. Nick heard himself say, "Hummingbird food."

The lair of The Illuminator. Silently, he ascended the cellar stairs.

Reaching a closed door at the top the detective heard voices coming from another part of the house. He listened, opened a crack, then swung the door open to find only a sparsely furnished home. Silently, he made way toward the voices.

The decor struck Nick as a mix of Brian Shockly and somebody else. There were posters of Jim Morrison and Bob Marley tacked up on the paneling. In the kitchen, chipped laminate and mismatched chairs. The hallway, root beer-colored shag carpet.

The improvised library set up in the living room marked a contrast – what seemed recent additions: an odd but expensive-looking lamp; framed drawings and sketches; Illuminated framed manuscripts like the ones in Graham's shop; several library shelves half-stacked with volumes; partially unpacked book boxes on the floor beside them.

Works of art leaned on shelves, against walls. Many of the objects left half-wrapped in newspaper – old friends of whoever had been impersonating Brian Shockly. Nick recognized these artifacts as the small comforts of culture that might've saved the occupant, Cassandra Shockly, from feeling alone in the world and served to define her identity – until insanity had taken over completely, as The Illuminator.

On a small worktable beside the window he saw the tools of Illumination – a pen rest, several styluses lined up in an almost military precision. They reminded Nick of surgical instruments. But over the past days he'd learned to read these signs.

Beside the styluses, the mortar and pestle his quarry had used in grinding gall to make ink. And in the center of the table, a page Nick immediately recognized, the last missing pages from Jim Stevens' journal.

He read:

This time when Gorgalo took me camping, at the last minute when we were leaving, he said we had to pick up another kid Timmy–seven or eight years old. Timmy was a patient, Gorgalo said . . ..

He had to tear himself from reading it – when again from down that hallway – came the voices.

Gripping the crow bar Nick moved toward them. Down a hallway. He stopped at a door where he heard a man and woman in heated conversation.

Crow bar raised beside his head at the ready, he leaned back from the jamb, took a breath, and kicked in the door.

Once inside he saw only the signs of hasty retreat. A makeshift recovery room in chaos: electric hospital bed half-stripped, a leaning intravenous pole, even a wall-mounted television that flickered the blue-white shadows of a daytime soap, its volume turned up loud.

Then the three hummingbirds – whizzing and darting – *at me* – defending their space.

He stepped through the chaos and switched off the set. Saw a steel basin on the floor filled with dried bloody bandages.

With the birds darting at the head of this intruder, Nick ducked his head, checked the closet – shelves of hospital whites and neatly folded blue scrubs. Drawers filled with bandaging, tubes of salves, ointments. When he picked up a sealed package of suture – *same dark blue* – he could almost see the gruesome letters embroidered upon the skin of Roache and Allengri – the three birds again darting and diving on him.

Retreating to The Illuminator's worktable, Nick read the page from Jim's journal in its entirety:

This time when Gorgalo took me camping, at the last minute when we were leaving, he said we had to pick up another kid Timmy–seven or eight years old. Timmy was a heart surgery patient, Gorgalo said, and it was follow-up support to visit this way, to camp out weekends with the doctor. I met his mother at their motel. The first night camping Gorgalo had me sleep in the tent. The second night it was Timmy in the tent, and I could hear, it was the same with him as Gorgalo did to me. Then the next day I saw the fresh scar on Timmy's chest when he changed the large dressing–I remember could see the small metal staple-stitches all in a row. He had the heart surgery three weeks before. He told me his mother didn't have money or insurance–Gorgalo was the hospital administrator. He operated for free. Gorgalo called those staples Timmy's 'zipper.'

Looking on from Cassandra Shockly's computer desk was a small, yellowed stone bust of Albert Schweitzer. Beside it stood an empty wine stem with a dot of dried red at the base of its bowl.

Nick took note of the volumes scattered about: King's Why We Can't Wait, Montesquiew's Spirit of the Laws, Kant's Critique of Aesthetic Judgment, and Bolivar's Decreto de Guerra a Muerta. Then, standing before the mantle, he could not help but admire the framed progressive fetal studies, etched with charcoal in The Illuminators' hand.

He next read a framed certificate of appreciation to Cassandra from Face the Children Foundation, for providing free reconstructive surgery to kids with birth defects in developing countries.

In examining this house Nick felt a confusing combination of admiration and regret, as if witnessing a mind's devolution.

In a corner of the room he came to an Illumination on rag stock, the Oath of Hippocrates, in what he guessed was The Illuminator's younger, less disciplined calligraphic hand. The bottom of the leaf bore attribution to the Vatican Library.

Nick read aloud, his words filling the silent house:
"I will bring no stain upon the learning of the medical art. Neither will I give poison to anybody though asked to do so, nor will I suggest such a plan . . ."

Tales Cassandra Shockly had at one time told herself.

The computer's screen saver whirling calm-colored spirals then caught Nick's eye.
Search her drives.

He sat at her computer, and like hearing a confession, followed links she'd left so obvious, leading to her several web cams.

Nick recognized Roache's house. What had been Gorgalo's – now a charred and frozen field of black cinders that denied engagement with even the sun's slightest ray. Another house, glass and steel, framed by tree limbs which he recognized as the house of Richard Allengri, the camera obviously located in the woods behind it. Another cam displayed only a dimly lit stone wall, perhaps the inside of a stone room.

A cave? Cavern, Boother had said. Like that story of the Spider Miracle . . .

What Nick saw on the fourth camera brought a start. It was his own home, viewed from the front. No. . .from the vacant lot across the street. Suddenly the connection was unmistakable: *that kid installing the For Sale sign. His face!* **Her face!**

Nick searched though directories that contained photos of Allengri and Roache. Their faces in different stages of transformation. The procedures on Roache. A gallery of horrors. As The Illuminator's moral scales.

Next he opened the directory: Animations.

He placed the cursor, ready to click on the file entitled: GorgaloFaceBodyMorph. Yet some instinct held him back; his index finger arrested in the air above the mouse button – part-way to making it click. He imagined The Illuminator – preparing, replaying, perfecting – this sequence. Savoring it. How many times had she tapped this same button? What thoughts had traveled through her mind?

Revenge? Or torture?

With all surgeries performed under anesthesia – painless, save for torment that came by the mirror, Nick wondered whether he might now be the subject of torture in witnessing this?

He had to admire her sense of theater: the glaze of ice on this house . . . Jim's journal page left on the table. . . even that he'd so easily discovered these files had to be a phase in The Illuminator's seduction.

Given all the history, he was vulnerable: a candidate to sympathize with her vengeance and he knew it. She'd even likely view him as a potential accomplice. And at that moment, these words came out of Nick's mouth: "God help me, Dr. Gorgalo, it would take someone as sick as *you* to bring *me* to take pleasure in viewing the Hell of this."

And he clicked.

The MorphAestetica logo flashed, then changed to a stopwatch icon, with the onscreen message: "loading morph sequence."

Then Nick saw – just as The Illuminator had planned: Gorgalo's lips swelling into a mass of flesh that gradually stretched outward, then turned downward into a crook that would pass for the beak of the Basilisk. Next the doctor's arms drew slowly away from his sides while from between wrists and armpits unfurled flaps of skin. The arms continued to lift as the sequence progressed and the lobes of skin stretched further, becoming leathery and dentate, now like parts of a kite to permanently link wrists and hands to hips to complete the wings the color and shape of a fleshy pterodactyl.

The legs lost all form we know as human and the two became one, tapering into tail of a serpent.

Nick wiped sweat from his forehead, took out his phone and tapped **chief**.

The image rotated, until the eyes of the Basilisk stared straight into Nick's.

When he heard Robertson's voice Nick said, "You can call off the troops in Colombia. And you better get hold of a search warrant for Brian Shockly's house and get a team over here."

Sitting before The Illuminator's computer screen looking at Dr. Gorgalo turned Basilisk, Nick thought he whiffed the musk of decay.

To the chief, he added, "And find somebody to come take care of these hummingbirds." Then he hung up, bathed in sweat, never before having before been so consumed by the case. A seasoned   detective who hadn't even noticed he'd missed Christmas.

CHAPTER 15

The motor home sat parked a quarter mile from Wiggins Caverns, out of sight on a dirt road, camouflaged beneath cut pine branches.

A garland of bats had been added to the Caverns' usual billboard overlooking the Interstate, with the words *Happy Holidays* in a cartoon-bubble emerging from the ghastly sketch of the corkscrewed angel-demon.

Drivers passing this billboard would be engrossed in the demands of merrymaking. Unaware of The Illuminator within, farthest from the cavern's public entrance: deep bowels of the Earth, blind to the sun.

The Illuminator had chosen the place in remembrance of Brian's spelunking trips.

Workmen would be off duty till after New Years. It was a big job; stalactites had begun parting the caves' ceilings, now a potential hazard, due to the years of temperature flux in heating the Caverns for tourists' comfort.

By now throughout the rooms and passages that made up the attraction's haunting collections, the eroding tooth-like formations had been clothed in wire mesh, awaiting a sprayed-on concrete coat. Others had already received their gunnite finish. And interspersed among these rebuilt stalactites, the ceilings had been decorated with roughed-out Styrofoam oddities: ghoulish faces and gobblinesque creatures, each awaiting a final concrete shell.

The Illuminator toiled within the Cavern's largest vaulted space – the Chamber of Horrors – surrounded by a spectacle of petrified wild animals and warring wax gladiators. Over them presided a towering colossus in its final stages of construction: Lucifer's Turn.

At the base of this blood-curdling figure, a respirator exchanged machine-driven rhythm for the soul's work – each lisp, pull and reset another breath to sustain Dr. Gorgalo's recovery from cartilage harvest.

Beneath the machine noise was the sound of off-season trickle, the River Styx, which coiled and wound through each of the Caverns' various chambers and features, marked by the signs she had calligraphed herself: *Water Sleeps, but Enemy is Sleepless.*

The Illuminator had warmed the place, lighting propane *Dragon* heaters left on site by construction workers. She'd always kept Brian's camp axe in the motor home, and had today dressed its bit on a hard Arkansas stone to split kindling from an ample wood supply beside the Chamber of Horrors' huge stone hearth.

The room now flickered with firelight as The Illuminator worked to fill a filigree-sculpted vessel in brilliant white marble, its broad yet shallow bowl perched on a wineglass pedestal. An integral prop in her specially-configured Chamber of Horrors: as central feature, The Font stood out before the mostly-finished feature Lucifer's Turn.

She had chosen this vessel for its particular history. Stolen it from a museum.

Oh Font.

Exalted Cup.

Origin of The Styx.

A moment in waiting.

In the way of Contrapasso with this vessel, The Illuminator planned to wash, very literally, the sin of Dr. Gorgalo.

When Detective Giaccone arrived he would find this climax of The Illuminator's catechism in the unsleeping waters of The Font.

Lucifer's Turn, a serpentine, colossus stands the height of the great cavern, floor to ceiling: It modeled the angel Lucifer, in the moment of being Transmogrified by God into Satan. Its immensity rises as a spiral out of Cavern floor's very stone.

The creature's flowing robes of black and white coil too – from base to shoulders – appearing as opposing rivers: scintillante white and light-abasing black. Wherever these drapes parted, they revealed along the creature's corkscrewed axis, the metal rungs and spokes of the devil's purposely exposed support framework, in the form of a gleaming double-helix.

Up high, the figure's great sneering face and head seemed to float high above the Chamber's floor, bound by filaments to the room's circular glass ocular – a leaded glass skylight that during the day admits sun, and by night, starlight. From a face of tortured arrogance, the partly-constructed fiend's crystalline eyes already catch and intensify the Chamber's firelight like immense sizzling embers.

On the helix framework within this creature's garments, The Illuminator has set staging planks in the way of a concealed and level bivouac. From this promontory she will direct The Goddard Drama's final act.

Now dressed for rough work in overalls, Cassandra struck a fist along the Chamber's walls until she heard a hollow. She dug out putty with her pocket knife, then backed out screws, reached inside and opened a valve. She heard water. Saw it spill, through a sluiceway she'd improvised, that deposited these waters into The Font. When she opened the valve further, the trickling sound became a gush.

She moved nearer, stood over The Font and looked down into it, watching it fill, the water swirling in circles, currents ever spinning from bottom to top, refracted firelight lacing the vessel's white marble sides with golden, iridescent threads.

The Font was perfect. The room's crowning touch. Vessel of her Magnum Opus.

She'd heard the story of the Baptismal Font the poet

Dante had shattered with a sledge hammer to save a drowning child. *Her* version, here, would be constructive. Instructive. In *this* vessel would mix histories more pressing. Once her surgery on Gorgalo was complete.

Once filled, water poured forth over the vessel's spillway lip, caught by a marble sluice – pitched very slightly toward the Chamber wall. There another trough she'd improvised exited through a pipe to sustain the underground river's twists.

Midway between the Font and the fireplaces' great blaze lay another of the place's attractions – the Heart Stone – an altar-like rock, its edges carved by time and the waters of some river into the anatomical shape of a human heart. The Illuminator's operating table and surgical theater, center stage.

Dr. Gorgalo lays there cocooned in wraps, suspended by narcotics' gracious filaments.

Soon his essence will be introduced to the waters for the Font, forever stirred, eternally to sleep.

The Illuminator planned next to set up equipment for the broadcast. But first she opens her laptop to play back footage from the cameras she'd installed in her brother's house, making certain the visiting detective has made arrangements for her three strong little birds.

BOOK IV

CHAPTER 1

With media now surrounding Brian's house Nick felt like a hostage. Last thing he'd seen on the computer screen was himself, from above, on a camera the Illuminator had placed – apparently just for him.

Minutes later the chief was by his side, search warrant in hand, scolding Nick for the break-in. But the gleam in his eye said otherwise.

Then Nick found himself drawn -- his eyes drifting to the photo: Brian Shockly and Gary Boother, in front of stone outcroppings that appeared to be a cave, reminding Nick of that image on the palimpsest. St. John the Baptist standing guard on the Day of Innocents. The Spider Miracle. Quite a sharp contrast between that image and the Giotto bas relief that made Brian's grave marker so bleak.

Then he put it together. Boother and Shockly, spelunking in the Caverns. The caverns were being renovated as tourist destination. That billboard -- advertising a new Chamber of Horrors.

"Fish & Game doesn't do hummingbirds," one uniformed officer was telling the chief.

Nick set the photograph back on the mantle, took out his cell phone and told the patrolman, "Let me try calling someone." The proprietor of Urban Birds' voice sounded panicked when Nick got him on the phone. But once he heard the request, Siggi Kraus couldn't hide his excitement, "Of course, detective! I'd be delighted to have such specimens as my guests." Kraus would leave immediately and care for the birds "until something can be arranged."

Canon Nailor intervened when he heard this. He had a colleague at Brauser College who'd be happy to lend the use of his aviary. The decision was made final.

Good thing, thought Nick. He had a cavern to visit.

CHAPTER 2

After final snips and stitches on Dr. Gorgalo, The Illuminator stripped off slickened latex gloves and let them drop to the cave's sand floor. Through the Chamber's great glass ocular above, she could see that day had given over to night.

Then she practiced Capoeira – exercising the art of approach – acrobatic contests with danger, gravity, and leverage. Her muscles answered these tests, endorphins bubbling through her, ready for the confrontation she knew was coming on fast.

To fortify for the conflict she prepared freeze-dried rations on a small propane camp stove. Then sat on the sand floor to take nourishment, surrounded by the Caverns' silent legions of wax warriors, knowing this meal might well be her last. It was a fate she shouldered happily, after what happened to her parents when she'd taken flight with them, and then all Brian had suffered in her absence – Penance due for inabilities in saving any one of them.

As she ate she reviewed The Work. From its beginnings, she had never swayed, never questioned her Commitment. She was now nearing Curandera Rosario's equal; only the jungle had become different. Here in this Chamber, eating field rations amidst a host of wax soldiers, she imagined herself seated on the straw and dirt floor of Rosario's *choza*, accepted as an equal with the other Chibcha children.

The curandera told tales at night. Blood-curdling. Rural myths and traditional stories designed to discourage children from straying.

The legend of *Patasola*, the hideous "one foot," who appeared vampire-like to male hunters or loggers in the wilds.

Or *Hobre Caimen*, the alligator man who appears on St. Sebastian's day to hunt human victims like a werewolf.

Mohan, a supernatural being who lay in wait within the barren forest lands, able to manipulate matter and souls of the dead beyond human comprehension.

There were many stories. Each more chilling than the last.

Rosario ended each of these late-night sessions by reciting collected rules:

Never let your house run out of sugar. Or salt. Or you will have bad relations and make mistakes.

If you keep at least a little money in your pocket through the midnight of New Years Eve, you will not lack in the coming year.

A *mosca*, housefly, in the house means company will come. If the *mosca* is big and fat, the guest wants to borrow.

The one who sets their wallet, coin, or paper money upon any bed will come to illness.

If you encounter the *mariposa negra*, the black butterfly, expect a death.

Those who take their own lives must complete their task of existence anyway, but with more difficulty in the body of another.

Cassandra broke from her daydream, washed out her mess kit, drank bottled water, and then tossed her sleeping bag up onto her scaffolded nest within Lucifer's robes. She easily swung her weight up the series of metal rungs. At the top heaved herself onto the deck. There she rolled out the bag, perfectly positioned to monitor her patient, who lay recovering, restrained upon the altar of the Heart Stone.

Each night since moving operations to the Caverns, she lit candles, making the area surrounding Gorgalo like a cathedral shrine. She imagined each of the fragile kindled wicks as one of the Innocents, each tiny flame another prayer for healing.

Here she would hold vigil for her pursuer, in full regalia of The Illuminator.

She unpacked her armor from its purple velvet wraps.

Removed her shirt and donned each piece: the brilliant breast plate – kissed by firelight, its gold coining blinking back flamelight against the Chamber's shadowed expanse. Beneath her armor, held tight to her breast, the Book of Souls.

She adorned herself with the matching gauntlets – shimmering the promise to protect the powerful muscles and veins of her wrists. She put on the armlets that would keep her biceps free from the cut of any foe. And the anklets that would guard the tops of her Achilles tendons and the tops of feet she kept bare for fighting.

Last, she concealed a small hand mirror at the ready, within her breast plate, and then tucked the Taser inside a belt compartment. The big syringe lay close, upon the platform.

Resplendent, ready for battle, she stood and surveyed the Chamber below – mentally mapping tactical positions – the archway through which Nick would make his entrance – the path he would take once inside The Chamber. Where she would face him.

BOOK IV

CHAPTER 3

Robertson and Canon Nailor sat waiting in the chief's office. Beyond the two men, nearer the window, sat another man. From the cut of clothes and cropped hair, Nick bet FBI.

It was no time to make acquaintances. He told the chief, "Set me up." But before he got the words out, what he saw on the Robertson's desk made his throat almost shut. A manila folder, turned face-down.

Not another case.

Nick was almost relieved to hear Canon Nailor issue warnings. It had all been too easy, the professor argued: Candy wrappers. The Illuminated manuscript. The palimpsest message beneath the manuscript's skin. The Old Scout piece. Tiny stones embedded in Campmaster Roache that had led Nick directly to the angel at Hillside Cemetery. And now, Wiggins Caverns. All of them come-hither clues.

Maybe stalking Nick replaced some psychodrama she'd played out trying to fix her brother Brian, the professor summed up.

Nick fired back he wasn't worried. If she'd wanted, he'd

already be dead: the **For Sale** sign. Breaking into his house to steal journal pages. And then to place that painting depicting the Saint's denial. All these things proved it.

The chief's hand moved to the manila folder.

A look of recognition on the chief's face suggested his friend's vigilance had not gone unnoticed.

"She's leading you!" Nailor warned. "Don't you get it, Nick? Wiggins Caverns is her ultimate 'trap rock!'"

Then Braxton Jewell walked into the room. "Bailey said you wanted me."

Nick was astounded to see the chief address the Chairman more directly than he'd ever before witnessed. "Go take a seat in the hallway, Brax."

A patrolman who'd come in on Jewell's heels placed a hand on the Chairman's shoulder to turn him gently, but firmly.

Jewell contemptuously shrugged off the touch.

But the patrolman stuck.

"What's going on here?" he demanded of the chief. Then Jewell faced the agent seated by the window. "And who the Hell're you?"

"Agent Connolly. FBI." The man flashed credentials and stood.

"About time something's getting done around here!"

"Its not what you think, Ed." The chief's triumphant smirk now unmistakable. Voice, more crooning than usual.

The professor threw a knowing glance toward the thin dossier on the chief's desk, then perhaps the ghost of a smile toward the chief, and then toward the man seated at the window – who almost smiled in return.

When the chief turned over the dossier, Nick could recognize Nailor's handwriting on the tab. **Braxton Jewell, Real Estate Fraud.**

The combination of these set Jewell's eyes aflair.

"Assist agent Connolly," Chief Robertson told the patrolman – all business. But he added, "And make sure Mr. Jewell gets a brand new holding cell."

"This way . . . " said the patrolman, leading a fuming Braxton Jewell. Connolly a step behind him reaching into his beltline for a set of cuffs to make the arrest.

It took only seconds for Nick to put it together. Jewell's scam. Bailey had picked up the thread and now the chief had pounced. Hereafter Goddard's departed would be spared eviction from Hillside Cemetery, in the event Jewell's little scheme failed and ended in foreclosure.

What Nick *didn't* know was that the chief had cut a deal with the Feds. Hearing details about downed officer Jim Stevens it was agreed they'd take the collar for Jewell. The chief would then repay Nick for his troubles by granting that he move in on The Illuminator. The detective would want it this way, and after thirty-five years' service had certainly earned the right to decide on safety issues – regardless of the professor's warnings. The chief also knew Nick would never have asked for these arrangements, knowing what he did about the chief's commitment to serve Pinecrest's Headmaster.

"I owe it to Jim . . .," Nick looked at the chief, and then at Nailor. He tried to explain, "and I promised The Headmaster at Pinecrest Academy to deliver clean house. . ."

A nod from Canon Nailor. Without another word the chief reached down and pulled out a desk drawer, then slid Nick's revolver across his desk.

Nick caught the bluing-bare .38 snub-nose and slid it into his jacket pocket. Then he drew his detective shield from his wallet, slid it across the desk toward the Chief, opened the office door and walked out.

BOOK IV

CHAPTER 4

A diaphanous net unwound itself around the night in knots of varied brilliance. Beneath these twinklings Nick hurtled down a lonely stretch of highway toward Wiggins Caverns. He was thinking of the horrific video he'd witnessed on The Illuminator's work station. Gorgalo's face and body – melting, reshaping. The crooked beak and bat-like wings forming like magic. Each time Nick blinked now, the Basilisk loomed large as his windshield.

He decided he would go in immediately after midnight. That would make it December 28.

Catch her sleeping. Or in some ceremony of vengeance.

After passing the billboard for Wiggins Cavern, the detective exited the freeway for an all night diner. He wanted to be strong. So from a picture menu ordered the Grand Slam breakfast: eggs, sausage, hash browns – even a cup of coffee.

Awaiting his food Nick overhead a radio program the short-order cook had turned up loud, at the request of patrons seated at the lunch counter.

The talk show host was taking callers. Every one rattling on about The Illuminator crimes.

As Nick dug in, a caller was saying: "I can't understand! Why is it that plastic surgery is considered a luxury when it makes some people beautiful? But a crime when it helps kids recognize monsters?"

There was a commercial break.

After the break another voice started off: "Someone should give The Illuminator a medal. I mean, if women aren't allowed to choose the fates of their bodies, why shouldn't the same for some men?"

The parking lot for Wiggins Caverns was black and empty, except for Nick's Police Interceptor. He sat solitary, motionless, anonymous as dark. His breath fogged the windows.

A search of Brian Shockly's house had turned up repair receipts for an older model motor home, still titled to Brain's now-deceased father. *Probably running it on stolen plates.* Her means of abducting and moving patients, Nick figured. Too smart to park it here.

At midnight he stood facing a waxy corrugated sign that was wired to the Caverns' iron gate. **Closed for Remodeling. Keep out.**

On the ground before the door, he saw a glint. A case hardened chain and padlock. Severed clean by bolt cutters.

One hand on the chilled steel door, something made him pause and look up.

And then to hold the gaze and let his eyes adjust.

Brilliant, almost close enough to touch, he saw Orion – the hunter's belt a shimmering chain of diamonds.

Nick drew his gun. The door's rusted hinges whined

nasal when he pushed it. *Slow.* To move the iron door slowly enough to avoid the sound, his feet were numb by the time he had swung it enough to get past.

By the thin, filtered starlight cast into this entryway, Nick could make out a ticket window, its torn green shade gapped and sagging. Stenciled across the fabric were the words "Sorry, Closed."

A feeling of eyes on him – cruel eyes that pulled at his arrival from the window shade's darkened rips and gaps. He couldn't see the camera she had placed so carefully – in fact would not notice any of them. *Nick was thinking: Focus. Let the eyes adjust.*

Camouflaged amidst the robes of Lucifer's Turn, on her laptop The Illuminator watched his approach. *Good, the Aspirant is engaged.* She looked out over the Chamber's wax gladiators, felt connected to these silent Legions, and then at Gorgalo upon the Heart Stone where Nick could soon witness the Basilisk's newskinned wings. *All of it – Breathtaking!* She felt the sparkle of golden knowing effervesce within her. Felt delicious, with a *w h o o s h*.

At this same moment, miles away in his Cambridge antiquities shop, Jorge Graham stands before an ancient stoneware crucible burning dried eucalyptus leaves, as part blessing, part prayer and part *limpiesa al la casa*. Beside the smoking vessel, open to scrawled observations gathered while living among the Chibcha tribe, the old scholar's worn filed notebook.

The old scholar now reads aloud some incantations, stares without blinking into the fragrant white billows, and in the voice of a medium pronounces: "The detective now goes in . . . "

Another moment and Nick's eyes adjusted; enough to make out yellow directional arrows stenciled along the floor. Following these arrows, he stepped through a slitted cold-curtain – the thick, slick, type of translucent plastic ribbon-barrier often hung at the mouth of a meat locker.

Blind dark.

Nick reached. Felt a narrow corridor. Walls of sweat-damp stone. Chilled, rough wall – he tested, groped with an outstretched foot. Tipped and projected the toe of his heavy oxford, but the shoe came against nothing.

Off balance, he tilted, stumbled forward. Coming down shocked his knee. Something skidded – hollow sound rolled then stopped. Down hill now, shoulder braced against the rough wall. Turning, then another step. Steep. Tilting. Something crunched underfoot.

Down on a knee, arms outstretched, fingers spread, waving in darkness just above the floor: crushed styro cup. Soda cans. To the side a squashed plastic bottle. *Workers' breaks,* he thought, *I'd never put up with this on my jobsite.*

But this wasn't Nick's job.

He stood. Took a step. Something cool brushed his cheek and he imagined kelp.

He reached up, brushed the thing, chased it – batting a hand against dead air, his head going woozy. Caught it and pulled till it snapped. He bunched it in has palm and tossed it: plastic streamers to tickle the face – part of the act.

Forward, downward, the floor pitched and tilted, *Circular. A broad spiral?* Nick could feel she was close. Death, too, maybe. And for sure, the bloody sight of the half-formed Basilisk. The words of Dr. Bacon, the Boston pathologist, rung in his head: *They'll have to flay the leg bones. The foot bones.* The only way Nick could quietly advance quietly was to crouch, kneel, lift each piece of litter, and place it outside of his path. Painfully slow. But his progress was sure.

A warm draft now, from within the tunnel. Like a great beast's musty breath. He saw faint flashes in the distance. Between them, black spots. Eyes half-adjusted, he picked his way.

A few more steps. A sharp turn. Nick found himself standing in a large chamber filled with harsh orange light. Above him the inverted gray moonscape of the cavern's ceiling. In here it was almost warm. His numb feet had begun to thaw, felt like they were expanding inside his shoes. His eyes were catching up, but against the obnoxious orange glow, burning gray orbs formed and floated. An enormous, round vault. He sensed the faces before he could see them.

The high frieze encircling this room, faces of a thousand ghouls stared down at him: swirling cast of tortured concrete masks – gaping, twisted mouths, filled with frozen terror-shouts and broken-toothed laments. Some hungry. Below this circumference, just overhead, torches on long, bronze stanchions ringed the room, lit by false electric flames, alive – staccato tongues flickering strobe-like between split filaments.

Nick held still. When he pivoted, the sound of his leather sole grinding sand echoed. In the sand, he saw the parallel tracks of a wheel chair. Blood spots.

When Nick looked up he saw stalactites, half-repaired in jag-meshed steel and cement. Threatened to fall and split him. How had he spiraled so deep? The place could collapse. Looking up dizzied him. He put a hand to the wall, yanked it back. A milky stream leaked down along the cavern wall, stained the sand below. Limestone-infused water, rich with carbonic acid – the stuff stalactites are formed of. Nick heard a trickling. Distant. Too loud for this leak.

Ahead he saw an arched wooden bridge. Skull-shapes capped the handrails. Below it a shallow river, banks heaped with skeletal bits and chunks made of plastic. A sign burned in a wooden plank: "River Styx." A script hung from the bridge's railing that read: "Water Sleeps, But Enemy Is Sleepless."

Nick recognized the calligraphic hand.

A quick memory of Dante's shattered baptismal font.

Stepping closer . . . *Is that water crimson?*

Watching him on the screen of her laptop, The Illuminator could almost see Nick thinking it.

An unwilling Pilgrim who'd yet come so far. Having read the page from Jim's journal about Dr. Gorgalo by now, surely Nick would have gotten Religion. Silently, she urged him along.

Nick knelt beside the bridge to dip red water. He whiffed. Almost tasted, but remembered. A lesson learned as a boy. Once he'd nicked a finger sitting on the workbench at his father's factory. Blood and iron taste alike.

He glanced upstream. A crusted spillway trickled reddish liquid. Rusty pipes? Standing, he felt something sticky grab at the knee of his pant-leg. He bent to brush it. Cool and quashey in his hand, he examined the wad: dirty white tape and partially coagulated blood-gauze.

Beyond the bridge another sign spelled in fake bones: "The Wrathful."

CHAPTER 5

On her screen The Illuminator watched Nick's advance.

At a distance he spotted another sign hanging above. A severed arm that terminated in a sinewy closed hand. Its lank and large-knuckled index finger crookedly pointing the way. Obviously cast in plaster. It looked fraudulent – a sharp contrast with the cool, bloody reality of the wad Nick held in hand.

The sign directed: **The Chamber of Horrors. Behold Lucifer's Turn – If you dare.**

I dare. The finger pointed toward a Gothic arch. To each side of the arch towered cast cement Roman sentries. Between axes born by each hung a drape, inscribed with Gothic script: **Abandon All Hope Who Enter Here.**

Nick recognized the phrase from readings of <u>The Inferno</u> that he'd begun after that first meeting with Canon Nailor. It was a welcome to Hell.

The great terra cotta keystone above the arch bore the casting of a face, ferocious – but with eyes and cheeks that bulged hilarity, a mouth bursting forth a tongue unbound in raucous laughter. Below, partly blocking the tunnel's gape, an accumulation of lumber scraps, spent brown paper cement sacks, and empty work-stained plastic pails. The hulking Roman sentries to either side scowled, made Nick feel dwarfed.

Inside the low tunnel, he encountered a forest of shoring timbers jammed this way and that.

Glued to her screen, The Illuminator watched Nick enter the tunnel's mouth.

He ducked and bent to get around the angled posts, brushed concrete dust from his greatcoat, and moved forward. Farther, he had to feel along the route through an absolute absence of light.

Nick's body then registered some presence. His throat went tight. Sensed The Illuminator. Gorgalo. Beyond. *Inside that Chamber.*

A flash of memory: the computer morph sequence of the doctor's face, the lips and nose melting into –.

Keep moving.

Nick threw up a hand, ducked another shoring timber, just shy of cracking his head on the rough wood. Forward, shoulder following a slight turn in the tunnel. Past the curve he encountered the orange lume. Warm wind on his face. He moved into it.

. . .a serpentine body. . .

There! An elongated, light-colored shape on the tunnel floor. Traces of rude orange light glanced from the object. Nick knelt, reached, took the cool, slick thing in hand. Bone, partly wrapped in bloody blue scrub cloth. Flesh, and the tendon that ties it, clung to one end. From Gorgalo's leg or foot, Nick guessed.

For a split second he was in The Illuminator's clinic again. Bloody bandages and the hummingbirds flitting, diving on him.

Closer.

From beyond he could hear – what? Nick closed his mouth, tried to still his breathing. His own pulse resounding within his ears. He exhaled and moved forward.

Now. A draw. A puff. Then – hiss. The rhythms of mechanical breath.

Beyond, beneath it – the sound of water. Not trickling, like the rust-colored River Styx he had encountered running under the bridge. This was a rushing. Splashing. Volume uncontained.

Why is he stopping? Enraptured, The Illuminator reveled in the thunder of her own pounding heart.

The cold bone in hand. Dr. Bacon's concluding words: *"They'll have to remove the leg bones – the foot bones – the genitals they'll have to tuck or cut."*
Concentrate. Listen. Sort. Think. Despite the bone – Gorgalo still lived – or so told these sounds of mechanized breath. What might remain of the physician-predator?

Cool, sticky-damp bone.

Nick tipped his hand to allow the relic to slide away, heard it fall upon the sand.

Another step. Warm wind brushed his cheeks, lifted the edge of his hair like a touch.

Then he began to sweat. First his palms. His gun grip felt slick. Then his chest. His trunk, a sauna, drained rivulets to soak his belt line. Down the spine he felt warm vapor, as if scooped down the back of his neck by some malevolent wing. His face was on fire and his forehead slipped drops. Voluminous, it seemed, as the rushing water he could hear within The Chamber.

Onward, arms outstretched in combat stance, Nick bladed his body. Above musty cave scent he smelled wood smoke.

A ventilator can run itself. But a wood fire? She's here! She's near!

Close indeed. She was expecting him. December 28. Nick was right on time.

And the detective knew he was walking into an ambush. It wouldn't be the first time. Ever since discovering Jim's box of records a part of him knew he'd let the Rookie down. Retirement, getting out of Goddard for good, would mean nothing till he sorted that out.

Crazy or sane it was more than curiosity; he would find out what The Illuminator had been trying to say.

Nick had always been a listener. And now he tried to distinguish among the layers of sound. Above the splashing watery sounds. Beneath the mechanical strokes of the breathing machine. There – a jetting, guttural roar.

Stepping through another turn in the tunnel he saw a glow – the way out marked by pilasters – but partly obstructed: pallets piled waist-high. Stacked with sand bags and paper sacks of Portland cement.

Its bulk would provide cover: a vantage point to safely scope the room – the depths of Hell – or even worse, their contrivance.

Nick crouched there, took in the layout, the cement sacks his embattlement. A soldier again.

What he saw in the Chamber made his heart pound. A crowd. Life-sized gladiators and wild beasts of every description that crowded the room. All clashing in blood sport. Chips of harsh firelight exposed blinks of bared teeth. Flash of weapon edge. Claws on skin. Bronze shields clinched in sinewy fists. Glaring, frightened eyes.

Fighting silently?

Each jungle beast within the multitude engaged – reared up, snarling – some sinking sharp teeth into the throats of their human opponents, others run through by sword or spear. Gladiators decapitated – half-fallen, limbless, or left on the ground where the flame light lapped at shining pools of red.

Then Nick felt his face flush – shamed even in absence of an audience. The crowd of gladiators was stock still, petrified in fight. In strobe effect, the electric torches' licking tongues of flare blinked back from phony lacquer blood-pools. Reflected flames, red enough to be real.

A sham. A tourist hoax. Breathing out, Nick hiked his shoulders. He felt stupid.

Another successful illusion, The Illuminator congratulated herself.

Nick visually inventoried the Chamber. Circular like the last room, smaller diameter –more refined. Two, maybe three stories. No stalactites. A high vaulted ceiling with the intersecting chains of a Gothic arch. At the apex a Great Ocular, its leaded panes a circular Palladian skylight. Now a dimly reflective portal to a frozen night sky.

Directly beneath the glass towered the archangel Lucifer, caught, it seemed, during transformation into the demon Satan.

From floor to skylight Nick's eye followed the helix structure beneath the figure's robes.

She could be in there.

Nick moved to take in the rest of the Chamber. Among the battling wax figures, there towered stout wood shoring posts. Their upper cross trees support for repairs to the vaulted ceiling.

Where's she hiding in all this?

Nick searched for movement.

Then he read the sand floor.

Through the shadows, in the bits of light, he could make out wheel chair tracks that abruptly ended: footstep-smeared blood spots – marked some struggle – but not the scuffle of fight. More, a shift. Parallel chair tracks. Then, only footsteps.

She had lifted her sedated patient from the wheel chair, then carried him. It made sense to Nick, the space between the archway and the stack of cement sacks had been too narrow to fit an occupied wheel chair. She had pushed the chair until reaching the obstacle. Quicker, then, to lift and carry her patient to her operating theater.

Damned strong.

However, Nick realized, should The Illuminator have instead chosen to move a couple cement sacks, she could have pushed Gorgalo's chair straight through.

Usually so disciplined. Was this haste? Or its imitation designed to throw me?

Lines in the sand told Nick she'd then returned for the chair, collapsed and then stowed it nearer her patient.

Planning ahead. She's running clear.

Crouched at her perch The Illuminator measured and weighed the detective's every move.

Years ago Cassandra had built tree stands while hunting with brother Brian. In an austere roost as high as this one in the Chamber, she had spent long, cold days with a Nikon and long lens.

Watching Nick below her, she recalled that warm November day with her brother, drawing lessons in patience, stamina and stealth from him, perched in his own tree within view – awaiting big game with a compound bow. She had photographed Brian, his face intent – for an entire day resisting any urge to allow dropping temperatures or lesser impulses to distract him into making the slightest movement or noise – until at dusk, she'd been pulled from momentary distraction by the whip of Brian's bow string – the sound of whispering fletch – and then the hollow thump.

Glancing toward her brother – she had seen the still poise of his bow, on his face the recognition of a hit. Only then did Cassandra look past him, downward and to the left, to find the arrow – weighing less than an ounce – where its razor head had silently found its place just behind the animal's shoulder. Then the rustling when the two hundred thirty pound, twelve-point buck went down upon the carpet of crinkly, dry leaves. It had kicked twice, and then gone still.

They had waited in their cold roosts for another hour to let the deer bleed out, when she could finally congratulate Brian on the clean kill.

That day at her dusky outpost, The Illuminator had learned what most wildlife photographers or meat archers take as rule – that the antlered white tail's vigilance and grace never tires – not in rut, forage, nor fight. But often to its demise, rarely, if ever, does a buck look up.

Now high above the Chamber of Horrors, The Illuminator experienced the rush of her own hunt. She savored Nick's every movement, who, locked in combat stance behind the barrier of concrete sacks, read this, her Third Act, through pistol sights. She admired Nick, how he unwrapped each element of his surroundings with his eyes – his face one moment betraying recognition, and in the next, disbelief.

The Illuminator was well prepared in breathtaking armor. Enjoyed the safe stiffness of her gilded breastplate. With each breath, the close-cropped shearling lining answering the alignment of her shoulders, chest, her muscular abdomen. The comforting fuzz of the shell's close-cropped lamb's fur edge came to contact her throat, her loins, and she noted these as boundaries of safety and vulnerability. The armlets, gauntlets, and anklets she wore promised protection as well. But more, these things reminded her she was a warrior. She placed a hand on the Taser on her belt.

For a moment Nick wondered at the room, how its hideousness resembled, generically, a host of old childhood nightmares. As if planned.

Along the far wall he regarded the source of flickering light: a large hearth, almost the height of Nick's shoulder, and again one and one-half times across like a gigantic infernal gape. Hemmed by massive brass andirons, its raging blaze. Before this mouth stood a hefty log chopping block, the silvery honed bit of an axe masked in its annual rings.

Not far from the block he saw **The Illuminator**'s patient – gauzed, taped, and draped. Difficult to make out through spaces between those wax fighters: wrapped in white fabric like some kind of hideous larval pest.

Gorgalo!

It fit the basic shape. But as curious as Nick had been, he wanted to deny what he saw.

He ducked, stretched to take another angle of sight.

Yes. The gauze-wrapped Basilisk lay upon what appeared

to be – bilaterally iniquitous in cold stone: the shape of the human heart.

Nick had seen photos of the Heart Stone on the Cavern's web site. But now, the sight of such a cold, disembodied shape awakened a profound sense of gravity.

He shut his eyes – not only to escape the sour masks that rung the room, and that frigid granite heart – but to sort and re-sort, to shuffle sounds: the rush and gush of water over there – from a series of troughs and spillways that fed a large, round, white marble vessel balanced atop an ornately carved pedestal – the mechanical respiration, three-part and haunting – the endless roaring of *Dragon* construction heaters.

Nick opened his eyes. Half-blinded by the heaters that whipped yellow beards of flame upward against metal blast shields. Barely containing the flames, the metal shields glowed and shimmered between white to pink to red to white. The yellow jets colored the limestone walls with the papery hues of fury.

And originating from the base of each roiling sheet metal silo, winding among the fierce battlers' feet, fueling unison of all these devices – a tangle of fat black rubber gas hoses connected to silver-painted canisters, stenciled, ominously in black lettering:

CAUTION

PROPANE

Nip a gas hose. An explosion waiting to happen.
Arms outstretched, pistol leading, Nick stepped from behind his embattlement. He wove through the bloodthirsty wax beasts and petrified gladiators. Reaching the center of the room he stopped beside the scaffolding – no idea she lay

waiting above him, belly-down, hidden beneath a scrap of tarpaulin.

Watching through holes in the aluminum walk board, she gauged his every movement, tic and step.

Nick raised a hand to grip a cross-brace. The vibration of his touch telegraphed upward through the tower. Her exuberance bubbled. She could have had him there and then. But tonight she wanted to watch him see her work. Partake of its intoxicating effect.

Nick opened the buttons of his great coat, felt heat escape, relieved at the added mobility. Quietly picked his way forward.

It brought a start when hearth logs shifted in the blaze, crackled and popped and shot red sparks. Recently placed logs that had barely caught fire that told Nick: *She's here.*

In front of the hearth he eyed the stack of split oak, the chopping block, the axe. Firelight danced along the smile of its curved, honed edge.

Nick's sense of smell had been impeccable since losing the tobacco. But nearing Gorgalo he caught the whiff of peroxide – sharp, wakeful.

But that was nothing. It was the sheer number of bones he saw.

The bones of a single leg total four. Each foot, twenty-six. Nick counted sixty. Enough for both legs.

The same number as his years on Earth. Most carried gristle and pink-red scraps of flesh.

A few steps closer gave him a perfect view of the carnage

laid out on the Heart Stone, the white-wrapped mass. An un-dulating tube went in at the top end – its breath – delivered by the mechanical source of the wheezing sound. Thinner tubes and plastic sacs that kept the patient hydrated and drained. Gorgalo – now the shape of the Basilisk – alive, present, yet not of this world.

Nick felt his mind begin to whirl. But experience pre-vailed and he shifted from revulsion to rescue. Pocketing his revolver he rushed to the being's side.

Then, despite an adult life spent saving lives – the detec-tive halted.

There had been his good friend Jason Aquilla in Viet Nam, who he'd rushed on his shoulder to a chopper, taking fire at every step. There had been that town kid who got a bad batch of blotter acid one night and ended up at the quarry with a belief he could fly. Nick had spent two hours climb-ing down to fasten a rope about the teen's waist – still very much alive but horribly frightened, the kid's jacket caught by the limb of a stubborn cliff-side maple. And the time he had plucked a toddler from a Jeep overturned in a gully, gas-oline dripping from the carburetor upon the red-hot exhaust manifold – while he untangled the car seat – and had gotten himself and the child clear of the wreck just before the mush-room cloud.

Now, to Nick, the only thing certain was his doubt.

Black nylon straps held the Basilisk fast. No eyes showed. Wrapped completely in white gauze blotched with crimson, wound with white tape and in places ripped sheeting, the ta-pering shape was a bird wrapped in rose-print – or a beaked and blood-blotched maggot – the wrapped head shaped hawkish, its arm-wings bound but still clearly present – then the elongated trunk, stretching toward a lizard-like terminus. Beside where Gorgalo lay, a small table was covered with an array of surgical tools designed to part flesh and chip bone – all in need of a good cleaning.

To make the rescue he'd need the wheelchair. *There, beyond that spillway . . .* He took a few steps.

Nearing it he could not ignore The Font, the blood spatter. *What could possess a soul –?*

Nick couldn't fathom it. He looked again at the sluice-way, a jury-rigged watercourse that poured into an immense, round white marble vessel atop a winestem-shaped stone pedestal.

An Illumination identified it as: **The Font**.

The calligraphy an exact match for the message he'd discovered in the bottom of that carton:

You will comprehend Jim Stevens' suffering after you have looked into the depths of The Font.

Overflowing by design, waters entering The Font ran clear as glycerin. Going out, the fluid held the crimson hue of lightly diluted wine, pouring along the marble sluice to where it terminated at larger, corroded metal pipe that exited through the chamber's wall.

Nick remembered the bridge he had crossed, the corroded iron pipe: *The River Styx.* Its red waters. The quashy blotch of crimson gauze. The sign that had read: *Water Sleeps–.*

Captivated, he stepped toward the marble vessel and its curious sluiceways, drawn by some hypnotic force. Hesitantly, cautiously, something squirmed in his gut. He felt another scrap of bone beneath his shoe.

What is this Gorgalo?

And what is this Illuminator?

When Nick glanced back toward Gorgalo, contempt for this doctor in *any* and all forms rose in his gullet as black bile. Another step toward The Font. Hesitated mid-step. But was already there.

Nick rested hands upon The Font's marble circumference. Leaned forward, peering into its swirling depths.

Circulating at the bottom of this basin – amidst a floating, ever-changing chain design of unworldly delicacy, laced by that streaming thread of shadow so singular to the ways of rattled water and bent light – traced hypnotic strands upon the striated ghost-white marble – harsher even than Hell: Gorgalo's bloody genitals – continually stirred by the spilling waters of The Font.

You will comprehend Jim Stevens' suffering after . . .

Nick vomited into The Font.

Not once. His retching tore at his finer tissues, again and again. His forehead dripped perspiration. Bracing a body exhausted and weakened by the chase, he clung with both hands to the rim of the great, thick white marble bowl. His back arched, convulsed, and flung each recursive retch.

Nick could name the parts that pleaded to leave him: the spleen, intestines, stomach, liver, kidneys, webs of muscle and tissue. His expulsion a tug of war against his solar plexus, forcing and convulsing, between thrusts the tears flowing from his eyes, slipping salty into his mouth and he would have his lungs go too if they let him.

His face would not open wide enough – cords beneath the skin of his neck stretched and his clavicles seemed ready to pop loose atop his chest. Top to bottom his body was a catapult: lower back arched, calves and tendons stretched, both temples burning with jaw muscle fatigue.

Nick wished he could spit out his heart.

Then.
Suddenly.
It was over.

Now Nick felt a clear, clean space inside, and he began to catch his breath.

His whole being hurt.

He was all right.

No organs had escaped him to be floated in the Font.

And when he glanced again at this Basilisk through tear-washed eyes, Detective Nick Giaccone believed that the lowly white wrapped and spiderlined form might even have been figment of his own revulsion.

He realized, very sadly: the many, many years since he had inhabited himself as fully as he had in this sacrament of expulsion.

BOOK IV

CHAPTER 6

Nick's purgation was Cassandra's Grande Opera. Entering, she'd watched his brow pique in question. Then upon first glance at Gorgalo, the contempt registering in the swelling bite of the detective's jaw. Ribbed sands of his brow deepening to ruts as he'd contemplated whether the doctor should be rescued, or had gotten what was coming to him.

Nick's body had answered these questions with revulsion. Then the slack regret on his mouth when he wiped it.

This was the reason she had lured him. The reason she'd created this Theater of Blood. To do for Jim Stevens' mentor what she could not do for herself.

And to watch Nick's absorption of fact, his progression toward pity, resignation, purgation and then, reinhabitance of his own body, Cassandra knew. She could begin to mourn her brother Brian. Her silent stream of tears answered: *At last!*

Until Nick donned dispassion as the mask of the lifesaver, thinking:

Get an ambulance.

He jammed a hand into his great coat for the mobile phone, scrolled: **chief** and pressed **send.**

No signal.

In denial Nick again pressed **send.** And again. Till his thumb hurt, hoping beyond all to connect with a world bathed in sunrays. He gripped the phone, punched **send** one more time, and then gave up on its annoying voicelessness.

He looked down: gas hoses at his feet snaking everywhere, a danger amidst these flames.

Nip a hose – these fires – and that's the end of it.

He shoved the phone into his pocket and looked around. Shoulder muscles ratcheting taught.

She's close. Watching.

His eye went back to Gorgalo. To his mind, the policeman's rescue reflex.

At the chopping block he yanked the axe, rushed toward Gorgalo and severed the restraints.

He parted bandages to check this creature's eyes for life.

Its pupils shifted, focused, drew in Nick's face. Something deep and draining in these eyes, as if, even in this drugged and listless state, Gorgalo sought to draw *from* Nick – something very deep, far behind Nick's eyes – as if this creature sought to assume the aggregate: thoughts, needs, fears, and weaknesses. Nick could almost feel the Basilisk clutching after *his very own* vessel.

He had to turn away.

Noticed the axe in his hand. Gripped. Raised slightly?

Nick let out a sigh, and rested this garden tool against the Heart Stone. Lifted the creature into the wheel chair, careful with all those plastic tubes.

Ready to push off toward the archway, once again Nick felt her eyes on him. He glanced. Saw flash of firelight grinning along the axe's curved and polished edge.

Why pass up a tool that will double as a weapon?

He set it upright in the chair alongside Gorgalo's gauze-wrapped shape. Before moving onward – like answering an itch, he again pulled back the gauze – to once again peer straight into the eyes of the Basilisk.

He saw a single silver tear swell from one corner. The droplet broke and fell, following an arc of sutured skin along the beak, then disappeared, wicked into the gauze.

Nick didn't trust it.

Something inside him clicked. He draped Gorgalo's form with a sheet from the Heart Stone, covering those eyes – concealing that axe. Then straightened his spine, neck upright, and stood slightly taller.

He thought of his life, his role: keeper of law and order – and in contrast, the Basilisk, a flightless contradiction of slither and wing. Dr. Gorgalo, a surgeon whose once-skilled and disciplined hands had held hearts, saved lives. Allengri, Roache, and Gorgalo – answering for Jim Steven's death. Cop killers.

Nick wiped his own tear with a pocket square.

Clarity. It washed over him like a wave of ice water. Nick would play his role: a *technical* observance of law, to move a sack of flesh to the next step in legal process.

Perched above in Lucifer's folds, The Illuminator could almost hear her adversary working the moral math. Holding still, legs lithe and taut beneath her, she rolled ever so slightly on the balls of her feet. Arms outstretched, knuckles down upon her scaffolding perch, she flexed the strong, supple muscles in her calves, poised and ready in a four-point crouch, pleasured by her shoulder muscles' response to the slight rocking – forcing her to remember gravity, balance, and tension, answering muscular hunger brought on by months of training, observation, and fantasy. Head to toe raced its deliciousness.

The ventilator. With effort Nick managed the wheeled, metal box a distance. It stopped short of reaching the wheelchair.

The power cord.

He surveyed the machine's knobs and gauges, ran a hand behind its metal housing and felt a toggle. Leaning, he read: *Battery Backup.*

He gambled, threw the switch, then pulled the plug.

The machine's wheeze, shush, and push came to a stop. The needle gauge fell to zero.

From within the unit's metal housing, Nick could hear a monotonous hum. He glanced at the power cord lying in the sand. Then heard a click.

The Basilisk's form shuddered.

Unsure if the machine would support the rescue, Nick considered saving only his own hide. Leave Gorgalo plugged in, to live out his final hours in this Hell cave.

Then: **ker-clunk.** *Inside the machine.* Then a **tic   tic   tic.** *Working.*

Something caught. The rush of bellows. *Air!*

The needle gauge jumped. And the rhythmic breathing resumed.

Nick glanced toward the archway leading out. Thought of carrying the body. What of this machine? To carry Gorgalo would tie up his pistol hand.

Stick with the chair. He pushed – weaving to get by the beasts and gladiators – around wood posts – at times lifting to help the chair wheels past those rubber gas tubes along the cavern floor. *Push – inch it along.*

From high above him The Illuminator's voice was sharp, cutting, sarcastic: "I can't let you take him. You haven't signed a release."

She flung back the Colossus' fabric robes – crouched, arms curled forward, ready to pounce. Firelight danced across the bug eye lenses of those sunglasses.

Nick drew the pistol from his great coat.

"I wouldn't," she said, Taser already drawn from her belt and leveling the weapon at Nick. "Judging by your body mass index, Detective, you might not survive being Tazed."

Nick let his gun hand drop limply to his side. But he didn't let go of the pistol.

Assured of her dominance in this contest, she tucked away the Taser. Her voice, taunting, "Much better."

Gold shards of light off her breastplate stung Nick's eyes.

Hands to hips, shoulders thrown back, she regarded the detective as a subaltern. "Now we can have that chat. After all these years. . ." She peeled off her big sunglasses and tossed them to the sand at Nick's feet.

"Sounds fun," Nick shot back, measuring. The Illuminator's concerted movement, compact strength. Firelight danced smartly, hypnotically across the gold-leaf coins of her breastplate and gauntlets like from dragon scales. Entranced, Nick's eye went to the gold-skinned protective armlets that entwined her biceps and triceps. He could sense a power pent within her.

Her armor, its stunning craftsmanship, seemed a perfect union of corporeal and sublime. Then Nick spied that one foreign object – the fat barrel of a large plastic syringe peeking from the edge of one armlet.

It must have registered in his eyes.

"You guess correctly that this spike's for you," she said, bringing a hand to the syringe. "To honor my Festivity of the Innocents."

Nick indicated the wheel chair. Hoarsely he said, "I'm taking Dr. Gorgalo to a hospital." He reached, lifting the front of the chair over a gas line and pushed. "Basilisk or not . . .it's a lousy rendition," he said, to test of her pride of craftsmanship.

"Basilisk!" The Illuminator insisted. Her eyes betrayed a deep pleasure in playing to an audience. "So, policemen *can* read," she sneered, "The paperwork, I've heard, can be a nightmare."

Nick studied her face, chin, jaw line and taut cheeks, all painted by yellow-orange strobes of flame. Something there frightened Nick, scarier than the needle and the Taser. It was her looks, identical to Brian's in every literal detail. Yet somehow, from a place beneath the skin –she looked as severe as her brother had looked innocent. The way she wore it, the face was a weapon in its own right.

Gorgalo jerked suddenly in the wheel chair, dislodging Nick's fascination with his adversary.

The Illuminator reached to her armlet. Drew forth the long, sheathed spinal needle. Its sheer length brought terror. Nick was about to raise his gun, but as if in nonverbal answer to his thought, The Illuminator reached to grip the Taser in her belt.

Using the extreme hypodermic setup as her pointer, The Illuminator indicated the Basilisk. "You know this one won't make it past seeing himself. His fate has run its course. So has his utility. Leaving *me* and *you* –." She brought the plastic tip guard to her teeth, bit down to uncap the syringe, and spat it over her shoulder. The cover clacked against the metal helix on its way down.

Nick sized her. The bare, brilliant stainless steel needle.

Her eyes glowering fiery satisfaction. He noticed a quickening in the way her golden breastplate rose and fell. He could not help but wonder, this slight yet powerful being. Casually, to ease without betraying perception or plan, Nick gestured about their environs, defiantly asking, "Who do you think you are helping here?"

"Mankind!" Her lip quivered. Eyes narrowed, voice taught, raspy, "I'm teaching! Casting daylight onto shadow!"

He could feel the eyes, traveling up his neck, face and throat – measuring where best to apply the spike.

Pointing her silver lance toward the heavens, The Illuminator tilted her head back and mixed words with laughter, "Think of The Work as Archimede's Death Ray." Then she drilled him with her eyes, "You know it? The Death Ray?" She depressed the syringe to send a short burst of its paralyzing contents skyward.

Nick leveled his gun at her. "Why don't I just shoot you?"

"Because Detectives are curious. Like Brian. Maybe you get off on risk."

Around the knot tightening in his throat, Nick said, "So then teach me about this ray."

She obliged. "When Archimedes legions focused their mirrored shields toward their aggressors, the concert of sun's rays turned that armada of Romans ships to ash – right where they floated. What if every injured kid shined their light?" She pointed the silvered tip toward Gorgalo, "How many of *them* would still be in business? Eh, Detective?"

Nick shouted, "First, you're not a *kid*, even if you wear

the face of one. Second, there are other ways to rig a ray. And third, you're hiding out in a cave. Not exactly beaming sunshine. But a lovely suit of shining armor. . . "

"Technically correct," she sliced off his sentence, "*They* took Brian years ago. Wearing his likeness, I'm his avenger."

Nick had hit upon it. To unmask any fanatic, hit square in the ideology. Upset her balance. "Noble avenger? Or the tired nurse?" was Nick's retort. "True. Your brother Brian's condition was serious. But not fatal. *Brian* pulled the trigger, not *them*," Nick said forcefully: "Let me read it back to you: *You* made a pact with him – a promise to visit Contrapasso upon your brother's persecutors – should he ever actually *harm* himself. You didn't *dissuade* Brian from ending it. You provided *incentive*. Why? Your own satisfaction. Maybe to quell your *guilt*."

"Brian took *himself* out!"

"You showed him the door!"

She sprung into Capoeira, turning a brilliant cartwheel, magnificent chain of gold reflections blazing Nick's senses.

Nick got a shot off but missed.

Landing at Lucifer's feet she dropped low. Drove a shoulder hard below Nick's sternum and pushed upward.

Pain flew through him. He reeled back, wind blast to empty his lungs. Gasping, he felt his heels leave the ground. A shoring timber hard and solid along his spine. Could not believe the power of her little mass.

She reared. Delivered the needle overhand.

When Nick threw a hand up to block, his pistol skidded in the sand.

Teetering on the tips of toes, he felt the sting in his palm. He pulled. It wouldn't budge. Pinned to the timber by her needle like a specimen.

He felt the shoring post budge and wobble. Reached with his free hand to yank the needle but when he pulled, the timber shifted. He hooked a foot to steady it.

When he looked up, loose mortar bits and lime from the ceiling rained into his eyes. Clapping his lids, Nick felt sharp bits grinding his corneas. The burn of lime mortar. He brought the free hand to wipe his eyes. The timber again shifted. Something tore in his pinned hand. A falling brick glanced his shoulder. He shrieked in agony.

Opening his eyes he caught the scent of surgery. Her cold eyes inches from his own. Felt hot breath. The twin hard darts of her Taser jammed hard to his collarbone.

"You have a *couple* good points there," Nick cracked sarcastically, reaching his free hand to take hold of her wrist.

"Glad to have your attention," The Illuminator rasped. "So here's the lesson. Why I brought you here. Better listen: only the fairer are strong enough to be victims," she lectured, "To feel defeat, fight back, rebuild."

"People tell me I'm a fair guy."

Her face betrayed no amusement. Instead it glowed in the pleasure of battle. She hissed: "Think I'm play acting? I'll have your innards for my jump ropes!"

Pain when she jammed the Taser harder against his collarbone. Nick became a statue. Still holding her wrist.

"I've tried it *all*, Detective. Clara Barton, war nurse. Florence Nightingale. Guardian angel with a vengeance. Now I'm living the life of Brian," she said.

The Taser points hurt, hard against his collarbone.

Blood dripped on his face from his pinned hand. With nothing left to lose, Nick snapped: "Seems I've got you, in a case of over-nursing. But why me? What do you *want*?"

She flicked her eyes upward to his fastened hand, to

remind this adversary of his predicament, "Your hands look as bloody as anyone's, Detective. *Those bastards* **made** Brian break. The social worker told my brother: 'Call your attorney.' The lawyer said: 'Call the police.' Then Brian called your police station, Detective, and asked for you. The desk sergeant took a message and said: 'Sounds like a civil matter, call your lawyer.' That's the spiral that killed my brother. And now the town of Goddard makes a *God* of Jim Stevens."

The wheelchair was within Nick's reach. If only he could distract her, then reach for the axe. *Ideology.* "Fight monsters figuratively – not physically, not literally," Nick said, and let go of her wrist. "In here –." Tapped his temple with the index finger of his free hand, "Transform those childhood monsters in the closet back into a meaningless pile of laundry."

As he spoke he worked the syringe stuck through his hand, feeling skin and tissue tear. Gripped its barrel with his fingertips. Hot searing of muscle. A burn, the chemical entering him. He had injected himself, or the wood – or both.

Nick rocked the hand, like pulling a nail with a claw hammer, levering wrist against timber, the needle's steel shaft against small bones and tendons. Felt something snapping within his hand.

"One little point, Detective . . ." She was hypnotically waving the Taser, its twin-barbed contacts like venomous fangs before his eyes, unaware of his maneuvers, ". . . to be a survivor, one must first acknowledge being a victim. Brian was never allowed that. Men think it's too – *girly*. So he could never accept the vulnerability. In fact he defied it."

"I believe Brian *could* have been a survivor," Nick allowed, wondering when the Taser's barbs would whip his muscles into frenzy, boost his heart rate, make his mouth froth, teeth clamping tongue. *She wants to talk, not Taze me,* he thought. To test her he asked defiantly, "But then, what do you call a *survivor* who takes his own life?"

"Take his own **life!**" she hissed. "Knots tied as a Youth Camper shouldn't have to be cut! Brian couldn't take more than an hour in a therapist's office," The Illuminator hissed, tapping her own index finger to her temple, "So he shot the monsters up *here*, instead of talking, telling, asking, hoping – *learning* to make it better. He wanted his *final* answer. And he wanted the answer *now!*"

Nick felt no narcotic effect yet from being pinned by her needle. Wondered if the dose had been too slight. Nodding toward Gorgalo, to distract his adversary, he reached, felt the pain in the hand that remained pinned above his head – and extended his free hand toward the wheel chair far enough to grasp it – barely able to pull it closer.

Meanwhile in his high hand, Nick felt the needle working loose. The syringe now *his* weapon. But he kept it there, bluffing, clutching the barrel –.

He thought of high school wrestling. And so began his greatest fake.

Reading periphery, Nick mapped location of the archway at the position of ten o'clock. The fireplace at one o'clock. And not far away, at four o'clock, the canister marked

CAUTION

PROPANE

When he reached his free hand into sheeting that covered Gorgalo to swing the axe it slashed The Illuminator's face. Knocked her Taser to the sand.

He brought the spike down hard at her. Pushed the plunger. Felt it glance from a bone. Or her breastplate.

She pivoted.

The syringe hit the sand.

The Illuminator stepped back.

One hand up to her cheek, the other to her shoulder where he'd stuck her.

What – in her eyes –. Flash! Envy? Admiration?

She'd raised a fingertip to the small slice beneath her eyelid. A succession of dark droplets formed, fell, and traced the curve of her young but masculine cheek, washing her younger brother's face with tears of deep crimson.

Examining a painted fingertip The Illuminator glowered, first toward Nick, then toward the figure in the wheel chair. Desperate. She switched back and forth – shifting eyes to Nick, to her colored finger, to the Basilisk – one to the other to the other, finally resting her gaze upon the Basilisk. "You call *this* Basilisk fake, Detective?" She tested, voice intent, desperately persuasive. "Gorgalo and the others were already the very *pictures* of monsters. I came on the scene to *develop* them."

Nick now felt the drug. The edges of things going cottony. His taut and ready muscles began to slump. He wondered if it would take him down. He managed to say, "I see –. Like they developed Brian."

"Reviled him. Revised him," she recited. "Have you forgotten what those animals did to your young friend Jim Stevens?" The Illuminator challenged, nudging Gorgalo's wheel chair with her knee in a way that made him move slightly, seem suddenly less inert, "Or is this wheel chair filled with *dirty laundry*?"

Nick's musculature was going dumb. Foundering. Though he made a show of looking down toward Gorgalo's beaked face, hoping he would again be able to bring up his own head, heavy as a Hubbard squash. He stepped one foot toward her, turned slightly sideways. Caught sight of his pistol on the floor. Though at that moment, his vision seemed to be playing tricks.

Maybe it was the drug. Or fatigue. Because when Nick now looked at Gorgalo – the fearsome Basilisk – he saw only a heap of soiled laundry. Whether or not his eyes deceived made no difference now. What Nick saw in the wheel chair was soiled linen – like a crappy pile of bed sheets. "*Dirty laundry, it seems,*" Nick giddily replied, tongue going thick, attempting to mask his affliction, but feeling kind of loose and talkative. "In fact, shit-streaked," he said, smirking, going cloudy behind the eyes, but awake enough to place his attention upon the pistol close to The Illuminator's feet. *It has to be now*, he thought.

The Illuminator was unpersuaded. "So tell me, Detective, are you just going to stand there? Or are you going to arrest me?"

"No handcuffs," said Nick, with a bloodied hand lifting one side of his great coat to reveal an empty belt line.

It had taken her off mark. He dropped. Rolled. Faced her with the gun. "So I guess I'll have to shoot you."

The Illuminator dove.

Nick fired.

But she'd cart wheeled.

Nick saw the graze mark on her breastplate.

Amazed, he again leveled the pistol.

Her one hand aimed the Taser, the other steadying as she went down on one knee, "Unless I kill you first, detective. Though you and me are birds of a feather. That's why I brought you here."

"Brought me?"

"You didn't think I knew you'd take the first manuscript to Professor Nailor? The string that undid the seedbag, Detective."

"And so here we are," Nick said cavalierly, refusing her the moment, waving his free hand, caked with drying blood. In the other hand he felt pistol weight, the crook of an index finger against the trigger's hard edge. But his head was a dizzy pillow of feathers; he wondered how much of the drug had entered his system. "So let's both die. Because if you're morally correct, we'll have Eternity to chat."

"You might shoot me, Detective," said The Illuminator, eying the revolver. "But you'll never kill The Work. Legions will spring from these sands."

She eyed him, still waving the Taser.

Nick knew that to go on this way – to feed her delusion – was crucial. He said, "That's where you're wrong."

"Let's talk about *you*," she said, arching her back, stepping carefully in a semi circle around him, clapping a hand on her shoulder to message tired muscles, it seemed, to convey a casual upper hand. "You might have a little work done, Detective Giaccone. We can start with injectables around the eyes. I'll make you – let's see – how about lady justice, the *greatest* grotesque – guaranteed numbed and painless." In the way a flame flares yellow with an impurity, so just then did her eyes.

"Let's talk about your so-called *work*," countered Nick. He shifted a foot, stepped toward the wheel chair. "You don't *make* monsters," he said, feeling the toe of his shoe against the gas hose at his feet. Close by lay the axe. A small cut in the propane hose and *whoosh!* He decided to convey the belief to The Illuminator. He shot an eye to the axe – testing The Illuminator's vigilance.

Her gaze flicked to follow the slightest motion of his own.

"You know, technically," Nick said, another try to distract her, slowly bringing up one hand so she could see it – then, in order not to startle The Illuminator into striking, using this hand to draw back the corner of the sheet covering Gorgalo, "if you had created a *true* Basilisk – *technically* speaking – I should already be dead," Nick said. "After all, I have stared into this one's eyes."

The Illuminator's eyes glowed rage at such impudence.

Again Nick flicked his eyes – from the axe – to the gas hose upon the floor – to the flames in the fireplace – to –. "You know, a *real* Basilisk kills with its stare. Not sometimes. *Always.*" He shifted his own stare to the flames licking the fireplace, hearty now with the new logs fully inflamed – watched her eyes following his. "So tell me, do I look dead?" He smirked, pried a question out of her face.

He'd hit a nerve. The Illuminator's eyes shot back to the axe, now at twelve o'clock. Getting ahead of him, consumed herself with his next move, forgetting to plot out her own tactics.

Given over to preemption, her composure now belonged to Nick. Unless she was faking, Nick thought, to convince him of his *own* dominance.

To defend her handiwork, The Illuminator drew the pocket mirror like it was a pistol, and stepped closer to the Basilisk. "Acid test," she replied, flipping the compact. "I expected this question," she sneered, lowering the mirror before the Basilisk's eyes. 'Watch!"

At the sight Gorgalo lurched, convulsed, pitched forward. Unable to abide his mirror image.

The Basilisk hit the sand. Writhed. Tape broke loose. Bandages split. Gauze unwound, revealing an awful spiral of stitch and half-dried fluids. The reptilian monstrosity tried to rise from the sand floor. When it did the abbreviated appendages of the upper half pried loose from the sticky body and revealed themselves as malformed skin wings.

But the creature's strength was gone. It fell to the sand, beak first. A serpentine terminus whipped sand, grains adhering to half-healed and salve-coated skin. The scaly growths at the tip appeared to be outgrown toenails.

About the form Nick noticed neat lines of blue-black sutures. Stainless steel staples holding the skin closed. The plastic breathing tube had slid out, connected by mucous webs to where it lay upon the sand, undulating in concert with the whooshing ventilation machine.

Nick wanted to look away, but the ridged plastic tubing thing caught his eye.

Thrashing. Then, beak opened, extubated, a transmogrified Dr. Richard Gorgalo emitted small grunts. The body writhed more, drew short, howling inhalations. Its extremity whipped. Then, a protracted expulsion of whatever kind of life had been stored in Dr. Gorgalo's body in the form of a final, hissing, utterance:

"m - e – e – e - d - i - c - c - c - i - n - e."

Laying still, to Nick this monster now seemed far smaller.

He flipped the ventilator switch to OFF.

Then all was still. But for the roiling flames and cascading bloody font water.

Nick noticed that she'd in fact allowed him the freedom to attend to the ventilator's switch.

He could see her emotions sway from distress to something more dangerous, like the swing of a compass needle and felt small triumph.

As a wrestler Nick had practiced using peripheral vision, in order to read a ring without eye movement betraying intention.

There, the archway out – at nine o'clock – beyond The Illuminator. He also saw the light colored curve of the axe handle – at three o'clock – within arm's reach. *I could swing low for it. Get a shot off and dive behind the pallet of concrete sacks.*

To bait her he met her eyes, looked directly at her Taser, nodded, then slowly, ceremoniously, he turned to face the Basilisk. Slowly he made a motion of bowing his head. Humbling his shoulders. Making the sign of the cross on his forehead, chest, and shoulders. He kissed his fingertips to show reverence.

Upon The Illuminator's face – a momentary satisfaction. *It's working.*

To draw out this Supplication, the detective smoothly went to one knee, then lifted the sheet that had fallen to hide the Basilisk's face.

He would give anything to stop this insanity. His life, if need be.

He stood calm-faced. Gently smoothed his supple great coat as if to show respect through best appearances. Then, quickly, turned his head and eyed the bottle marked:

CAUTION

PROPANE

The Illuminator's face registered the gesture.

And Nick spun, scooping the axe handle, raising it high, as if to come down across a gas hose and kill them both.

Had drawn her fire.

The sudden, hot spear of a Taser dart burned in Nick's

chest. Electric current coursing through his muscles, he let go of the axe, dropped, rolled, and got off one shot at the silver PROPANE canister – then dove behind the stacked sacks of cement.

Whipping yellow-orange fangs of flame hungrily engulfed the room above him, scorching his face.

Blur – Illuminator's armor toward Lucifer's robes.

The shattering ocular was the last thing Nick heard – its falling glass shards' a metallic tinkling against Lucifer's great and tangled helix framework.

Then he was out.

CHAPTER 7

Nick got his wits back lying on a stretcher. He shivered in the cold, taking oxygen into his lungs through a cannula. His mouth felt dry as dust, his lips like vinyl and his face was tight – two sizes too small. He ran fingers over his facial skin and thought: *taut as a tomato.* His vision blurred, The Illuminator's words rung in his mind, *"I'll make you lady justice –."*

He reached.

"All still there," came a cheery a woman's voice.

Too cheerful for The Illuminator.

His vision began to clear, his eyes caked with dried muck and mortar so he could only see shapes. At least the colors were comforting, *the blue wash of squad car lights over there. And there, to the other side, those red strobes must be an ambulance, or a fire truck.* Nick used a parched hand to clean crusts from his eyes.

Then, overhead, lines of leafless branches crisscrossing his view. Entering his field of vision was a blue uniform sleeve, and then the rest of the emergency medical technician.

"I'm Francine," said the medic. "And you're OK." She gently tugged at his great coat. "Good thing you dressed warm. Thick coat blocked one of the Taser darts. Probably saved ya."

"My face." With a hand he searched cheeks and forehead, in places gathered like parchment.

"A little sun burned. Give it three days," the woman told him, "Four days, tops. Use aloe. Though you're short a pair of brows." Nick's ribs hurt, but he was exuberant as he heard the low chopping of the three media copters. Saw them hovering low, above the bare trees.

"Where is she?" Nick asked.

"She who?"

Nick hoisted himself slowly. "Didn't you find anyone in there? Somebody else? The Illuminator?"

"They found you up *there*." She pointed toward the crest of a large, stony hill above and beyond the tourist trap's entrance. "Some kind of skylight for the Caverns. Lucky you didn't get buried in the explosion. The collapse."

"Collapse?" Nick looked around at a blurred world, breathing in cold, fresh air that felt like skim ice. Feeling thanks for life, until slowly, the shapes within his view began to congeal, edges restored, becoming objects he could identify. He saw all the fire trucks, ambulance, the Coroner Dr. Fogg's black Chevrolet Suburban.

"Who carried me up? The Illuminator?"

"Maybe you climbed out in your sleep. You're Rip Van Winkle. Been out a while . . . Firefighters dug out a – a *thing* –." Francine struggled for words as she wiped salve upon his face. "A *horrible* thing. Human, maybe. Probably another one of those *transmogs,* like in the newspapers. . ."

It took a while to take things in.

He saw his Police Interceptor where he'd left it. Nick loved that car. Parked beside it, Professor Nailor's high-horse-powered dragon. A sudden wave of dizziness made Nick slump.

"Easy there, boy," he heard Francine say. "Take it easy." She made him lie back.

"A woman," he insisted. "Inside the Caverns–."

"Ain't it always a woman with you heroes?" the medic replied, her tone so tart that Nick could grasp the texture of worn humor beneath.

He remembered the briefing at headquarters, and protested weakly, "There should be a motor home."

But Francine's voice instructed, "You just rest right there, Officer Motorhome, while I give you something to help. . ." he felt his sleeve being pulled upwards, roughly, without nonsense by the medic's able hands, a jab in the crook his arm as she inserted another IV.

Nick saw TV crews getting in place, Goddard Police holding back a growing crowd of onlookers.

"Hey – you were *inside* Wiggins Caverns. . . " The medic's voice became conspiratorial, "My kids have been hounding – what's *Lucifer's Turn* all about?"

"It isn't finished," Nick murmured.

Later he got to see all the footage. Nothing had been found of The Illuminator, except for a collection of bones, saws, mallets and other surgical implements arranged at the base of that ever-circulating attraction, The Font.

No motor home was ever discovered.

Since this was the Monday after Christmas, no one had yet reported theft of The Font, stolen from Worchester's Higgins Armory Museum, still closed for the holiday weekend.

The Higgins Museum holds the largest and finest collection of Medieval and Renaissance armor and weaponry in the western hemisphere. The Friday evening before, The Illuminator had attended a Patron's holiday Medieval costume feast disguised in the trappings of a courtly page.

That night as festivities drew to a close she'd slipped behind a tapestry in the museum's great hall, a three-story arcade housing armored riders ready to joust, as well as a breathtaking boy's suit of armor worn by a mannequin, poised to deliver a message to a shining mounted knight.

Created by armor smiths of the era as a calling card to display the finest of their craft, the boy's suit of armor had fascinated her.

Once the affair was over, the armory's doors locked for the holiday weekend, she'd silenced the alarm and then found the museum's Chapel.

There she'd lit a votive and knelt.

That night in the empty museum, with vacant suits of armor her overseers, The Illuminator had borrowed an ornate white marble vessel that would serve as The Font. With the assistance of a pallet jack, using straps to secure the piece, she'd moved it to the freight elevator, and then to the first floor from the loading dock and into her motor home.

The remaining hours of that the night had been spent in moving The Font to center of the Chamber of Horrors where Nick was to finally behold it.

The white marble Font was one of legend. Chosen carefully by the Higgins Armory museum's founder, a man accustomed to giving thanks for his good fortune as a leading steel industrialist. And he had spared no expense to acquire The Font.

And because of its history, The Illuminator had spared no amount of risk or effort to incorporate the piece into her *Grande Finale.*

Because The Font had at one time, long ago, served as quenching vessel, beside the forge of a sword smith, while outfitting warriors for the Crusades.

CHAPTER 8

Dropping off his final report at Headquarters, to stand before Jim Steven's bronze-cast face, felt very different. This time, no questions tugged at Nick. No whisper within naming ways he might have failed Jim. No more bright ideas to fix it.

A week later, with the sale of his second residence closed and paid in full, Nick boarded a plane at Boston Logan Airport. In eight hours: Rome, and he would check into the Albergo Abruzzi, take his usual room overlooking the Pantheon, stay a few days to purchase clothes for the climate, tour museums, and best of all, sample the fare. Later, the high-speed train would take him to Naples, and by taxi, he could reach the family home in Positano.

All through December, Nick had looked forward to each of these things. Had rehearsed them in his mind to keep himself going in pursuit of The Illuminator.

But now, he took his seat on the plane a changed man. He felt no sense of excitement. Instead he was filled with a certain strength. And behind that new strength, a solid ray of self-assurance that could cut through any darkness.

He reached into his pocket for his key ring. And holding Jim's key, his mind was on the crimes against children and adolescents he'd uncovered in Goddard, an evil that still lurked in the hearts of some men, unbounded by barriers of language, or geography. To think about it, his fingernails dug into the armrest. Because he was thinking of the places that evil still crept. And as the engines roared, and the wheels of the jet left the ground, he knew in blood and bone: never again would he close his eyes to it. In retirement Nick would be scanning for it, if not hunting it down.

Others had long been counting on this.

A boiler room in the basement of the Pinecrest Academy Administration Building had become a place to store old desks and derelict bookshelves since the nineteen seventies oil shortage, when the school had converted its heating system from steam. Now the dismal space was tidy, bathed white in halogen light, and alive with new wires. The blinking lights of computer equipment made a stark contrast to the pair of diesel blackout generators, and a tabletop emergency HAM radio. Along the room's longest wall, a bank of flat-screen video monitors hung above a stretch of white laminate desk surface that harshly reflected the lights. Empty cardboard cups littered the length of it.

Through that night The Headmaster and Canon Nailor had poured over every minute of video footage from The Illuminator case, taken from cameras located across from Nick's house, from those inside it, and toward the end of the ordeal, within the confines of Wiggins Caverns.

Once the last clip was shown, after a long silence, Nailor asked, "So, what do you think?"

The Headmaster pointed out, "Nick Giaccone went back for his man, Jim Stevens. Even though it was all so many years ago. In the only way he could. You don't find men like that."

The Headmaster further explained, "I've been asked to build a special team."

"Same agency?"

The Headmaster nodded. "SEETHROUGH. Nick will be our man to watch the Adriatic." It had come from the top.

Nailor asked, "Does Giaccone know you plan to bring him in?"

The Headmaster did not reply.

That same day, another flight took off from an undisclosed military airstrip in New England. Designed to transport large loads such as heavy ordinance, or even a small army of troops, today the C-130 carried a very light payload in its belly.

Five hours later, after touching down in Bogotá, Colombia, the flight crew dropped the aft ramp and a convoy of onyx-black sports utility vehicles drove onto the tarmac, each armored and sporting blacked-out and bulletproof windows.

Some miles away, in a Mission clinic outside a small village to the north, The Illuminator lay recovering from surgery.

By noon the motorcade of Navy SEALs traveled with air support of Blackhawk helicopters – raising dust through small villages, and eyebrows among the locals.

The Illuminator heard the copters well before their arrival. She donned a surgical mask in the hope of preserving identity.

When the vehicles pulled up, half the armed men piled out and scrambled into position around the armored cars to protect the Mission clinic's entrance from any ambush. The

other half of the SEALs scattered to surround the humble
building. They wore black uniforms with body armor
beneath. And the Blackhawks' rotors chopping the air, hovering above.

From the rear cargo area of the third vehicle in line two
heavily armored men slid a large shape, shrouded in white
fabric. A quick radio check for final go-ahead, and they
wheeled their mysterious cargo toward the clinic's front door.

Waiting in her room within the Mission clinic, the Illuminator was unarmed. Except for the Book of Souls.

New powers, from her recent addition of a page marked
Dr. Gorgalo, had allowed her to slip through customs at
Boston Logan Airport, and then onto a plane, unnoticed.

It would be some time before the pages' cumulative
powers granting her invisibility would be explained by
science. She'd discovered it by accident, adding the leaf
capturing Gorgalo's scant soul, and knew by instinct: this
power granted her, this invisibility, was a distillation of what
causes a community to blind itself to the harm of its children – and a tincture of whatever allowed certain sinners to
practice violence unnoticed – that thing that causes some
to pretend they do not see what's truly monstrous. Now,
reversed by Providence, she would use this power's every
particle to undo such wrongs.

The discovery had been overwhelming. But now she held
the Book in both hands. So fear did not present itself.

When the door of the Illuminator's room swung open
and the two SEALs wheeled their odd delivery inside, a pair
of armed comrades came in behind them as cover.

Following them a uniformed U.S. Marine pushing a hand
truck entered to unload cases marked: Nek-Tar.

The two men unshrouded the large shape, now at the foot of her bed.

Cassandra stood.

Before her, a large flight cage. Inside flitted her three hummingbirds: The Purple-backed Thornbill, the Copper-headed Emerald, and the Velvet-purple Coronet.

She said, "You're right on time."

At the sound of Cassandra's vice, Antonio Narino, Simon Bolivar, and Cortez hovered close to the mesh.

One of the SEALs told her, "SEETHROUGH sends compliments…"

The other added, "Until next mission." And they were gone.

Cassandra Shockley opened the cage door to let the three birds fly free, took off her mask, and then stepped before the mirror.

ENDPAPERS

Passages that describe the face of Simon Allengri are taken, almost verbatim, from Bram Stoker's Dracula. In the same vein, I adapted a passage from Robert Louis Stevenson's Dr. Jekyll & Mr. Hyde which describes what Nick sees rendered by The Illuminator upon the face of George Roache in the scene at Mass General Hospital. I thought it vital to transplant these two monstrous descriptions Illuminator style, in keeping with her odd methods of keeping such writings alive.

The passages from Beowulf quoted in this work are taken from Seamus Heaney's translation of that poem.

The floral iconography web site that rare book expert Jorge Graham consults is Phagat's Garden.

The language I use to describe the eyes of the dog named Fancy in the scene at the Boother residence is cut, Illuminator style, from Edgar Allen Poe's short story, "The Telltale Heart." The passage is taken from the opening of that story in which the narrator describes the eyes of the man who will become his subject of homicide – the description of those eyes at once providing motive and identification of the subject as predator.

The poem my character Jorge Graham recites in his shop is "Tampico," by Grace Hazard Conklin. I use it a little astonished it came to my attention, and with all the greater thanks.

ABOUT THE AUTHOR

Tom Lukas left his career as master carpenter and licensed homebuilder at age thirty-three to earn a degree in English Literature because he wanted to become a writer. At Virginia he found a home at the eText Center and in the American Studies program which emphasized electronic publishing, and applied this new form of craftsmanship as project manager for the National Endowment for the Humanities award-winning literary archive *The World of Dante*, and in editing the New York Public Library's first electronic literary archive *African American Women Writers of the Nineteenth Century*. At age fifty he published his first work in *North American Review*.

Special Operations is Tom's first novel, which he also illustrated and rendered as an eBook that features sound as well as graphic art. He lives in Seattle, Washington.

For more on Tom Lukas, visit SPYCARBOOKS.COM